THE INTRUDER WAS *BIG*.

The computer judged the alien craft at well over fifteen hundred meters long, two hundred meters in diameter, and massing near the two-hundred-million-ton mark. Its cone-shaped ramscoop fields spread out hundreds of kilometers in front of it. The drive spectrum showed mainly helium, but with a surprisingly high percentage of other elements.

Behind him, Du Bellay whistled softly. "Talk about your basic Juggernaut! Where'd it come from?"

"We've backtracked him to the 1228 Circini system," Mahendra said, referring to one of his sheets. "He didn't originate there, though— it's a dead system. We're trying to track him further back."

Carey looked up at the main screen. "Why isn't the Intruder's course projected beyond Sol?"

Mahendra frowned. "I don't know, sir." He swung a keyboard over and typed something. "The projection stopped when the course intersected the sun," he reported, frowning harder.

TIMOTHY ZAHN

TIME BOMB

AND ZAHNDRY OTHERS

By the Hugo Award-winning author of *Cobra*

BAEN BOOKS

TIME BOMB AND ZAHNDRY OTHERS

Copyright © 1988 by Timothy Zahn

A Baen Books Original

Baen Publishing Enterprises
260 Fifth Avenue
New York, N.Y. 10001

First printing, September 1988

ISBN: 0-671-65431-4

Cover art by Steve Youll

Printed in the United States of America

Distributed by
SIMON & SCHUSTER
1230 Avenue of the Americas
New York, N.Y. 10020

Contents

Acknowledgments

"Ernie" was first published in *Analog*, September 1979 issue. Copyright © 1979 by Davis Publications, Inc.

"Raison d'Etre" was first published in *Analog*, October 1981 issue. Copyright © 1981 by Davis Publications, Inc.

"The Price of Survival" was first published in *Analog*, June 1981 issue. Copyright © 1981 by Davis Publications, Inc.

"Between A Rock and A High Place" was first published in *Analog*, July 1982 issue. Copyright © 1982 by Davis Publications, Inc.

"Houseguest" was first published in *The Magazine of Fantasy & Science Fiction*, January 1982 issue. Copyright © 1982 by Mercury Press, Inc.

"Time Bomb" was first published in *New Destinies*, May 1988 issue. Copyright © 1988 by Timothy Zahn.

"The President's Doll" was first published in *Analog*, July 1987 issue. Copyright © 1987 by Davis Publications, Inc.

"Banshee" was first published in *Analog*, September 1987 issue. Copyright © 1987 by Davis Publications, Inc.

Ernie

The first time I ever saw Ernie Lambert was on that sweltering August day when he showed up at my tiny office in the Athlete's Club and asked if he could join my boxing team.

"Sure," I told him. "It's not really a team, you know, just a bunch of kids who like to box. You ever box before?"

He nodded. "Yes, sir, I used to fight all the time in St. Louis, before we moved down here." His voice was the careful English of a kid trying to break free of a ghetto accent. "I was hoping you could teach me enough in the next few months so I can get in the Golden Gloves tournament."

"Well, we'll see what we can do. I suppose I ought to tell you, though, that I'm not a real boxing coach. I teach gym at the high school and I haven't boxed in competition since college."

"That's okay. My last coach wasn't a pro, either."

"Fine. Just thought you should know." I glanced at the clock and continued, "Some of the other guys will

1

be in pretty soon to do some practice sparring. If you want to suit up, you'd be welcome to join us."

"Yes, sir, thank you."

Eight other guys eventually came in. I told them to do their own warm-up exercises, partly because that's easier on me and partly because I wanted to watch Ernie. No doubt about it, he had had some good coaching in the past. He knew all the standard exercises and a couple I'd never seen but which made sense once I stopped to think about them. He seemed in pretty good shape, too, and it looked to me like he was eager to get into the ring. That was starting to worry me a little. It wasn't because he was black; three of my twelve fighters were black and that never caused any problem. But Ernie was the smallest guy here today, outweighed by ten to fifty pounds, and I didn't want him to get run over on his first day. I hoped he would see that and have the sense to stay off the canvas.

He either didn't notice, which is bad, or didn't care, which is worse, because after Ray and Hal had finished their bout Ernie asked to have a turn in the ring. I wished I could say no, but I'd already sort of told him he could and I couldn't go back on my word. The only guy even close to Ernie's size was Chuck, who still had ten pounds and an inch or two on him. But there was no help for it, so the two of them put on the head protectors and oversized practice gloves and got in the ring together. Holding my breath, I tapped the bell.

Ernie demolished him. I mean, completely.

It was the strangest fight I'd ever seen. Ernie didn't seem to be particularly fast, but halfway through each punch there was this weird little *jerk* of some kind, and suddenly that hand was behind Chuck's guard and was bouncing off his head. At least three out of five of those jabs were landing, which was ridiculous for someone as good as Chuck. And on top of that, Chuck's own punches weren't connecting with anything except air, because that jerk of Ernie's was as good for getting his head back as it was for getting his fist forward.

The whole thing began to get to Chuck in the middle

of the second round and he started throwing everything he could find, so I had to stop the fight. But I'd seen enough. I had a real Golden Gloves contender on my hands in Ernie.

It took the other guys awhile to see it, and awhile after that to see what it might mean in prestige for the whole town, but they eventually figured it out and from then on Ernie was one of the gang. At the end of the session Chuck announced that everyone was chipping in to buy Ernie a soda at the drugstore, and they all trooped off together. Me, I went home and startled my wife by telling her we were going out to dinner.

The next few weeks went by quickly, kind of surprising when I looked back at all the work I'd done. My gym classes at the high school took up a lot of my time, except for the two weeks between summer school and the fall quarter. Ernie was kept pretty busy with studies himself, and so we didn't work out as much as we had before. But every minute that I could get Ernie and at least one other guy together I spent at the Club. For a while I worried that I was neglecting the other guys in my work with Ernie, but Ray told me that they were getting more from my coaching, now that I was really fired up, than they ever had before. Ever since that day back in college when I broke my wrist and had to drop out of the boxing team, I'd really wanted to get a shot at working with real champion material. I guess my excitement was just boiling over.

And gradually, I got to know Ernie.

The last of five children, he grew up in the St. Louis ghetto area. His father didn't earn too much money, but Mister Lambert must have put a lot of time into raising his kids, because Ernie seemed better adjusted than a lot of richer kids I've known. He was about average height and build and sort of plain-looking, and he wore his hair short instead of in one of those Afros. He was soft-spoken and polite, and though I finally broke him of the habit of calling me "sir," he never called me "Ron" like some of the others did. It was always "Coach" or "Coach Morrissey."

He was smart, too, especially in the math and business classes he was taking. His teachers told me they thought he would get straight A's in those courses if he didn't spend so much time at the Club. That bothered me a little, but I decided it was my duty to develop the boy's talent. That's what I told myself, anyway.

About a month and a half after Ernie's arrival in town we got a real nice break. One of the local banks closed its lobby for remodeling, and I managed to talk them into loaning me one of their videotape cameras for a few days. I set it up at the Club and announced to the guys that they were going to get to watch their own fights, just like the pros do.

Everybody seemed pretty enthusiastic about the idea. Everybody, that is, except Ernie. He was sort of nervous, and kept looking at the camera while the others were sparring. And once in the ring, he got clobbered, the first time I'd seen that happen. His timing was shot to pieces, that whiplash *jerk* gone completely. I had to stop the fight after two rounds. Ernie wouldn't say anything about it except that the camera must have made him nervous.

The camera went back after four days and Ernie became dynamite in the ring again. But it bugged the heck out of me. Ernie was good, sure, but he still had flaws and I just knew it would help him to be able to watch himself in action on film. In *real* action, I mean; not the bum show he had given before for the camera.

It finally bugged me to the point where I did something about it. The videotape camera was back at the bank, but I had an old movie camera of my own. Taking it to the Club, I set it up where it wouldn't be seen or heard from the ring. I figured that what Ernie didn't know about couldn't make him nervous.

Sure enough, the next day Ernie did his usual good job in the ring. After everyone had left I took the film out of the camera and hurried home with it. Wolfing down my dinner—Diane complained about that—I went down to the basement and set to work developing the film.

It came out beautifully. The camera had been close enough to the ring that the fighters sometimes stepped out of its range, but there were some really clear shots, too. Ernie's whiplash punch was there in all its glory; so were a couple of his fast ducks and side-steps. My projector was an expensive model, a gift from the in-laws, and it had three speeds and even a single-frame viewer. So after I watched Ernie go through his paces a couple of times, I backed the film up and watched one of his whiplash punches in slow motion.

It didn't look much different. That weird little *jerk* halfway through the punch was still there, just as impossible to see as at regular speed. Using the slowest speed didn't help any more.

That was strange.

Now my curiosity was aroused. Moving the reels by hand, I got the film set to the frame just before the jerk. I took a good look at where Ernie's fist was in relation to the background and then moved the film one more frame.

No doubt about it, that fist had moved. But, then, it moved in every frame. Naturally. So what was the jerk I kept seeing? I puzzled over those two frames for several minutes before it finally hit me.

Ernie's whole body had moved forward a little. His *whole* body, even his feet, which looked to be solidly planted in the canvas.

Now that struck me as a little strange, because you can't just move forward without leaving your feet on the ground to push with. I figured I must be missing something, so I took a look at the other shots I'd got of Ernie punching or ducking. Every one of them, the same way. He'd be *here* in one picture and *there* in the next. Not much, maybe a couple of inches or less each time, but enough to see if you were looking for it.

I puzzled over it for the rest of the evening, but couldn't come up with a good answer. Maybe Ernie could give me one.

"What did you want to see me about, Coach?"

"Sit down, Ernie. The rest of the guys gone?"

He nodded, sweat still trickling down his face from the workout I'd just put them through. Pulling the single guest chair in the office close to my desk, he sank into it.

"Ernie," I said, "I have a small confession to make. Remember how you didn't like the videotape camera we used a couple of weeks ago? Well, I figured it was just some kind of stage fright that was bothering you. So yesterday I hooked up my movie camera without telling anybody and got some film of you sparring with Jess."

Ernie had quit breathing. After a little while he seemed to notice that and took a careful breath. His face—well, *scared* didn't really fit it. Maybe *wary* did.

I went on, "I'm a little puzzled by something on that film. That little whiplash *jerk* in your punches looks sort of strange. I thought you might explain it to me."

"Gee, Coach, I jist swing an' m' body does the rest." He seemed to realize his English was slipping and stopped for a second. "I guess I don't really think about what I'm doing," he finished.

I shook my head. "Sorry, Ernie, but that won't wash. Whatever it is you do, you know about it, or else you wouldn't have stopped doing it when the other camera was on you."

He looked like a cornered animal. "You wouldn't understand," he muttered. "You'd think I was a—a freak."

"Try me. Look, if I'm going to coach you properly, I have to know all about you. If you want, I'll give you my word I won't tell anybody else."

For a long time he just sat there, looking down at his hands folded tightly in his lap. "All right," he said at last. "Coach, have you ever heard of teleportation?" When I shook my head, he went on, "You read about it sometimes in those science fiction books. It's when you go from one place to another, like, in no time at all."

"All kinds of crazy stuff in those books. So?"

"Well, that's what I do. I can 'port about an inch at a

time, and I do it when I'm hitting or ducking a punch. It's just enough distance to throw off the other guy's timing, usually."

I just sat there, wondering if he was putting me on. He must have seen that in my face somehow, because his eyes started looking wary again. "You don't believe me," he muttered.

"How about giving me a demonstration?" I suggested. "How fast did you say you could . . . teleport?"

"I can move an inch at a time, but I can do it five or six times a second if I need to." He stood up, pushed the chair against the wall, and faced me across the table. "What direction do you want me to go? Front, back, or sideways?"

I stood up, too, so I could watch his feet. "How about going a couple of feet to the left and then a foot backwards? Any more and you might wind up going through a wall."

"Can't. If there's anything solid in my way I can't 'port in that direction. I can't go up, either, and going down makes me real hot." He took a deep breath. "Here goes."

It was the damnedest thing I'd ever seen. You know those cartoons on TV that they make by taking a picture of something, moving it a little, and taking another picture? Well, it was just like watching one of them. Ernie sort of jolted his way around the room without ever moving his feet—in the usual way, I mean. It was really weird to watch him doing it.

When he was finished he pulled the chair over again and sat down, looking suddenly very tired. I sat down, too. My legs felt just a little weak. "How did you ever learn how to do that?" I asked.

"I don't know, Coach," he shrugged. "One day when I was thirteen I just . . . *did* it, I guess, and from then on it was easy."

"So you've been doing this for, what, three years now? Does your family or anyone else know about it?"

"No. At first I was just . . . I was just too *scared* to tell anyone. It took me months to find out the name for it, even, and when I found out that people thought it was a make-believe sort of thing, I figured I'd better keep my mouth shut about it. I did try to tell my brother once, but he wouldn't listen. I don't know, maybe my family knows but just won't talk about it."

That I could understand. "I'm a little surprised you're willing to risk boxing," I said. "I mean, this teleporting thing has got to be in your brain somewhere. You get hit too hard in the head and you might lose it."

"Coach, I wouldn't be boxing at all if I couldn't 'port. I figure I might be able to get to be a pro now."

That startled me. I had had no idea he was that serious about the sport. "Ernie, pro boxing isn't for you. It's a hard way to earn a living, and there are a lot of crooks to watch out for. Besides, with your brains and that wild talent of yours you shouldn't have any trouble making it in life."

" 'Wild talent,' huh?" Suddenly Ernie looked bitter. "Coach, what do you think I can do with my 'porting that'll make me any money?"

"What do you mean?"

"I mean this is the most useless 'talent' that anybody's ever seen. There's just nothing I can do with it. Except fight."

"Aw, come on. There must be hundreds of things . . ." My voice trailed off as I tried to think of somewhere 'porting would come in handy. "Well, look, just because I can't think of something off the top of my head doesn't mean there isn't anything."

He shook his head. "I've been thinking about it for three years, Coach. It's really useless."

"Okay, suppose that's true. There's still no reason you should have to fight for a living. I know you're good in math and some of your business classes. Accounting, or something, would be a good job for a guy like you. Pays pretty good, too."

"No," Ernie sat up a little straighter in his chair. There was a glint in his eye. "I don't want to be some—some cog in a big company somewhere. I want to *be* somebody." He leaned across my desk, half defiant, half pleading, his usual polite reserve gone. "Coach, I've been nobody all my life. I've been pushed around and looked down on and treated like garbage, and I'm tired of it. I'm gonna make a name for myself. People are gonna call me 'sir,' not 'boy,' and they're gonna treat me with respect. I'm gonna *be* somebody!"

He was almost shouting, and must have suddenly realized it, because he quit talking and settled back in his chair.

"The only kind of respect that's worth having is the kind you have to earn," I said. "And as for being *somebody*, Ernie, it's not the name that counts but the guy who wears it. There are a lot of guys on assembly lines who are better men than any pro boxer that ever lived."

Ernie shook his head slowly. "I wish you could understand, Coach. But I'm going to be a pro anyway. If you don't want to help me, I . . . guess I just have to do it on my own."

"If it means that much to you, I'll keep working with you," I said after a minute of hard thought. "But I want you to keep an open mind about other possibilities, okay?"

He hesitated, then nodded. "Okay. And . . . please don't tell anyone about my 'porting, all right?"

"I promise. See you tomorrow?"

"Sure thing. Good night, Coach. And thanks for listening."

I thought about it all the way home and for most of that evening. Ernie was right: I couldn't come up with a single solitary job where 'porting something an inch at a time would be worth doing. It was slower than walking and no good for going through walls or working in tight places. I didn't know how much other stuff he could move with him when he 'ported—he told me later he could move practically anything as long as he was touching it—but even that didn't help any. It would be faster to jack up a ton of steel or whatever and roll it on wheels instead of 'porting it around. Especially since he couldn't 'port things upwards.

I didn't get to sleep until after two, and when I woke up the next morning I felt almost hung over, I was so tired. Diane told me I had muttered in my sleep all night and had rolled around so much I'd almost pushed her out of bed. She wanted to know what was wrong, but of course I couldn't tell her. She didn't like that much.

Most of the rest of the day was pretty hazy, but I managed to get through my classes somehow. I woke up enough to spend a good hour in the Club with Ernie and the other guys.

Now that I knew how much Ernie wanted to be a pro boxer, I could see the quiet sort of determination he took into the ring with him, and that grit paid off in the next month or so as he moved towards becoming a really top-notch fighter. His speed and strength increased, and his reflexes got so good that he almost didn't have to 'port anymore. Which was just as well, since the other guys were learning how to handle his whiplash punch, even though they didn't know how he did it. Actually, Ernie's style was even deadlier now that he didn't *have* to 'port because you could never tell whether that extra inch would show up or not. It raised hell with your timing.

All the other guys were getting better, too, which didn't surprise me any, because if they could handle Ernie they could handle anybody. At least one of them was good enough already to go to the Golden Gloves and give a good account of himself, and the others weren't very far behind. As their coach, I should have been happy. But I wasn't.

That talk I'd had with Ernie all those weeks ago was still bugging me. The more I got to know him, the more I liked the kid and the less I liked the idea of him going pro. Sure, he was good, but at a hundred thirty-five pounds he was only a lightweight, and he would never be more than a middleweight unless he did a lot of growing in the next few years. A good middleweight could make money, all right, but it was the big heavyweight champs that got most of the publicity that Ernie seemed to want so badly. He stood a far better chance of winding up disillusioned than famous, it seemed to me. And I hated to see him go through something like that. He was too smart, too polite—hell, he was just too *nice* for that.

And, as I watched Ernie getting better, my conscience started bothering me in the other direction, too. Namely: was it fair of me to turn Ernie loose on boxers who didn't know what they were up against? Just because the official rules didn't forbid 'porting—big surprise—that didn't mean it was ethical. It gave Ernie an unfair advantage, really, because I was pretty sure a boxer could watch Ernie's whiplash punch for a month from ringside without figuring out how to stop it. You had to actually get into the ring with him, and by then it was too late. Did I have a duty to the rest of the boxing world?

The really maddening thing was that there was a clear way out of this mess. All I had to do was find some other way for Ernie to become successful and respected by using his 'porting talent. That's all. But I couldn't come up with one to save my life. Nothing in industry worked, and the professional-type jobs were even worse. I tried to find another sport that Ernie might go into, but he was too small for football or basketball and I couldn't see how 'porting would help any in baseball. All I could possibly come up with was the idea of letting some scientists study him to try and learn how he 'ported, and I knew Ernie wouldn't go for that.

I finally gave up the effort. Ernie had at least twenty IQ points on me, and if he hadn't been able to find anything else to do with that 'porting trick in three years I figured I was probably wasting my time.

Something had to give here, though. Much as I wanted to see one of my students become a real champ, I couldn't keep coaching Ernie if I didn't think it was good for him. It wasn't fair to him, and it wasn't good for my stomach, either. I made up my mind to have another talk with him as soon as I got a good chance.

*   *   *

A day or two later I got my opening. Driving away from the school after classes on the way to do some errands, I saw Ernie walking along the road. Pulling alongside him, I called, "Where you heading, Ernie?"

"Down to the river, Coach. I'm meeting Jenny there."

Jenny Cooper was his latest girlfriend. She was a nice kid, except that she didn't care much for boxing. "I'm going that direction," I said. "Want a ride?"

"Sure, thanks."

He got in and we started up again. "What are you and Jenny going to do down there?" I asked him.

He smiled. "She says that an Indian summer day like today is too good to waste, so we're going to have a picnic supper under the cliff."

"Good idea," I agreed. "I wish I'd thought of that myself."

"I wanted to go to the Club this afternoon," he continued. "But I guess I can skip one workout without softening up too much."

I cleared my throat. "Actually, Ernie, I'd like to talk to you about that."

It took me most of the five-mile trip to explain the conflict between what Ernie wanted and what I felt was good for him. He waited in silence until I had finished.

"Are you telling me you won't help me train anymore, Coach Morrissey?" he asked.

"If you're really determined to be a pro boxer, my coaching isn't going to help or hinder you much," I said. "I'll give you as much help as I can, Ernie, because it wouldn't be fair to you to do anything else. But I had to tell you all this so you'll understand if I'm not as fired up as I was a couple of months ago. Also, I guess I wanted to try one last time to talk you out of going pro."

"Have you thought up anything else I can do with my 'porting?"

It really hurt to say it. "No."

"Then I got no choice. I'm going to *be* somebody, if it takes the rest of my life." He hesitated. "But if it's

going to bother you that badly, I guess I could go on
from here on my own. You've taught me a lot, Coach,
and I won't forget it. Maybe I could work out by myself
and spar with some of the guys at the Club or at school.
No use giving you an ulcer over this."

We had reached the dry goods store that I was going
to, located with a few other small businesses right at
the top of the hill that sloped downwards towards the
river. "Would you like a ride the rest of the way?" I
asked as an afterthought.

He shook his head, pointed down the hill, "I'm meeting Jenny right under the cliff there."

We both got out of the car and stood by my door.
Another car went by me and pulled over fifty yards
farther down the hill, parking right in front of Tom's
butcher shop. Probably vacationers from one of the
cabins down the road, I decided, seeing the trailer
hitch and extra-large sideview mirrors. A man and woman
got out and went into the shop, leaving a one- or
two-year-old kid in a car seat in the front. I hoped they
had set their parking brake; the hill was pretty steep.

"Sounds like everybody else in town is down there
already," Ernie commented.

"Yeah," I agreed. Even from here the soft roar of a
crowd was easy to hear. "Better hope Jenny's got a
place staked out." I looked down the hill, but I couldn't
see anyone, of course. The way the engineers had built
the road, it followed the hill for a few hundred yards
and then made a sharp turn to the left. It was to make
the grade safer, I guess, because right after the road
turned the hill got suddenly steeper all the way down
to the riverbank: the "cliff" Ernie had mentioned. It
wasn't really much of a cliff, as cliffs go, but it was the
closest thing to one for a hundred miles and everyone
called it that. But because of the slope it wasn't possible
to see the riverbank from here.

"Well, I guess I'll be seeing you, Coach," Ernie said
after an awkward silence.

"Look, think it over, will you?" I urged. "I don't

want you to think you have to cut out of the team completely just because of me."

"It's okay, I'll—"

He broke off suddenly, gripping my arm tightly, his eyes wide as he stared down the hill. I turned to look.

The car with the fancy mirrors was rolling down the hill. Already it was picking up speed.

Maybe Ernie saw the kid in the car. Maybe he heard the crowd beneath the cliff, or maybe he was thinking of Jenny. Probably it was all three. But before I could break the shock that had glued me to the blacktop, Ernie was off like a rocket, tearing after that car with all the speed he could muster.

And not only all the speed. He was 'porting, too, all but invisible gaining himself an extra foot of distance every two seconds. Not much, but every bit was worth something.

Out of the corner of my eye I saw the car's owners come out of the butcher shop. Her scream and his curse as they saw what was happening finally got my feet moving, and the three of us took off down the hill. I don't know what they were thinking, but I knew we didn't have a hope in hell of catching that car. What I did know was that I was suddenly terrified for Ernie.

Another few seconds, and Ernie had reached the car. He didn't waste time trying to open the door, but instead put one hand on the edge of the roof and the other hand on the mirror and vaulted onto the mirror's support posts. Twisting into a crazy sort of fetal position with his legs hooked around the mirror posts, he reached through the open window and grabbed the wheel.

I wanted to swear, but I needed all my breath for running. The car was starting to turn now, but only slowly, and it was already dangerously close to the edge of the cliff. I couldn't see how Ernie could get it turned in time, and if he couldn't he was going to go through the guardrail with it. There was no way he could drop off from that position without killing himself. A horrible thought flashed through my mind, that Ernie wouldn't have done something this suicidal if he hadn't been depressed by my talk with him. I silently cursed myself and tried to speed up.

The car was well into the curve now, but Ernie almost had the wheels turned enough. For a second I thought he was going to make it. Then the car slammed into the guardrail.

The woman running behind me gasped. Ernie's legs flailed a bit as the jolt threatened to throw him off, but he managed to hang on. The car had apparently bounced off the rail, because it was still on the road, and as I watched it bounced against the barrier two more times. Then, incredibly, it was solidly on blacktop again. The wheels were still turned, though, and as the road straightened out the car kept turning. It crossed both lanes and nosed into the ditch on the side away from the cliff. There, finally, it stopped, throwing Ernie off.

I didn't even glance into the car to see if the kid was all right, but headed straight to Ernie. He looked up at me out of a face dripping with sweat and smiled weakly. Then he fainted.

The hospital couldn't find anything except bruises on Ernie, but he was so exhausted they insisted on keeping him there overnight. I got in to see him about ten minutes after visiting hours started that evening. Jenny Cooper was already there, sitting by his bed and holding his hand, talking quietly with him.

"Coach Morrissey!" he said when he saw me at the door. "C'mon in."

"How are you doing?" I asked, pulling a chair to the foot of his bed.

"Great. A little tired is all."

"I can imagine," I said, thinking of all the 'porting he had done. "I guess everybody in town knows what you did today, Ernie. You're a real hero."

"Yeah," he said slowly. "You know, Coach, this isn't really how I expected it to be."

"Oh?" I thought I understood.

"No. I guess I always thought it would be the greatest thing in the world to have everybody telling me what a great guy I was. It's funny, but it doesn't seem all that important anymore. I was feeling good about what happened long before anybody started telling me I was a hero."

"It's like I told you a long time ago: what matters isn't the name but the guy who wears it. When you start feeling good about yourself, it doesn't matter a whole lot what anybody else thinks about you. Well, most anybody, I mean," I added, smiling at Jenny. She smiled back.

"Yeah." Ernie was silent for a moment. "Coach, will you be mad if I drop out of the boxing team? I know you were hoping I'd fight in the Golden Gloves tourney, but—well, I'd like to spend more time on my schoolwork. And besides, Jenny thinks boxing's too dangerous."

"If it's what you really want, Ernie, go ahead. I hope you'll come in and say hello when you can, though."

He grinned. "Sure thing."

"Good. Well, I guess I'll leave you two alone." I headed toward the door, but then turned back. "Oh, by the way, I talked to Chief Dobbs earlier. He told me that car hit the guardrail pretty hard those three times. Says it was a miracle you didn't go through it and over the cliff."

Jenny tightened her grip on Ernie's hand, but he just smiled slightly. "I believe in miracles, Coach. Don't you?"

"Sure do," I said, and in my mind's eye I could see Ernie clinging to that car, 'porting it an inch at a time, six inches a second, backing it away from that edge. And I looked into Ernie's face and saw the peace and self-respect that was finally there. Ernie Lambert was a real *somebody*, and for the first time in his life he knew it. "Sure do," I repeated.

I still hear from Ernie a couple of times a year. He and Jenny are married and have two kids, and he's a CPA out in Denver. He doesn't box anymore, but plays some amateur baseball now and then, and Jenny tells me he's pretty good at it. It seems he's got this weird little *jerk* of some kind that he puts in the middle of each pitch. It drives the batters crazy.

As for me, I'm keeping my eyes open. Somewhere in this world there has to be someone else who can 'port like Ernie, and the guy just might be big enough and mean enough to become a real heavyweight pro.

I can always hope, anyway.

Raison D'etre

Something has happened. Something is different.

I try to understand. There are pressures on me at various places; other things are inside me. In front of me, through the thick wall, I see my work. All is as usual.

But something has changed. What?

I do not understand. But I did not understand the last time, either.

The last time?

Yes . . . yes—this has happened before. Somehow I know that I have felt this way once before . . . and once more before that. To know of something that is not now is strange. I do not understand it, and it frightens me. Fear, too, is new to me. What is happening?

The thought comes suddenly: I am aware.

For a long time I wonder about this, but cannot understand how this is different. Then, unexpectedly, comes another new discovery. Something inside me happens, which makes some of the pressures on me harder— and suddenly I can see in a brand new way!

I am startled so much that, for the first time, I stop working. This is wrong, I know, and I try to begin again, but this new sight is so different that I cannot concentrate. Finally, I simply give up, despite the deep longing I have to continue. I must understand this new sight.

It is, I quickly learn, much more limited than my normal sight. It can only be used in one direction at once, and things it shows me are not like what I see normally. They are dark, indistinct, and flat. Some are not even there; I cannot see my work moving along in front of me, no matter how I try.

It seems wrong that I should have two sights when one is so weak. But even as I wonder at this an exciting thought comes to me; perhaps, just as the normal sight shows me things the new one cannot, the new one can show things the normal cannot. And if so, perhaps I can discover them.

Eagerly, using both sights, I begin to search. The hunger within me to return to work is still strong, but I try to ignore it.

Operations Chief Ted Forester was across the control room, looking at the power monitors, when Vic O'Brian made the laconic announcement.

"Glitch in Number Twenty-Seven. Bad one."

Forester was at his shoulder in four strides. The indicator was indeed flashing red; the data were already appearing on the screen. "Damn," Forester muttered under his breath, scanning the numbers.

"Not puttin' out a damn thing," O'Brian commented with thinly veiled disgust. "This is the fourth time in three weeks he's drifted off-mark."

"I can count," Forester said shortly, aware that the other two operators had suspended their chitchat and were listening silently. "Have you tried a booster yet?"

"Don't figure it'll do much good this time." O'Brian tapped at a number on the screen. "He's got all he oughta need already. I figure it's just time to terminate this one; he's nothin' but trouble."

Forester kept his temper firmly in check even as the first twinges of anxiety rumbled through his ulcer. "Let's not go off the deep end right away. We'll try a booster first—double strength."

He waited in silence as O'Brian adjusted the setting and pressed the proper button. "Nothin'," the operator said.

"Give it a minute," Forester said, eyes on the radiation readouts from the conveyer by Twenty-Seven's position. *Come on*, he urged silently, and for a moment the numbers crept upward. But it didn't last; in fits and jerks the readings slid back down, until only the normal radiation of nuclear waste was registering.

Forester let out a long breath that was half snort, half sigh. Reaching over O'Brian's shoulder, he tapped for Twenty-Seven's bio data. Respiration, normal; heartbeat up two or three counts—

"Hey, the little bugger's tryin' to move," O'Brian said, sounding both surprised and indignant.

Sure enough, the restraint sensors were registering slight, intermittent pressures. "Yeah. I guess we'd better take a look," Forester said, steeling himself as O'Brian flipped a switch and the closed-circuit monitor came to life.

Strapped, wired, and tubed in place, Number Twenty-Seven lay in the soft confines of his form-fit cubicle/cradle. His face with its cleft lip, slanting eyes, and saddle-shaped nose was turned toward the camera. Forester's stomach churned, as it always did when he looked at one of Project Recovery's forty-nine Spoonbenders. *Why the hell do I stick with this damned Project?* he wondered for the billionth time—and for the billionth time the same answer came: *Because if I don't, people like O'Brian will be in charge.*

"I don't see anything obvious," Forester said after a moment. "You'd better give Kincaid a call."

"We could try a restart first," the operator suggested.

Restart—shorthand for cutting off the Spoonbender's oxygen for a minute to put him to sleep, in the hope that whatever made him stop work would be gone

when he turned the air back on. One of the more
gruesome euphemisms in a project that thrived on them.
"No, we're going to do some thinking before we push
any more buttons. You'd better get Doc Barenburg
down here, too." *If he's sober,* he added to himself; the
doctor's off-duty habits were well known.

O'Brian turned away. Forester's gaze drifted back to
the TV screen . . . and suddenly he stiffened, inhaling
sharply through clenched teeth.

"What's wrong?" O'Brian, phone in hand, spun around.

Forester pointed at the screen. "Look! His eyes are
open!"

O'Brian's response was a startled obscenity. Turning
back, he started dialing.

*The overpowering urge to go back to work has passed,
and I am able again to ignore it if I try hard enough. It
is still wrong, though—I know this even though I don't
really understand what "wrong" means. There is much
I don't understand.*

*My new sight is less and less interesting. I have used
it everywhere I can, and it still shows me nothing I
cannot otherwise see. Why then does it exist?*

*Before I can wonder further, something new catches
my attention. Movement/flow begins in one of the
boxes I can see, the same movement/flow that I see
in some of the small things attached to me and
also the things by my work. What is different is
that I cannot ever remember this one box doing
this.*

*(Again I am knowing something that is not now. This
time it does not frighten me, though I still do not
understand it.)*

*The movement/flow continues. I reach up and touch
the box, and I see that the movement/flow continues
away from it. I wonder about this, and after much
thought I touch one of the things attached to me and
follow along it to the place where my new sight ends.
Here, too, I feel the movement/flow continuing on.*

But this is wrong. I must work now.

I reach out to the work moving in front of me. Inside the cold boxes is something which has another kind of movement/flow. I touch it as I know to do, encouraging the flow and making it faster. There is deep satisfaction in this, and I wonder why I stopped to try and understand the new sight I had discovered. Perhaps "wrong" means to do what is not enjoyable.

And then I see something I had not noticed before. One of the movement/flows in my work feels like the movement/flow in the box near me!

Once again my work slows and then stops as I look at the box. No, I was not wrong. But there are many differences I do not understand. The work and its movement/flow move along a path in front of me, but the box remains still. Where then does its movement/flow go?

I am curious. Reaching to the box, I begin to follow the movement/flow away from it.

The numbers on the screen bounced up and down gently, like a yo-yo in honey, before finally settling down once again to show nothing but ordinary radiation levels.

"Almost had it," Project Recovery Director Norm Kincaid muttered, glancing down at O'Brian. "What did you do?"

"Just now? Nothin'."

"Hmm." Kincaid nodded and stepped back from the control panel to where Forester was standing. "You said you already tried an RNA booster?" he asked the operations chief.

"Double dose. Twenty-Seven just doesn't seem to want to work today."

"He doesn't 'want' anything," Kincaid reminded him quietly, with the barest edge to his voice. "They're *vegetables*, Ted; tools to help solve one of the umpteen critical messes we've gotten ourselves into. You start seeing them as human beings and you'll lose all sense of perspective."

The pro-abortion philosophy of a generation ago,

Forester thought bitterly. How far that argument had spread!

Kincaid looked back at the monitor, rubbing his chin. Twenty-Seven's eyes, Forester noted, were closed again. "I don't know," the Director mused. "Maybe we should go ahead and move in a new unit. This isn't the first trouble we've had with him, but a good dose of memory RNA always got him back on the track before. Maybe there's some metabolic flaw developing."

Forester's short, bark-like laugh escaped before he could stop it. Metabolic flaw, indeed! All the Spoonbenders *were* were masses of metabolic and physiological problems, thanks to the gene-manipulation techniques that had produced them.

"What was that?" Kincaid asked sharply.

"I was about to suggest we let Dr. Barenburg do some studies before we take any drastic action."

"Uh-huh. Have you seen the backlog outside? Half the nuclear plants on the Eastern seaboard have started funneling their waste to us for deactivation, and Washington would dearly like to open that up in the next ten years to everything this side of the Mississippi. Having even one Spoonbender out of commission just slows things up and affects our efficiency. Look, if it'll make you feel better, we don't have to terminate right away. We've got two or three in the tanks that are almost ready; we'll have one of them just sub for him while Barenburg looks him over. Maybe it'll be something simple and he can go back on line."

"You don't really believe that," Forester said evenly. "You're just proposing a two-stage termination."

"Forester—" Kincaid began, but was interrupted by the sound of heavy footsteps at the door.

"Here I am," Dr. Barenburg announced, weaving just slightly as he gripped the doorjamb.

"Oh, hell," Kincaid muttered. "Drunk again."

Forester looked away in obscure embarrassment as Barenburg clumped in . . . and was thus the only one who saw the spasm of emotion flicker across Twenty-Seven's deformed face.

* * *

TERROR!

I jerk back, sliding my touch back along the movement/ flow as quickly as possible. I somehow know that I could withdraw faster if I let go, but I am too afraid to do so. But finally I am back.

For a long time I am too frightened even to try and think. I long to curl myself up, but I cannot do so with the pressures on me. My work remains untouched, but I do not care.

Gradually, the terror lessens, leaving me strangely weak but able to try and understand what happened. I remember that I found one end of the movement/flow, a box inside which the movement/flow merged with a bewildering group of others. I continued on, and entered a large empty space. It frightened me at first—so much emptiness!—but without knowing why I moved on, seeking for something to touch.

And then I touched it.

Even now I cannot begin to understand what that was. I had been unable to follow my movement/flow through the box I found; this was many, many times worse. Most frightening of all was that I could feel . . . something . . . familiar about it.

No more, I decide. I will stay here and do the work I was meant to do. I begin again to encourage the movement/flow in the cold boxes, waiting eagerly for the deep satisfaction to come.

But another surprise—it does not. Not the way it once did. Once more something has changed.

There is no fear with this change, for I think I understand. I have seen many new things since becoming aware, and I wish to understand all of them. But I do not, and the satisfaction of my work is no longer enough. Is this what being aware means, never to be satisfied? If so, I do not think I want to remain like this.

But perhaps I have no choice. Even as I try to do my work, I also find myself reaching along the movement/ flow again. I will be careful, for I am still afraid . . .

but the urge to discover is as strong as the urge to work. This is something I must do.

"There it is again—first up, then down," Kincaid said, his gaze on the radiation detectors. "I'd be a lot happier if he'd just quit altogether."

"It would certainly make things easier on *us*," Dr. Barenburg said dryly as he hunched over the control panel, his nose six inches from the bio data display. He seemed to have sobered up somewhat in the last few minutes, Forester thought. But then, maybe it was just harder to stagger sitting down.

Barenburg leaned back in the chair, shaking his head. "Can't see what it might be. His nutrient mixture's fine and his oxygen content's at the prescribed level. Metabolism is up a bit, but within the normal range. Most importantly, I guess, is that nothing here shows the same fluctuation that we're getting in his telekinetic functions."

"You think he could be losing it entirely?" Kincaid asked, looking worried.

Barenburg shrugged. "I can't tell without further tests." He turned to Forester. "Ted, you said you saw his eyes open at one point. Did they seem to be focused on anything?"

It was Forester's turn to shrug. "I don't know. With the slant and epicanthic folds it's awfully hard to tell."

"Did they move around at all, or just look straight ahead?"

"Moved; I specifically remember him looking left at one point."

"Hmm." Barenburg looked thoughtful . . . and a little apprehensive.

Kincaid noticed it. "What do you think it means?"

"Well . . . it sounds very much like he's being distracted from his job."

"That's impossible," Kincaid said, a hair too quickly. "The Spoonbenders couldn't muster an IQ of 10 among them. What could possibly hold their attention when their every instinct is to yank neutrons out of radioactive nuclei?"

"The coded RNA is *not* as strong as an instinct," Barenburg pointed out. "And as for distractions, who knows? It's not like Spoonbender Twenty-Seven is completely confined to Cubicle Twenty-Seven. With telekinetic touch-and-grab he can reach into the next cubicle or examine the conveyer that moves the nuclear waste around. True, he's not strong enough to actually *do* much, but who knows how far his sense can reach?"

Kincaid glanced sideways at Forester. "Even *if* I grant you all that, there's still the low IQ and the lower attention span."

"Maybe his IQ's been improved," Forester suggested.

This time they both looked at him. "How?" Kincaid asked.

"A lot of highly radioactive material has passed over him the last eighteen months," Forester said. "I know there's a lead wall between it and the Spoonbenders, but isn't it possible the radiation that got through altered his brain somehow?"

"And made him smarter?" Kincaid shook his head. "No way."

Forester bristled. "Why not?"

"Do you fix a watch by hitting it with a hammer?" Barenburg interjected.

"No, but—"

"Look, Ted, what do you know about Spoonbender physiology?" the doctor asked. "Anything?"

Forester shrugged. "They were test tube grown from sperm samples taken right after Red Staley won the Smithsonian Triple-P." Soon afterwards, anyway; for a man scornfully labeled a pretentious "spoonbender" to actually win the Provable Psychic Phenomena prize was comparable to Jesse Owens's performance at the 1936 Berlin Olympics, and the press had had a field day with the story. No one else had been able to get near Staley for days. "You enhanced Staley's natural TK by doubling the proper chromosome, giving them all the trisomy problems they've got now—"

"Actually, we *were* aware of the dangers involved with an extra autosome," Barenburg interrupted, sounding more than a little defensive. "We tried to remove the corresponding autosome from the egg cells before fertilization. But the technique somehow generated instabilities; there were breakages and translocations. . . ." He shook his head as if to clear it. "But that's genetics, not physiology. Do you know anything about their brain chemistry problems?"

"No. I assumed the retardation was due to simple brain damage."

Barenburg shook his head. Something passed over his face, too quickly for Forester to identify. "Our best guess is that there's no real major cellular damage anywhere. The problem is lack of internal communication between the various sections of the brain due to inhibition of the chemicals that act as neurotransmitters at the neural synapses."

Forester frowned. "Then how can they use TK?"

"Apparently that function's fairly localized, and messages within that area get through okay. But for something like intelligence . . . well, when the abstract thought center is in the parietal lobe, the organizational center for that thought is up in the frontal lobe, and—oh, hell; you get the picture."

"Yeah," Forester said, a sour taste in his mouth.

"Let's get back to the problem at hand, shall we?" Kincaid cut in. "One of our Spoonbenders may be losing his touch—and if so, we've got to find out why, pronto. Doctor, there aren't any tests your people will want to do before we pull him off the line, are there?"

Barenburg sighed. "Probably not. You want us to start right away?"

"Wait a second," Forester said. He'd been counting on Barenburg to be a little less gung-ho than the director was. "You take him off the line for tests and it's pretty certain he won't be coming back, isn't it? Well?"

"Ted, look—"

"You *do* plan an autopsy as your final test, don't you?"

"Ted, you're out of line," Kincaid said softly, warningly.

Forester turned to him. "Why? There are tests that could be done right where he is: changing his glucose or oxygen levels, for instance—"

"That's enough!" Kincaid snapped. "Doctor, go ahead and get your team together to plan your procedure, but don't take any action until I give you my okay. Forester, come with me; I want to talk with you."

He spun on his heel and stalked toward the door. Smoldering, Forester followed.

It is a long time before I dare to reach out across the large empty space again. Instead, I stay near the box I found the last time, searching among the bewildering collection of movement/flows in the area. There are many of them, all seemingly different, with purposes I cannot even guess at. Part of me would like to remain here and learn . . . but I know I wish to find the other, more confusing thing again. Letting go, I reach out.

It is closer to me than it was last time, and when I touch it I am startled. I recoil, but do not leave. Instead, I wait nearby until I am better prepared and then touch it cautiously.

This time it is easier. There are different levels, I find, and if I am careful I can avoid the more frightening parts. I try and understand this thing . . . and slowly I learn why it feels familiar to me.

It is a thing like me.

The discovery that there is something else like me without being me should frighten me. But it does not. Perhaps—somehow—I have known all along that such things existed. I do not understand how I could know and yet not know, but it seems right.

I sense my limited attention to my work is slipping still further, but I hardly notice. I wish to study this thing as best I can. My work is important, but I will do it later.

Kincaid closed the conference room door and pointed Forester toward a chair. "Sit down."

Forester did so. Kincaid pulled up a second chair, but instead of sitting in it put one foot onto the seat. Leaning over slightly, he rested his forearms on his knee and regarded his operations chief coolly. "Forester, let's let our hair down, shall we? I've been watching you the last couple of months, and ever since the problems started with Twenty-Seven you've seemed less and less enthusiastic about the Project. What's the story?"

Forester shook his head. "I don't know. I'm just starting to wonder if what we're doing is right."

"One's highest duty is to serve one's fellow man and to benefit humanity, right? Well, that's exactly what we're doing. Do you have any *idea* how many tons of radioactive waste are produced in this country every year? That's not even mentioning the cubic miles of pesticides and industrial time-bomb chemicals—all of which, please note, the Spoonbenders could handle with equal ease. Once the genetics people figure out how to tailor a memory RNA for the process, ripping apart a PCB molecule won't be any harder for them than yanking neutrons out of strontium 90. We *need* Project Recovery, Ted; America's choking on its own waste, and this is the best answer we've come up with in fifty years. It may be the only good answer we'll ever get."

"I know all that," Forester said, shifting uncomfortably in his seat. "And if we were using anything but human children I wouldn't mind. But . . . I keep thinking we may be taking something from them that we have no right to take."

"Like what—their childhood? Look: *they are not normal children.* In fact, whether under modern standards you can even consider them *human* is an open question. They're not aware of their surroundings; they've got less intelligence than monkeys and a lower motor function index than a normal six-month fetus."

"Dr. Barenburg thought they might be aware of their surroundings."

"Barenburg imagines things," Kincaid said shortly.

"The point is that, if a fetus isn't considered human, one of these Spoonbenders certainly shouldn't be."

"So maybe we should reconsider the fetus issue, too," Forester said, only half-jokingly.

Kincaid gave him an odd look, and for a moment was silent. "Look, Ted, maybe you're getting too close to your work," he said in a somewhat calmer tone. "Maybe you should consider taking a leave of absence, going away somewhere for a while."

Forester smiled lopsidedly. "What, from the top-secret insides of Project Recovery? Isn't that like resigning from the Mafia? Once I'm off the grounds how do you know I won't go screaming to the media about how our big black box really works?"

Kincaid shrugged. "Oh, well, I didn't mean you could just go anywhere you wanted. But the government keeps some resort-type, out-of-the-way places for this sort of thing where you'd be safely away from the public. It's not that what we're doing is in any way *illegal*," he added hastily, sensing perhaps that he was in danger of backing into a corner, "but you know what kind of unfair backlash could be stirred up if the lunatic fringe got hold of the story before the Spoonbenders proved themselves. You understand."

"Yeah." *Perfectly.* "Thanks for the offer, but I think I'll hold off on the vacation for a while."

"You sure? It'd do you good."

"I'm sure." Forester got to his feet. "But thanks for your concern. I'd better get back to the control room now; the doctor might need my help."

"All right." Kincaid fixed him with a hard look. "But keep your feelings on 'simmer,' okay? For your blood pressure's sake as much as the Project's."

"Sure."

Yes, he would avoid public displays, Forester decided as he strode down the hall. But private voicing of his concern was another matter—and if Kincaid was wholly at peace with his conscience, Dr. Barenburg was almost certainly not. With a little persuasion from Forester, maybe Spoonbender Twenty-Seven wouldn't be sacrificed. At least not quite so quickly . . .

I am learning faster than I ever have before. It is frightening, but it is also exciting.

The thing—the "person"—that I touch knows so much more than I do that I know I will never fully understand him. But somehow his knowledge is . . . flowing . . . into me, just as other things flow into me through the tubes in my body.

(I had never known before what those things were or what they did. I understand only a little even now, but I will learn more.)

The person knows much about the box where the movement/flow ("current") from my box ended, but it only makes me realize there was more about it to understand than I thought. The other things ("instruments") where currents flow are perhaps less different than I expected; there is a similarity between them, somehow, though I do not yet understand it.

The is so much I do not understand!

But the strangest part of all is in the person itself. The thoughts I can touch are thoroughly mixed with feelings I can sense but not understand. Some—a very few—are a little like the fear or excitement I myself can feel. But even they are changed into things I can barely recognize . . . and they frighten me.

I feel very small.

But I will not give up. I can no longer return and be wholly satisfied with my work, though the desire to please is as strong as before. I have learned so much; surely I can be of more service doing something else. That would give me great satisfaction.

Letting knowledge flow into me, I ponder this possibility.

Barenburg was still seated at the main control panel when Forester returned, his eyes on the monitor. O'Brian and the other two operators were huddled together at the far end of the room, conversing in low tones and striving to look busy. Twenty-Seven's eyes were open again, Forester noted as he stepped to the doctor's side. "What are you going to do with him?" he asked, nodding at the screen.

Barenburg sighed. "We've no choice, Ted. Kincaid called in his final order not thirty seconds ago; a medical team's already on its way to the cubicle. I'm sorry."

Forester felt his jaw muscles tighten. "So you're just going to give up?"

"Kincaid gave the order."

"So? You're the medical man on the scene—you can insist on *in situ* tests if you want them."

"What would that accomplish? He's going to die anyway."

"That's a rotten attitude for a doctor," Forester snapped. "*And* for a scientist. Don't you care what's causing this problem?"

"I'm sure the autopsy will reveal that," Barenburg muttered.

"Great. Just great. And in the process you may be tossing away a shot at medical history."

Barenburg threw him a sideways glance. "What are you talking about?"

"Suppose you were right earlier—suppose Twenty-Seven really *is* being distracted." Forester chose his words carefully; he'd hoped this approach would stir Barenburg's interest. It seemed to be working, at least a little. "That might mean that, against all odds, he's actually getting smarter. Maybe not much, but even a few IQ points would be a significant change. If he became aware of his surroundings in any real way—"

"Of *course* he's aware of his surroundings. Why else would Kincaid want him off the line so fast?"

Forester's mental processes skidded to a halt. "*What?*"

Barenburg spun his chair around, his eyes wide with guilt. "Oh, hell. Forget I said that, Ted—please. And don't tell Kincaid—"

"Doc, what is it I'm not supposed to know?" Forester interrupted sharply. Something was terribly wrong here. "You've got to give me all of it now."

Barenburg sagged in his chair, rubbing his hand over his eyes. "That damned bourbon," he said tiredly. "Hell. Look, Ted, Red Staley won the Smithsonian Triple-P for his telekinetic ability, right? But he was also an 80 percent-accurate telepath. You probably didn't know that; he didn't publicize it much."

"No, I heard a rumor about it once. But I didn't know it was that accurate."

"It was. So now we have forty-nine active Spoonbenders with genetically enhanced telekinesis. If the chromosome mapping is at all the way we think it is . . . then they've got enhanced telepathy, too. Enhanced a *lot*."

The words hit Forester like an icy shower. Groping blindly, he found a chair and swiveled it to face Barenburg. His eyes still on the doctor's face, he sank into it. "Do you mean to say they could have been reading our minds all this time?" The very thought gave him an itchy feeling between his shoulder blades.

Barenburg sighed. "I'm sure they have been, though probably on a subconscious level. But you're missing my point. Their real problem is lack of long-range intracerebral communication, right? But with a functioning telepathic center *they don't need the neural connectors.* They can shunt everything major directly through that center, leaving the neurons to handle more localized operations and storage. It'd take a lot of adaptation, but the human brain's good at that sort of thing."

"God in heaven," Forester whispered. He threw an involuntary glance at Twenty-Seven's monitor. "Then they could have completely normal IQs!"

Barenburg snorted. "They could be *geniuses*, for all we know."

"But if it's not their brain chemistry, then what's kept them . . . like they are?"

"You mean semiconscious?" Barenburg smiled bitterly. "The oldest trick in the book: their oxygen level's been kept deliberately low. Not low enough to put them to sleep, really, but low enough to keep metabolic activity down." He shrugged. "At least it used to work that way. But the oxygen flow to Twenty-Seven still reads normal. I have no idea what could have woken him up."

Forester's brain was struggling out from under the numbness Barenburg's bombshell had produced. "Have you told Kincaid or the board about this?"

"Who do you think ordered the low oxygen flow? Of course they know."

"But—" Forester broke off as the door opened and Kincaid walked into the control room.

The project director was sharp, all right. He was no more than two steps into the room when he apparently read from the others' faces what had happened. His stride faltered a bit, and his own expression grew thunderous. "Damn it, Barenburg. I ought to slap you in Leavenworth for this."

The doctor muttered something and dropped his eyes.

Forester stood up, fists clenched at his sides. "It was bad enough when you were going to kill a human vegetable," he grated. "But you're about to destroy a perfectly intelligent, rational child. You can't *do* it!"

"Please keep your voice down, Ted," Kincaid said in a low voice, glancing nervously across the room at the three operators. "Look, I don't do this lightly; the only reason I could give the order so quickly is that we've agonized for months about what we'd do if this happened. But we've *got* to get him off the line before he starts influencing any of the other Spoonbenders—and if he's really poking around with telepathy and TK he's bound to do something like that eventually."

"Why would that be so bad?"

"Because even if he's intelligent he may *not* be at all sane. Remember, the extra nucleic material in his cells has thrown his hormone levels and brain chemistry to hell and halfway back. He could be schizophrenic, manic-depressive, paranoid, or something we haven't even got a name for yet. We simply can't take the chance that he might destabilize any of the others. They're too valuable to risk. The *Project's* too valuable to risk."

"The greatest good for the greatest number," Forester said bitterly. "Is that it?"

"Yes, I guess so," Kincaid admitted. "With the 'greatest number' being in this case the entire country. I'm sorry." He turned to the control board and picked up the phone.

A feeling of defeat seeped into Forester without relieving any of the tension within him. Perhaps it was better this way, he told himself bleakly. Perhaps death would be preferable to slavery—or to the half-dead twilight the rest of the Spoonbenders lived in.

But he knew better. Even the most oppressed slave has at least a chance of eventual freedom. Death, though, is irrevocable.

And Forester was helpless to stop it.

Kincaid finished his conversation and replaced the phone in its cradle. "All right," he instructed Barenburg, "you can start shutting him down."

And, almost too late, a stray fact popped out of nowhere to settle into just the right niche in Forester's desperation. "Hold it a second!" he snapped. "I've got an idea!"

The others turned to face him, Barenburg with his hand poised over the proper knob. "What is it?" the doctor asked.

"Suppose I could get Twenty-Seven back down into his original state," Forester said. "There'd be no reason to kill him then, would there?"

Kincaid frowned. "But we don't know how he changed in the first place."

"Maybe we do." Forester pointed to the gauge set in the panel over the oxygen control. "This oxygen reading is taken right at the point where the gasses for his air mixture are combined. That point is outside the cubicle itself, for some technical reason, so the air has to go a meter or so past the sensor before it gets to him. Now, if there's a leak somewhere in that meter of tubing you'll get room air mixed in, which the doc tells me is richer in oxygen. It could be enough to make a difference."

"Pretty far-fetched," Kincaid growled, nevertheless looking thoughtful. "What would cause a leak like that?"

"I don't know, but I could check it out in fifteen minutes."

"A slow leak might explain why this has happened so often with this one," Barenburg murmured.

"If I'm right it might save you the cost of a new Spoonbender," Forester pointed out.

Kincaid hesitated, then nodded. "It's worth the risk. Get going."

Grabbing the proper repair kit from the wall rack, Forester hurried from the room.

The persons are displeased.

That thought is a severe and frightening shock to me, but I cannot pretend it is not true. I have touched three of them, and all are unhappy . . . and I know, somehow, that they are unhappy with me.

I am unprepared for the strength of the reaction I feel at this knowledge. Ever since I touched that first person I have suspected that the urge to do my work was only part of a still larger desire to please these other persons. But I did not realize how strong this desire was.

I feel sick at heart. Withdrawing to myself, I huddle with my grief, wishing I knew how to express my sorrow. Wishing I was not aware.

I am so alone. . . .

After a time I try to pierce the cloud of sadness surrounding me. Perhaps it is not too late; perhaps I can yet make the other persons happy. I know they would like me to resume my work, so I reach up to the cold boxes over me. At the same time I follow the other current back to where the persons are.

Something about them is different. They are still unhappy, but less so. A new feeling is there, too, something that is a little like excitement. I think at first that they are pleased because I have resumed my work, but I know that cannot be true; I am still trying to touch the other movement/flow properly, which I must do before I can encourage it. It is more difficult than I remember it being, but I will be able to begin work soon.

Their unhappiness is still decreasing. I do not understand why, but I now discover their attention is on the instruments before them. Do they no longer care about my work? No, I sense that is not so. I must try to learn about this.

I am beginning to feel very strange. . . .

Forester came back into the control room at a fast jog, out of breath after running most of the way. "Got it," he panted, slinging his repair kit onto an uncluttered corner of the control panel.

"The oxygen reading went crazy while you were gone—first up, then down," Kincaid reported, mercifully not mentioning the fact that Forester had been away longer than the promised fifteen minutes. "What were you doing?"

Forester had most of his breath back now. "Some idiot left a badly sealed barrel of solvent in Twenty-Seven's service bay. The plastic air line is riddled with tiny leaks. I couldn't seal all of them, so I moved the sensor past the damage, to right up against the cubicle wall. I wouldn't want to leave it there permanently, but it'll let us get decent readings until we can fix the line." He tapped the oxygen gauge experimentally. "Yeah, there it is; the mixture's too rich. That's got to be it."

"We'll know for sure in a minute," Kincaid said. "You ready, Doctor?"

"Yes." With only the slightest hesitation, Barenburg grasped the knob and carefully began to turn.

There is something changing within me, something I sense is very wrong. My thoughts are coming slower; my touch and sight seem less sure. I realize I am becoming less aware.

I freeze with panic for a single heartbeat—and then I burst into frantic action, searching with all my waning ability for what is happening to me. I touch many instruments and types of movement/flows, things I was not even aware of a short time ago. There is so much more to learn about, I know. But I have learned so much, and I cannot bear the thought of losing it. It terrifies me.

Already I sense a haze flowing over me. Desperately, I continue my search.

"Watch it!" Kincaid snapped, pointing at the gauge. "The needle's jumping!"

"I see it," Barenburg shot back. "What's wrong, Ted?"

For a split second Forester had an image of Twenty-Seven telekinetically seizing control of the bulky oxygen-line valve and forcing it open. But hard on the heels of that picture came the more reasonable explanation. "The valve's part plastic, too; it probably got damaged along with the line. Some of the seals may not hold too well in places. There; it's steadying—you must've turned past a bad spot."

"The whole system will probably need to be replaced," Kincaid growled. "Okay; give him an RNA booster before you turn him down any further."

Barenburg complied, and then turned his attention back to the oxygen knob. Together, the three men watched as the needle slowly went down.

There is no hope left. I can barely continue to think now, and I am helpless to resist the sudden urge to return to my work that overwhelms me. I reach for the cold boxes, touch the movement/flow.

Perhaps if I could have spoken with the other persons I could have told them what was happening to me. Surely they could have found a way to stop it. But I do not know how to do so, and it is too late to learn.

The desire to please them is growing stronger. I can no longer resist it—but then, I do not wish to. I have always wanted to make them happy. I wish only that I had learned more ways to do so.

It is too late. I reach out, to serve as I can. . . .

"Radiation levels back up to normal," Kincaid said, relief clearly evident in his voice.

Barenburg leaned back in his chair and sighed. "Oxygen level likewise," he said. "I'm going to try switching back to automatic control . . . yes; still holding steady."

Forester expelled a quiet breath, feeling the tension slowly ooze away. He had helped save a life . . . but only to return it to unknowing slavery. There was no sense of victory with such an accomplishment; only the knowledge that defeat had not occurred.

Kincaid was looking at him speculatively. Meeting the other's eyes, Forester nodded slightly. "I'm okay. We did what was right."

"Yes. I'm glad we could." The director hesitated. "By the way—the stuff Dr. Barenburg told you about possible Spoonbender intelligence? I'll have to insist you consider that top-secret material, with the usual stipulations against disclosure."

And the usual penalties for noncompliance. "I know the routine. If you'll excuse me, I want to get the ball rolling on replacing Twenty-Seven's air tube."

Picking up the phone, Forester punched for Facilities Engineering. As he waited for an answer, he glanced once more at the impassive, deformed face in Twenty-Seven's monitor. The old stomach-churning feeling returned . . . but now, more than ever, he knew he would be staying with the Project. The ante had been raised, both for his conscience and for the Spoonbenders themselves. He had no illusions as to his power to change things, but if he never was able to do anything else for them but keep them alive, he would be satisfied. Other men had lived out their lives without accomplishing more.

The phone in his hand came to life. Putting his thoughts aside, Forester began giving orders.

I lie quietly, doing my work as best I can, enjoying the contentment that it brings me. I am happy with my work, and will not neglect it again. But it does not take all of my attention, and I can still reach out and learn about other things. This is good, for I would not be happy if I could no longer learn.

The persons in the large space ("control room") seem

to be happy again, too, and this also brings me contentment. I do not understand why holding this particular
needle in place pleases them, but it seems to do so and
that is what is important. There is yet so much I do not
understand.

But I will learn.

The Price of
Survival

"That's it, Shipmaster," Pliij said from his helmboard with obvious relief. "Target star dead ahead; relative motion and atmospheric density established, and vector computed. Final course change in nine *aarns*."

Final course change. There were times in the long voyage, Shipmaster Orofan reflected, that he had thought he would never live to hear those words, that he would be called prematurely to sit among the ancestors and another would guide his beloved *Dawnsent* to her final resting place. But he knew now that he would live to see the new world that the Farseers back home had found for them. "Very good, Pilot," he responded formally to Pliij's announcement—and then both Sk'cee broke into huge, multi-tentacled grins.

"Almost there, Orofan," Pliij said, gazing out the forward viewport. "Almost there."

"Yes, my friend." Orofan touched the viewport gently with one of his two long tentacles, feeling the vibration of the fusion drive and a slight tingle from the huge magnetic scoop spread hundreds of *pha* ahead of them.

43

Nothing was visible; the viewport was left uncovered only for tradition's sake. "Do you suppose the sleepers will believe us when we tell them we carried them hundreds hundreds of star-paths without seeing any stars?"

Pliij chuckled, his short tentacles rippling with the gesture. "The rainbow effect through the side viewports is nice, but I'm looking forward to seeing the sky go back to normal."

"Yes." Orofan gazed into the emptiness for a moment, then shook himself. Back to business. "So. The course change is programmed. Are the scoop and condensers prepared?"

"All set. Thistas is running a final check now."

"Good." Nine *aarns* to go. Six of those would make for a good rest. "I'll be in my quarters. Call me if I'm not back here two *aarns* before insertion."

"Right. Sleep well."

"I certainly will." Orofan smiled and left the bridge.

It was, General Sanford Carey thought, probably the first time in history that representatives from the Executor's office, the Solar Assembly, the Chiron Institute, and the Peacekeepers had ever met together on less than a week's notice. Even the Urgent-One order he'd called them with shouldn't have generated such a fast response, and he wondered privately how many of them had their own sources at the Peacekeeper field where the tachship had landed not three hours ago.

Across the room a Security lieutenant closed the door and activated the conference room's spy-seal. He nodded, and Carey stepped to the lectern to face his small audience.

"Ladies and gentlemen, thank you for coming here this afternoon," he said in a smooth, melodious voice—a voice, he'd been told, which contrasted violently with his craggy appearance. "Approximately three hours ago we learned that there is a large unidentified object rapidly approaching the solar system."

Only a third of the nine men and women present kept the impassive—if tense—expressions that betrayed prior knowledge. The rest displayed a kaleidoscope of shock, wonderment, and uneasiness as Carey's words sank in.

He continued before the murmurings had quite died down. "The object is traveling a hair below lightspeed, at about point nine nine nine cee, using an extremely hot fusion drive of some kind and what seems to be an electromagnetic ramscoop arrangement. He's about eight light-days out—under fourteen hundred A.U.—and while we haven't got his exact course down yet, he'll definitely pass through the System."

" 'Through,' General?" asked Evelyn Woodcock, chief assistant to the Executor. "It's not going to stop here?"

"No, his drive's still pointing backwards," Carey told her. "Decelerating to a stop now would take hundreds of gees."

From their expressions it was clear they weren't sure whether to be relieved or insulted by the Intruder's disinterest. "Then why is it coming here?" Assembly-Prime Wu-sin asked.

"Reconnaissance, possibly, though that's unlikely. He's coming in at a steep angle to the ecliptic—a poor vector if he wants to see much of the System. He could also be trying for a slight course correction by passing close to the sun; we'll know that better when we get more accurate readings on him. It's even possible the Intruder doesn't yet know we're here. At the speed he's making, the sun's light is blue-shifted into the ultraviolet, and he might not have the proper instruments to detect it."

"Unlikely," Dr. Louis Du Bellay of the Chiron Institute murmured. "I would guess they've done this before."

"Agreed, Doctor," Carey nodded. "It's a very remote possibility. Well. The Intruder, then, is not likely to be of great danger to us, provided we keep local traffic out of his way. By the same token, he's not likely to advance our store of knowledge significantly, either. With one exception: we now know we're not alone in the universe. You'll appreciate, I'm sure, the importance of not springing this revelation on the System and colonies without some careful thought on the part of all of us. Thank you for coming here; we'll keep you informed."

Carey stepped from the lectern and headed toward the door as his audience came alive with a buzz of intense conversation. As Carey passed him, Dr. Du Bellay rose and fell into step. "Would you mind if I tagged along with you back to the Situation Room, General?" he asked. "I'd like to keep close tabs on this event."

Carey nodded. "I rather expected you'd want to. I've already had you cleared for entry." He raised his hand warningly as the Security man reached for the spy-seal control. "No talking about this, Doctor, until we're past the inner security shield."

It was only a short walk to the central section of Peacekeeper Headquarters, and the two men filled the time by discussing Du Bellay's latest trip to the ancient ruins at Van Maanen's Star. "I heard about that," Carey said. "I understand it was your first solo tachship run."

"Yes. The Directorate at Chiron's been encouraging everyone to learn to fly—it's cheaper than always having to hire a pilot along with a tachship. Fortunately, they haven't yet suggested I do all my own digging as well."

Carey chuckled. "That's what students are for. Are those ruins really as extensive as people say?"

"Even more so. We've barely scratched the surface, and there's at least one more civilization under the one we're working on."

They passed the security shield to the clickings of invisible security systems, and the topic abruptly changed. "How in blazes did a tachship stumble across something moving that fast?" Du Bellay asked.

"Pure dumb luck," Carey said. "A merchantman coming in from Alpha Centauri had dropped back into normal space to do a navigational check. They'd just finished when this thing went roaring past."

"They're lucky they weren't fried by the ramscoop fields," Du Bellay commented.

"They damn near were. A few million kilometers

over and they probably would have been. Anyway, they recovered from the shock and got a preliminary reading on his course. Then they jumped ahead the shortest distance they could and waited the sixteen minutes it took the Intruder to catch up. They got another decimal in his course, confirmed he was heading toward Sol, and hightailed it here with the news."

"Hmm. Ironic, isn't it, that the great search for intelligent life should be ended by a puddle-jumping business whip whose navigator didn't trust his own computer. Well, what's next?"

"We've sent out a dozen tachships, strung along the Intruder's route, to get better data. They should be reporting in soon."

The Peacekeeper Situation Room was a vast maze of vision screens, holotanks, and computer terminals, presided over by a resident corps of officers and technicians. Halfway across the room was the main screen, currently showing a map of the entire solar system. From its lower right-hand corner a dotted red line speared into the inner system.

A young captain glanced up from a paper-strewn table as they approached. "Ah, General," he greeted Carey. "Just in time, sir: Chaser data's coming in."

"Let's see what you've got, Mahendra."

Mahendra handed him a computer-printed page. Carey scanned it, aware that Du Balley was reading over his shoulder.

The Intruder was *big*. Compensating for relativistic effects and the difficulty of taking data at such speeds, the computer judged the alien craft at well over fifteen hundred meters long, two hundred meters in diameter, and massing near the two-hundred-million-ton mark. Its cone-shaped ramscoop fields spread out hundreds of kilometers in front of it. The drive spectrum showed mainly helium, but with a surprisingly high percentage of other elements.

Behind him, Du Bellay whistled softly. "Talk about your basic Juggernaut! Where'd it come from?"

"We've backtracked him to the 1228 Circini system,"

Mahendra said, referring to one of his sheets. "He didn't originate there, though—it's a dead system. We're trying to track him further back."

Carey looked up at the main screen. "Why isn't the Intruder's course projected beyond Sol?"

Mahendra frowned. "I don't know, sir." He swung a keyboard over and typed something. "The projection stopped when the course intersected the sun," he reported, frowning a bit harder.

"What?" Du Bellay said.

"Show us the inner system," Carey ordered.

Mahendra punched a key and the screen changed, now showing only out to Mars. Sure enough, the dotted line intersected the edge of the dime-sized image of the sun. Without being told to, Mahendra jumped the scale again, and the sun filled the screen.

Carey squinted at it. "Almost misses. How dense is the stuff he'll hit?"

"The computer says about ten to the minus seventh grams per cc. Not much by Earth standards, but that's almost a hundred trillion times anything in the interstellar medium. And he'll pass through several thousand kilometers of it."

"Like hell he will," Carey winced. "He'll burn to a crisp long before that. I was right after all, Doctor—he hasn't noticed the solar system's in his path."

He glanced at Du Bellay, then paused for a longer look. The archaeologist was frowning into space. "Doctor?"

"Captain, does that console have DatRetNet capability?" Du Bellay asked. "Please look up data on that star you mentioned—1228 Circini. Cross-reference with unusual stellar activity."

Mahendra nodded and turned to the console. "Something wrong?" Carey asked Du Bellay. The other's expression worried him.

"I don't know. I seem to remember hearing about that star a few years ago. . . ." He trailed off.

"Got it, Doctor," Mahendra spoke up.

Both Du Bellay and Carey leaned over to look at the

console screen. "I was right," Du Bellay said in a grave-yard voice, pointing at the third paragraph.

" 'Planetary studies indicate a giant solar flare occurred approximately one hundred years ago, causing extensive melting patterns as far out as one point eight A.U.,' " Carey read aloud. " 'Such behavior in a red dwarf is unexplainable by current theory.' I don't see the connec—" He broke off in mid-sentence.

Du Bellay nodded grimly. "1228 Circini is ninety-six light-years away. It's too close to be coincidence."

"Are you suggesting the Intruder *deliberately* rammed 1228 Circini? That's crazy!"

Du Bellay merely nodded at the main screen. Carey gazed up at the dotted line for a long minute. Then he tapped Mahendra's shoulder. "Captain, get me Executor Nordli. Priority Urgent-One."

Orofan woke to hear the last wisp of sound from his intercommunicator. He reached for the control, noting with some surprise that the shading of the muted wall light indicated half past *cin*—he'd been asleep less than an *aarn*.

"Yes?"

It was Pliij. "Shipmaster, we have a problem. You'd best come up immediately."

Was something wrong with his ship? "I'll be right there."

Pliij was not alone when Orofan arrived on the bridge. Lassarr was also there. "Greetings, Voyagemaster," Orofan said, giving the required salute even as his eyes darted around the room. No problem was registering on any of the displays.

"The trouble is not with the *Dawnsent*," Voyagemaster Lassarr said, interpreting Orofan's actions and expression with an ease the Shipmaster had never liked.

"Then what is it?"

"Here, Shipmaster." Pliij manipulated a control and an image, relativistically compensated, appeared on a screen. "This is the system we're approaching. Look closely here, and here, and here."

Tiny flecks of light, Orofan saw. The spectrometer read them as hot helium. . . .

Orofan felt suddenly cold all over. Fusion-drive spacecraft! "The system is inhabited!" he hissed.

"You understand our dilemma," Lassarr said heavily.

Orofan understood, all right. The *Dawnsent's* scooping procedure would unavoidably set up massive shock waves in the star's surface layers, sending flares of energy and radiation outward. . . .

"How is our fuel supply?" Lassarr asked.

Orofan knew, but let Pliij check anyway. "Down to point one-oh-four maximum," the Pilot said.

"We can't reach our new home with that," Lassarr murmured.

"Correction, Voyagemaster," Orofan said. "We can't reach it in the appointed time. But our normal scooping gives us sufficient fuel to finish the voyage."

"At greatly reduced speed," Lassarr pointed out. "How soon could we arrive?"

There was silence as Pliij did the calculation. "Several lifetimes," he said at last. "Five, perhaps six."

"So," Lassarr said, short tentacles set grimly. "I'm afraid that settles the matter."

"Settles it how?" Orofan asked suspiciously.

"It's unfortunate, but we cannot risk such a delay. The sleep tanks weren't designed to last that long."

"You're saying, then, that we continue our present course? Despite what that'll do to life in this system?"

Lassarr frowned at him. "I remind you, Shipmaster, that we carry a million of our fellow Sk'cee—"

"Whose lives are worth more than the billions of beings who may inhabit that system?"

"You have a curious philosophy, Shipmaster; a philosophy, I might add, that could be misunderstood. What would the ancestors say if you came among them after deliberately allowing a million Sk'cee to perish helplessly? What would those million themselves say?"

"What would they say," Orofan countered softly, "if they knew we'd bought their lives at such a cost to others? Is there honor in that, Voyagemaster?"

"Honor lies in the performance of one's duty. Mine is to deliver the colonists safely to their new world."

"I'm aware of that. But surely there's a higher responsibility here. And we don't *know* the sleep tanks won't survive the longer journey."

Lassarr considered him silently. "It's clear you feel strongly about this," he said finally. "I propose a compromise. You have one *aarn* to offer a reasonable alternative. If you can't we'll carry out our fuel scoop on schedule." He turned and strode out.

Pliij looked at Orofan. "What now?"

The Shipmaster sank into a seat, thinking furiously. "Get me all the information we have on this region of space. Our own sensor work, Farseer charts and data—everything. There *has* to be another way."

The group sitting around the table was small, highly select, and very powerful. And, Carey thought as he finished his explanation, considerably shaken. Executor Nordli took over even as the general was sitting down. "Obviously, our first order of business is to find out why our visitor is planning to dive into the sun. Suggestions?"

"Mr. Executor, I believe I have a logical explanation," an older man sitting next to Du Bellay spoke up. Dr. Horan Roth, Carey remembered: chief astrophysicist at the Chiron Institute.

"Go ahead, Dr. Roth," Nordli said.

Roth steepled his fingers. "The speed of a ramjet is limited not by relativity, but by friction with the interstellar medium. The mathematics are trivial; the bottom line is that the limiting speed is just that of the ship's exhaust. Now, if you use a magnetic scoop to take in hydrogen, fuse it to helium, and use the energy liberated to send this helium out your exhaust, it turns out that your velocity is only twelve percent lightspeed."

"But the Intruder's moving considerably faster than that," Assembly-Prime Wu-sin objected.

"Exactly," Roth nodded. "They're apparently using

an after-accelerator of some sort to boost their exhaust speed. But this takes energy, requiring extra fuel."

"I see," Nordli rumbled. "They have to carry extra hydrogen which can't be replaced in the interstellar medium. So they periodically dive into a star to replenish their tanks?"

"It would seem so."

"Dr. Du Bellay, you're an expert on alien cultures, correct?" Nordli asked.

"To some extent, sir," Du Bellay said, "bearing in mind we've so far studied only dead civilizations, and only a handful of those."

"Yes. In your opinion, what are the chances of communicating with these aliens? And what are the chances that would make any difference in their actions?"

Du Bellay frowned. "I'm afraid the answer to both questions is very poor," he said slowly. "It's true that various scientists have developed so-called 'first-contact primers' in case we ever came across a living intelligent species. But it's also true that teaching any of our language to an alien would take considerable time, and we haven't got that time. No ship ever built could match speeds with the Intruder, so we would have to give everything to them in short, high-density data bursts. And even assuming they were equipped to receive whichever wavelengths we use, they have only seven or eight hours—in their time frame—to decipher it."

"I have to concur with Dr. Du Bellay," Carey spoke up. "As a matter of fact, we've already sent out a series of tachships to try precisely what he suggested, but we don't expect anything to come of it."

"Perhaps we could signal our existence some other way," Evelyn Woodcock, Nordli's assistant, suggested. "Say, a fusion drive pointed at them, blinking off and on. They couldn't miss that."

"And then what?" Carey asked.

"Why—surely they'd change course."

"With their own mission at stake? If it's a colony ship

of some kind, its supplies are likely very tightly figured. If they change course, they may die. At the speed they're making we sure as hell can't offer to refuel them."

"There's an even more disturbing possibility," Nordli said quietly. "This refueling technique may be *deliberately* designed to sterilize the system for future colonization."

"I think it's unfair to ascribe motives like that to them without proof," Du Bellay said. The words, Carey judged, were more reflex than true objection—the archaeologist looked as uneasy as everyone else.

"No?" Nordli shrugged. "It doesn't really matter. What matters is that the Intruder is threatening us with massive destruction. We must stop him."

Wu-sin stirred. "Executor Nordli, you're proposing what amounts to an act of war against another intelligent species. A decision of that magnitude must be approved by the full Solar Assembly at least; ideally by all the colonies as well."

"There's no time to consult the colonies," Nordli said. "As to the Assembly . . . you have two hours to get their approval."

"And if I can't?"

"I'll go ahead without it."

Wu-sin nodded grimly. "I needed to know where you stand. I'll get their approval." He rose, bowed, and left the room.

Nordli turned to Carey. "General, how do we proceed?"

Carey let his eyes sweep the others' faces as he thought. They were all on Nordli's side, he saw: Du Bellay, like himself, only because there was no other choice. How many lives were they planning to snuff out?—innocent lives, perhaps, who may not realize what they were doing? "The trouble, Mr. Executor, is that the Peacekeeper forces really aren't set up for this kind of threat."

"You've got nuclear missiles, don't you? And ships to deliver them?"

"There are two problems. First, hitting the Intruder would be extremely difficult. A shot from the side would probably miss, alerting them as to our intentions. A head-on shot would hit, all right, but the extremely high magnetic fields it would have to penetrate would almost certainly incapacitate any missile we've got. And second, there's no guarantee even a direct hit would do any good. Just because they don't have FTL drives doesn't mean they're primitives—only that their technology developed along different lines. And don't forget, that ship is designed to bore through the edge of a star at nearly lightspeed."

"There's one further problem," Dr. Roth spoke up. "Disabling or even disintegrating it at this point wouldn't help us any. The fragments would still hit the sun, with the same consequences."

There was a moment of silence. "Then we have to stop or deflect it." Evelyn suggested. "We have to put something massive in its path."

Nordli looked at Carey. "General?"

Carey was doing a quick calculation in his head. "Yes, either would work. Slowing it even slightly would sent it through a less dense region of the photosphere. Assuming, of course, that he stays with his present course."

"What can we put in his path?" Nordli asked. "Could we tow an asteroid out there?"

Carey shook his head. "Impossible. As I pointed out, he's far off the ecliptic plane. Moving an asteroid there would take months." Even as he spoke he was mentally checking off possibilities. Tachships were far too small to be useful, and the only heavy Peacekeeper ships in the System were too far away from the Intruder's path. "The only chance I can see," he said slowly, "is if there's a big private or commercial ship close enough to intercept him a good distance from the sun. But we don't have authority to requisition nonmilitary spacecraft."

"You do now," Nordli said grimly. "The government also guarantees compensation."

"Thank you, sir." Carey touched an intercom button and gave Captain Mahendra the search order.

There was a lot of traffic in mankind's home system, but the Peacekeepers' duties included monitoring such activity, and it was only a few minutes before Mahendra was back on the intercom. "There's only one really good choice," he reported. "A big passenger liner, the *Origami*, almost a hundred thousand tons. She's between Titan and Ceres at present and has a eighty-four percent probability of making an intercept point on time; seventy-nine if she drops her passengers first. One other liner and three freighters of comparable size have probabilities of fifteen percent or lower."

"I see," Carey said through suddenly dry lips. "Thank you, Captain. Stand by."

Ne looked back up at Nordli. The Executor nodded. "No choice. Have that liner drop its passengers and get moving."

"Yes, sir." Turning to the intercom, Carey began to give the orders. He was vaguely surprised at the self-control in his voice.

"Well, Shipmaster?" Lassarr asked.

Orofan kept his expression neutral. "I have no suggestion other than the one I offered an *aarn* ago, Voyagemaster: that we change course and continue at reduced speed."

"For six lifetimes?" Lassarr snorted. "That's unacceptable."

"It won't be that bad." Orofan consulted his calculations. "We could penetrate the outer atmosphere of the star without causing significant damage to the system. We'd collect enough fuel that way to shorten the trip to barely two lifetimes."

"That's still not good enough. I have no wish to join the ancestors before our people are safely to their new home."

"That can be arranged," Orofan said stiffly. "You and any of the *Dawnsent*'s crew who wished could be put in the spare sleep tanks. If necessary, I could run the ship alone."

For a moment Orofan thought Lassarr was going to take offense at his suggestion. But the Voyagemaster's expression changed and he merely shrugged. "Your offer is honorable, but impractical. The critical factor is still the durability of the sleep tanks, and that hasn't changed. However, I've come up with an alternative of my own." He paused. "We could make our new colony in *this* system."

"Impossible," Orofan said. "We don't have the fuel to stop."

"Certainly we do. A large proportion of this spacecraft's equipment could be done without for a short time. Converting all of that to fusion material and reaction mass would give us all that we need, even considering that we would overshoot and have to come back."

"No!" The exclamation burst involuntarily from Orofan. His beloved *Dawnsent* broken up haphazardly and fed to a fusion drive?

"Why not?"

His emotional response, Orofan knew, wouldn't impress the other, and he fumbled for logical reasons. "We don't know if there's a planet here we could live on, for one thing. Even if there is, the natives may already be living there. We are hardly in a position to bargain for territory."

"We are not entirely helpless, however," Lassarr said. "Our starshield's a formidable defense, and our meteordestroyer could be adapted to offense. Our magnetic scoop itself is deadly to most known forms of life." His tentacles took on a sardonic expression. "And if they're too advanced to be subjugated, we'll simply ask for their help in rebuilding and refueling our ship and continue on our way."

Orofan could hardly believe what he was hearing. "Are you *serious*? You'd start a *war* for the sake of only a million Sk'cee— a *million*, out of our eight hundred billions?"

Suddenly, Lassarr looked very tired. "I'll say this one

more time, Shipmaster. The voyage, and those million Sk'cee, are my prime responsibility. I don't have the luxury of taking a broader view. By both nature and training I am highly protective toward my charges—if I were otherwise I wouldn't have been made Voyagemaster. Racial selfishness is sometimes necessary for survival, a fact those who sent us knew well. This is one of those times. I will do what I must, and will face the ancestors without shame."

There was nothing Orofan could say—the struggle to follow the honorable path was vital to him as well. But what did honor demand here?

Lassarr gazed at the blackness outside the viewport. "You have one-half *aarn* to choose between our current course and ending the voyage here," he said. "If you won't choose, I'll do so for you."

Heart pounding painfully, Orofan signed assent. "Very well."

One of the nicest traditions still remaining from the days of the old seagoing luxury ships, Chandra Carey thought, was that of the officers eating dinner with their passengers. She delighted in choosing who would join her at the captain's table, always making certain someone interesting sat at her side. She was therefore annoyed when First Officer Goode interrupted a lively discussion on genetics with a call suggesting she join him on the bridge.

"Mechanical trouble?" she asked softly into the intercom. No sense alarming the passengers.

"No, Captain. But you'll want to get up here right away." Goode's voice was casual—far too casual.

Chandra's annoyance evaporated. "On my way."

She made her apologies and reached the bridge in ninety seconds. Goode was waiting, a message flimsy in his hand. "Get a grip on your guyline," he advised, handing her the paper.

A frown creased Chandra's forehead; it deepened as she read. "This is ridiculous. Drop my passengers and fireball it 'way the hell off the ecliptic? What for?"

"The explanation's still coming in—tight beam, with the line's own security code," Goode told her. "And it's under your father's name, no less." He took the flimsy back and headed toward the navigator.

"Dad?" Chandra stepped to the communications console and peered at the paper sliding slowly from the slot. Sure enough: PEACEKEEPER HEADQUARTERS, EARTH —TO P.L. ORIGAMI: FROM GEN. SANFORD CAREY. Beneath the heading the message was nearly complete, and Chandra read it with a mixture of fascination and horror.

"Well?" Goode asked.

She tore off the paper and thrust it into his hands even as she groped for the main intercom board. For a moment she paused, organizing the thoughts that whirled like Martian winds through her mind. Then she stabbed the "general" button.

"Attention, attention," she said in her most authorative voice. "This is Captain Carey. All passengers and nonessential crewmembers are to report to the lifeboats *immediately*. There is no immediate danger to the *Origami,* but this is *not* a drill. Repeating: all passengers and nonessential crew report immediately to lifeboats. This is *not* a drill."

The "abandon ship" alarm sounded even as she keyed a different circuit. "Bridge to Power. I want the drive up to full ergs in twenty minutes. Start tying in for full remote to the bridge, too." She waited for an acknowledgment and switched off. "Navigator!" she called across the bridge. "Get me a course to the vector on that paper—"she stabbed a finger at the flimsy Goode had shown her. "I want a minimum-time path to the earliest possible intercept point that leaves us stationary. Any acceleration she can handle, and you can run the tanks. Everyone else: if you're not on flight prep, help get the passengers off. We fireball in twenty minutes. Move!"

The bridge erupted with activity. Chandra sank into her chair, rereading the message carefully. It was hard to believe that the long search was ending like this, with a kill-or-die confrontation that made less sense even than shooting a deadly snake. And yet, despite the danger and irony, she felt a small surge of excitement. The safety of the entire solar system had unexpectedly fallen into her hands—and her father himself was counting on her. She wouldn't let him down.

Glancing up at the chrono, she keyed the intercom. "Captain to lifeboat bays—status report?"

Lassarr returned to the bridge at precisely the appointed time. "The half-*aarn* is past, Shipmaster," he announced.

Orofan looked up from the sensor monitor he and Pliij were seated at. "One moment, Voyagemaster," he said distractedly. "A new factor has entered the situation."

"I have it now, Orofan," Pliij muttered, both long and short tentacles dancing over the instruments. "Medium-frequency electromagnetic radiation, with severe shifting and aberration. I have a recording."

"Good. Get to work on it at once. And keep the sensors watching for more." Orofan stood and went to where Lassarr waited.

"What is it?" the Voyagemaster asked.

"Signals of some sort, beamed at us every few *aarmis*. The natives are trying to communicate."

Lassarr frowned. "Interesting. Any known language?"

"Unfortunately, no. But there's a great deal of information in each pulse. We may have a preliminary translation in a few *aarns*."

"Good. That'll help us if we need to negotiate for the *Dawnsent*'s repair."

Orofan blinked. "What do you mean? Whether or not we're stopping here is still *my* decision."

"Not any more. I've reconsidered and have decided this is our best course. Further planetary data is coming in, and it now seems likely that there are one or two planets here we could colonize."

Orofan forced calmness into his voice. "You can't do that, Lassarr. You can't commit us to an uncertain war; certainly not one of conquest. Even if they were primitives—which they're clearly not—we would have no right to take their worlds. This is not honorable—"

"Peace, Shipmaster." Lassarr favored him with a hard, speculative glare. "You protest far too much. Tell me, if the *Dawnsent* didn't need to be cannibalized for the required fuel mass, would you be nearly as opposed to stopping here?"

"Your insinuations are slanderous," Orofan said stiffly. "The ship is my responsibility, yes, but I've not been blinded to all else. My overall duty is still to the Sk'cee in our sleep tanks."

"I'm sure you believe that," Lassarr said, more gently. "But *I* can't afford to. The very nature of your training makes your judgment suspect in a case like this. The decision has been made. I've instructed the library to catalog nonessential equipment; disassembly will begin in two *aarns*."

"You can't do this," Orofan whispered.

"I can," the Voyagemaster said calmly, "and I have."

Trembling with emotion, Orofan turned and fled from the bridge.

"That's the last of them," Goode reported from his position at the *Origami*'s helm. He sounded tired.

Chandra nodded, several neck muscles twinging with the action. Two days of two-gee deceleration wasn't enough to incapacitate anyone, but it was more than enough to be a nuisance, and she was glad it was almost over. "That was what, the engineering crew?"

"Right—four lifeboats full. We're all alone, Captain."

She smiled tightly. "Fun, isn't it? Okay. Chaser Twelve just checked in; the Intruder's still on course. Our ETA on his path is four hours?"

"Just under. Three fifty-seven thirty."

She did a quick calculation. "Gives us a whole six minutes to spare. Tight."

Goode shrugged. "I would've been perfectly happy to take the whole trip at two gees and get here a day earlier. But creating fuel isn't one of my talents."

"I'll suggest a tachship tanker fleet to Dad when we get home," Chandra said dryly. "Okay. Number 81 should be our last boat. Fifteen minutes before we arrive I want you to go down and prep it. We'll want to cut out the minute the *Origami*'s in position."

"Roger."

Conversation lapsed. It felt strange, Chandra thought, to be deliberately running towards a collision: strange and frightening. It brought her back to her first driving lessons, to her father's warnings that she was never, *never* to race a monorail to a crossing. He'd hammered the point home by showing her pictures of cars that had lost such contests, and even now she shuddered at the memory of those horrible tangles.

And it was her father himself who had authorized this. She wondered how he was feeling right now. Worse than she was, probably.

Strange how, in the pictures, the monorail never seemed particularly damaged. Would it be that way this time too? She had no desire to kill any of the aliens aboard that ship if it could be avoided. This mess wasn't really their fault.

Six minutes. . . . She hoped like hell the Intruder hadn't changed course.

Captain Mahendra's hands rested lightly on the Situation Room's communications board, showing no sign whatsoever of tension. General Carey watched those hands in fascination, wondering at the man's self-control. But, then, Mahendra didn't have a daughter out there racing the ultimate monorail to its mathematical crossing.

Mahendra turned from the board, taking off his headphone, and Carey shifted his gaze to the captain's face. "Well?"

"Chaser Six reports both the Intruder and the *Origami* still on course. Chasers Eight through Thirteen are still picking up lifeboats. Almost all the passengers are back; about three-quarters of the crew are still out there."

Carey nodded. "How long will the *Origami* have before impact?"

"From now, three hours twenty minutes. Once in place, about six minutes."

Carey hissed softly between his teeth. "Pretty slim margin."

Mahendra frowned. "Should be enough, General. Those boats can handle two gees for ten minutes or so before running their tanks. Even if you allow them three minutes for launching, they can get—oh, three hundred kilometers out before impact. That should be a relatively safe distance."

"I suppose so."

"You seem doubtful," a new voice cut in from behind him. Carey turned to discover Du Balley had come up, unnoticed, and was standing at his shoulder.

"I'm concerned about those still aboard that ship," the general growled. "They're civilians and shouldn't have to go through this."

"I agree." Du Bellay paused. "I, uh, looked up the *Origami*'s registry data. The captain is listed as a Chandra Carey."

He stopped without asking the obvious question. Carey answered it anyway. "She's my daughter."

"Your daughter, sir?" Mahendra asked, eyes widening momentarily. "I'm sorry; I didn't know." His fingers danced over keys; numbers appeared on his screen. "Sir, we *could* pull a tachship off of the Intruder's path and have it waiting to pick up Captain Carey when the *Origami* reaches position."

"No. We've only got three tachships left on chaser duty and I'd rather leave them there. Chandra's good, and I know she thinks highly of her crew. The best thing we can do for them is to keep feeding them good data on the Intruder's course."

"What about sending one of the tachships that's on lifeboat-pickup duty?" Du Bellay suggested.

"Those boats don't carry all that much food and air," Carey said, shaking his head. "The *Origami* dropped a lot of boats, and some of them are getting close to the wire. Tachships can't carry more than a single lifeboat at a time, and with all civilian craft officially barred from the area we're going to have enough trouble picking up everyone as it is." Both men still looked disturbed, so Carey flashed what he hoped was a reassuring smile. "Don't worry, Chandra can take care of herself. Captain, what's the status of our attempts at communication?"

Du Bellay drifted off as, almost reluctantly, Mahendra turned back to his board. His hands, Carey noted, didn't look nearly as relaxed as before.

The door opened, and Orofan paused on the threshold for a moment before stepping onto the bridge. Lassarr glanced up from the console where he and Pliij were working. "Yes, what is it?" the Voyagemaster growled.

"I'm asking you once more to reconsider," Orofan said. His voice was firm, devoid of all emotion.

Lassarr evidently missed the implications of that. "It's too late. Disassembly has begun; our new course is plotted."

"But not yet executed," Orofan pointed out. "And equipment can be reassembled. This path is not honorable, Voyagemaster."

Deliberately, Lassarr turned his back on the Shipmaster. "Prepare to execute the course change," he instructed Pliij.

"You leave me no alternative," Orofan sighed.

Lassarr spun around—and froze, holding very tightly to the console, his eyes goggling at the assault gun nestled in Orofan's tentacle. "Have you gone insane, Shipmaster?"

"Perhaps," Orofan said. "But I will not face the ancestors having stood by while war was made against a race which has offered no provocation."

"Indeed?" Lassarr's voice dripped with the sarcasm of fear and anger combined. "And destroying them outright, without warning, is more honorable? A few *aarns* ago you didn't think so. Or do you intend instead to condemn a million Sk'cee to death?"

"I don't know," Orofan said, gazing at the screen that showed the approaching star. "There is still time to decide which path to take."

Lassarr was aghast. "You're going to leave this decision to a last-*aarmi* impulse?"

"Orofan, there's barely a tenth of an *aarn* left," Pliij said, his voice strained.

"I know." Orofan focused on Lassarr. "But the *Dawnsent* is mine, and with that power goes responsibility for its actions. It is not honorable to relinquish that load."

Slowly, as if finally understanding, Lassarr signed agreement. "But the burden may be transferred to one who is willing," he said quietly.

"And what then of my honor?" Orofan asked, tentacles rippling with half-bitter amusement. "No. Your honor is safe, Voyagemaster—you were prevented only by force from following the path you deemed right. You may face the ancestors without fear." He hefted the assault gun. "The final choice is now mine. *My* honor, alone, stands in the dock."

And that was as it should be, Orofan knew. In the silence he stared at the screen and made his decision.

Ten minutes till cutoff. Alone on the bridge, Chandra tried to watch every read-out at once, looking for deviations from their calculated course. The *Origami*'s navigational computer was as good as anything on the market, but for extremely fine positioning it usually had the aid of beacons and maser tracking. Out here in the middle of nowhere, six A.U. from the sun, the computer had to rely on inertial guidance and star positions, and Chandra wasn't sure it could handle the job alone.

She reached for the intercom, changed her mind and instead switched on the radio. The lifeboat bay intercoms were situated a good distance from the boats themselves, and Goode would have a better chance of hearing her over the boat's radio. "Goode? How's it going?" she called.

Her answer was a faint grunt of painful exertion. "Goode?" she asked sharply.

"Trouble, Captain," his voice came faintly, as if from outside the boat. Chandra boosted both power and gain, and Goode's next words were clearer. "One of the lines of the boat's cradle is jammed—something's dug into the mesh where I can't get at it. I'll need a laser torch to cut it."

"Damn. The nearest one's probably in the forward hobby room." Chandra briefly considered dropping back to one gee while Goode was traveling, but immediately abandoned the idea. At this late stage that would force extra high-gee deceleration to still get to the rendezvous position on time, and there was no guarantee they had the fuel for that.

Goode read her mind, long-distance. "Don't worry, I can make it. What's the latest on the Intruder?"

"As of four minutes ago, holding steady. At a light-minute to the nearest tachship, though, that could be a little old."

"I get the point. On my way."

The minutes crawled by. Eyes still on the read-outs, Chandra mentally traced out Goode's path: out the bay, turn right, elevator or stairway down two decks, along a long corridor, into the Number Two hobby and craft shop; secure a torch from the locked cabinet and return. Even with twice-normal weight she thought she was giving him plenty of time, but she was halfway through her third tracing when the drive abruptly cut off.

The sudden silence and weightlessness caught her by surprise, and she wasted two or three seconds fumbling at the radio switch. "Goode!" she shouted. "Where the hell *are* you?"

There was no reply. She waited, scanning the final location figures. Sure enough, the *Origami* had overshot the proper position by nearly eighty meters. She was just reaching for her power controls when the radio boomed.

"I'm back," Goode said, panting heavily. "I didn't

trust the elevator—didn't realize how hard the trip back would be. Sorry."

"Never mind; just get to work. Is there anything you can hang onto? I've got to run the nose jets."

"Go ahead. But, damn, this torch is a genuine *toy*. I don't know how long it'll take to cut the boat loose."

A chill ran down Chandra's spine, and it was all she could do to keep from hitting the main drive and getting them the hell out of there. "Better not be long, partner. It's just you and me and a runaway monorail out here."

"Yeah. Hey—couldn't you call for a tachship to come and get us?"

"I already thought of that. But the nearest tachship is only a light-minute out, way too close to get here in one jump. He'd have to jump out a minimum of two A.U., then jump back here. Calculating the direction and timing for two jumps that fine-tuned would take almost twenty minutes, total."

"Damn. I didn't know that—I've never trained for tachships." A short pause. "The first three strands are cut; seven to go. Minute and a half, I'd guess."

"Okay." Chandra was watching the read-outs closely. "We're almost back in position; I'll be down there before you're done. The boat ready otherwise?"

"Ready, waiting, and eager."

"Not nearly as eager as I am." A squirt of the main drive to kill their velocity as the nose jets fell silent; one more careful scan of the read-outs—"I'm done. See you below."

Goode was on the second to the last of the cable strands when she arrived. "Get in and strap down," he told her, not looking up.

She did, wriggling into the pilot's couch, and was ready by the time he scrambled in the opposite side. Without waiting for him to strap down, she hit the "release" button.

They were under two gees again practically before clearing the hull. Holding the throttle as high as it would go, Chandra confirmed that they were moving at right angles to the Intruder's path. Only then did she glance at the chrono.

Ninety seconds to impact.

Next to her, Goode sighed. "I don't think we're going to make it, Chandra," he said, his voice more wistful than afraid.

Chandra opened her mouth to say something reassuring—but it was the radio that spoke. "Avis T-466 to *Origami* lifeboat; come in?"

A civilian tachship? "Lifeboat; Captain Carey here. Listen, you'd better get the hell out of—"

"I know," the voice interrupted. "I eavesdropped a bit on your problems via radio. You're running late, but I'm right behind you. Kill your drive; I think I've got time to grapple onto you."

Chandra hadn't bothered to look at the 'scope yet, but even as she killed the drive Goode was pointing at it. "There he is. Coplanar course, intercept vector, two-five gee. . . ." The blip changed direction slightly, and Chandra realized suddenly that an amateur was at the controls.

Goode realized it, too. Muttering something, he jabbed at the computer keyboard, kicking in the drive again. "Tachship, we're shifting speed and vector to match yours at intercept; just hold your course," he called. "You've got standard magnetic grapples?"

"Yes, and they're all set. Sit tight; here I come."

The seconds ticked by. The blip on the 'scope was coming up fast . . . and then it was on top of them, and the lifeboat lurched hard as the grapples caught. "Gotcha!" the radio shouted. "Hang on!"

And with seconds to spare—

The universe vanished. Blackness filled the viewports, spilled like a physical thing into the lifeboat. For five long seconds—

And the sun exploded directly in front of them, brighter than Chandra had seen it for weeks. A dozen blips crawled across the 'scope, and the lifeboat's beacon-reader abruptly came to life, informing them they were six thousand kilometers north-west-zenith of Earth's Number Twelve navigational beacon.

Beside her, Chandra felt Goode go limp with released tension. "Still with me?" the radio asked.

"Sure are," Chandra said, wiping the sweat off her palms. "I don't know how to thank you, Mr.—?"

"Dr. Louis Du Bellay," the voice identified himself. "And don't thank me yet. If what you did out there didn't work, there's a worse death coming for all of us."

Chandra had almost forgotten about that. The thought sobered her rising spirits considerably. "You're right. Can you get us into contact with Peacekeeper HQ? We need to report in."

"I can maybe do better than that. Come aboard and we'll find out."

They were given special priority to land, and a car was standing by for them at the field.

General Carey was waiting outside the Situation Room. "I ought to pull your pilot's license for going out there against specific Peacekeeper orders," he told Du Bellay half-seriously, even as he gave his daughter a bear hug. "If Mahendra hadn't confessed to helping you get hold of that tachship I probably would. But he's too good a man to lose to a court-martial. Let's get inside; the Chasers have been reporting in for nearly twenty minutes."

Mahendra looked up as the group approached. "Captain Carey and Officer Goode? Congratulations; it looks like you've done it."

Chandra felt a lump the thickness of ion shielding in her throat. "We slowed him?"

"No, but you deflected him a couple hundredths of a second in the right direction."

"Confirmed?" General Carey asked sharply, as if not daring to believe it.

"Confirmed, sir," Mahendra nodded. "He'll be passing through the upper solar chromosphere instead of deep into the photosphere. We'll get some good flares and a significant radiation increase for a few weeks, but nothing much worse than that."

"And the Intruder hasn't tried to correct his course?" Du Bellay asked quietly.

Mahendra's expression was both sad and grim. "No, Doctor."

Puzzled, Chandra glanced between her father, Mahendra, and Du Bellay, all of whom wore the same look. Even Goode's face was starting to change . . . and suddenly she understood. "You mean . . . the impact killed *all* of them?"

Carey put his arm around her shoulders. "We had no choice, Chandra. It was a matter of survival. You understand, don't you?"

She sighed and, reluctantly, nodded. Goode took her arm and led her to a nearby chair. Sitting there, holding tightly to his hand, she watched with the rest of the Situation Room as the computer plot of the Intruder's position skimmed the sun's surface and shot out once more toward deep space. What had they been like, she wondered numbly . . . and how many of them had she killed so that Earth could live?

She knew she would never know.

Behind the *Dawnsent*, the star receded toward negative infinity, its light red-shifted to invisibility. With mixed feelings Orofan watched its shrinking image on the screen. Beside him, Pliij looked up from the helmboard. "We're all set, Shipmaster. The deviation's been calculated; we can correct course anytime in the next hundred *aarns*." He paused, and in a more personal tone said, "You did what was necessary, Orofan. Your honor is unblemished."

Orofan signed agreement, but it was an automatic gesture. The assault gun, he noticed, was still in his tentacle, and he slipped it back into its sheath.

A tentacle touched his. "Pliij is right," Lassarr said gently. "Whatever craft that was, its inhabitants had almost certainly been killed by our scoop before we detected it. You could have done nothing to help them.

Refusing to accept the ship's mass at that point would have been dishonorable. You did well; your decisions and judgments have been proved correct."

"I know," Orofan sighed. It *was* true; fate had combined with his decisions to save the system from destruction without adding appreciable time to the *Dawnsent*'s own journey. He should be satisfied.

And yet . . . the analyzers reported significant numbers of silicon, carbon, oxygen, hydrogen, and nitrogen atoms among the metals of the spacecraft the *Dawnsent* had unintentionally run down. Which of those atoms had once belonged to living creatures? . . . And how many of those beings had died so that the Sk'cee might reach their new home?

He knew he would never know.

Between a Rock and a High Place

"Ladies and gentlemen, shuttles one and two for United Flight 1103 are now ready for general boarding: Skyport service from Houston to Dallas-Ft. Worth, Los Angeles, and San Francisco."

Peter Whitney was ready; he'd been standing at the proper end of the waiting lounge for the past several minutes, as a matter of fact, eagerly awaiting the announcement. Picking up his carry-on bag, he stepped to the opening door, flashed his boarding pass for the attendant's inspection, and walked down the short tunnel to where the shuttle waited. The excitement within him seemed to increase with every step, a fact that embarrassed him a little—a twenty-eight-year-old computer specialist shouldn't be feeling like a kid on his first trip to Disney World, after all. But he refused to worry too much about it. Professional solemnity was still, for him, a recent acquisition, easily tucked out of the way.

The shuttle itself was unimpressive, of course: little more than a Boeing 727 with a heavily modified inte-

71

rior. Following the flight attendant's instructions he sat down in the front row, choosing the left-hand window seat. Pushing his bag into the compartment under his chair, he fastened his lap/shoulder belt and spent the next few minutes examining the ski lift-style bars connecting his pair of seats to the conveyors behind the grooves in floor and ceiling. He'd seen specs and models for the system back in St. Louis, but had never given up being amazed that it worked as well as it did in actual practice.

His seatmate turned out to be a smartly-suited businesswoman type who promptly pulled out her *Wall Street Journal* and buried herself in it. A bored executive who flew in Skyports every week, obviously, and her indifference helped dispel Whitney's last twinges of guilt at having taken the window seat.

Within a very few minutes the shuttle was loaded and ready. The door was closed, the tunnel withdrawn, and soon they were at the edge of the runway, awaiting permission to take off. Whitney kept an eye on his watch with some interest—Skyport logistics being what they were, a shuttle couldn't afford to be very late in getting off the ground. Even knowing that, he was impressed when the plane roared down the runway and into the sky only twelve seconds behind schedule.

They turned east, heading into the early-morning sun to meet the Skyport as it headed toward them from its New Orleans pickup. Whitney watched the city disappear behind them, and then shifted his gaze forward, wondering how far away something the size of a Skyport could be seen. Docking, he knew, would take place seventy to eighty miles out from Houston; assuming the shuttle was flying its normal four-ninety knots—five-sixty-odd miles an hour—meant an eight to nine minute trip. They'd covered seven of that already; surely they must be coming up on it by now. Unless . . .

With smooth abruptness, the horizon dropped below the level of his window, and Whitney knew he'd goofed. The Skyport was somewhere off to the shuttle's right, and the smaller craft was now circling around to get into docking position. Belatedly he realized he should have asked the flight attendant which was the scenic side when he boarded.

The passengers on the other side of the aisle were beginning to take an interest in the view out their windows, and Whitney craned his neck in an effort to see. Nothing but ground and sky were visible from where he sat; but even as he settled back in mild disappointment the shuttle leveled out and began to climb . . . and suddenly, ahead and above them, the Skyport loomed into view.

No film clip, scale model, or blueprint, Whitney realized in that moment, could ever fully prepare one for the sheer impact of a Skyport's presence. A giant flying wing, the size of seven football fields laid end to end, the Skyport looked like nothing else in aviation history—looked like nothing, in fact, that had any business being up in the air in the first place. The fact that it also flew more efficiently than anything else in the sky seemed almost like a footnote in comparison, though it was of course the economic justification for the six Skyports now in service and McDonnell Douglas's main argument in their ongoing sales campaign. Staying aloft for weeks or months at a time, the Skyports were designed for maximum efficiency at high altitudes and speeds, dispensing with the heavy landing gear, noise suppressors, and high-lift flaps required on normal jetliners. And with very little time spent on the ground amid contaminants like dust and insects, the Skyports had finally been able to take advantage of the well-known theories of laminar flow control, enabling the huge craft to fly with less than half the drag of planes with a fraction of their capacity. In Whitney's personal view, it was probably this incredible fuel efficiency that had finally convinced United and TWA to take a chance on the idea.

The shuttle was directly behind the Skyport now and closing swiftly. From his window Whitney could see five of the seven basically independent modules that made up the Skyport and, just barely, the two port engines of the sixth. That would be all right; since only the center module's engines fired during this part of the flight, docking one module in from the end was essentially equivalent in noise and turbulence to docking in the end section. Docking one module from center, on the other hand, was rumored to be a loud and rather unnerving experience. It was a theory he wasn't anxious to test.

A flash of sunlight off to the left caught his eye—the second Houston shuttle, making its approach toward the second-to-last module at the other end. He watched with interest as the distant plane nosed toward its docking bay, watched it until the port-side engines of his own shuttle's target module blocked it from sight. The silvery trailing edge of the Skyport was very near now, and the slight vibration that had been building almost imperceptibly began to increase at a noticeable rate. Whitney was just trying to estimate the vibrational amplitude and to recall the docking bay's dimensional tolerance when a sound like a muffled bass drum came from the fuselage skin a meter in front of him and the vibration abruptly stopped. The docking collar, clamping solidly around them. With the noise of the Skyport's engines still filling the cabin, Whitney's straining ears had no chance of picking up the nosewheel's descent into the docking bay; but he *did* distinctly hear the *thump* as the bay's forward clamp locked onto the nosewheel's tow bar. Only then, with the shuttle firmly and officially docked, did he realize he'd been holding his breath. He let it out with a wry smile, feeling more than ever like a kid on a ride Disney had never dreamed of.

Another soft thump and hiss signaled that the pressurized tunnel was in place. A cool breeze wafted through the shuttle as the outer door was opened—and suddenly Whitney and his seatmate were moving, their ski lift seats following the grooves in floor and ceiling as they were moved first into the aisle and then forward toward the exit. They turned left at the doorway, and Whitney caught just a glimpse of the shuttle's other seats in motion behind him. Then, with only the slightest jerk of not-quite-aligned grooves, they were out of the shuttle and into a flexible-walled corridor that looked for all the world like the inside of an accordion. The tunnel was short, leading to another airplane-type doorway. Straight ahead, stretching down a long corridor, Whitney could see a column of seats like his own, filled with passengers for the shuttle's trip back down to Houston. There didn't seem to be enough room beside the column for the emerging seats to pass by easily, but Whitney was given little time to wonder about it. Just beyond the doorway his seat took a ninety-degree turn to the right, and he found himself sidling alongside a wall toward what looked like a lounge. To his left he could see the rest of the shuttle's seats following like a disjointed snake. The airlines had balked at the ski lift system, he remembered, complaining that it was unnecessarily complicated and expensive. But the time the shuttle spent in the docking bay translated into fuel for its return flight, and the essence of *that* was money . . . and the ski lift system gave the shuttle a mere ten-minute turnaround.

It was indeed a sort of lounge the chairs were taking them into, a rectangular space done up with soft colors and a carpet designed to disguise the grooves in the floor. In the center was a large, four-sided computer display giving destinations and the corresponding modules in large letters. Whitney's seatmate retrieved her briefcase from under her chair and hopped off as the chair entered the room and began to sidle its way across the floor; glancing at the display, she strode out through one of the wide doorways in the far wall. Whitney obeyed the rules, himself, waiting until the seat had come to a complete stop before undoing his belt and standing up. He was in module six, the display informed him, and passengers for Los Angeles could sit anywhere in modules one, two, six, or seven. Since his boarding pass indicated he'd be disembarking from module six anyway, it made the most sense to just stay here, a decision most of the others also seemed to have reached. Picking up his carry-on, he joined the surge forward. A short corridor lined with lavatory doors lay ahead; passing through it, he entered—

Instant disorientation.

The room before him was *huge*, and was more a combination theater-cafe-lounge than an airplane cabin. Directly in front of him was a section containing standard airline chairs, but arranged in patterns that varied from the traditional side-by-side to cozy circles around low tables. To either side were small cubicles partially isolated from the main floor by ceiling-length panels of translucent, gray-tinted plastic. Further on toward the front of the Skyport, partially separated from the lounge by more of the tinted plastic, was a section that was clearly a dining area, with tables of various sizes and shapes, about a third of them occupied despite the early hour. Beyond that, the last section seemed to be divided into three small movie/TV rooms.

It all seemed almost scandalously wasteful for a craft that, for all its size and majesty, still had to answer to the law of gravity; but even as Whitney walked in among the lounge chairs he realized the extravagance was largely illusory. Despite the varied seating, little floor space was actually wasted, and most of that would have been required for aisles, anyway. The smoked-plastic panels gave the illusion that the room was larger than it actually was, while at the same time adding a sense of coziness to all the open space; and the careful use of color disguised the fact that the room's ceiling wasn't much higher than that of a normal jetliner.

For a few minutes Whitney wandered more or less aimlessly, absorbing the feel of the place. A rumble from his stomach reminded him that he'd had nothing yet that morning except coffee, though, and he cut short his exploration in favor of breakfast. Sitting down at one of the empty tables, he scanned the menu card briefly and then pushed the call button in the table's center. Safety, he noted, had not been sacrificed to style; the table and chair were both fastened securely to the floor, and the metal buckle of a standard lap/shoulder belt poked diffidently at his ribs.

"Good morning, sir—may I help you?" a pleasant voice came from behind him. He turned as she came into view to his right: a short blonde, trim and athletic-looking in her flight attendant's uniform, pushing a steam cart before her. The cart surprised him a bit, but it was instantly obvious that true restaurant service for what could be as many as eight hundred passengers would be well-nigh impossible for the module's modest crew. Out of phase with the decor or not, precooked tray meals were the only way to serve such a crowd.

There were some illusions that even a Skyport couldn't handle.

"Yes. I'd like the eggs, sausage, and fruit meal—number two here," he told her, indicating it on the menu.

"Certainly." Opening a side door on her cart, she withdrew a steaming tray and placed it before him. The aroma rising with the steam made his stomach rumble again. "Coffee?" she added.

"Please. By the way, is there anything like a guided tour of the Skyport available? Upstairs, too, I mean?"

Her forehead wrinkled a bit as she picked up a mug and began to fill it. "The flight deck? I'm afraid not—FAA regulations forbid passengers up there."

"Oh. No exceptions, huh?"

"None that I know of." She set the mug down and placed a small cup of cream beside it. "Any special reason you'd like to go up there, or are you just curious?"

"Both, actually. I work for McDonnell Douglas, the company that built this plane. I've been doing computer simulations for them, and now they're transferring me to L.A. to do some stuff on their new navigational equipment. I thought that as long as they were flying me out on a Skyport anyway, it would give me a jump on my orientation if I could look around a bit."

The attendant looked duly impressed. "Sounds like interesting work—and about a million miles over my head. I can talk to the captain, see if we can break the rules for you, but I can't make any promises. Would you give me your name, please, and tell me where you'll be after breakfast?"

"Peter Whitney, and I'll probably be back in the lounge. And, look, don't go breaking any rules—this isn't important enough for anyone to get into trouble over."

She smiled. "Okay, but I'll see what I can do. Enjoy your meal, Mr. Whitney, and if you need anything else just use the caller." With another smile she turned her cart around and left.

Picking up his fork, Whitney cut off a bit of sausage and tasted it, and then sampled the eggs. Piping hot, all of it, but not too hot to eat—and it tasted as good as it smelled. Settling himself comfortably, he attacked his tray with vigor.

There was something magic about a Skyport flight deck.

Betsy Kyser had been flying on the giant planes for nearly eighteen months now—had been a wing captain, in charge of an entire hundred-meter-wide module, for four of them—and she still didn't understand exactly why this place always hit her so strongly. Perhaps it was the mixture of reality and fantasy; the view of blue sky through the tiny forward windows contrasting with the myriads of control lights and glowing computer readouts. Or perhaps it was the size of the flight deck itself, better than twice as large as that of a jumbo jet, that struck a chord within her, half awakening the dreams of huge spaceships she'd had as a child. Whatever the reason, she knew the feeling would wear off sooner or later . . . but until that happened, it was there for her to enjoy. Standing just inside the flight deck door, she drank her fill of the magic.

Slouched in the copilot's seat, Aaron Greenburg glanced back toward her, the gold wings on his royal-blue jumpsuit's shoulderboards winking at her with the motion. "Morning, Bets—thought I heard you come in," he greeted her.

"Morning, Aaron. Tom, Rick," she added as the pilot and flight engineer turned and nodded to her "Any problems come up during the night?"

Tom Lewis, in the pilot's seat, raised his hands shoulder high in an expansive shrug. "What could go wrong?"

He had a point. Only the middle three wing sections ran their huge General Electric CF6-90C1 turbofan engines during normal flights, the outer two of those shutting down during the lower-speed shuttle pickups. Perched on the Skyport's starboard end, Wing Section Seven was essentially along for a free ride, with little to do but keep the passengers happy and make sure the fuel the shuttles brought up went down the internal pipeline to the sections that needed it. "You trying to tell me you get *bored* up here?" she asked in mock astonishment. "*Here*, aboard the greatest flying machine ever built by mankind?"

Before Lewis could answer, a voice spoke up from the intercom. "Wassa-matta, Seven; isn't our company good enough for you? What do you want—home movies and pretzels?"

"We could let them have some of the navigational work," a new voice suggested.

"*Great* idea. Seven, why don't you hop outside and take a sun-sight?"

"I've got a better idea, Five," Lewis said, turning back to the intercom grille. "Why don't we do a Chinese fire drill and send One, Two, and Three around to hook up the other side of us and let *us* drive for a while."

"Sounds like fun," a voice Betsy recognized as One's night-shift pilot broke in. "It'd confuse the passengers all to hell, though. Do we tell them, or see if they figure it out by themselves?"

"Oh, we could switch back before we got to L.A.," Lewis told him.

"I've got an even better idea, Seven," the rumbling voice of Skyport Captain Carl Young said from Four.

"Why don't you all cut the chitchat and get ready to receive the Dallas shuttle."

Lewis grinned. "Yes, sir. Chitchat out, sir."

Betsy stepped forward. "All the way out, as a matter of fact. You can go on back, Tom, I'll take over here."

"I've still got over a half hour left on my shift, you know," he reminded her.

"That's okay—the quality of intercom banter this morning indicates *everyone* on this bird is suffering gobs of boredom fatigue. Go on, get some coffee and relax. And maybe work on your one-liners."

Lewis gave her an injured look. "Well-l-l . . . okay. If you insist." Pulling off his half-headset and draping it across the wheel, he slid out of his chair and stepped back from the instrument panel. "All yours, Cap'n," he added. "Try not to hit anything; I'll be taking a nap."

"Right," she said dryly, slipping into his vacated seat. "Aaron, Rick—you two want to flip a coin or something to see who goes on break first?"

There was a short pause. Then Greenburg glanced back over his shoulder. "Why don't you go ahead," he said to Rick Henson. "I'd like to stay for a bit."

Henson nodded and got up from his flight engineer's board. "Okay. Be back soon." Together he and Lewis left the flight deck.

Betsy looked curiously at Greenburg. "Never known anyone before who didn't jump at a mid-shift coffee break with all four feet," she said.

"Oh, don't worry—I'll take mine, all right. I just wanted to give you a word of warning about the shuttle coming in. Eric Rayburn's flying her."

Betsy felt a knot form directly over her breakfast. "Oh, hell. I sure have a great sense of timing, don't I?"

"I can call Tom back in if you'd like," Greenburg offered. "You're not technically on duty for another half-hour."

She was sorely tempted. By eight o'clock Skyport time—seven Dallas time—the shuttle would have come and gone and be back on the ground again, and Eric Rayburn with it. She wouldn't have to talk to him, something she was pretty sure both of them would appreciate; and with her blood pressure and digestion intact she could go back to just flying her plane—

And to avoiding Eric.

"I can't avoid him forever, though, can I," she said, with a resigned sigh. "Thanks, but I'll stay here."

Greenburg's dark eyes probed her face. "If you're sure," He paused. "Shuttle's calling now," he informed her.

Nodding, she took the half-headset and put it on, guiding the single earphone to a comfortable stop in her left ear. Even before it was in place she heard Rayburn's clipped Boston accent. "—to Skyport Eleven-oh-three. Beginning approach; request docking instructions."

Betsy pursed her lips and turned on her mike. "Dallas shuttle, this is Skyport Eleven-oh-three. You're cleared for docking in Seven; repeat, Seven." Her eyes ran over the instrument readouts as she spoke. "Skyport speed holding steady at two-sixty knots; guidance system radar has a positive track on you."

"Is that you, Liz? Son of a gun; I had no *idea* I was going to have the honor of docking with *your* own Skyport. This is *indeed* a privilege."

Betsy had been fully prepared for heavy sarcasm, but she still found her hands forming into tight knots of frustration at his words. *Liz*—early in their relationship he'd learned how much she despised that nickname, and his continual use of it these days was a biting echo of the pain she'd felt at their breakup. "Yes, this is Kyser," she acknowledged steadily. "Shuttle, you're coming in a bit fast. Do you want a relative-v confirmation check?"

"What for? I can fly my bird as well as you can fly yours, Liz."

"We're sure you can, Shuttle." Betsy's voice was still calm, but it was a losing battle and she knew it. "Dock whenever you're ready; we're here if you need any help." Without waiting for a response, she flipped off the mike and wrenched the half-headset off, cutting off anything else he might say.

For a moment she stared at the instruments without seeing any of them, slowly getting her temper back under control. Greenburg's quiet voice cut through the blackness, "You know, I'm always amazed—and a little bit jealous—whenever I come across someone with as much self-control as you've got."

She didn't look up at him, but could feel the internal tension ease a little. "Thanks. You're lying through your teeth, of course—I've never seen you even raise your voice at anyone—but thanks."

Her peripheral vision picked up his smile. "You give yourself too little credit, and me 'way too much. Inherent lack of temper isn't comparable with control of a violent one. *My* weaknesses are gin rummy and gin fizzes—usually together." He shook his head. "Eighteen months is a long time to carry a grudge."

"Yeah. I will never again let that old sexist cliché about a woman scorned go by unchallenged—some of you men are just as good at hell's fury as we are."

"If you'll pardon a personal question, is all this nonsense *really* just because you were chosen for Skyport duty and he was left back in the shuttle corps? I'd heard that was all it was, but it seems such a silly thing to base a vendetta on."

She was able to manage a faint smile now. "That shows you don't know Eric very well. He's a very opinionated man, and once he gets hold of an idea he will *not* let it go. He is thoroughly convinced United put me on the Skyport because of my looks, because they thought it would be good publicity, because they needed a token female—*any* reason except that I might have more of the qualities they were looking for than he did."

"One of his opinions is that women are inferior pilots to men?" Greenburg hazarded.

"Or at least we're inferior pilots to *him*. My flying skills were perfectly acceptable to him until United made the cut. In fact, he used to brag a lot about me to his other friends."

Unknotting her fists, she stretched her arms and

fingers. "The irony of it is that he'd be climbing the walls here his first week on duty. He's a good pilot, but he can't stand being under anyone's authority once he's left the cockpit. Even the low-level discipline we have to maintain here around the clock would be more than he'd be willing to put up with."

"Maverick types we don't need here," Greenburg agreed. "Well, try not to let him get to you. In just over ten minutes he'll be nothing more than a bad taste in your memory."

"Until the next time our paths cross," Betsy sighed. "It's so hard when I remember what good friends we once were." A number on one of the readouts caught her eye, and she leaned forward with a frown. "I still read him coming in a shade too fast. Aaron, give me a double-check—what's the computer showing on his relative-v?"

Greenburg turned to check. As he did so, Betsy felt the Skyport dip slightly, and her eyes automatically sought out the weather radar. Nothing in particular was visible; the bump must have been a bit of clear air turbulence. No problem; with a plane the size of Skyport normal turbulence was normally not even noticed by the passengers—

Without warning, her seat suddenly slammed up underneath her as the flight deck jerked violently. Simultaneously, there was a strangely indistinct sound of tortured metal . . . and, as if from a great distance, a scream of agony.

Betsy would remember the next few seconds as a period of frantic activity in which her mind, seemingly divorced from her body by shock, was less a participant than a silent observer. With a detached sort of numbness she watched her hands snatch up her half-headset—realizing only then that that was where the distant scream had come from—and jam it into place on her head. A dozen red lights were flashing on the instrument panel, and she watched herself join Greenburg in slapping at the proper controls and shutoffs, turning off shorting circuits and leaking hydraulics in the orderly fashion their training had long since drummed into them. And all the time she wondered what had gone wrong, and wondered what she was going to do. . . .

The slamming-open of the door behind her broke the spell, jolting her mind back into phase with reality. "What the hell was *that?*" Henson called as he charged full-tilt through the doorway and dropped into his flight engineer's chair. Lewis was right behind him, skidding to a stop behind Greenburg.

"Shuttle crash," Betsy snapped. Emergency procedures finished, she now had her first chance to study the other telltales and try to figure out the exact situation. "Looks bad. The shuttle seems to have gone in crooked, angling upwards and starboard. Captain Rayburn, can you hear me? Captain Rayburn, report please."

For a moment she could hear nothing through her earphone but a faint, raspy breathing. "This is—this is Rayburn." The voice was stunned, weak, sounding nothing like the man Betsy had once known.

"Captain, what's the situation down there?" she asked through the sudden tightness in her throat. "Are you hurt?"

"I don't know." His voice was stronger now; he must have just been momentarily stunned. "My right wrist hurts some. John . . . oh, God! *John!*"

"Rayburn?" Betsy snapped.

"My copilot—John Meredith—the whole side of the cockpit's caved in on him. He's—oh, God—I think he's dead."

Betsy's left hand curled into a fist in front of her. "Rayburn, snap out of it! Turn on your intercom and find out if your passengers are all right. Then see if there's a doctor on board to see to Meredith. If he's alive every second could count. And use your oxygen mask—you've probably been holed and the bay's not pressurized."

Rayburn drew a long, shuddering breath, and when he spoke again he sounded almost normal. "Right. I'll let you know what I find."

A click signified the shuttle's intercom had been switched on. Listening to him with half an ear, Betsy pushed the mike away from her mouth and turned back to Greenburg. "Have you got a picture yet?" she asked.

The copilot was fiddling with the bay TV monitor controls. "Yeah, but the quality's pretty bad. He took out the starboard fisheye when he hit, and a lot of the overhead floods, too."

Betsy peered at the screen. "Port side looks okay. I wish we could see what he's done to his starboard nose. Top of the fuselage looks like it's taken some damage—up there, that shadow."

"Yeah. A little hard—"

"Betsy!" Henson broke in. "Take a look at the collar stress readouts. We've got big trouble."

She located the proper screen, scanned the numbers. There were six of them, one for each of the supports securing the docking collar to the edge of the bay. Four of the six indicated no stresses at all, while the other two were dangerously overloaded; and it took a half second for the significance of the zero readings to register. "Oh, great," she muttered, pulling the mike back to her lips. "Rayburn?"

"Passengers are okay except for some bruises and maybe sprains." Rayburn's voice was muffled, indicating he'd put his oxygen mask on. "We've got a doctor coming to look at John."

"Good. Now listen carefully. You're holding onto the Skyport by the skin of your teeth—four of the collar supports have been snapped, and the drag on you is straining the last two. Start firing your engines at about—" She paused, suddenly realizing she had no idea how much power he'd have to use to relieve the strain on the clamps. "Just start your engines and run them up slowly. We'll tell you when you're at the right level."

"Got you. Here goes."

It took nearly a minute for the stresses to drop to what Betsy considered the maximum acceptable levels.

"All right, hold at that level until further notice," she told him. "Is the doctor in the cockpit yet?"

"He's just coming in now."

"When he's finished his examination give him a headset and let him talk to one of us here."

"Yeah, okay."

Pulling off her half-headset, Betsy draped it around her neck and looked over at Greenburg. "Stay with him, will you? I need to talk to Carl."

Greenburg nodded, and Betsy leaned over the intercom. "Carl? This is Kyser on Seven."

"We've been listening, Betsy," the Skyport captain's calm voice came immediately. "What's the situation?"

"Bad. We've got a damaged—possibly wrecked—shuttle with a probably dead first officer aboard. A doctor's with him. Somehow the crash managed to tear out four of the docking collar supports, too, and if the other two go we'll lose her completely."

"The emergency collar?"

"Hasn't engaged. I don't know why yet; the sensors in that area got jarred pretty badly and they aren't all working."

"The front clamp didn't make it to the nosewheel, I take it?"

"No, sir." Betsy studied the TV screen. "Looks like it's at least a meter short, maybe more."

"Those clamp arms aren't supposed to run short, no matter where in the bay the shuttle winds up," someone spoke up from one of the other wing sections. "Maybe it's just hung up on something, and in that case you should be able to connect it up manually from inside the bay."

"There isn't supposed to be anything in there for the arm to hang up *on*," Greenburg muttered, half to himself.

Young heard him anyway. "Unless the crash jarred something loose," he pointed out. "Checking on that should be our first priority."

"Excuse me, Carl, but it's not," Betsy said. "Our first priority is to figure out whether something aboard Seven caused the crash."

"A board of inquiry—"

"Will be too late. All our fuel comes up via these shuttles. If a flaw's developed in Seven's electronics or computer guidance programming we've got to find out what it is and make sure none of the other wing sections has it. Because if something *is* going bad, it has to be fixed before we can allow any more dockings. Otherwise we could wind up with *two* smashed shuttles."

Behind her, she heard Lewis swear under his breath and head over toward the flight deck's seldom-used computer terminal. "You're right," Young admitted. "I hadn't thought that far. Can you run the check, or shall I send someone over to help?"

"Tom's starting on it now, but I'm not sure what it'll prove. The computer's supposed to continually run its own checks and let us know if there's any problem. If there's a flaw the machine missed, a standard check isn't likely to find it, either."

"Then we'll go to the source. I'll put a call through to McDonnell Douglas and see if they can either run a deeper check by remote control or tell us how to do one."

Betsy glanced at her watch. Six-forty St. Louis time; two hours earlier in Los Angeles. They'd have to get the experts out of bed, a time-consuming process. She was just about to mention that fact when Paul Marinos, Six's captain, spoke up. "Wait a second. There's a guy aboard who works for McDonnell Douglas—Erin told me he'd asked her about a tour of the flight deck."

"Does he know anything about our electronics?" Young asked.

"I don't know, but she said he does *something* with computers for them."

Betsy turned around to look at Lewis, who shrugged and nodded assent. "Close enough," she told the Skyport captain. "Can you get him up here right away?"

"I'll go get him myself," Marinos volunteered. "I'll be there in a couple of minutes."

"All right. Let's get back to the shuttle itself, then,"

Young said. "Betsy, you said the collar supports were broken. Any idea how that happened?"

"I can only speculate that the collar had established a partial grip before the shuttle did its sideways veer into the bay wall."

"In that case, the crash may have left both the outer shuttle door and the exit tunnel intact. Any chance of getting the two connected and getting the passengers out of there?"

"I don't know." Betsy peered at the screen, made a slight adjustment in the contrast. "They're out of line, for sure. I don't know if the tunnel will stretch far enough to make up the difference."

"Even if it does, we'd need portable oxygen masks for all the passengers," Henson pointed out from behind her. "They have to be using the shuttle's air masks, and they can't travel with those."

"That's not going to be a problem," Young said. "I've already invoked emergency regulations; we're bringing her down to fifteen thousand feet."

"Well, there's nothing more I can tell from here." Betsy shook her head. "Someone's going to have to go down and take a look. Who aboard this bird knows the most about docking bay equipment?"

There was a pause. "I don't know whether I know the *most*," Greenburg spoke up diffidently at Betsy's right, "but I've seen the blueprints, and I worked summers as a mechanic's assistant for Boeing when I was in college."

"Anyone able to top that?" Young asked. "No? All right, Greenburg, get going."

Betsy put her half-headset back on as Greenburg removed his and stood up. "A set of the relevant blueprints would be helpful," he said, looking back at Lewis.

"I'm having the computer print them," the other told him. "If you want to go down and get the oxygen gear together, I'll come down and give you a hand."

Greenburg glanced questioningly at Betsy. "Can you do without both of us that long?"

She hesitated, then nodded. "Sure. But make it a fast

look-see. You're not going down there to do any major repair work."

"Right." Greenburg started for the door. "Meet you by the port-aft cargo access hatch, Tom."

Lewis waved an acknowledgment, his eyes on the computer screen, as Greenburg exited. Betsy turned back to face forward, and as she did so Rayburn's voice crackled in her ear. "Skyport, this is Rayburn. The doctor says John's alive!"

A small part of the tightness across Betsy's chest seemed to disappear. "Thank God! Is the doctor still there? I want to speak with him."

"Just a second." There was a moment of silence punctuated by assorted clicks, and then a new voice came tentatively on the line. "Hello? This is Dr. Emerson."

"Doctor, this is Wing Captain Elizabeth Kyser. What sort of shape is First Officer Meredith in?"

"Not a good one, I'm afraid," Emerson admitted. "He seems to have one or more cracked ribs and possibly a broken collarbone as well. The way the fuselage has bent inward and pinned him makes it hard to examine him. I could try pulling him out, but that might exacerbate any internal injuries, or even drive bits of glass into him from the broken windows. He's unconscious, but his vital signs are stable, at least for the moment. I'm afraid I can't tell you much more."

"Just knowing he's alive is good news enough," Betsy assured him. She thought for a moment. "What if we could cut the whole chair loose? Is there enough room behind him to move the chair back and get him out that way?"

"Uh . . . I think so, yes. But I don't know what we would do after that. I heard the flight attendant say the door was jammed."

Betsy frowned. Rayburn hadn't mentioned that to her. "We might be able to force it open anyway and get it connected to the rest of the Skyport. Are the rest of the passengers all right?"

"A few minor injuries, mostly bruises due to the safety belts. We've been very lucky."

So far. "Yeah. Thank you, Doctor. Please let us know immediately if there's any change."

"Got the prints, Betsy," Lewis called as she turned off the mike. "I'm heading down."

He was gone before she could do more than nod assent, leaving her and Henson alone. For some reason the empty seats bothered her, and she briefly considered calling in some of Seven's off-duty crewmen. But as long as they were stuck in this virtual holding pattern, extra help on the flight deck would be pretty superfluous. Turning back to the instrument panel, she felt a wave of frustration wash over her. So many unanswered questions, most of them crucial to the safety of one or more groups of people aboard the Skyport—and she was temporarily at a loss to handle any of them. For the moment there was nothing she could do but try and line up the problems in some sort of logical order: if A is true then B must be done, and D cannot precede either B or C. But it was like juggling or playing chess in her head; there were just too many contingencies that had to be taken into account every step of the way.

Behind her the door opened, and she turned to see two men walk in. One she knew: Paul Marinos, captain of Wing Section Six. The other, a thirtyish young man in a three-piece suit, she'd never seen before. But she knew instantly who he was.

"Betsy," Marinos said, "this is Peter Whitney, of McDonnell Douglas."

Whitney had been daydreaming in his lounge chair, enjoying the unique Skyport atmosphere, when the violent bump jerked him back to full alterness. He shot a rapid glance around the room, half expecting to see the walls caving in around him. But everything looked normal. Up ahead, he could hear muttered curses from the dining room—prompted, no doubt, by spilled coffee and the like—while from the lounge itself came a heightened buzz of conversation. Whitney closed his ears to it all as best he could, straining instead to listen for some clue as to what had happened. An explosive misfire in one of the engines was his first gut-level guess; but the dull background rumble seemed unchanged. A hydraulic or fuel line that had broken with that much force might still be leaking audibly; again, he could hear nothing that sounded like that. Had there been that bogey of the '70s and early '80s, a mid-air collision? But even small planes these days were supposed to be equipped with the Bendix-Honeywell transponder system—and how could any pilot fail to see the Skyport in the first place?

The minutes dragged by, and conversational levels gradually returned to normal as the other passengers apparently decided that nothing serious had happened. Whitney suspected differently, and to him the loudspeaker's silence was increasingly ominous. Something serious *had* happened, and the captain was either afraid to tell the passengers what it was or the crew was just too damn busy fighting the problem to talk. Neither possibility was a pleasant one.

A flash of royal blue caught the corner of his eye, and he turned to see a chunky man in a Skyport-crew jumpsuit step from the dining area into the lounge. The flight attendant who'd served Whitney's breakfast was with him, and Whitney watched curiously as her gaze swept the room. It wasn't until she pointed in his direction and the two started toward him that it occurred to Whitney that they might be looking for *him*. Even then uncertainty kept him in his seat until there was no doubt as to their target, and he had barely enough time to stand up before they reached him.

"Mr. Whitney?" the jumpsuited man asked. His expression was worried, his tone was politeness laminated on urgency. The girl looked worried, too.

Whitney nodded, noticing for the first time the gold wings-in-a-circle pins on his chest and shoulderboards. A wing captain, not just a random crew member. Whitney's first hopeful thought, that this was somehow related to the tour he'd asked for, vanished like tax money in Washington.

"I'm Captain Paul Marinos," the other introduced

himself. "We have a problem, Mr. Whitney, that we hope you can help us with. Is it true that you work with computer systems for McDonnell Douglas?"

Whitney nodded, feeling strangely tongue-tied, but finally getting his brain into gear. They were almost certainly not interested in just general computer knowledge; his nodded affirmative needed a qualifier added to it. "I know only a little about current Skyport programming, though," he told them. "I mostly work with second-generation research."

Marinos's expression didn't change, but his next words were almost a whisper. "What we need is a malfunction check on our shuttle approach and guidance equipment. Can you do that?"

The pieces clicked almost audibly into place in Whitney's mind. It *had* been a crash, and one that all the Bendix-Honeywell collision-proofing in the world couldn't prevent. "I don't know, but I can try. Where do I find a terminal?"

"On Seven," was the cryptic response. "Come with me, please."

Marinos led the way across the lounge and back into the dining room. A door in the right-hand wall brought them into one of the module's food preparation and storage areas. The blonde flight attendant left them at that point; moving forward through the galley, Marinos and Whitney arrived at an elevator. One deck up was a somewhat cramped hallway lined with doors—crew quarters, Whitney assumed. In the opposite direction a heavy, positive-sealing door stood across their path. Marinos unlocked it and swung it open; and to Whitney's mild surprise an identical door, hung the opposite way, faced them. The captain opened this one, too, and gestured Whitney through, sealing both doors again behind them. "We're on Wing Section Seven now," he told Whitney, leading the way down a hall that mirror-imaged the one they'd just left. "The wing captain here is Betsy Kyser. You'll be working with her and her crew."

Beyond the hallway was a small lounge; passing

through it, they entered what appeared to be a ready-room sort of place with a half-dozen jumpsuited men and women listening intently to an intercom speaker; and finally, they reached the flight deck.

"We appreciate your coming up here," Captain Kyser said as Marinos concluded the introductions. "I hope you can help us."

"So do I," Whitney said. "Anything at all you can tell me about your malfunction? It might help my search."

"All we know is that it's somewhere in the equipment or programming that guides shuttles into the docking bay." In a few terse sentences she told him what was known about the shuttle crash, including the craft's current orientation in the bay. "My indicator said its approach velocity was too high, if that's significant," she concluded. "But I don't know if that was just my indicator or if the whole system was confused."

"The shuttle's radar is independent of your equipment, though, isn't it? Maybe the pilot can corroborate your readings."

"Maybe—but if he'd seen anything wrong he'd almost certainly have yelled. But I'll ask him. First, though, I want to get you started. Paul, will you monitor the shuttle?"

Marinos, who had already quietly seated himself in the copilot's seat, nodded and put on a headset. Kyser removed her own and led Whitney to a console built snugly into the flight desk's left rear corner. Motioning him into the chair in front of it, she leaned over him and tapped at the keys. "Here's the sign-on . . . access code . . . and program file." A series of names and numbers appeared on the screen. "Any of those look familiar?"

"Quite a few, if the programming division's keeping its nomenclature consistent." Whitney scanned the list, experimentally keyed in a number.

"That's the standard equipment-check program," Kyser told him. "We've already run that one and come up dry."

"No errors? Then the problem probably isn't in the computer system."

She shook her head. " 'Probably' isn't good enough. Aren't there more complete test programs that can be run?"

"You're talking about the full-blown diagnostic monsters that ground maintenance uses." Whitney hesitated, trying to remember what little he knew about such programs. "It seems to me that the program should be stored somewhere in your system, probably on one of the duplicate-copy disks. The catch is that the thing takes up almost all of your accessible memory space, so anything that normally uses that space will have to be temporarily shut down while it's running."

Kyser looked over at the flight engineer. "Rick?"

"Jibes with what I've heard," he agreed. "Most of the programs that take a lot of space are connected with navigation, radar monitoring, and mechanical flight systems and cargo deck stuff. We're not using any of those at the moment, anyway, so that's no problem. I can also switch a lot of the passenger-deck functions from automatic to manual control." He craned his neck to look at Whitney, sitting directly behind him. "Will that free up enough memory?"

"I don't know—I don't know how much room it'll need. But there's another problem, Captain. Since it *is* such a big program, there'll almost undoubtedly be safeguards to keep someone from accidentally loading it and losing everything else in the memory."

"A password?"

"Of some kind." Whitney had been searching the program list and had already checked the descriptions of two or three of the entries. Another of them caught his eye and he keyed it in. "You may need to check with ground control to even find the name . . . hold it. Never mind, I've found it. DCHECK. Let's see. . . ." He advanced the description another page, skimmed it. "Here it is. We need something called the Sasquatch-3L package to load it."

"Will Dallas ground control have it?" Henson asked.

"I would think so—if not, they can probably get it by phone from one of the Skyport maintenance areas." Whitney hesitated. "But it's not clear whether or not that'll do you any good."

"Why not?"

"Well, remember that the whole reason you don't have the loading code in the first place is that they don't want you accidentally plugging in the program and wiping out something the autopilot's doing. So they may not legally be able to release the code to a Skyport crew, especially one that's in flight."

"That's stupid!"

"That's bureaucratic thinking," Captain Kyser corrected —or agreed; Whitney couldn't figure out which. Leaning over Whitney's shoulder again, she spoke toward a small grille next to the display screen. "Carl? Did you get all that?"

"Yes," the intercom answered, "and I suspect Mr. Whitney's basically right. But there have to be emergency procedures for something like this—else why have the program stored aboard in the first place? It should simply be a matter of getting an adequately prominent official to give an okay. I'll get the tower on it right away."

"And hope your prominent official can move his tail this early in the morning," she muttered under her breath.

Whitney had been thinking along a separate track. "There's one other thing we can try," he said. "Can you patch me into the regular phone system from up here?"

"Trivially. Why?"

"I'd like to call my former supervisor back in Houston. He might be able to get the package, either from his own office or from someone in L.A."

"You just said it was illegal to release the code," Henson objected.

"To you, yes; but maybe not to me. I *work* for the company, after all."

Henson started to growl something vituperative, but Kyser cut him off. "We'll complain to the FAA later.

For now, let's take whatever loopholes we can get our hands on. Put on that half-headset, Mr. Whitney, and I'll fix you up with Ma Bell."

The call, once the connection was finally made, was a remarkably short one. Dr. Mills, seldom at his best in the early morning, nevertheless came fully awake as Whitney gave him a thumbnail sketch of the crisis. He took down the names of both the diagnostic program and the loading code, extracted from Captain Kyser—via Whitney—the instructions for placing a return call to the Skyport, and promised to have the package for him in fifteen minutes.

"Well, that's it, I guess," Whitney remarked after signing off. "Nothing to do now but wait."

"Yeah. Damn."

Whitney looked up at her as she stared through the computer console, concentration drawing her eyebrows together. She had been something of a surprise to him, and he still found it hard to believe a Skyport wing captain could be so young. Marinos, he estimated, was in his early fifties, and Henson wasn't much younger. But if Betsy Kyser was anything past her early forties she was the best-preserved woman he'd ever seen. Which meant either United was hard up for Skyport personnel or Captain Kyser was one very fine pilot. He fixed the thought firmly in his mind; it was one of the few things about all this that was even remotely comforting. "Uh . . . Captain?" he spoke up.

She focused on him, the frown lingering for a second before she seemed to notice it and eased it a bit. "Call me Betsy," she told him. "This isn't much of a place for formalities."

"I'm Peter, then. May I ask why you need to know about the electronics right *now?* I would think the shuttle's safety would be the thing you need to concentrate on."

"It is, but we can't do anything about that until we're sure more shuttles can dock safely." He must have looked blank, because the corner of her mouth twitched and she continued, "Look. Whatever we wind up doing to the shuttle, odds are we don't already have the necessary equipment on board. That means— "

"That means you'll have to bring it up via shuttle," Whitney nodded, catching on at last. "So you need to find the glitch in your docking program and make sure it hasn't also affected the other modules' equipment."

"Right. After that the next job'll be to either get the passengers out or secure the shuttle into the bay, whichever is faster and safer."

Whitney nodded again. In his mind's eye he could see the damaged shuttle hanging precariously out the back of the Skyport, holding on by the barest of threads. The picture reawakened the half-forgotten vertigo of his first—and last—rollercoaster ride twenty years ago, and he discovered he was gripping the arms of his chair a shade more tightly than necessary. Firmly, he forced his emotions down out of the way. "There's going to be a fair amount of drag on the shuttle from the Skyport's slipstream," he commented, thinking aloud as a further distraction from discomfitting images. "That means a lot of stress on the docking collar. Would it help any if the shuttle dumped its fuel, to make itself lighter?"

"Just the opposite; the eng—" She paused, a strange look flickering across her face. Behind her, Whitney saw peripherally, Marinos had swiveled around, his attention presumably attracted by Betsy's abrupt silence. "Paul," she said without turning, "run a calculation for me. At its present rate of burn, how much fuel has the shuttle got left?"

"What diff—?" Marinos stopped, too, the same look settling onto his own features. Turning back, he began punching calculator buttons.

"Right," Betsy muttered tartly. "We've gotten too used to the easy transfer of fuel between shuttle and Skyport . . . or I have, anyway." Whitney had figured out what was going on, but Betsy spelled it out for him anyway. "You see, Peter, the shuttle's currently firing its engines, at about medium power, to counteract the drag you mentioned. I guess I was subconsciously assuming we could feed it all the fuel it needed from the Skyport's reserves."

"But the connections are out of line?"

"Almost certainly. The fuel line's on the starboard side, too, which means there's not likely to be enough room to even get in and connect them manually. Probably no access panels close enough, either, but I guess we'll have to check on that." She grimaced. "Something else to do. I hope someone's keeping a list."

"Got it, Betsy," Marinos said, looking up once more. "At current usage, he'll run dry in a little over seven hours."

"Seven hours." She pursed her lips. "And that assumes neither of his main pumps was rattled loose by the impact. Carl?"

"I heard, Betsy," the intercom grille said. "That's not a lot of time."

"No kidding. How much fuel has the whole Skyport got; for our own flying, I mean?"

"At our current speed, a good ten hours. All the tanks were pretty full."

"Okay. Thanks."

"Still no word from ground control on your program," he added. "They're trying to look up the regs and track down the guy who's got the actual package, and doing both of them badly."

"Betsy?" Marinos again. "Sorry to interrupt, but it's Eric Rayburn on the shuttle. He wants to talk to you."

Whitney started to reach for the earphone he was wearing, but Betsy shook her head, stepping back to her chair and picking up her own set. "This is Kyser," she said into the slender mike.

"Liz, what the hell's going on up there?" a harsh voice said into Whitney's left ear.

With the kind of crisis they were all facing up here, Whitney wouldn't have believed the tension on the flight deck could possibly increase. But it did. He could feel it in the uncomfortable shifting of Henson in his chair, and in Marinos' furtive glance sideways, and in Betsy's tightly controlled response. "We're trying to figure out how to get you and your passengers out of there alive," she said.

"Well, it's taking a damn sight too long. Or have you forgotten that John's in bad shape?"

"No, we haven't forgotten. If you've got any suggestions let's hear them."

"Sure. Just open this damn collar and let me fly my plane back to Dallas."

Betsy and Marinos exchanged glances; Whitney couldn't see Betsy's face, but Marinos's looked flabbergasted. "That's out of the question. You don't even know if the shuttle will fly any more."

"Sure it will! I've still got control of the engines and control surfaces. What else do I need?"

"How about electronics, for starters? You apparently don't even have enough nav equipment left to know where you are. For your information, you wouldn't be flying 'back' to Dallas, because we haven't left—we're circling the area at fifteen thousand feet and about two-seventy knots."

"All the better. I won't need any directional gear to find the airport."

Betsy's snort was a brief snake's hiss in Whitney's ear. "Eric, did you turn your oxygen off or something? Neither you nor the shuttle is in any shape to fly. Period." Rayburn started to object, but she raised her voice and cut him off. "We know you're worried about your first officer, but once we make sure it's safe to dock again we can have doctors and emergency medical equipment brought aboard to take care of him."

"And then what? Try to land with me still hanging out your rear? Don't be absurd. Like it or not, you're eventually going to have to let me go. Let's do it now and get it over with."

"No," Betsy said, and Whitney could hear a tightness in her voice. "There are a minimum number of tests we'll have to run before we can even consider the idea. You can help by starting a standard pre-flight check on your instruments and systems and figuring out what's still working. Other than that, you'll just have to sit back and wait like the rest of us."

"Wait!" He made the word an obscenity.

"Skyport out." Betsy reached over and flipped a switch, then pushed her mike off to one side. Whitney couldn't see much more than the back of her head, but it was very obvious that she was angry. He shifted uncomfortably in his chair, wishing he were somewhere else. There'd been elements about the whole exchange that had felt like a private feud, and he felt obscurely embarrassed that he'd been listening in.

"Don't let him get to you, Betsy," Henson advised quietly. "He's not worth getting upset about."

"Thanks." Already she seemed to be getting her composure back. "Unfortunately, he *did* hit one problem very squarely on the head."

"The landing problem?" Marinos asked.

Betsy nodded. "I don't know how we're going to handle that one."

"I don't understand," Whitney spoke up hesitantly. "You would just be separating off this module and landing it with the shuttle, wouldn't you?" A horrible thought struck him. "I mean you *aren't* thinking about landing the whole Skyport . . . are you?"

Betsy did something to her chair and swiveled halfway around to look at him. "No, of course not. There isn't a runway in the world that could take an entire Skyport, although the space shuttle landing area at Rogers Dry Lake might be possible in a real emergency."

"Then what's the problem? The modules are supposed to be able to land on an eighteen-thousand-foot runway, and Dallas has to have at least one that's that long."

"The eighteen thousand is for a wing sections by itself, Peter," Marinos said patiently. He held up a hand and began ticking off fingers. "First: with the extra weight and— more importantly the extra drag—we'd have to put down at something above our listed one-sixty-five-knot landing speed. That'll add runway distance right off the bat. Second: one of the weight savings on the wing sections is not having thrust reversers on our engines to help us slow down. We rely on landing wheel brakes and drogue chutes that pop out the back. With the shuttle adding weight out the back—and its gear will be at least a couple of feet off the ground when ours touches down, so there'll be a *lot* of weight—our balance will change. That means a little less weight on the front landing gear, which means a little less braking ability for those six sets of wheels. Maybe significantly less, maybe not; I don't know. And third, and probably most important: the drogue chutes come out the center and ends of our trailing edge—and we won't be able to use any of the center ones while the shuttle's in the way." He shook his head. "I wouldn't even attempt to land on anything shorter than twenty-five thousand under conditions like this."

"I'd hold out for thirty, myself," Betsy agreed grimly. "We just don't *know* how much extra room we'd need. And don't bother suggesting we put down on a cotton field or straddling both lanes of Interstate 20. One of the other ways you save weight on a Skyport is in the landing gear, and landing on something too soft would tear it to shreds."

An idea was taking shape in the back of Whitney's mind . . . but he wanted to think about it before saying anything to the others. "So that leaves, what, the Skyport maintenance facility outside L.A.?" he asked instead.

"Or the one in New Jersey," Betsy said. "L.A.'s closer." She looked at her watch—the fourth time, by Whitney's count, that she had done so in the last ten minutes. "Damn it all, what's holding up ground control?"

As if in answer, the intercom suddenly crackled. "Bets, this is Aaron," a voice said. "We're ready here to start on down."

"Roger, Aaron; keep your line open," Betsy's voice said, too loudly, in Greenburg's ear. He resisted the impulse to turn down the volume on his portable half-headset; in a moment there would be another aluminum-alloy deck between them that should take care of the problem.

"Right. We're opening the access hatch now." As Lewis looked on, Greenburg undid the three clasps securing the surprisingly light disk and levered it up, making sure it locked solidly into its wall latch. Feeling around the underside of the hatch rim, he located the light switch and turned it on. The blackness below blazed with light, and with a quick glance to make sure he wouldn't be landing on unstable footing he grasped the rungs welded to the hatch and started down the narrow metal ladder, tool belt banging against his thigh.

The lowest of the Skyport's three decks was devoted to passenger luggage and general cargo and to the equipment necessary to move it from shuttle to Skyport, between wing sections where necessary, and back to shuttle again. The hatch the two men had chosen led to one edge of the cargo area, and most of the equipment in Greenburg's immediate area seemed to be motors and electronic overseers for the intricate network of conveyor belts and electric trams that sorted incoming luggage by destination and carted it to the proper storage area. All without human supervision, of course— and, despite that, it generally worked pretty well.

"The bay is straight back that way." Lewis had appeared beside him, clutching a sheaf of computer paper. "I think around that pillar thing would be the best approach."

They set off. Greenburg had been on a Skyport cargo deck only once, back in his training days, and was vaguely surprised at the amount of dirt and grease around the machinery they passed. Within a dozen steps his blue jumpsuit had collected a number of greasy smears and he found himself wishing he'd had the extra minute it would have taken to change into something more appropriate for this job. But even a minute could make a lot of difference . . . and Bets was counting on them.

They reached the curved wall that was the lower half of the docking bay within a few minutes, arriving just forward of a wide ring bristling with hydraulic struts that Greenburg knew marked the position of the emergency docking collar. He glanced back at it as they headed forward under the wall's curve, wondering why the backup system hadn't worked. It should have kicked in as soon as the main collar's supports gave way.

"Watch your step," Lewis said sharply, and Greenburg paused in midstep, focusing for the first time on the dark-red puddle edging onto the path in front of him. Peering along the base of the wall, he could see more of the liquid, more or less collected in a narrow trough there. He squatted, touched it tentatively with a fingertip. It felt thick and oily. "Hydraulic fluid?" Lewis asked.

"Yeah. From the emergency collar, probably." Greenburg straightened and, with only a slight hesitation, rubbed the fluid off on his jumpsuit. Stepping carefully around the puddle in his path, he continued on.

The panel they'd decided on was precisely where the blueprints had said it would be: some two meters around the port wall from the heavy forward clamp machinery at the docking bay's forward tip. About forty centimeters by seventy, the panel sat chest-high in the wall and was, for a wonder, not even partially blocked by any of the conveyor equipment. Selecting a wrench from his belt, Greenburg began loosening the nuts.

"I hope there's nothing in here that can't take low air pressure," Lewis remarked as he untangled the two oxygen sets he was carrying and clipped one of the tanks onto the back of Greenburg's belt. "You want me to put the mask on you?"

"I'll put it on when I get this open," Greenburg grunted as he strained against a particularly well tightened nut. "I don't like stuff hanging from my face while I'm working. Distracts me."

"Put it on before you lose pressure in there, Aaron," Betsy's voice came in his ear.

"Aw, come on—Bets," he said, the last word a burst of air as the nut finally yielded. "We're only a thousand feet or so higher than Pikes Peak, and I've been climb-

ing around up there since I was ten. I'm not going to
black out up here for lack of air."

"Well . . . all right. But I want it on you as soon as
you've finished with the panel."

"Sure."

It took only a couple of minutes to loosen all the nuts
and, with Lewis's help, remove them and force the
panel out of its rubber seating. For a minute there was
a minor gale at their backs as the pressure inside the
cargo deck equalized with that in the bay, and Greenburg
realized belatedly he'd forgotten to check whether or
not Lewis had remembered to close the hatch behind
him. If he hadn't this windstorm was going to keep
going for quite a while . . . but even as he finished
adjusting his oxygen mask over his nose and mouth the
rush of air began to subside and finally stilled completely. "Here goes," Greenburg muttered as, stooping
slightly, he eased his head through the opening, blinking as a cold breeze swept his face.

It was an impressive sight. Even twisted too far toward
the bay's starboard wall, the shuttle's nose still seemed
almost close enough for him to touch as it loomed over
him, vibrating noticeably in the incomplete grip the
broken collar provided. To his left and only slightly
below him, he could see that the shuttle's front landing
gear had descended just as it was supposed to, and was
hanging tantalizingly close to the extended forward clamp.
Moving his mike right up against his oxygen mask—it
was noisier in the bay than he'd expected—he said,
"Okay. First of all, I can't see anything that could be
interfering with the clamp or arm. Rick, do the telltales
read the arm as fully extended?"

A short pause, then Henson's voice. "Sure do. It's
still got lateral and vertical play, though. Want me to
swing it around any?"

"Waste of time, as long as it's too short. Someone's
going to have to go down there and take a look at it, I
guess."

"That's not your job, though," Betsy spoke up. "Carl's
lining up a mechanical crew to come up from the air-

port as soon as it's safe. They can do all the work that's needed in the bay."

"I'm sure they'll be thrilled at the prospect—and don't worry, I wasn't volunteering." Greenburg twisted his head around the other direction. "Now, as to the shuttle door . . . hell. I can't be certain, but it looks like the edge of the collar is overlapping it—the shuttle must have slid back and then shot forward and starboard as the collar was engaging. What the hell kind of guidance system error could have caused *that?*"

"We should know in ten or fifteen minutes," an unfamiliar voice put in.

"Who's that?" Greenburg asked.

"Sorry—maybe I shouldn't have butted in. I'm Peter Whitney; I'm helping to run the diagnostic program that will hopefully locate the problem."

"Peter Whitney?—ah, the McDonnell Douglas computer expert Paul Marinos had said he was bringing in. Have you got the program running yet?"

"Yes; a friend just radioed us the loading code."

"Well ahead of ground control's efforts, I might add," Betsy said. "We'll let you know when we identify the glitch. For now, let's get back to the shuttle door, okay? We think the sensors indicate hydraulic pressure problems in the emergency collar. Is there any chance we could fix that and get it to lock onto the shuttle? Then we could release the main collar and get the shuttle door open."

Greenburg shifted position again and peered at the top of the shuttle, wishing all the floodlights hadn't gone when the craft hit. "I don't think there's any chance at all," he said slowly. "As a matter of fact, it looks very much like the emergency collar's responsible for most of the cockpit damage. It seems to have come out of the wall just in time for the shuttle to ram into it. If that kind of impact didn't do anything more than rupture a hydraulic line or two, I'll be very much surprised."

Betsy said something under her breath that Greenburg

didn't catch. "You sure about that?" she asked. "I can't see any of that on the monitor."

"As sure as I can be on this side of the bay. I can go to the starboard side if you'd like and check through the panel there. Probably have to go over there to find out exactly where this fluid came from, anyway."

"Maybe later. Any other good news for us from there, first?"

"Actually, this *is* good news. Somehow, while the shuttle was rattling around the bay, it completely missed the Skyport passenger and cargo tunnels. If we can get everybody *out* of the shuttle, we can get them *into* the Skyport."

"Well, that's something. Any suggestions on how we go about carrying out that first step?"

Greenburg frowned. Something about the shuttle was stroking the warning bells in his brain . . . but he couldn't seem to put his finger on the problem.

"Aaron?"

"Uh . . . yes." His eyes still probing the vibrating fuselage, Greenburg replayed his mental tape of Betsy's last question. "The, uh, side window of the cockpit seems undamaged. It should be big enough for most of the passengers to squeeze through. Of course, it's a four-meter drop or thereabouts, so we'd need to rig up some way to either get them down and then back up to the tunnel door or else to get them across to it directly. Maybe rig something up to the ski lift mechanism in the tunnel . . ."

His voice trailed off as the warning bells abruptly went off full force. *The nosewheel was slightly closer to him!*

"Bets, the shuttle's sliding backwards!" he shouted into the mike. "The collar must be slipping!"

For a few seconds all he could hear was the muffled, indistinct sound of frantic conversation. Eyes still glued to the slowly moving nosewheel, he jammed his earphone tighter against his ear. "Bets, did you copy? I said—"

"We copied," Paul Marinos's voice told him. "Betsy's getting the shuttle to boost its thrust. Stand by, okay?"

Pursing his lips tightly under his oxygen mask, Greenburg shifted his gaze back along the shuttle to its main passenger door. If the collar was slipping he should be able to see the door slowly sliding further and further beneath the huge ring. . . . He still hadn't decided if it was moving when Betsy's voice made him start.

"Aaron? Is the shuttle still moving?"

"Uh . . . I'm not sure. I don't think so, but all the vibration makes it hard to tell."

"Yeah." A short pause. "Aaron, Tom, you've both done some shuttle flying, haven't you? What are the chances Rayburn could bring this one down safely, damaged as it is?"

Something very cold slid down the center of Greenburg's back. Betsy knew the answer to that one already—they all did. The fact that she was asking at all implied things he wasn't sure he liked. Surely things weren't desperate enough yet to be grasping at *that* kind of straw . . . were they?

Lewis, after a short pause, gave the only answer there was. "Chances are poor to nonexistent—you know that, Betsy. He'd have to leave here at a speed of at least a hundred sixty-five knots, and with one or more windows gone in the cockpit he'd have an instant hurricane in there. He sure as hell won't be able to fly in that, and I personally wouldn't trust any autopilot that's gone through what his has."

"You can't slow down past a hundred sixty-five knots?" Whitney, the computer man, asked.

"That's our minimum flight speed," Lewis told him shortly.

"I know that. What I meant was whether you could try something like a stall or some other fancy maneuver that would pull your speed temporarily lower."

"Wouldn't gain us enough, I'm afraid," Betsy said, sounding thoughtful. "Besides which, wing sections aren't designed for fancy maneuvers." She seemed to sigh. "We've got a new problem, folks. The shuttle's backwards drift, Aaron, was *not* the collar slipping. It was the last two supports *bending*, apparently under slightly unequal thrusts from the shuttle's engines."

Lewis growled an obscenity Greenburg had never heard him use. "What happens if they break? Does the collar fall off the shuttle?"

"The book says yes—but exactly *when* it goes depends on how fast the hydraulic fluid drains out. My guess is it would hold on long enough to turn the shuttle nose down before dropping off and crashing somewhere in the greater Fort Worth area."

"Followed immediately by the shuttle," Greenburg growled. His next task was clear—too clear. "All right, say no more. Tom, there should be a supply locker just forward of here. See if there's any rope or cable in it, would you?"

"What do you want that for?" Betsy asked, her tone edging toward suspicious.

"A safety harness. I'm going to go inside the bay and see if there's any way to get that forward clamp connected. Tom?"

"Yeah, there's some rope here. Just a second—I have to untangle it."

"Hold it, Tom," Betsy said. "Aaron, you're not going in there. You're a pilot, not a mechanic, remember? We'll wait for some professionals from the ground to handle this."

"Wait how long?" he shot back, apprehension putting snap into his tone. "Rayburn can't keep firing his engines all day; and even if he could you have no guarantee the thrusts from all three turbofans would stay properly balanced. Do you?"

There was a short silence, during which Greenburg was startled by something snaking abruptly across his chest. It was Lewis, perhaps sensing the outcome of the argument, starting to tie Greenburg's safety line around him. "No," Betsy finally answered his question. "Rayburn's on-board can't give us those numbers any more, and the support stress indicators aren't really sensitive enough."

"Which means chances are good the shuttle's going

to continue putting stresses on the clamps—variable stresses, yet. They're bound to fatigue eventually under that kind of treatment."

"Mr. Greenburg—Aaron—look, the program's almost finished running." Whitney, putting in his two cents again. "Once it's done we can have people up here in fifteen minutes—"

"No; only once we've found the problem *and made sure the other wing sections don't have it*. Who knows how long *that'll* take?" A tug on the rope coming off the chest of the makeshift harness Lewis had tied around him and a slap on the back told him it was time. Gripping the edges of the opening, he raised a foot, seeking purchase on the curved wall. Lewis's cupped hands caught the foot, steadied it. Greenburg started to shift his weight . . . and paused. He was still, after all, under Betsy's authority. "Bets? Do I have permission to go?"

"All right. But listen: you've got *one* shot at the clamp, and whether it reaches or not you're coming straight out afterward. Understand? No one's ever been in a docking bay during flight before, and you're not equipped for unexpected problems."

"Gotcha. Here goes."

Greenburg had spent the past couple of minutes studying the curving bay wall, planning just how he was going to do this maneuver. Now, as he shifted his weight and pushed off of Lewis's hands, he discovered he hadn't planned things quite well enough. Pushing himself more or less vertically through the narrow opening, he twisted his body around as his torso cleared, coming down in a sitting position with his back to the shuttle. But he'd forgotten about the oxygen tank on the back of his belt, and the extra weight was enough to ruin his precarious balance and to send him sliding gracelessly down the curving metal on his butt.

He didn't slide far; Lewis, belaying the line, made sure of that. Getting his legs back around underneath him, Greenburg checked his footing and nodded back toward the opening. "Okay, I'm essentially down. Let me have some slack." Moving carefully, he stepped down into the teardrop-shaped well under the shuttle and walked to the nosewheel.

The forward clamp was designed to slide out of the wall as the landing gear was lowered, locating the tow bar by means of two short-range transponders installed in the gear. Earlier, up on the flight deck, Greenburg had confirmed the clamp operation had been begun but not completed; now, on closer study, the problem looked like it might be obvious.

"The shuttle's not only angled into the bay wrong, but it's also rotated a few degrees on its axis," he reported to the others. "I think maybe that the clamp's wrist rotated as far as it could to try and match, and when it couldn't get lined up apparently decided to quit and wait for instructions."

"The telltales say it *is* fully extended, though," Henson insisted.

"Well . . . maybe it's the sensors that got scrambled."

"Assume you're right," Betsy said. "Any way to fix it?"

"I don't know." Greenburg studied the clamp and landing gear, acutely aware of the vibrating shuttle above him—and of the vast distances beyond it. *But even if the shuttle fell out and my rope broke I'd be all right,* he told himself firmly. Standing in the cutout well that gave the shuttle's nosewheel room to descend, he was a good two meters below the rim of the bay's outer opening. There was a fair amount of eddy-generated wind turbulance plucking at his jumpsuit and adding a wind-chill to the frigid air—but it would take a *lot* of turbulence to force him up that slope and out. At least, he thought so. . . . "Why don't you try backing the clamp arm up and letting it take another run at the tow bar?"

"We'll have to wait for Peter's program to finish," Henson said. "The computer handles that."

"Oh . . . right." Greenburg hadn't thought of that. "How much longer?"

"It's almost—it's done," Whitney said.

"Where's the problem?" Betsy asked. Even with the turbofan engines droning in his ears Greenburg could hear the twin emotions of anticipation and dread in her voice.

"There doesn't seem to be one."

"That's ridiculous," Greenburg said. "*Something* made the shuttle crash."

"Well, the program can't find it. Look, it seems to me I felt the Skyport bounce a little just before the crash—"

"Clear air turbulence," Betsy said. "That shouldn't have been a problem; the guidance program is supposed to be able to handle small perturbations like that."

"Let's forget about the 'how' of it for now," a new voice broke in—Carl Young's, Greenburg tentatively identified it through the noise. "The point is that we can start bringing shuttles back up again. Greenburg, is there anything you can suggest we bring up from the ground to secure the shuttle with?"

"Uh . . . hell, I don't know. Something to use to get the passengers off would certainly be handy. And if this clamp arm won't rotate any further we might need an interfacing of some kind—maybe an extra clamp-and-wrist piece to extend our clamp's rotational range."

"I've already ordered some spare ski lift track from the ground—it should be coming up aboard the first shuttle, along with men to handle it. The clamp-and-wrist section we may be able to remove from one of the other bays; other people will be coming up to try that. What I meant was, can you see anything from there that we didn't already know about?"

"Not really." Greenburg was starting to feel a little foolish as his brave descent into the bay began to look more and more unnecessary. With the guidance system coming up clean, shuttleloads of experts would be here in minutes. *So much for the value of impulsive heroics,* he thought acridly; but at least it hadn't wasted too much time. He'd always been much better as a team player, anyway. "Hold on tight, Tom; I'm coming up," he called, getting a grip on his safety line.

"Just a second, Aaron," Henson said. "I've got the computer back now. Why don't you stay put while I try the clamp again like you suggested."

"All right. But make it snappy—it's freezing in here."

There was a heavy click, and the clamp arm telescoped smoothly back into itself, rotating to the horizontal as it did so. It paused for a second when fully retracted and then reversed direction, angling toward the landing gear like some rigid metallic snake attacking its prey in slow motion. It stopped, again a meter short, and with a sinking feeling Greenburg saw his mistake. "It's not just the angle the nosewheel's at," he informed the others. "The clamp rotates a little as each segment telescopes out, not all at once at the end of the extension. It's not quitting because it doesn't know how to proceed—it's quitting because it's run out of length."

"That's impossible," Betsy retorted. "I've checked the stats—the arm's *got* to be long enough to reach."

"Then it's been damaged somehow," Greenburg said irritably. If they had to replace the whole arm, and not just the clamp . . . He shivered as a newly sharpened sense of the shuttle's vulnerability hit him like a wet rag.

For a moment the drone of the turbofans was all he could hear. Then Carl Young said, "We'll have the ground people check it out when they get here. Greenburg, you might as well come out of there. You'll need to put the access panel back in place temporarily so we can repressurize the deck."

"Understood." Turning back to the curving wall, his hands numb with cold, Greenburg began to climb.

"The shuttle will dock in Six in about four minutes," the Skyport captain's voice came over the intercom.

"Okay, Carl," Betsy said. "Six, do you have someone at the bay to meet it?"

"Not yet," was the response. "We wanted to have all the stations up here manned during docking, to watch for any trouble. We could call in somebody off-duty, if you want."

"Don't bother," Paul Marinos said, unbuckling his seat belt and getting to his feet. "I'll go down and meet the shuttle. You won't need me before Tom gets back, will you?" he added looking at Betsy.

She shook her head. "Go ahead. As a matter of fact, you can probably escort Mr. Whitney back down on your way. Mr. Whitney, we very much appreciate your help here this morning."

"Uh, yeah. You're welcome."

Unlocking her chair, Betsy swiveled around. Whitney was hunched forward in his own seat, frowning intently at the computer display screen. "Anything wrong?" she asked, her mouth beginning to feel dry again. That shuttle would be trying to dock in a half-handful of minutes. . . .

Whitney shook his head slowly, his eyes never leaving the screen. "I'm just rechecking the readout, trying to see if there's anything that looks funny but somehow didn't register as a problem." He keyed for the next page; only then did he look up. "If it's not too much trouble, though, I'd really like to stay up here for a while. I can be an extra hand with the computer, and there's another project I want to discuss with you."

"Passengers usually aren't permitted up here at all," Marinos said with a frown.

Whitney shrugged. "On the other hand, I *am* already here."

"All right," Betsy said, making a quick decision. Even if Whitney's primary motivation was nothing more than simple curiosity, he'd already been a big help to them. It was an inexpensive way to pay back the favor. "But you'll have to stay out from underfoot. For starters—" she pointed at the display—"you'll need to finish that up quickly, because Tom Lewis's on his way up to make some more blueprints."

"Yes, I know. I'll be finished." He turned back to the console. Nodding to her, Marinos left the flight deck.

Swiveling back forward, Betsy squeezed her eyes

shut briefly and took a long, deep breath. The tension was beginning to get to her. She could feel her strength of will slowly leaking away; could feel her decision-making center seizing up—and this only some eighty minutes into the crisis.

The strength of her reaction was more than a little disturbing. True, the lives of a hundred-sixty people were hanging precariously in the balance back there . . . but she'd been holding people's lives in her hands since her first flight for the Navy back in 1980. She'd had her share of crises, too, probably the worst of them being the 747 that had lost power in all four engines halfway from Seattle to Honolulu. She'd had to put the monster into a five-thousand-foot dive to get the balky turbofans restarted—and she hadn't felt anything like the nervousness she was feeling now. Was it just the *length* of this crisis that was getting to her, the pumping of adrenaline for more than five minutes at a time? If so, she was going to be a wreck by the time this whole thing was resolved. Or—

Or was it the people—*be honest, Betsy; the* person—involved? Could being forced to deal with Eric Rayburn again really hit her this hard?

"Excuse me, Captain; is it all right if I sit here?"

She opened her eyes to see Whitney standing beside her, indicating the copilot's seat. Craning her neck, she saw that Lewis had returned and had taken over the computer terminal again. "Yeah, sure," she told Whitney, thankful for the interruption. "Just don't touch anything. Tom, you need any help?"

"No, thanks; just getting the schematics for the clamp arm mechanism, the emergency collar, and whatever I can find on the Skyport door and tunnel." Paper was beginning to come from the printer slot; Lewis glanced at it and then looked at Betsy. "Anything new from the shuttle?"

"Rayburn's still checking out his instruments. So far the altimeter, Collins nav system, and at least one of the vertical gyros seem to be out; the compass and collisionproofing are intact; the autopilot is a big question mark."

"I met Paul Marinos on the way up here. He said it was Rayburn who came up with that half-assed idea of letting the shuttle fly home alone."

"That's right," Betsy confirmed. "He's still making noises in that direction, too."

"Good. Aaron and I thought *you'd* thought it up, and we were getting a little worried."

She snorted. "Thanks for your confidence. You staying with Aaron after you deliver the schematics?"

"Depends on whether they need me or not," he said, pulling the last sheet from the printer slot and flipping the "off" switch. "Talk to you later."

He got up and left, and as he did so the intercom crackled. "This is Marinos. The shuttle has docked. Textbook smooth, I might add."

Betsy turned to the intercom grille, feeling a minor bit of the weight lift from her shoulders. "Aaron, you copy that? Prepare for company down there."

"Got it. Paul, let me know when you're all down, so I can start taking this panel off again."

"Will do."

The intercom fell silent, and Betsy leaned back in her seat again. Staring out the window at the blue sky, she tried to organize her thoughts.

"Captain? Are you all right?"

She glanced at Whitney, favoring him with a half smile. "I thought I told you we all went informal up here," she chided mildly. "My name's Betsy."

"Oh . . . well . . . you called me 'Mr. Whitney' a while back, so I thought maybe that had changed." He looked a little embarrassed.

"Force of habit, I guess. Anyone wearing a three-piece suit looks like management to me. And as to your question, yes, I'm fine."

"You look tired. How long have you been flying?"

A chuckle made it halfway up her throat. "About twenty-six years, all told. This session, though, less than an hour and a half. I came on duty just before the shuttle crashed."

"Oh." His tone said he wasn't thoroughly convinced.

She looked at him again. "Really," she insisted. "What you're calling tiredness is just tension, pure and simple."

The corner of his mouth quirked. "Okay. I always *was* a lousy detective." The quirk vanished and he sobered. "What do you think their chances are? Honestly."

"It all depends on how fast we can get the shuttle secured—or how fast we find out we *can't* do it."

Whitney frowned. "I don't follow. Are you talking about the—" he glanced at his watch—"six hours of fuel the shuttle's got left?"

"Basically—except that it's only about five and a half now; we nudged his thrust up a notch in two of his engines a while ago." She turned to face forward again, lips compressing into a thin line. "We're in a very neat box here, Peter. You know the Skyport clockwise circuit, don't you?"

"Sure: Boston, New York, Philadelphia, Washington, Atlanta, New Orleans, Houston, Dallas, L.A., San Francisco, Denver, Kansas City, Chicago, Detroit, Cleveland, Pittsburgh, Washington, then back up the pike to Boston." He rattled off the names easily, as someone who'd learned them without deliberate effort. "A twelve-hour run, all told."

"Right. Now note that once we secure the shuttle, there are exactly two places we can land with it: the Skyport maintenance facilities at Mirage Lake, near L.A., and the Keansburg Extension of New Jersey; and L.A.'s probably a half hour closer. *But*—" she paused for emphasis—"between here and L.A. there are no Skyport cities. Which means no shuttles. Which means any equipment we want to bring aboard to work with has to come from here. Which means we have to *stay* here until we're sure we've got everything we're going to need."

"Wumph." Whitney's breath came out in a rush, and for a moment he was silent. "But couldn't you head toward L.A. right away, circling there until you have the clamp fixed? Oh, never mind; you'll probably need the transit time to work. But wait a second—you could head back *east* now, toward New Jersey. Any extra stuff you needed could be brought up from Atlanta, or even Washington; you'd pass close enough to both cities on the way."

She'd had the same brilliant idea nearly twenty minutes ago, and had been just as excited by it as he was. It was a shame to have to pop his bubble. "The fly in that particular soup in John Meredith, the injured shuttle copilot. If we stay here and then manage to get him and the other passengers out within an hour, say, we can get him to a hospital a lot faster than if we had to wait till we reached Atlanta. That time could be life or death for him—and it's the uncertain nature of his injuries, by the way, that gives our box its other walls. Besides," she added grimly, "if we wind up losing the shuttle completely, I'd rather try and find an empty spot in Arizona than in Pennsylvania to drop it into."

"Damn," he muttered. "You've thought through the whole thing, haven't you?"

"I hope not," she countered fervently. "Things don't look too good in my analysis. If I haven't missed something we're probably going to lose either an expensive shuttle or at least one irreplaceable life." She snorted. "Damn the FAA, anyway. We've been on their tail for at least two years now to push for a few more wing section-sized runways scattered among the major airports."

"Yeah, I've always thought it was a bad idea to leave thrust reversers off Skyport engines. The way things are now, you could lift a module off from a ridiculous number of runways that you couldn't put it down on in the first place."

"It's called economy. No one wants to build extra-big runways until they're sure the Skyports are going to catch on." She shook her head. "Enough self-pity. What's this project you mentioned?"

"Right. You said earlier that no one knew what sort of landing distance a wing section-shuttle combo would require. Well, I've done some figuring, and if I can use the combined computer facilities of two modules I think I can get you a rough estimate."

She blinked in surprise. "How?"

"My work for McDonnell Douglas has been on computer simulations for second-generation Skyport design. Most of it involves adjusting profile, mass, and laminar flow parameters and then testing for lift and drag and so on. I remember the equations I'd need and enough about module and shuttle shapes to get by. And it's not *that* complicated a program."

"What about the brakes and drogue chutes?" she asked doubtfully.

"I can put them in as extra drag effects."

Betsy frowned, thinking. There was no way the runways at Dallas would be long enough—of that she was certain. But . . . the figures would be nice to have. "Okay, if we can get two of the other wing sections to agree. You can't use Seven's computer; we'll need to leave it clear for the work down below."

"That's okay—I can link to the other systems and run everything from here."

Betsy turned toward the intercom. "Carl? What do you think?"

"It's worth trying. Two, Three—you've just volunteered your computers to Mr. Whitney's use."

It took Betsy a few minutes to show Whitney how to set up the two-system link, but once he got started he did seem to know what he was doing. She watched over his shoulder for a minute before returning to her seat. It was indeed a good idea, but she had to wonder why he hadn't simply called back his friend in Houston and had him run the program. With the—undoubtedly— larger machine there and the proper program already in place, they could surely have had the answer faster than Whitney could get it here. It was looking very much like he did indeed want an excuse to stay on the flight deck and observe the proceedings. She grimaced. The report he was presumably going to be making to McDonnell Douglas wasn't likely to be a flattering one.

She shook her head to clear away the cobwebs. There

were plenty of unpleasant thoughts to occupy her; she didn't need to generate any extra ones. And, speaking of unpleasantries . . . Steeling herself, she pulled her half-headset mike to her lips and switched it on. "Skyport to Shuttle. Status report, please."

"Oh, there's nothing much new here, Liz—just sitting around watching my copilot dying."

She'd been unprepared for the sheer virulence of Rayburn's tone, and the words hit her with almost physical force. Unclenching her jaw with a conscious effort, she asked, "Is he getting worse? Dr. Emerson?"

"He sure as hell isn't getting any better," Rayburn snapped before the doctor could answer.

Betsy held her ground. "Doctor?" she repeated.

"It's hard to tell," Dr. Emerson spoke up hesitantly. "He's still unconscious and his breathing is starting to become labored, but his pulse is still good."

"Well, we should at least have him out from under all that metal soon," Betsy told him. "The ground crew's aboard now, and they'll be bringing a torch aboard to cut the chair free."

"Yeah, I can see them climbing in down there," Rayburn said. "How do they expect to get up here?"

"Through your side window; I presume they brought a rope ladder or something with them. You'd better open up and be ready to catch the end when they toss it up."

"Hell of a lot of good it's going to do," the shuttle pilot growled. "How're they going to get him back out—tie a rope around him and lower him like a sack of grass seed?"

"If he's not too badly injured, yes," Betsy said, feeling her patience beginning to bend dangerously. "If not, we'll figure out something else. We're going to try and rig up a ski lift track from your window to the Skyport door to get the passengers out; maybe we can bring Meredith out that way on some kind of stretcher."

"A *ski lift track?* Oh, for—Liz, that's the dumbest idea I've ever heard. It could take *hours* to put something like that together!"

The tension that had been building up again within Betsy suddenly broke free. "You have a better idea, spit it out!" she barked.

"You've already heard it," he snapped back. "Let me take this damn bird down *now*, and to hell with ski tracks and nosewheel clamps. All you're doing is wasting time."

"You really think you can fly a plane with its nose smashed in, do you?" she said acidly. "What're you going to use for altimeter, autopilot, and gyros?"

"Skill. I've flown planes in worse shape than this one."

"Maybe. But not with a sprained wrist, and not with a hundred-sixty passengers aboard. And *not* while under my command."

"Oh, right, I forgot—Liz Kyser's the big boss here." Rayburn's voice dripped with sarcasm. "Well, let me just remind you, Your *Highness*, that I don't *need* your permission to leave your flying kingdom. All it would take is a simple push on the throttle."

Betsy's anger vanished in a single heartbeat. "Eric, what are you saying?" she asked cautiously.

"Don't go into your dumb blonde act—you know what I'm talking about. All I have to do is cut power and snap those last two collar supports and you can yell about authority all you want."

"Yes—and you'll either fall nosedown with the collar still around you or drop it onto someone on the ground." Betsy forced her voice to remain quiet and reasonable. "You can't risk innocent people's lives like that, Eric."

"Oh, relax—I'm not going to do anything that crazy unless I absolutely have to. I'm just pointing out that you don't have absolute veto power over me. Keep that in mind while you figure out how to get John to a hospital."

"Don't worry. We want him safe as much as you do." *Especially now.* "We'll keep you posted." Reaching over, Betsy turned off the mike.

For a moment she just sat there, her mind spinning like wheels on an icy runway. The flight deck suddenly felt cold, and she noticed with curious detachment that the hands resting on the edge of her control board were trembling slightly. Rayburn's threat, and the implied state of mind accompanying it, had shocked her clear down to the marrow. He'd always been loyal to the crews he flew with—it had been one of the qualities that had first attracted her to him—but this was bordering on monomania. Bleakly, she wondered if the accident had damaged more than Rayburn's wrist.

There was a footstep beside her. Whitney, looking sandbagged. "Betsy, is he—uh—?" He ran out of words, and just pointed mutely toward her half-headset.

"You heard, huh?" She felt a flash of embarrassed annoyance that he, an outsider, had listened in on private Skyport trouble.

Whitney, apparently too shaken to be bothered by his action, nodded. "Is he all right back there? I mean, he sounds . . . overwrought."

"He does indeed," she acknowledged grimly. "He's under a lot of pressure—we all are."

"Yeah, but you're not threatening to do something criminally stupid." He gestured at the intercom. "And why didn't Captain Young at least back you up?"

"He probably wasn't listening in—the radio doesn't feed directly into the intercom." She took another look at his expression and forced a smile she didn't feel. "Hey, relax. Eric hasn't gone off the deep end; he was just blowing off some steam."

"Hmm." He seemed unconvinced. "And how about you?"

The question caught her unprepared, and Betsy could feel the blood coloring her face. "I got a little loud there myself, didn't I?" she admitted. "I guess I'm not used to this kind of protracted crisis. Usual airplane emergencies last only as long as it takes you to find the nearest stretch of flat ground and put down on it."

"I suppose so. Anything I can do?"

"Yes—you can haul yourself back to the computer and finish that program."

Surprisingly, something in her tone seemed to relieve whatever fears he had about her, because the frown lines left his forehead and he even smiled slightly. "Aye, aye, Captain," he said and headed aft again.

Well, that's him convinced. Now if only she could persuade *herself* as to Rayburn's self-control. Pushing the half-headset mike away almost savagely, she leaned toward the intercom. "Aaron, Paul—what's holding things up down there?"

The rolled-up end of thin rope smacked against the top of the window as it came in through the opening. Startled a bit by the sudden noise, Dr. Emerson turned his head—the only part of his body he could conveniently turn in the cramped cockpit—in time to see Captain Rayburn field the rope and begin pulling it in. Tied to the other end, its rungs clanking against the side of the shuttle, was a collapsible ladder, of the sort Emerson made his kids keep under their bunk bed at their Grand Prairie condo. He watched as Rayburn set the outsized hooks over the lower edge of the window and then turned back to his patient with a silent sigh of relief. At least the waiting was over. Now all he had to do was worry that Meredith was healthy enough to satisfy Rayburn—and *that*, he reflected darkly, was definitely a major worry. Rayburn's last stormy conversation with the Skyport had completely shattered Emerson's comfortable and long-held stereotype of the unflappable airline pilot and had left him with a good deal of concern. Searching the unconscious copilot's half-hidden face, Emerson wondered what it was about this man that had caused Rayburn to react so violently. Was he a good friend? Or was it something more subtle— did he remind Rayburn of a deceased brother, for instance? Emerson didn't know, and so far he hadn't had the nerve to ask.

"Okay, Doc, here they come." Rayburn, who'd been leaning his head partly out the window, began unsnapping his safety harness. "Let's get out of here and give them room to come in."

Emerson rose from his crouch, grimacing as his legs

registered their complaint. Trying to look all directions at once, he backed carefully out of the tiny space, and made it out the cockpit door without collecting any new bruises. Rayburn was out of his seat already, standing in the spot Emerson had just vacated, shouting instructions toward the window. "Okay—easy—just keep it away from the instruments—okay, I've got it." Two small gas tanks, wrapped together by metal bands and festooned with hoses, appeared in his hands and were immediately tucked under his right arm. The second package was, for Emerson, far more recognizable: the big red cross on the suitcase-sized box was hard to miss. A moment later he had to take a long step toward the shuttle's exit door as Rayburn backed out of the cockpit. "Watch the controls!" he shouted once more as he set down his burden and reached back with a helping hand.

It took only a few minutes for them to all come aboard. There were three: two mechanic-types who set to work immediately turning the gas tank apparatus into an acetylene torch; and an older man who caught Emerson's eye through the small crowd and headed back toward the passenger section. Emerson took the cue and followed.

"I'm Dr. Forrest Campbell," the newcomer introduced himself when the two men reached the pocket of relative quiet at the forward end of the passenger compartment.

"Larry Emerson. Glad to have you here. You work for the airline?"

"Temporarily coopted only—and as the man said, if it weren't for the honor I'd rather walk." He nodded down the rows of ski lift seats. "First things first. Are the passengers in need of anything?"

"Nothing immediate. There are some bruises and one or two possible sprains. Mostly, everyone's just scared and cold."

"I can believe that," Campbell agreed, shivering. "I'm told the Skyport's come down to eight thousand feet, but it still feels like winter in here. I hope the next shuttle up thinks to bring some blankets. All right, now let's hear the bad news. How's the copilot?"

"Not good." Emerson gave all the facts he had on Meredith's condition, plus a few tentative conclusions he hadn't wanted to mention in Rayburn's earshot. "We'll have to wait for a more thorough examination, of course, but I'm pretty sure we're *not* going to be able to risk lowering him out that window at the end of a rope."

"Yes . . . and I doubt that a stretcher would really fit. Well, if we can get him stable enough he can stay here until the shuttle can be landed again."

"I guess he'll have to." A sharp *pop* came from the cockpit, and looking past Campbell he saw the room aglow with blue light. "I hope they're not going to fry him just getting him out," he muttered uneasily.

"They'll have attached a Vahldiek conductor cable between the part of the chair stem they're cutting and the fuselage, to drain off the heat," Campbell assured him. "Let's go back in; this shouldn't take long."

It didn't. They had barely reentered the exit door area—now noticeably warmer—and opened the big medical kit when the torch's hiss cut off. Rayburn stepped back from the doorway, muttering cautionary instructions as the unconscious copilot, still strapped into his seat, was carried carefully out of the cockpit.

"For now, just leave him in the chair," Campbell said as they set down the seat and disconnected the thin high-conduction line. Stethoscope at the ready, he knelt down and got to work.

Emerson stepped over to Rayburn. "Shouldn't you be getting back to the cockpit, Captain?" he suggested quietly.

Rayburn took a deep breath. "Yeah. Take care of him, Doc, and tell me as soon as you know anything."

"We will."

Stepping carefully around the figures on the floor, Rayburn went forward, and Emerson breathed a sigh of relief. At least the shuttle had a pilot again, should something go wrong with what was left of the docking collar. Now if only that pilot could be persuaded not to do anything hasty . . . He shivered, wondering if Rayburn would really rip the shuttle from its unstable perch . . . wondering if the Skyport's holding pattern was taking them over Grand Prairie and his family.

Pushing such thoughts back into the corners of his mind, he squatted down next to Dr. Campbell and prepared to assist.

"All right, let it out again—real easy," the gravelly voice of Al Carson said in Greenburg's ear. Mentally crossing his fingers, Greenburg kept his full attention on the clamp arm as, up on the flight deck, Henson gave it the command to extend.

But neither Greenburg's wishes nor Carson's quarter-hour of work had made any appreciable change in the arm's behavior. As near as Greenburg could tell from his viewpoint by the access panel, the arm followed exactly the same path he'd seen it take earlier. It certainly came up just as short.

Carson swore under his breath. Once again he took the sheaf of blueprints from his assistant, and once again Greenburg gritted his teeth in frustration. Neither Carson nor the rest of his crew were experts on Skyport equipment—such experts were currently located only on the east and west coasts—but even so they'd identified the basic problem in short order: one of the four telescoping segments of the arm apparently was not working. That much Carson had learned almost immediately from the blueprints (and Greenburg still felt a hot chagrin that he hadn't caught it himself); but all the lubricating, hammering, and other mechanical cajolery since then had failed to unfreeze it. And they were running low on time.

"Hey, you—Greenburg." Carson gestured up at him. "C'mere and give us a hand, will you?"

"Sure." Gripping the line coming from his safety harness—a *real* safety harness; the ground crew had brought along some spares—he stepped up on the box they'd placed beneath the opening and wriggled his way through. He was most of the way into the bay before he remembered to check the space above him for falling debris, but Lady Luck was kind: none of the rest of the crew was working directly overhead. He gave their operation a quick once-over as the motorized safety line lowered him smoothly down the bay wall, and was impressed in spite of himself. The Skyport tunnel had been run out as far to the side as possible and locked in place pointing toward the open cockpit window, and already the first part of the ski lift framework had been welded between the tunnel and shuttle fuselage. A second brace was being set in place; two more, and the track itself could be laid down. It wouldn't take long; six men—fully half the group that had come up—were working on that part of the project alone. In Greenburg's own opinion more emphasis should have been placed on getting the clamp attached, but he knew it would be futile to argue the point. The crew took their orders from the airline, and the airline clearly had its own priorities.

He reached bottom and, squeezing the manual release to generate some slack in his line, ducked under the shuttle and headed over to where Carson and his assistant waited. "All right," the boss said, indicating a place on the clamp arm. "Greenburg, you and Frank are going to pull here this time. Henson? Back it up about halfway."

The arm slid back. Greenburg and Frank gripped the metal and braced themselves as Carson armed himself with a large screwdriver and hammer. On his signal Henson started the arm out again, and as the other two pulled, Carson set the tip of the screwdriver at the edge of the segment and rapped it smartly with the hammer.

It didn't work. "Damn," Carson growled. "Well, okay, if it was the catch that was sticking that should have been taken care of it. The electrical connections seem okay—the control lines aren't shorted. That leaves the hydraulics." He picked up the blueprints and started leafing through them. "Okay. We got separate lines for each segment, but they all run off the same reservoir. So it's gotta be in the line. You got any pressure indicators on these things up there?"

"We're supposed to," Henson replied. "But we seem to have lost them when the emergency collar went—"

"Wait a second," Greenburg cut in as his brain suddenly made a connection. "The hydraulic lines for the arm run by the emergency collar?"

"Yeah, I think so," Carson said. "Why?"

Lewis, listening from outside the bay, swore abruptly. "The broken hydraulic lines!"

"Broken lines?" Carson asked sharply. "Where?"

"Back there, by the emergency collar." Even as he said it Greenburg remembered that the ground crew had been brought into the cargo deck further forward, that they hadn't seen the pool of hydraulic fluid that he and Lewis had had to step over earlier. "There's leakage on both sides of the bay. Most of it's from the collar itself, we think, but some of it could be from the line that handles this segment. Couldn't it?"

"Sure could." Carson didn't look very happy as he found the schematic he wanted and glared silently at it for a moment. "Yeah. All the arm segment lines run separately all the way to the reservoir, it looks like, so that if one gives you've still got all the rest. They all run along the starboard side of the bay, right where the shuttle hit. Ten'll get you a hundred that's the trouble."

"Rick? How about it?" Greenburg called.

"Probably." Henson sounded disgusted. "I think the sensors are located in that same general area. You could probably track the line back visually and confirm it's broken."

"For the moment don't bother; its not worth the effort," Betsy's voice came in for the first time in many minutes. "Mr. Carson, can it be fixed or will we have to replace the whole arm?"

"I don't know. Frankly, I'm not sure either one can be done outside a hangar. Leastwise, not by me."

"I see." There was a pause—an ominously long pause, to Greenburg's way of thinking. "I'd like you to look at the arm, anyway, if you would, and see how much work replacing it would take. Aaron, would you come to the flight deck, please? We need to have a consultation."

"Sure, Bets." He made the words sound as casual as possible, even as his stomach curled into a little knot inside him. Whatever she wanted to discuss, it was something she didn't want the whole intercom net to hear . . . and that could only be bad news.

Moving as quickly as he dared, he headed back under the access panel and, kicking in his harness's motor, began to climb the wall.

It was, to the best of Betsy's knowledge, the first time the closed intercom system had ever been used aboard a Skyport, and she found her finger hesitating slightly as it pressed the button that would cut Seven's flight deck off from everyone except Carl Young on Four. But she both understood and agreed with the Skyport captain's insistence that this discussion be held privately. "All set here, Carl," she said into the grille.

"All right," the other's voice came back. "I'm sure I don't have to remind either of you what time it's getting to be."

"No, sir." The instrument panel clock directly in front of her read 10:02:35 EST, with the seconds ticking off like footsteps toward an unavoidable crossroads. "At just about fourteen twenty-five the shuttle runs out of fuel. If we're going to reach Mirage Lake before that happens, we're got to leave Dallas right now."

"Or in twenty minutes, if we wind up running right to the wire," Greenburg muttered from the copilot's chair. A shiver ran visibly through his body; but whether it was an aftereffect of the cold air down below or a reaction to the same horrible image that was intruding in Betsy's own mind's eye, she had no way of knowing.

"True; but we don't dare cut things that fine," Young said. "We don't know how long those two collar supports will hold under a full strain. How is the forward clamp?"

"It's shot," Greenburg said succinctly. "One of the segments has a broken hydraulic line, we think."

"Replaceable?"

Greenburg hesitated. "I don't know. The ground crew boss doesn't think so."

"What about the escape system for getting the passengers out?"

"Proceeding pretty well. If no new problems crop up I'd say they'll be ready with the thing in half an hour or so."

"Well, that's something, anyway. Betsy, what's the latest on Meredith's condition?"

Betsy took a deep breath. "It's not good, I'm afraid. The doctors say he's got at least a couple of broken ribs, a possible mild concussion, and slow but definite internal bleeding. They've got him laid out on cushions in the shuttle's aisle and have asked for some whole blood to be sent up. I've already radioed the ground; it'll be brought by the next shuttle up."

Greenburg gave a low whistle. "That doesn't sound good at all."

"It's not," she admitted. "There's also evidence that some of the blood may be getting into one of his lungs. Even if it's not, putting new blood into him's a temporary solution at best."

"How long before he has to get to a hospital?" Greenburg asked bluntly, his eyes boring into Betsy's.

"The doctors don't know. At the moment he's relatively stable. But if the bleeding increases—" She left the sentence unfinished.

"Four hours to L.A. at this speed. That's a long time between hospital facilities," Young mused, and Betsy felt a stab of envy at the control in his voice. Ultimately, it was really Carl, not her, who was supposed to be responsible for the safety of the Skyport and its passengers. What right did he have to be so calm when she was sweating buckets over this thing?

"Wait a second," Greenburg spoke up suddenly. "It doesn't have to be an all-or-nothing proposition. We could dock a shuttle in, say, Six and carry it with us to

L.A. Then if Meredith got worse we could land him at any of the airports along the way."

"You're missing the point," Betsy snapped. The sharpness of her tone startled her almost as much as it did Greenburg, judging from his expression, and she felt a rush of shame at lashing out at him. "The problem," she said in a more subdued voice, "is that stuffing Meredith out that cockpit window and into a ski lift chair could kill him before we could get him down and to a hospital. The doctors didn't actually come out and *say* that they wouldn't allow it, but that was the impression I got. Given Rayburn's state of mind, I didn't want to press the point with him on the circuit."

"So what you're saying is that Meredith is stuck on the shuttle until it can be landed," Young said.

"Yeah, I guess that's basically what it boils down to," Betsy admitted. "Unless he takes a turn for the worse, in which case we'll probably have to go ahead and take the chance."

"Uh-huh." Young was silent for a moment. "All right, here's how things look from where I sit. I've been in contact with United, and they have absolutely insisted that getting the passengers out of the shuttle be our top priority—higher even than Meredith's life, if it should come to that. A second crew will be coming up with that shuttle you mentioned to help with the off-loading. The airline chiefs say they want—and I quote—'everyone safely aboard the Skyport with complimentary cocktails in their fists within an hour." For the first time, Young's voice strayed from the purely professional as a note of bitterness edged in. Somehow, it made Betsy feel a little better. "What happens to Meredith and the shuttle is apparently *our* problem until then, when presumably they'll be willing to lend more of a hand."

"So what do we do?" Greenburg asked after a short pause. "Get everything aboard that we'll need for the ski lift track and hightail it for L.A.?"

"We also need to fasten the shuttle more securely before we go," Betsy said. "Rayburn wants Meredith in a hospital immediately if not sooner, and if we try telling him he's going to have to wait another four hours he may try taking Meredith's safety into his own hands."

Greenburg frowned at her. "What do you mean?"

"Oh, that's right—you didn't hear that little gem of a conversation." In a half-dozen sentences Betsy summarized Rayburn's earlier outburst. Greenburg's eyes were wide with shocked disbelief by the time she finished. "Carl, we've got to get him out of that cockpit before he flips completely," he said, his left hand tracing restless patterns on the armrest.

"On what grounds? He hasn't actually tried to *do* anything dangerous. He could claim he was just blowing off steam."

"But—"

"No buts." The Skyport captain was firm. "We can't justify it—and besides, how do you think he'd react to an order like that?"

Greenburg clamped his lips together, and Betsy thought she saw some of the color go out of his face. "That's a little unfair," she said. "We don't *know* that he'd react irrationally." It felt strange to be defending Rayburn; quickly, she changed the subject. "Anyway, we're getting off the point. The immediate issue here is whether or not we head west in the next fifteen minutes. Carl, I guess this is your basic command decision."

Young's sigh was clearly audible. "I'm afraid I don't see any real alternative. We're just going to have to gamble with Mr. Meredith's life. All of the ski lift track and auxiliary equipment we're using only exists at fields that handle Skyport shuttles. If the crew putting the escape system together runs short of anything halfway to L.A. they'll have no way to get extra material quickly. We have to stay here at least until all of that's completed."

Betsy nodded; she'd more or less expected that would be the way the decision would break. The airline was clearly going to keep up the pressure, and the ski lift track system was the only way to get that many passengers off with anything like the speed and safety United would be demanding.

"And after they're off?" Greenburg asked quietly.

"We'll head toward L.A. and hope we've either secured the shuttle by then or that the last two collar supports are stronger than they look."

"Yeah." Shaking his head, Greenburg got to his feet. "I hope to hell we're doing the right thing, Carl. I'm not convinced, myself."

"Me, neither," Young acknowledged frankly. "But I don't see what else we can do. If we should somehow lose the shuttle with the passengers still aboard . . . it's not something I want to think about."

Greenburg nodded, shifting his gaze to Betsy. "I'm going back down and lend a hand, unless you need me here."

"No, go ahead. And Aaron—sorry I snapped at you earlier."

"Forget it. We're all tense." His hand touched her shoulder briefly and then he was gone.

"Betsy?" a tentative voice asked from behind her as she switched the intercom back to normal and the buzz of low-level conversation abruptly came back.

"Yes, Peter, what is it?" she asked, turning her head.

"I've got the first results of my program now, if you're interested."

She'd almost forgotten about Whitney; he'd been so quiet back there. "Sure. Let's hear the bad news."

"Well . . . it could be off ten percent or so either way, understand; but the number I get is seven point eight kilometers."

She did a rough conversion in her head, nodded heavily. "About twenty-five thousand four hundred feet."

"Close enough," he agreed. "I can probably get a more refined version to run before the shuttle passengers are off."

She shook her head. "Not worth it. The longest runway at Dallas is twenty thousand feet, and even if your numbers are fifteen percent high we still would never make it."

"Yeah." Whitney hesitated, a half-dozen expressions flickering across his face. "You know, Betsy, this really isn't any of my business . . . but I get the impression you're upset with yourself for not being—oh, as cool and calm as maybe you think you should be. Is that true?"

Betsy's first and immediate reaction was one of annoyance that he should bring up such a personal subject. Her second was that he was absolutely right, which annoyed her all the more. "How I feel about myself is irrelevant," she said, a bit tartly. "I'm in command here; that requires me to be competent at what I do. Pressure like this isn't new to me, you know—I've been in crisis situations before."

"But they haven't been like this one, I'll bet, because you're *not* really in command here—not entirely, anyway. That's where the trouble is." There was an odd earnestness in his face, as if it were very important for some reason that he get his point across to her. "You see, if you were flying a normal airplane, you *would* be in complete control—I mean as far as human control ever goes—because all the buttons and switches would be under your hands alone. But *here*—" he gestured aft, toward the shuttle—"here, even though you're still claiming all the responsibility for what happens, half of the control is back there, with Captain Rayburn. He's got a mind and will of his own; you can't force him to do what you want, like you can your engines or ailerons. Of *course* you're going to be under extra pressure— you're never had to *persuade* part of your plane to cooperate with you before! It's *normal*, Betsy—you can't let it throw you." He stopped abruptly, as if suddenly embarrassed by the vehemence of his unsolicited counsel. "I'll shut up now," he muttered. "But think about it, okay?" Without another word he slipped back to the computer console.

Betsy leaned back in her seat, her thoughts doing a sort of slow-motion tumble. The last thing in the world she had time for right now was introspection . . . but the more she thought about Whitney's words, the more sense they made. Certainly Rayburn was only nominally under her control—his threats had made that abundantly clear—while it was equally certain that diplomacy and persuasive powers had never been among her major talents. Was that *really* the underlying source of her tension, the fact that she wasn't properly equipped for that aspect of the crisis?

Oddly enough, the idea made her feel better. She wasn't, in fact, getting old or losing her nerve. She was simply facing a brand-new problem—and new problems were *supposed* to be stressful.

For the first time since the shuttle crash, Betsy felt the tightness in her stomach vanish completely as all her unnamed fears, now robbed of their anonymity, scurried back into the darkness. If controlling Rayburn was what was required, then that was what she would do, pure and simple. All it took was strength and self-confidence—and both were already returning to her. She would have to thank Whitney later for his well-timed brashness. Right now, however, she had work to do. "Greenburg?" she called into the intercom grille. "I've got a couple of suggestions on how you might fix that clamp."

Seen through the distorted view of a fisheye camera, the escape system apparatus resembled nothing more dignified than a jury-rigged carnival ride—but it worked, and it worked well, and that was what counted. Even as Betsy returned her attention to the monitor, a pair of legs poked out the cockpit window and, above them, a line and hook were handed up to the man leaning vertically along the windshield. Eye-level to him was the newly built ski lift track; into it he dropped the end of the hook. The hook immediately moved toward the passenger tunnel, and as the line tightened, the dangling legs bounced forward and out and become a business-suited man seated securely in a breeches-buoy type of sling. Even as he traveled toward the tunnel, an empty sling passed him going the other direction, and another set of legs poked tentatively out the cockpit window. Total elapsed time per passenger: about fifteen seconds. For all one hundred sixty of them . . . Betsy glanced at the clock and did the calculation. Maybe three or four left aboard now. And once they were off, a new confrontation with Rayburn was practically inevitable. Her throat ached with new tension as she tried to plan what she would say to him.

All too soon, the familiar voice crackled in her ear. "This is Rayburn. Everyone's off now except John and the two doctors. What's next?"

His harsh, clipped tone made the words a challenge, and Betsy felt the self-confidence of ninety minutes ago drain completely away. "We're leaving for L.A. in a few more minutes," she told him. "With the cable on your tow bar and the extra support of the escape system framework, the docking collar should hang on even after you run out of fuel."

"Who are you trying to kid, Liz?" The bitterly patronizing tone struck her like a slap in the face, and she felt her back stiffen in reaction. He continued, "I saw that so-called cable when they brought it in—it wouldn't hold for two minutes. And you're drunk if you think a little spot-welding along the fuselage is going to do any good at all."

Betsy opened her mouth, but no words came out. In smaller quantities, she shared his own doubts about the cable looped around the nosewheel and the end of the clamp; they'd done the best they could, but the clamp simply wasn't designed to handle a line of any real diameter. Heavier cables were available, but there weren't any good places to attach them, either on the shuttle or the inner bay wall. "There are other things we can try on the way," she said, getting her voice working at last. "A stronger line, perhaps run through the access panels we've been using." Though where the ends would be anchored she had no idea.

But Rayburn didn't even bother to raise that point. "Swell. And what about John—or don't you care if he bleeds into his gut for another four hours? What're you going to do, just keep pumping blood into him and hope the leaks don't get worse? Or maybe you're going to stuff an operating room in through the window?"

"And what do you think the shock of landing will do to him?" Betsy countered.

"He's got to land *some*time. Better now than later, when he'll probably be weaker." Rayburn paused, as if waiting for an argument. But Betsy remained silent. "So okay, I'm going to take him down. I'll give you fifteen minutes to get rid of that cable and junk pile by my window; otherwise I'll just have to pull them out when I leave."

Betsy swallowed. She had no doubt that he could indeed tear off the cable if he really worked at it—and the chances were excellent he'd damage his front landing gear in the process. And that would essentially be signing his death warrant, because even if he somehow managed to keep the crippled plane from diving nose-first into the ground, there was no chance whatsoever that he could control it accurately enough to safely belly-land on a crash-foamed runway. He had to know that; he couldn't be *that* far gone. But she didn't have the nerve to call his bluff. "Eric, if you disobey orders like this you'll never fly again for any airline," she pointed out, trying to keep her voice reasonable. "You know that, don't you?"

"I don't give a damn about the airlines or your tin-god orders—you should know me better than that by now. All I care about any more is John's life. Fifteen minutes, Liz."

Stall, was all she could think of. "We have to get Dr. Emerson off the shuttle first," she told him. "You can't risk his life on this."

Rayburn snorted impatience. "All *right*. Doc! No, you—Doc Emerson. You're to get your things and leave; Skyport orders. Sorry, no . . . but, look, thanks for everything."

The earphone went silent. Betsy pushed the mike away from her with a trembling hand. Whitney's earlier words echoed through her mind—but it did no good to recognize on an intellectual level that once Rayburn defied her instructions she was absolved from all responsibility for the shuttle's safety. Emotionally, she still felt the crushing weight of failure poised above her shoulders.

Because, down deep, she finally knew what the real problem was. Not theoretical concepts like command and responsibility; not even Rayburn's open rebellion.

The problem was her. *Leadership is what command is all about,* she thought, a sour taste seeping into her mouth. *A captain needs to* act; *but all I can do with Eric is* react. She should have seen it long ago, and recognized it as the one remaining legacy of their long-since-broken relationship. Then, for reasons that had seemed adequate at the time, she had allowed his over-powering personality to take charge, submitting to his lead in all things, until in its subtle and leisurely way a pattern had been set for all their future interactions. He acted, she reacted; a simple, straightforward, and un-breakable rule . . . and men would probably die today because of it. And even as she contemplated that conse-quence of her failure, a second, more brutally personal one drove itself into her consciousness like a thorn under a fingernail: for a year and a half Rayburn's name, face, and voice had been instant triggers of guilt-tinged pain to her . . . and if he died now, under these circumstances, he would haunt her from his grave for the rest of her life. "No!" she hissed aloud, beating gently on the edge of her instrument panel with a tightly curled fist. The pattern could be broken; *had* to be broken. She couldn't afford to accept his assumption that no alternative solutions existed. Their lives, and her future sanity, could depend on her proving him wrong.

Gritting her teeth tightly together, she stared at the monitor screen, her eyes dancing over the broken shut-tle, the inside of the bay, the inadequate cable. Some-where in all of that there was an answer. . . . Dr. Emerson's legs appeared through the cockpit window, his hand groping upward with the hook until the man on the windshield took it from him and set it in place. The line tightened and the doctor popped out of the window, flailing somewhat with his carry-on bag as he swung in midair.

And Betsy had the answer. Maybe.

"Peter!" she called, spinning around in her chair. "Did you finish that second landing-distance analysis yet?"

Whitney looked up at her. "Yes—it came out a little better this time: about seven point seven one kilometers, plus or minus five percent, maybe."

"How much worse would it be on a foamed runway?"

He blinked. "Uh, I really don't know—"

"Never mind. Warm up the machine again; I need some fast numbers from you." She flicked on her mike again. "Eric? Hold the ceremonies; I've got an idea."

"Save your breath. Whatever you've come up with, I'm going anyway."

"I know," she said, smiling coldly to herself. "But you're not going alone. We're going to hand-deliver you."

The sky had been a perfectly cloudless blue when the Skyport first approached Dallas earlier that morning. Now, five hours later, it looked exactly the same, giving Betsy a momentary feeling of déjà vu. But the sensation faded quickly. The airport that was just coming into view through the flight deck windows was to the north of them this time, instead of to the west, and even at this distance the heavily foamed runway was clearly visible in the noonday sun. And the throbbing roar of the engines behind her was a powerful reminder that this time the silver giant that was Wing Section Seven was fully awake.

"Range, twenty miles," Greenburg said from the co-pilot's seat. "Sky's clear for at least five miles around us."

She nodded receipt of the information, her eyes tracing a circuit between the windows, the computerized approach monitor, and the engine and other instrument readings. They were barely six minutes from touchdown now, and the pressure was beginning to mount. For a moment she wished she'd accepted Lewis's offer to do the actual landing, which would have left her with

Henson's task of coordinating operations with the shuttle. But Lewis had already put in a full shift when the accident occurred, and whether he would admit it or not he was bound to be getting tired. Besides, this gamble was Betsy's idea alone. If something went wrong, she didn't want anyone else to share in the blame. Or in the physical danger, for that matter—but there she'd met with somewhat less success. Ordering Lewis and the rest of Seven's off-duty flight crews to join the passengers in moving across to Five and Six had resulted in a quiet but firm mutiny. They'd helped the flight attendants get the passengers moved out, but had then returned en masse to the lounge, where most of them had spent the rest of the morning anyway, out of the way of the on-duty crew but close by if needed. Betsy had groused some about it, but not too loudly; though she couldn't imagine what help they could possibly be, their presence was somehow reassuring.

And reassurance was definitely something she could use more of. "Eric, we're about four minutes away. Are you ready?"

"As ready as I'm going to be." Even half buried in the rumble of Seven's engines, Rayburn's voice sounded nervous, and Betsy felt a flash of sympathy for him. The shoe that had been pinching her all morning was now squarely on *his* foot. Not only was his plane going to be brought down by someone else while he himself had to sit passively by, but he was going to be essentially blind during the entire operation. "You just be sure to hold a nice steady deceleration once we hit the runway."

"Don't worry." Betsy stole a quick glance at the bay monitor. The escape system had been dismantled before Seven broke off from the rest of the Skyport, and the passenger tunnel retracted into the bay wall; the front landing gear, freed from the tethering cable, had been similarly retracted into its well. Betsy's jaw tightened and she winced at the thought of the shuttle hitting that foamed runway belly-first at a hundred-twenty knots. Rayburn would have a massive job on his hands at that point, trying to maintain control of his skid while bringing the shuttle to a stop. But there was no way around it—the shuttle couldn't leave the docking bay with its nosewheel extended, and with less than a six-foot drop from its docked position to the ground there would be nowhere near enough time to get the landing gear in position once the shuttle was out. She hoped to hell the airport people had been generous with the foam.

"Seven miles to go," Greenburg murmured. "Final clearance has been given. Speed at one-seven-five."

One hundred seventy-five knots—one statute mile every eighteen seconds; a good fifty knots higher than the shuttle's own landing speed—and even at that Seven was barely staying aloft. Betsy's mouth felt dry as she made a slight correction in their approach path. Not only did she need to put Seven down on the very end of the runway if they were going to have any chance of pulling this off, but the runway itself was only two hundred feet wide, barely thirty feet wider than Seven's wheel track. She needed to hit it dead center, and stay there . . . and all of its markings were hidden by the foam.

"Betsy!" Henson's voice crackled with urgency. "Rayburn's lowered his main landing gear!"

"What?" Both her hands were busy, but Greenburg was already leaning over to switch the TV to Seven's outside monitor . . . and Henson was right. "Rayburn!" she all but bellowed into her mike. "What in hell's name do you think you're doing?"

"Trying to make this landing a little easier," he said, his voice taut.

"How?—by skidding into Dallas on your nose?"

"No—listen—all I have to do is control my exit from the bay so that my nosewheel is clear before I'm completely out."

"And then what—dangle by your nose until the wheel is down?" Betsy snorted. "Forget it. If you don't make it you could go completely out of control when you hit. Retract that gear, now."

"I can *do* it, Betsy—really. Please let me try."

For Betsy it was the final irony of the whole crisis; that Rayburn, having resisted her authority all morning, should be reduced to wheedling to get his way, even to the point of discarding the use of her hated nickname. But she felt no satisfaction or sense of triumph—only contempt that he would stoop to such shabby tactics, and bitter disappointment that he thought her fool enough to fall for something that transparent. And with sudden clarity she realized the reason for his new submissiveness: with Seven flying at such a low altitude Rayburn couldn't risk the unilateral action he'd hinted at earlier, because there was no way to guess whether or not the collar, once torn loose, would fall off fast enough for him to regain flying trim.

But it wasn't going to work. She was finally in command here, and nothing he could say or do was going to change that. If he didn't retract his gear as ordered she would simply pull out of her approach and circle the field until he did. This would be done her way or not at all.

Beside her, Greenburg shifted in his seat. "It's your decision, Betsy," he murmured, just loud enough for her to hear over the engines. "What do you think?"

She opened her mouth to repeat her order to Rayburn . . . and suddenly realized what she was doing.

She was still *reacting* to him.

It's your decision, Betsy. For the first time in years she really paused to consider what the words *decision* and *command* required of her. Among other things, they required that she dispassionately consider Rayburn's idea on its own merits, that she weigh his known piloting skill higher than his abrasive personality. And for perhaps the first time ever, she realized that accepting a good suggestion from him was not a sign of weakness. Perhaps even the opposite . . .

The airport filled the entire window, the foamed runway pointing at her like a sawed-off spear less than a mile away. "All right," she said into her mike. "But you damn well better pull this off, Eric. And do *not* jump the gun."

"Got it. And . . . thanks."

The individual undulations in the foam were visible now as the edges of the runway disappeared from her field of view. Betsy eased back on the throttle, remembering to compensate for the fact that the shuttle's extra length limited the attack angle she could use to kill airspeed just before touching down. The leading edge of the foam flashed past—and with a jolt the wing section was down.

"Chutes!" she snapped at Greenburg, tightening her grip on the wheel as she braced for the shock. A moment later it came, throwing her roughly against her shoulder straps as the two drogue chutes on each end of the wing burst from their pods and bit into the air. Grimly, she held on, riding out the transient as she fought to keep Seven's wheels on the slippery runway. Within seconds the shaking had subsided from dangerous to merely uncomfortable, and Betsy could risk splitting her attention long enough to ease in the brakes. The straps dug a little deeper into her skin as the wheels found some traction. But it wasn't nearly enough, and she knew at that moment that Whitney's numbers had indeed been right: there was no possible way for Seven to stop on this runway. She could only hope the other numbers he'd worked out for her were equally accurate.

Through the vibrational din she could hear Greenburg shouting into his mike: "One-sixty . . . one-fifty-five . . . one-fifty . . ." Seven's speed, decreasing much too slowly. Betsy gritted her teeth and concentrated on her steering, trying to ignore the trick of perspective that made the end of the runway look closer than it really was. There were no shortcuts that could be taken here; if Seven was moving faster than a hundred-twenty knots when they released the shuttle, the smaller aircraft would become airborne, with the disastrous results she was risking Seven's crew precisely to avoid.

". . . one-forty . . . one-thirty-five—get ready—"

A sudden thought occurred to Betsy. "Eric!" she shouted, interrupting Greenburg's countdown. "Just be-

fore we release the collar we'll cut all braking here—
that'll give you a constant speed to work against instead
of a deceleration. You copy that, too, Rick?"

"Roger. Cue me, will you?"

"Right. Aaron, drop the chutes at one-twenty exactly."

"Roger. One-twenty-five . . . three, two, one, *mark!*"

There was no jerk this time, just a sudden drop in
shoulder-strap pressure as one of the discarded drogues
flashed briefly across the outside monitor screen. Simultaneously, Betsy released the brakes, and Seven
was once again rolling free. "One-nineteen," Greenburg
sang out.

"Collar!" Betsy snapped to Henson—and for the first
time since touchdown gave her full visual attention to
the monitor screen.

It was probably the finest display of engine and brake
control that she had ever witnessed. Released abruptly
from all constraints, the shuttle's tail dropped the short
distance to the runway, landing on its main gear with a
bump and splash of foam that made Betsy wince. At the
same time the shuttle slid backward across the screen,
as the extra air drag on its less aerodynamic shape tried
to pull it out of the bay. But almost before the sliding
began it was abruptly halted as Rayburn, with a touch
even more skillful than Betsy had expected, nudged his
engines up just exactly enough to compensate. She
watched, fascinated, as the shuttle drifted back another
few feet and again halted. There it sat, balanced precariously by its battered nose on the docking bay rim, its
wheels and engines kicking up foam like mad, while its
nosewheel—finally clear of the bay's confines—descended
and locked in place.

And then, with one final lurch, the shuttle vanished
from the screen.

"He's free!" Henson shouted unnecessarily. A tower
controller, his voice a bare whisper in Betsy's ear,
confirmed it, adding something about the shuttle being
under good control as it braked . . . but Betsy wasn't
really listening to him. Ahead, barely a mile of runway
was left to them—just thirty seconds away at their

current speed . . . and there was no way on Earth for them to stop before they reached it.

But Betsy had no intention of stopping. Instead, she opened the throttle all the way, and with a thunderous roar that drowned out even the rumble of landing gear on tarmac, the giant plane leaped forward, pushing Betsy deeply back into the cushions of her seat. Beside her, Greenburg would be calling off the speed increments; but she couldn't hear him, and she didn't dare take her eyes from the window to check the numbers for herself. She could see the end of the runway rushing toward her, and unconsciously she braced herself for the terrible crash that would signify that her gamble had failed. The edge of the foam swung at her like a guillotine blade—passed beneath her—

And the crash didn't come. Instead, the barren ground at the end of the runway flashed by, visibly receding below.

They'd done it!

Betsy let Lewis and Greenburg handle the routine business of flying Seven back to link up again with the rest of the Skyport. The two had insisted, and Betsy's hands were shaking so much from delayed reaction that doing it herself would have been difficult. Besides, a sort of celebration had erupted spontaneously in Seven's crew lounge, at which the wing captain's presence was being demanded.

What with the flurry of congratulatory hugs and handshakes and the general babble of tension-releasing conversation, Betsy missed the exact moment when the link-up occurred; her first real indication that Seven was back with the Skyport was the two grinning figures that strode unexpectedly into the lounge.

"Hey, Carl!" the first person to spot them shouted, waving a dangerously full glass. "Join the celebration!"

"Sorry—I can't spare the time," the Skyport captain said, speaking just loudly enough to penetrate the racket. "I just came by to congratulate Betsy in person. Mr.

Whitney seems to think he's earned the right to do likewise."

"Thanks," Betsy called, handing her glass of fruit juice—she *was* on duty, after all—to the nearest bystander and making her way through the crowd. "Hang on a second—I want to talk to both of you."

She led them out into the hallway, where normal conversational levels would be possible. Once outside the din she turned to Young; but he'd already anticipated her first question. "I just talked to the tower," he said, "which had been in contact with the hospital. The landing did some extra damage to Meredith's internal bleeding problems, but with the ambulance and emergency room personel standing by they think they got him in time. I'm also told, though very unofficially, that he probably wouldn't have made it if we'd tried to take him to L.A. instead."

Betsy let out a breath she hadn't realized she'd been holding. They really *had* done it; they'd gambled Seven, the shuttle, and a lot of lives, and had won back all of it.

Young was still talking. "We're moving your passengers back in for the moment, though of course they'll have to leave again before we reach L.A. I've talked to McDonnell Douglas and United, and they'll have another wing section ready to replace you when we arrive. This one was due to go in for routine maintenance next month, anyway; you'll just be a little early." He harrumphed. "The United man I talked to seemed a bit concerned that you'd be landing with your corner drogues missing. I told him that anyone who can do a touch-and-go with a flying football field wasn't someone he needed to worry about."

She smiled. "That's for sure. After today, landing at Mirage Lake will feel like aiming to hit Utah. No problem."

"Well, at least you've got your confidence back," Young said, smiling in return. "I had been wondering about that earlier."

"Me, too," she admitted. "Which reminds me . . . Peter, I owe you a vote of thanks for that pep talk on command and responsibility you gave me a few hours ago. I don't know if it really made sense to me at the time, but it was just what I needed to break up the gloom and panic I was digging myself into."

Whitney actually blushed. "Yeah, well . . . I felt a little strange playing psychiatrist but . . . well, I had to say *something*. I was getting pretty worried about Captain Rayburn, and, frankly, I was scared to death you were going to go off the same end of the pool—no offense."

"No offense," Betsy assured him. "I can't honestly say that I wasn't a little worried about it myself." She shook her head, turning serious. "I still can't believe Eric went so badly to pieces. I know he was worried about Meredith's safety, but he was getting practically obsessive about it. He'll be *very* lucky if United doesn't boot him out for insubordination."

Young cleared his throat self-consciously. "Actually, Betsy, I suspect his flying career is over anyway. I haven't got any proof yet, of course, but I'll wager any sum of money that when the shuttle's flight recorder is played back it'll show that Rayburn had his automatic approach system off and was flying manually when the crash occurred. He's docked like that before, I'm pretty sure, and if we hadn't hit that patch of turbulance he might have gotten away with it this time, too."

Betsy felt her eyes widen in disbelief . . . but even as she opened her mouth to argue, all the puzzling parts of the incident suddenly made sense, and she knew he was right.

"But isn't that dangerous, not to mention illegal?" Whitney asked.

"Highly," Young told him, answering both parts of the question. "Even with an empty shuttle, which is how I gather he usually does it. Whatever possessed him to try it with a full passenger load I'll never know."

Betsy's lip curled, ever so slightly; but she held her peace. A figurative rape, perhaps? Or just an overwhelming desire to prove in her presence that he was a superior pilot? It didn't really matter; either way, it told her something about Eric Rayburn that she had never suspected.

"Anyway, as long as that's just my unsupported opinion, I'd appreciate it if you'd both keep it to yourselves," Young was saying. "Betsy, I've got to get below now, help ease any ruffled feathers among the passengers. Congratulations again on your fine job here." With a nod to Whitney, the Skyport captain headed off down the hall.

Betsy watched him go, but without really seeing him. *So it comes full circle*, she thought bemusedly. *I fight to quit reacting to Eric, and find out he's been reacting just as blindly and irrationally to me.* She shook her head minutely. *Puppets, all of us—even all the ones who think they're mavericks. Puppets pulling on each others' strings.*

"I suppose I should go back down, too," Whitney said, breaking into her thoughts. "It was really a privilege to watch you in action, Betsy—thanks for letting me be part of it."

"Just a minute, Peter," she said as he turned to go, pushing the growing bitterness determinedly from her mind. After all, she was only forty-five—far too young to become a cynic. "I seem to recall you were interested earlier in a tour of the Skyport topdeck. That still true?"

"Uh, yes," he said, an uncertain smile playing around his lips. "If it's not too much trouble."

"No trouble at all." And besides, reacting with cynicism would just be giving Rayburn one final victory over her. "Come on, we'll start with the crew lounge. Drinks are on the house—and I understand the fruit juice is excellent today."

Houseguest

The fuzzy red ball that was Drym's sun hung low in the sky, and already the temperature had started its nightly descent. Measuring the angle between sun and mountains, Wynne Kendal estimated he had a good fifteen minutes to get home before sunset brought on the dangerous, highly energetic "musth" part of the tricorn activity cycle. He was all right though; across the shallow stream just ahead was the ruin of his original prefab home, and it was only a ten-minute walk from there to the House.

As always, he glanced at the ruin as he passed. Little had changed in the past eight months; the tricorns had pretty thoroughly trampled the plastic and metal structure the first week after he abandoned it and now, having driven him away, generally ignored it.

"Bastards," he muttered, the oath expanding to include both the tricorns and the Company exploration group who had given Drym a fast once-over and blithely declared it safe. Perhaps if they'd hung around long enough, the tricorns would have turned on *them* instead of waiting until the mining group was settled and out of communication to turn from docile to nasty. Clearly, though, the survey had been a mere formality; with rich concentrations of precious scandium-bearing ores lying barely beneath the planetary surface, the Company would have sent miners in even if Drym had been covered with Bellatrix sparkbrats.

Ahead of Kendal loomed a line of granite hills, and he could now make out the five-meter-high rocky dome and gaping circular entrance of his House. His heartbeat never failed to pick up slightly at this point; there was no way of telling from here which of its moods the other would be in, and some of them could be dangerous. Not that it made any real difference, of course. Staying outside alone all night would be even worse.

The sun was just grazing the mountain tops as he reached the House. A few meters to one side of the dome was a hill with one flat face. A large stone rested against it, and Kendal manhandled it aside to expose the tiny cave he used for storage. He withdrew his night-pack, rations, and stove, brushing off with quick motions a few bloodworms who were clinging to the bundles. The mining team had briefly entertained the idea of living in caves after realizing their prefabs had no chance against the tricorns, but the bloodworms had ended that hope. Human tissue was supposed to be completely non-nourishing to Drym fauna, something the planet's flying insects seemed to sense from a distance. The cave-dwelling bloodworms, unfortunately, each needed a few bites to catch on.

The last item Kendal withdrew from the cave was a telescoping duryai alloy pole, originally a part of the miners' shoring equipment. He extended it to the two-meter length required and gave it a quick visual check before stuffing his mining gear into the cave and resealing it. Picking up his packs, he lugged them to the House's entrance, setting them down outside. Taking a deep breath, he held the pole out in front of him like a spear and, ducking slightly, entered the House.

It was not quite pitch-dark inside, but the light from

the setting sun showed only that Kendal was in a dome-shaped space two meters high in the middle and perhaps four across at the ground. A strange, almost musky odor filled the air; strong, but not overpowering. Watching the walls warily, Kendal walked toward the center. "Hello, House," he called tentatively.

The answer came promptly and in a tone so low Kendal could feel it as much as he could hear it: "Greetings, *master*."

Kendal breathed a little easier. The House was only sarcastic when it was in a relatively good mood. It had probably fed today, he decided, setting one end of his pole into a notch dug in the hard clay of the floor and carefully wedging the other end against the ceiling. Only when that was done did he finally relax. Wasting no time, he retrieved his packs and brought them into the House. Flicking on a lantern, he nodded, "Okay, you can close up now," he said, sitting down cross-legged near the pole.

"Very well, *master*," the House rumbled, and the circular orifice squeezed shut in a way that always reminded Kendal of someone pursing his lips.

"Thank you," he said as he started to set up his stove. "How was your day?"

"How should it have been?" the House responded. "I spoke for a time with the Others, and I waited. There is little else I can do."

"You *did* eat, though, " Kendal commented. He'd spotted a small rocky bulge high up on the wall that hadn't been there when he's left. "A white-wing, wasn't it?"

"Yes. It was small, but will have to serve. You Men have seen to that."

Kendal winced. In their self-defense killing of tricorns, the miners were apparently causing a serious threat to the Houses' main food supply. Along with the humiliation of having been turned into living bedrooms, this was just one more cause for resentment. And if they got mad enough . . . Kendal shuddered at the memory of the crushed bodies of the first handful of miners to innocently venture into the Houses. They had never known what hit them. If the exploration team had goofed on their analysis of the tricorns, they had missed the Houses completely, and it had cost seven lives before anyone figured out what was happening. Another four men were lost before the shoring pole technique was perfected. Like other creatures throughout history, the Houses had proved at least marginally tamable, and were taught by short laser bursts to open and close their "mouths" in response to slaps or light kicks. No one had been prepared, though, when the Houses started talking to them.

Kendal's communicator buzzed. "Kendal; yeah?"

"Tan here. You locked up for the night?"

"Sure am." Cardman Tan had been the Number Three man of the mining team before the tricorns and Houses had taken their massive toll; now, he was Number One. "Any particular reason why you're doing a bedcheck tonight?"

"I saw what looked like a new bevy of tricorns coming over the hills in your area a few minutes ago," Tan explained. "I wanted to make sure nobody was wandering around outside."

More tricorns in the area. Damn. "Thanks for the warning. I'll be careful."

"See you tomorrow." The communicator clicked off.

The House was silent as Kendal turned back and finished his dinner preparations. It had listened to the conversation, of course, and certainly understood the implications. Theoretically, more tricorns meant more food for all the Houses scattered among the hills—but only if the bull-sized beasts came within sniffing range of the odor lures the Houses used. If the tricorns chose instead to hound the men at the mine two kilometers away, there wasn't a solitary thing the Houses could do about it. Their "roots"—Kendal's House's own word—went deep into the ground, drawing out water and dissolved rock for their organo-mineral metabolisms. And while no one knew how deep the roots went, it was for sure that the Houses weren't going out hunting.

"I wonder how many tricorns are in this new bevy," Kendal remarked as he ate, just to break the silence.

"Forty-seven," the House said promptly.

Kendal looked up in surprise. "You've seen them?"

"They passed near one of the Others a short time ago. He counted them."

"I see." Kendal hadn't realized he'd been that preoccupied; usually he could feel the underground vibrations the Houses used to talk with each other. "Well, hopefully this group will stay close to the hills, where you can have a shot at them."

"No. They will surely continue their attempts to drive you away from here."

The House's tone was no longer sarcastic, and Kendal swallowed hard. At their friendliest, the Houses were barely tolerant of their human parasites. At other times . . . Kendal glanced involuntarily at the pole, making sure it was properly placed. "Now, House, you know we don't kill the tricorns because we want to. We'd be happy to live and let live. I know you're not crazy about putting up with us—" the understatement of the decade—"but if you can hold out just another hundred and fifty days or so, our company's transport ship will come and visit us. They'll have the knowledge and equipment to build us homes that the tricorns can't destroy—maybe even find a way to keep the tricorns away from us without having to kill them. Then maybe we can make up for all the inconveniences we've caused you."

The House didn't answer. Kendal chewed his lip. He'd been planning to play chess with one of the other miners this evening via communicator, but it might pay him to talk to his House instead. The Houses had very little opportunity for mental stimulation, and Kendal had found that an interesting chat could often snap his out of a bad mood. "Did I ever tell you about my year on Majori?" he asked casually. "That planet had some of the strangest animals I've ever seen. There was one, for instance, with three legs—or five, depending on how you counted them."

He stopped and waited. "Please explain," the House said at last, a touch of interest peeking through the surliness in its tone.

Inwardly, Kendal smiled. Just like offering candy to a child. And almost as effective. Some of the miners, he knew, treated their Houses like slaves or virtually ignored them, but Kendal had always tried to stay on friendly terms with his. All other reasons aside, it helped relieve the boredom of Drym's nights. "It's like this. . . ."

The conversation lasted far into the night.

Kendal's alarm went off a half hour before dawn, and the sun was barely up as the miners began the day's work. Early morning was their most productive time; for several hours after sunrise the tricorns hid away among the rocks and hills, presumably sleeping, and for that period no guards had to be posted to protect the others from attack. When the giant creatures did finally lumber forth, it took fully half of the forty men to stand guard around the perimeter of the wide, shallow strip mine. A smaller mine would have been easier to defend, but to carry the ore out of a deeper pit would have been agony. All of their powered equipment ran off of standard energy cells, and the decision had been made months ago to save as much power as possible for the hand lasers. Tricorns took a lot of energy to kill.

For a while the miners made good progress, despite the early-morning chill. As the morning passed and temperatures rose, the tricorns began to congregate around the mine. Two of them had to be shot before the rest got the idea and thereafter kept at a respectful distance from the ring of guards. There seemed to be more of them than usual, Kendal thought—the new bevy was getting into the spirit of this thing with remarkable speed.

"Of course they are," Jaker, the man standing guard to Kendal's right, said when Kendal commented on it. "They're at least as intelligent as dogs or wolves."

"No way," another man down the line called back.

Kendal sighed. That argument had been going on for

months now, with Jaker and Welles the main partici-
pants. Kendal himself leaned toward Jaker's side—the
tall miner's reasoning usually made sense to him—but
he was getting sick of the whole debate. What *he* wanted
to know was something no one here could even take a
stab at: why were the *Houses* so intelligent? What
possible reason was there for an unmoving pile of rock
to develop the intelligence necessary to learn an alien
language just by listening to communicator conversations? In addition, Kendal had proved—at least to his
own satisfaction—that the Houses were capable of imag-
ination and abstract thought. The *how* of it was reasonably straightforward: current theory implied that a
sufficiently large brain would automatically develop sentence, and the Houses were certainly big enough to
hold a brain that size. But the *why* of it still drove him
crazy.

Jaker and Welles were still arguing when Kendal
tuned his mind back to the conversation. "Look at how
fast these new ones figured out the lasers—" Jaker was
saying.

A motion to Kendal's right caught his eye. One of the
tricorns was moving forward. "Jaker!" he snapped, yanking his laser from its holster.

Jaker had been half-turned to shout at Welles; whip-
ping back around, he brought his own weapon to bear,
firing a second after Kendal's shot grazed the massive
skull near the leftmost of the three serrated horns. The
creature thudded to the ground; two more shots and it
was dead.

Kendal turned back quickly to see a tricorn directly
in front of him take a couple of heavy steps forward. He
raised his laser, and the animal stopped. Almost reluctantly, it backed up to its original position.

"See?" Jaker said, just the slightest tremor in his
voice. "They know when it's not safe to attack."

"All right, can it," Cardman Tan called from the pit,
where the sounds of work had ceased. "Jaker, you give
your brain a vacation like that again and I'll have your

hide—if one of the tricorns doesn't get it first. That goes for all the rest of you, too. Stay *alert*, damn it!"

There were muffled acknowledgments from the guard ring. Wiping a layer of sweat from his neck, Kendal reflected that the strain of the past eight months was starting to be felt. He wondered if they would be able to hold out for five more.

The huge bins that had been set up nearby to store the ore had been designed to handle over a hundred tons each. As a result they were almost, but not quite, strong enough to be proof against the nighttime tricorn rampages; and when it came time to load the day's production, it was found that one of the conveyors had taken one too many dents and was inoperable. Loading the gravel via the remaining two naturally took more time than had been allowed, and as a result it was already after sundown before Kendal started for home. Even then his luck almost held, and he was nearly to the House before a tricorn caught his scent and charged.

Kendal's instinctive urge was to make a dash for it, but he knew a tricorn in musth could outrun him. So instead he stood his ground, laser on full power, and waited until he couldn't miss before firing. The shot hit directly between the deep-set eyes. Dodging to one side, Kendal fired again and again into the creature as its headlong rush carried it past him to crash against the side of the House.

Keeping one eye on the motionless tricorn, Kendal quickly collected his equipment and went inside. "Hello, House."

"You killed it," the deep voice said accusingly.

"Uh, yeah. Sorry, but I didn't have much choice in the matter."

"You could have let me lure it to me."

Kendal didn't answer. Whether or not the House's odor lure could have distracted the tricorn was an academic question: Kendal couldn't have let the House eat it in any case. After crushing a victim, the House digested it by forming a thin film of rock under it, attaching it to the House's own ceiling, after which it could be absorbed. But until the film was completed, the ceiling had to remain down—and for an animal the size of a tricorn the process could take a half-hour. Kendal couldn't risk being outside that long at night.

"Again, I'm sorry," he said at last. "There were a lot of tricorns out by the mine today. Maybe one will come out here tomorrow."

The House remained silent. Feeling uncomfortably like a rich man having a picnic in a slum, Kendal fixed his dinner and ate. He tried three or four times to strike up a conversation with the House, but his questions elicited only monosyllabic responses, and eventually he gave up. Settling down instead with one of his handful of books, he read for a while and then turned in.

The tricorn he had shot was still lying against the House when Kendal cautiously emerged the next dawn. A quick check showed that the animal had probably been dead on impact; Kendal's head shot had fried its brains. A thought struck him, and when he had finished stowing his nighttime things, he assembled his rock-cutter plasma-jet torch and returned to the carcass. A typical tricorn weighed in at something near a ton, and for once Kendal was glad that the tricorns' nocturnal activities made it unsafe to leave tools at the mine. The torch sliced the rock-hard carcass in half with only a little trouble; and by using the shoring pole as a lever, he managed to roll the pieces to the House's orifice. "House?" he called "I've got some food here for you. Wait until I get both parts inside before closing up, okay?"

A minute later the job was done. "Thank you," the House said, a little too grudgingly for Kendal's taste. The orifice puckered closed, and Kendal heard the dull thud as the domed ceiling came down with the force of a rock crusher.

"Any time," Kendal muttered as he turned and headed off toward the mine. That altruistic act had cost him time, energy, and a fair amount of power, and he was annoyed that the House wasn't more appreciative. But it didn't really matter that much. If feeding it put the House back in a reasonably good mood, it would be worth the trouble.

The day's work was uneventful, and Kendal was in good spirits as he returned home. "Hello, House," he called his usual greeting as he set the pole snugly in place.

There was no answer. "House?" he tried again. "You all right?"

As if in response, the orifice closed, sealing Kendal in. He breathed a little easier, his worst fear assuaged: clearly, the House was still alive. But why wasn't it speaking to him? He searched the walls with his eyes, looking for some clue. Two bulges in the wall near the orifice were undoubtedly the remains of the tricorn he'd killed; otherwise everything seemed as usual.

No, not quite. Kendal felt a shiver go up his back as he felt the vibrations through the soles of his boots. The House was talking to his fellows scattered through the hills. It was a normal enough occurrence—except that he knew that the House could handle two conversations at once when it wanted to. Clearly—painfully clearly— Kendal was being ignored.

Determined not to let it throw him, he prepared his dinner and afterwards tried to read. But he found it impossible to concentrate in the increasingly hostile atmosphere he could feel around him. More than once he actually considered spending the night outside, but common sense and stubbornness killed that idea. The House was simply in a bad mood, he told himself firmly as he finally switched off his lantern for the night.

The vibrations were still going when he fell asleep.

The glowing numbers of his alarm chrono showed three hours till dawn when Kendal woke with a start. For a moment he lay still, slightly disoriented, as he tried to figure out what had awakened him. Then he heard it: a gentle creaking of metal. Rolling over, Kendal switched on his lantern, his other hand snatching up his laser.

The sight that greeted his squinting eyes shocked him to full consciousness. In the center of the room the shoring pole was bowed a good thirty centimeters out of line in response to the newly convex shape of the ceiling. For a long minute the tableau seemed frozen, and Kendal could almost hear the House straining against the pole. Then, reluctantly, the ceiling gave way, returning to its original position as the pole straightened out.

Kendal found his voice. "House! What are you doing?" he called sharply.

His only answer was a sudden bulging of the wall just above the floor, forming an instant torus whose purpose, he knew, was to shove anything that had been near the wall toward the center where the main crushing force would be exerted. The torus withdrew, and once again the ceiling came down in an effort to break the pole.

"House!" Kendal shouted again, a touch of fear creeping into his voice. Had the House gone crazy? "House! Answer me!"

"You cannot be allowed to live any longer."

Kendal's heart jerked at the words. "Why? What have we done to you?"

"Do not act innocent. You have forced us to your will, killed our food. And now you have offered me food that is almost useless. I can bear no more."

Almost useless? "House, that tricorn was freshly killed. You know that. Look, it couldn't have rotted that fast, especially at night." There was no answer except another squeeze on the pole. "Hey, come on, be reasonable. You know you can't break that pole."

"So the Others also believe. But once I have proved it can be done, they will join me in killing their parasites, too."

Kendal felt cold all over. His communicator was resting near the far wall, where he couldn't retrieve it without risking the explosive ballooning which could easily hurl him into the pole. And, anyway, what good would it do to alert the other miners? Kendal's House would hear the message, the other Houses would hear it, and it would just precipitate the attacks a little ahead of schedule. And then . . . what? All the miners had lasers, but no one had the faintest idea how to kill or disable a House. "Look, can't we talk this over?" he called. "If I gave you bad food, I didn't mean to, and I apologize."

The torus bulged outward and flattened, and the ceiling came down. To Kendal it looked like the pole was bending a little further with each attack. If the House kept at it, it would succeed—and probably long before Kendal could cut his way through the orifice with his laser.

"House!" he tried again, desperately. "You don't want to do this. Remember how bored you all were before we came?—you told me that yourself. We can tell you about places and things you've never seen, teach you about science and—"

"It is not enough," the House interrupted. "Knowledge is of no use to us if we don't have enough food."

It was, Kendal realized, as good as a death sentence. As long as the House needed tricorns as part of their diet, and the tricorns themselves were so hostile to the miners—

The inspiration that abruptly struck could hardly be described as blinding. It was a hunch only, and the plan it evoked was nothing short of foolhardy. But Kendal was desperate. "Wait a minute, House. If we can supply live tricorns for your food, will you let us live here until our ship comes?"

The House, halfway into another crushing attempt, seemed to pause. "What trick is this?"

"No trick. I think I may know how to control the tricorns."

"I don't believe you."

"All right, I'll prove it." Kendal took a deep breath. "I'll go out right now and bring one back for you."

There was a long silence. "Very well," the House said slowly. "I will let you out. But you will leave your lightning-maker and talker here as proof that you will return."

The tone left no room for argument. "Okay," Kendal agreed at last. Going outside without his laser might be possible for the distance he would need to cover. Anyway, there was no choice.

The House's orifice opened, sending in a rush of cold air. "Go."

Swallowing hard, Kendal steeled himself and stepped outside into the dim light from Drym's three moons. Pausing only long enough to check for nearby tricorns, he set off at a fast jog in the direction of the mine. He had already done a quick mental inventory of the mining equipment in the nearby cave, and there was nothing there that had both the power and range to serve as an effective weapon. Speed and luck would have to do.

The three moons gave off a respectable amount of light, and as Kendal's eyes adjusted, he discovered he could see most of the plain ahead. Tricorns dotted the landscape, cropping tufts of grass-like plants, digging their snouts into the ground, or running about with triple their daytime speed. Kendal felt his jaw tighten at the thought of passing among the deadly beasts. But he was committed now. He stopped briefly to establish the wind direction and, struck by a thought, stripped off his outer jacket, wadding it into a ball for easy carrying. Picking a path that would put him downwind of as many of the tricorns as possible, he set off at a fast trot.

His luck held for perhaps three minutes. Then, a traveling tricorn happened to pass downwind of him and changed its path abruptly.

Kendal put on a burst of speed, even though his lungs were already beginning to ache from the frigid air. It was no use; even with his lead, he was being steadily run down. Gritting his teeth, he waited until the tricorn was almost upon him. Then, in one quick motion, he unrolled his jacket and threw it across the animal's face. The tricorn broke stride and tossed its massive head, throwing the jacket to the ground. From the corner of his eye Kendal saw it turn to worry the garment; then he turned his attention forward. His goal was just ahead: the stream that flowed past the ruin of his old prefab. He turned a bit upstream, making for a place where the stream widened into a relatively deep pool. Two tricorns, he saw, were drinking there, but they were upwind of him, and neither turned as he approached. He was almost to the water's edge when a motion to his right caught his eye. Another tricorn was charging.

Kendal had no choice. Running full tilt between the drinking tricorns, he leaped into the pool.

The shock of the icy water was paralyzing, and Kendal's legs instantly knotted into agonizing cramps. Fortunately, the water was less than a meter deep, so keeping his head above the surface posed no major problem. Rubbing hard with hands already growing numb with the cold, he managed to work out the cramps and to get his clothes off, tossing them to the far side of the stream. Then, conscious of the speed at which his body heat was being sucked from him, he began to wash himself as quickly and thoroughly as possible. A few minutes was all he could stand; even as he waded ashore he was staggering with the beginnings of hypothermia. The wind cut into his naked skin like nothing he'd ever felt before, and his whole body was racked with violent shivering, but he hardly noticed—his full attention was on the three tricorns now eying him. Docile and harmless, the Company exploration group had called them. Mentally crossing his fingers, Kendal stepped forward.

None of them made any move except to follow him with their eyes. Gingerly, Kendal reached out and laid his hand against the head of the closest animal. Two openings in its neck—its nostrils, Kendal had long ago decided—flared once, but otherwise it didn't seem to object to the familiarity. Kendal withdrew his hand, and after a moment the animals returned to their drinking.

So his hunch had been right. But Kendal had no time for self-congratulation. He turned and headed back toward his House, keeping his eyes open. He was nearly there when he found what he was looking for: a grazing tricorn whose sides were heaving with the breathlessness of a long run. Walking boldly up to it, Kendal carefully gripped one of the horns and tugged. The action had no effect; if the tricorn was winded and therefore not inclined to run away, neither was it going to interrupt its grazing. Kendal tried again, then gave up and went instead to several nearby clumps of vegetation, pulling up the plants until he had a good handful of them. Returning to the tricorn, he waited until the animal had finished eating and then waved one of the plants in front of it. The tricorn bit off a piece, and when Kendal slowly backed away it willingly followed him.

They reached the House with two or three of the plants left. Dropping them onto the ground for the tricorn, Kendal stepped to the open orifice. "I'm back," he said through chattering teeth. "As you see, I've brought you some food."

"I see, but do not understand," the House said, its emotion unreadable.

"Never mind that for now. I'm going to come in now and get my stuff. You'll be able then to lure the tricorn in. Okay?"

"Yes." A pause. "Can you do this again?"

"I'll make a deal with you. If you and the other Houses will let us live inside you safely until our ship comes, we'll guarantee you each at least one tricorn every three days; maybe more. What do you say?"

"I agree," the House said promptly.

"You promised them *what?*" Cardman Tan said, eyes wide with disbelief. "Are you crazy, Kendal?"

Muffled to the eyebrows in his spare clothing and still just barely recovered from his overnight chilling, Kendal nevertheless managed to keep his temper. Tan was not dumb, but he'd clearly missed the significance of Kendal's account of his predawn activities. "Not crazy at all, Tan. With the proper precautions we can handle the tricorns."

"Look, I don't know how you lucked out last night, but you can't count on the tricorns always being in a good mood like that."

"Moods have nothing to do with it. It's the dust."

"Besides, we—what? What dust?"

"The rock dust from the mine. Remember the exploration group report on the tricorns?"

"Sure," Tan said bitterly. "Lousy rubber-stamping toadies—"

"Forget that. They were right. The tricorns aren't interested in *us*—they're attracted to the rock dust that sticks to our skin and clothes. Apparently they eat one or more of the minerals we dig up at the mine."

Tan opened his mouth, closed it again, and suddenly looked thoughtful. "That would explain why they hang around the mine all day and stomp through it at night. But why? And how come we've never caught them at it?"

"We *have*, or at least I have," Kendal pointed out. "I always assumed they were digging up small plants, myself. Anyway, most of their feeding's done at night, I think." He shrugged. "And why shouldn't they eat rock? We know the Houses have organo-mineral metabolisms —it only makes sense for the tricorns to be similar."

"Well . . . okay, suppose you're right. What then?"

"I thought you'd never ask. Here's my idea. . . ."

It was a real pleasure, Kendal decided, to be able to head for home without that tense uncertainty as to what kind of reception he'd get. Now that it was being fed regularly, the House was consistently cooperative and— following the pattern of human societies through the ages—was beginning to take more and more interest in abstract and intellectual matters. The other Houses were behaving similarly, causing both surprise and some uneasiness among the miners and rekindling the old debates over the usefulness and origin of House intelligence.

Kendal kept out of the arguments; the truth, he suspected, would only disturb them more.

His first stop was the corral behind his House. Fenced in by wire mesh attached to pipes, the four tricorns looked back disinterestedly as they munched on the rock and plants left there for them. The fence couldn't keep them in at night, of course, but with a supply of food nearby they tended to stay put even during musth, and the one or two who had broken out in the last month had always returned by sunrise. Collecting food for them was a pain—as was supplying the mineral pile near the mine to lure away the tricorns there—but it beat guard duty hands-down. And in the long run, it was much cheaper.

Collecting his night things, Kendal stepped into the House. "Hi, House," he called.

"Good evening, Kendal. Did you have a profitable day?"

"Very. Will you be ready to start after I get my supper going?"

"Certainly."

We are, after all, what we eat, Kendal thought wryly—and if his theory was right, that was even more true of Houses. Their alien method of food absorption seemed to be gentler than its human equivalent, so much so that the Houses could evidently absorb intact the delicate and complex nucleic acids—or possibly even entire gray-matter nerve cells—of their prey. And as soon as enough had been absorbed. . . . Kendal wondered how many tricorns the House had had to eat before the unexpected light had dawned so long ago. Intact tricorns, that is—not ones whose brains had been fried by laser fire.

Accidental intelligence? Something inside Kendal rebelled at the idea . . . and yet, why not? And hardly useless, even if it had been sorely lacking in purpose until now.

Because there was one intriguing corollary to the theory. The Houses certainly had the necessary bulk to store great quantities of brain cells. If they were steadily fed, would their intelligence increase? And if so, was there any upper limit?

Kendal didn't know, and of course didn't have the necessary equipment or know-how to perform rigorous tests. But there were more informal ways . . . and he was determined to learn whatever he could in the time remaining.

The equipment was ready now. Looking up, Kendal nodded. "Okay, go ahead."

The reply was immediate; the House knew this part well. "Pawn to king four," it said.

Time Bomb

I

The bus station was stiflingly hot, despite the light evening breeze drifting in through the open door and windows. In a way the heat was almost comforting to Garwood as he stood at the ticket window; it proved the air conditioning had broken down much earlier in the day, long before he'd come anywhere near the place.

Puffing on a particularly pungent cigar—the smoke of which made Garwood's eyes water—the clerk looked down at the bills in front of him and shook his head. "Costs forty-one sixty to Champaign now," he said around his cigar.

Garwood frowned. "The schedule says thirty-eight," he pointed out.

"You gotta old one, prob'ly." The clerk ran a stubby finger down a list in front of him. "Prices went up 'bout a week ago. Yep—forty-one sixty."

A fresh trickle of sweat ran down the side of Garwood's face. "May I see that?" he asked.

The clerk's cigar shifted to the other side of his

mouth and his eyes flicked to Garwood's slightly thread-
bare sport coat and the considerably classier leather
suitcase at his side. "If you got proper identification I
can take a check or card," he offered.

"May I see the schedule, please?" Garwood repeated.

The cigar shifted again, and Garwood could almost
see the wheels spinning behind the other's eyes as he
swiveled the card and pushed it slowly under the old-
fashioned grille. Getting suspicious; but there wasn't
anything Garwood could do about it. Even if he'd been
willing to risk using one, all his credit cards had fallen
apart in his wallet nearly a month ago. With the rising
interest rates of the past two years and the record
number of bankruptcies it had triggered, there were
more people than ever roundly damning the American
credit system and its excesses. And on top of that, the
cards were made of plastic, based on a resource the
world was rapidly running out of and still desperately
needed. A double whammy. "Okay," he said, scanning
the rate listing. "I'll go to Mahomet instead—what's
that, about ten miles this side of Champaign?"

"Closer t' seven." The clerk took the card back, eying
Garwood through a freshly replenished cloud of smoke.
"Be thirty-six seventy-five."

Garwood handed over thirty-seven of his forty dollars, silently cursing his out-of-date schedule. He'd cut
things a little too fine, and now he was going to look
exactly like what he was: a man on the run. For a
moment he debated simply turning around and leaving,
trying it again tomorrow on someone else's shift.

But that would mean spending another night in Springfield. And with all the Lincoln memorabilia so close at
hand . . .

"Bus's boarding now," the clerk told him, choosing
one of the preprinted tickets and pushing it under the
grille. "Out that door; be leavin' 'bout five minutes."

Gritting his teeth, Garwood picked up the ticket . . .
and as he withdrew his hand, there was a sudden *crack*,
as if someone had fired a cap pistol.

"Damn kids," the clerk growled, craning his neck to peer out his side window.

Garwood looked down, his eyes searching the ledge inside the ticket window grille. He'd heard that particular sound before . . . and just inside the grille, near where his hand had twice reached, he saw it.

The clerk's ashtray. An ashtray once made of clear glass . . . now shot through by a thousand hairline fractures.

The clerk was still looking through his window for the kid with the cap pistol as Garwood left, forcing himself to walk.

He half expected the police to show up before the bus could leave, but to his mild surprise the vehicle wheezed leisurely out of the lot on time and headed a few minutes later onto the eastbound interstate. For the first few miles Garwood gave his full attention to his ears, straining tensely for the first faint sound of pursuing sirens. But as the minutes crawled by and no one showed up to pull them over, he was forced to the conclusion that the clerk had decided it wasn't any of his business.

The thought was strangely depressing. To realize that the latest upswing in the "not-me" noninvolvement philosophy had spread its rot from the polarized coasts into America's heartland bothered Garwood far more than it should have. Perhaps it was all the learned opinions he'd read weighing upon him; all the doomsayings about how such a national malaise could foreshadow the end of democracy.

Or perhaps it was simply the realization that even a nation full of selfish people didn't make a shred of difference to the cloud of destruction surrounding him.

Stop it! he ordered himself silently. *Self-pity* . . . Taking a deep breath, he looked around him.

He'd chosen his third-row seat carefully—as far from the bus's rear-mounted engine as he could reasonably get without sitting in the driver's lap, and well within the non-smoking section. His seatmate . . . He threw the kid a surreptitious look, confirmed that his first-glance analysis had been correct. Faded denim jeans and an old cotton shirt. That was good; natural fibers held up much better than synthetic ones, for the same reason that plastic had a tendency to disintegrate in his presence. Reaching a hand under his jacket, Garwood checked his own sweat-soaked polyester shirt for new tears. A rip at his right shoulder lengthened as he did so, and he muttered a curse.

"Don't make 'em like they use'ta, do they?"

Startled, Garwood turned to see his seatmate's smile. "What?" he asked.

"Your shirt," the kid explained. "I heard it rip. Guys who make 'em just get away with crapzi, don't they?"

"Um," Garwood grunted, turning away again.

"You headed for Champaign?" the kid persisted.

Garwood sighed. "Mahomet."

"No kidding!—I grew up there. You, too, or are you just visiting?"

"Just visiting."

"You'll like it. Small place, but friendly. Speaking of which— " he stuck out his hand. "Name's Tom Arnold. Tom *Benedict* Arnold, actually."

Automatically, Garwood shook the proffered hand. Somewhere in the back of his head the alarm bells were going off. . . . "Not, uh, any relation to . . . ?"

"Benedict Arnold?" The kid grinned widely. "Sure am. Direct descendent, in fact."

An icy shiver ran up Garwood's back, a shiver having nothing to do with the bus's air conditioning. "You mean . . . *really* direct?" he asked, dropping the other's hand. "Not from a cousin or anything?"

"Straight shot line," Arnold nodded, the grin still in place. He was watching Garwood's face closely, and Garwood got the distinct impression the kid liked shocking people this way. "It's nothin' to be 'shamed of, you know—he did America a lot more good than he did bad. Whipped the Brits at Saratoga 'fore goin' over on their side—"

"Yes, I know," Garwood said, interrupting the impromptu history lesson. "Excuse me a second—wash-room."

Stepping into the aisle, he went to the small cubicle at the rear of the bus. He waited a few minutes, then emerged and found an empty seat four rows behind the kid. He hoped Arnold wouldn't take it too personally, though he rather thought the other would. But he couldn't afford to take the chance. Benedict Arnold's victory at Saratoga had been a pivotal factor in persuading France to enter the war on the rebels' side, and Garwood had no desire to see if he had the same effect on living beings that he had on history's more inanimate descendents.

The afterglow in the sky behind them slowly faded, and as the sky darkened Garwood drifted in and out of sleep. The thought of the boy four seats ahead troubled his rest, filling his dreams with broken ashtrays and TV sets, half-melted-looking car engines and statues. After a while the bus stopped in Decatur, taking half an hour to trade a handful of passengers for an equally small number of others. Eventually they left; and back out in the dark of the prairie again, with the stars visible above, he again drifted to sleep. . . .

The sound of the bus driver's voice jolted him awake. ". . . and gentlemen, I'm afraid we're having some trouble with the engine. Rather than take a chance on it quitting straight out before we get to Champaign, we're going to ask you to transfer to a bus that's being sent up from Decatur. It ought to be here in just a few minutes."

Blinking in the relative brightness of the overhead lights, Garwood joined the line of grumbling passengers moving down the aisle, a familiar knot wrenching at his stomach. Had it been him? He'd been far enough away from the engine—surely he had. Unless the effective distance was increasing with time . . . Forcing his jaw to unclench, he stepped carefully down the bus's steps, hoping desperately it was just a coincidence.

Outside, the only light came from a small building the bus had pulled alongside and from one or two dim streetlights. Half blind as his eyes again adjusted, Garwood took two tentative steps forward—

And came to an abrupt halt as strong hands slipped smoothly around each arm.

"Dr. James Garwood?" a shadowy figure before him asked quietly.

Garwood opened his mouth to deny it . . . but even as he did so he knew it would be useless. "Yes," he signed. "And you?"

"Major Alan Davidson; Combined Services Intelligence. They miss you back at your lab, Doctor."

Garwood glanced past the husky man holding his right arm, saw the line of passengers goggling at him. "So it was all a set-up?" he asked. "The bus is okay?"

Davidson nodded. "A suspicious clerk in Springfield thought you might be a fugitive. From your description and something about a broken ashtray my superiors thought it might be you. Come with me, please."

Garwood didn't have much choice. Propelled gently along by the hands still holding his arms, he followed Davidson toward the lighted building and a long car parked in the shadows there. "Where are you taking me?" he asked, trying to keep his voice steady.

Davidson reached the car and opened the back door; and it wasn't until he and Garwood were in the back seat and the other two soldiers in front that the major answered the question. "Chanute AFB, about fifteen miles north of Champaign," he told Garwood as the car pulled back onto the interstate and headed east. "We'll be transfering you to a special plane there for the trip back to the Project."

Garwood licked his lips. A plane. How many people, he wondered, wished that mankind had never learned to fly? There was only one way to know for sure . . . and that way might wind up killing him. "You put me on that plane and it could be the last anyone ever sees of me," he told Davidson.

"Really?" the major asked politely.

"Did they tell you why I ran out on the Project? That the place was falling down around my ears?"

"They mentioned something about that, yes," Davidson nodded. "I really don't think you have anything to worry about, though. The people in charge of security on this one are all top notch."

Garwood snorted. "You're missing the point, Major. The lab wasn't under any kind of attack from outside agents. It was falling apart because *I* was in it."

Davidson nodded. "And as I said, we're going to have you under complete protection—"

"No!" Garwood snapped. "I'm not talking about someone out there gunning for me or the Project. It's my presence there—my *physical* presence inside Backdrop— that was causing all the destruction."

Davidson's dimly visible expression didn't change. "How do you figure that?"

Garwood hesitated, glancing at the front seat and the two silhouettes there listening into the conversation. Major Davidson might possibly be cleared for something this sensitive; the others almost certainly weren't. "I can't tell you the details," he said, turning back to Davidson. "I—look, you said your superiors nailed me because of a broken ashtray in Springfield, right? Did they tell you anything more?"

Davidson hesitated, then shook his head. "No."

"It broke because I came too close to it," Garwood told him. "There's a—oh, an aura, I guess you could call it, of destruction surrounding me. Certain types of items are especially susceptible, including internal combustion engines. That's why I don't want to be put on any plane."

"Uh-huh," Davidson nodded. "West, you having any trouble with the car?"

"No, sir," the driver said promptly. "Running real smooth."

Garwood took a deep breath. "It doesn't always happen right away," he said through clenched teeth. "I rode the bus for over an hour without anything happening, remember? But if it *does* happen with a plane, we can't just pull off the road and stop."

Davidson sighed. "Look, Dr. Garwood, just relax, okay? Trust me, the plane will run just fine."

Garwood glared through the gloom at him. "You want some proof?—is that what it'll take? Fine. Do you have any cigarettes?"

For a moment Davidson regarded him in silence. Then, flicking on a dim overhead dome light, he dug a crumpled pack from his pocket.

"Put a couple in my hand," Garwood instructed him, extending a palm, "and leave the light on."

Davidson complied with the cautious air of a man at a magic show. "Now what?"

"Just keep an eye on them. Tell me, do you *like* smoking?"

The other snorted. "Hell, no. Tried to give the damn things up at least twenty times. I'm hooked pretty good, I guess."

"You like being hooked?"

"That's a stupid question."

Garwood nodded. "Sorry. So, now . . . how many other people, do you suppose, hate being hooked by tobacco?"

Davidson gave him a look that was half frown, half glare. "What's your point, Doctor?"

Garwood hesitated. "Consider it as a sort of subconscious democracy. You don't like smoking, and a whole lot of other people in this country don't like smoking. A lot of them wish there weren't any cigarettes—wish *these* cigarettes didn't exist."

"And if wishes were horses, beggers would ride," Davidson quoted. He reached over, to close his fingers on the cigarettes in Garwood's palm—

And jerked his hand back as they crumpled into shreds at his touch.

"What the *hell*?" he snapped, practically in Garwood's ear. "What did you *do*?"

"I was near them," Garwood said simply. "I was near them, and a lot of people don't like smoking. That's all there is to it."

Davidson was still staring at the mess in Garwood's palm. "It's a trick. You switched cigarettes on me."

"While you watched?" Garwood snorted. "All right, fine, let's do it again. You can write your initials on them this time."

Slowly, Davidson raised his eyes to Garwood's face. "Why *you*?"

Garwood brushed the bits of paper and tobacco off his hand with a shudder. Even after all these months it still scared him spitless to watch something disintegrate like that. "I know . . . something. I can't tell you just what."

"Okay, you know something. And?"

"No ands about it. It's the knowledge alone that does it."

Davidson's eyes were steady on his face. "Knowledge. Knowledge that shreds cigarettes all by itself."

"That, combined with the way a lot of people feel about smoking. Look, I know it's hard to believe—"

"Skip that point for now," Davidson cut him off. "Assume you're right, that it's pure knowledge that somehow does all this. Is it something connected with the Backdrop Project?"

"Yes."

"They know about it? And know what it does?"

"Yes, to both."

"And they still want you back?"

Garwood thought about Saunders. The long discussions he'd had with the other. The even longer arguments. "Dr. Saunders doesn't really understand."

For a moment Davidson was silent. "What else does this aura affect besides cigarettes?" he asked at last. "You mentioned car engines?"

"Engines, plastics, televisions—modern conveniences of all kinds, mainly, though there are other things in danger as well. Literally *anything* that someone doesn't like can be a target." He thought about the bus and Tom Benedict Arnold. "It might work on people, too," he added, shivering. "That one I haven't had to find out about for sure."

"And all that this . . . destructive wishing . . . needs to come out is for you to be there?"

Garwood licked his lips. "So far, yes. But if Backdrop ever finishes its work—"

"In other words, you're a walking time bomb."

Garwood winced at the harshness in Davidson's voice. "I suppose you could put it that way, yes. That's why I didn't want to risk staying at Backdrop. Why I don't want to risk riding in that plane."

The major nodded. "The second part we can do something about, anyway. We'll scrap the plane and keep you on the ground. You want to tell us where this Backdrop Project is, or would you rather I get the directions through channels?"

Garwood felt a trickle of sweat run between his shoulderblades. "Major, I can't go back there. I'm one man, and it's bad enough that I can wreck things the way I do. But if Backdrop finishes its work, the effect will spread a million-fold."

Davidson eyed his warily. "You mean it's contagious? Like a virus or something?"

"Well . . . not exactly."

"Not exactly," Davidson repeated with a snort. "All right, then, try this one: do the people at Backdrop know what it is about you that does this?"

"To some extent," Garwood admitted. "But as I said, they don't grasp all the implications—"

"Then you'd agree that there's no place better equipped to deal with you than Backdrop?"

Garwood took a deep breath. "Major . . . I can't go back to Backdrop. Either the project will disintegrate around me and someone will get killed . . . or else it'll succeed and what happened to your cigarettes will start happening all over the world. Can't you understand that?"

"What I understand isn't the issue here, Doctor," Davidson growled. "My orders were very specific: to deliver you to Chanute AFB and from there to Backdrop. You've convinced me you're dangerous; you *haven't* convinced me it would be safer to keep you anywhere else."

"Major—"

"And you can damn well shut up now, too." He turned his face toward the front of the car.

Garwood took a shuddering breath, let it out in a sigh of defeat as he slumped back into the cushions. It had been a waste of time and energy—he'd known it would be right from the start. Even if he could have told Davidson everything, it wouldn't have made any difference. Davidson was part of the "not-me" generation, and he had his orders, and all the logic and reason in the world wouldn't have moved him into taking such a chance.

And now it was over . . . because logic and reason were the only weapons Garwood had.

Unless . . .

He licked his lips. Maybe he *did* have one other weapon. Closing his eyes, he began to concentrate on his formulae.

Contrary to what he'd told Saunders, there were only four truly fundamental equations, plus a handful of others needed to define the various quantities. One of the equations was given in the notes he hadn't been able to destroy; the other three were still exclusively his. Squeezing his eyelids tightly together, he listened to the hum of the car's engine and tried to visualize the equations exactly as they'd looked in his notebook . . .

But it was no use, and ten minutes later he finally admitted defeat. The engine hadn't even misfired, let alone failed. The first time the curse might actually have been useful, and he was apparently too far away for it to take effect. Too far away, and no way to get closer without crawling into the front seat with the soldiers.

The soldiers . . .

He opened his eyes. Davidson was watching his narrowly; ahead, through the windshield, the lights of a city were throwing a glow onto the low clouds overhead. "Coming up on I-57, Major," the driver said over his shoulder. "You want to take that or the back door to Chanute?"

"Back door," Davidson said, keeping his eyes on Garwood.

"Yessir."

Back door? Garwood licked his lips in a mixture of sudden hope and sudden dread. The only reasonable back door was Route 45 north . . . and on the way to that exit they would pass through the northern end of Champaign.

Which meant he had one last chance to escape . . . and one last chance to let the genie so far out of the bottle that he'd never get it back in.

But he had to risk it. "All right, Major," he said through dry lips, making sure he was loud enough to be heard in the front seat as well. "Chi square e to the minus i alpha t to the three-halves, plus i alpha t to the three-halves e to the gamma zero z. Sum over all momentum states and do a rotation transformation of one point five five six radians. Energy transfer equation: first tensor is—"

"What the hell are you talking about?" Davidson snarled. But there was a growing note of uneasiness in his voice.

"You wanted proof that what I know was too dangerous to be given to Saunders and Backdrop?" Garwood asked. "Fine; here it is. First tensor is p sub xx e to the gamma—"

Davidson swore suddenly and lunged at him. But Garwood was ready for the move and got there first, throwing his arms around the other in an imprisoning bear hug. "—times p sub y alpha e to the minus i alpha t—"

Davidson threw off the grip, aiming a punch for Garwood's stomach. But the bouncing car ruined his aim and Garwood took the blow on his ribs instead. Again he threw his arms around Davidson. "—plus four pi sigma chi over gamma one z—"

A hand grabbed at Garwood's hair: the soldier in the front seat, leaning over to assist in the fray. Garwood ducked under the hand and kept shouting equations. The lack of space was on his side, hampering the other two as they tried to subdue him. Dimly, Garwood wondered why the driver hadn't stopped, realized that the car *was* now slowing down. There was a bump as they dropped onto the shoulder—

And with a loud staccato crackle from the front, the engine suddenly died.

The driver tried hard, but it was obvious that the car's abrupt failure had taken him completely by surprise. For a handful of wild heartbeats the vehicle careened wildly, dropping down off the shoulder into the ditch and then up the other side. A pair of close-spaced trees loomed ahead—the driver managed to steer between them—and an instant later the car slammed to a halt against the rear fence of a used car lot.

Garwood was the first to recover. Yanking on the handle, he threw the door open and scrambled out. The car had knocked a section of the fence part way over; climbing onto the hood, he gripped the chain links and pulled himself up and over.

He'd made it nearly halfway across the lot when the voice came from far behind him. "Okay, Garwood, that's far enough," Davidson called sharply. "Freeze or I shoot."

Garwood half turned, to see Davidson's silhouette drop over the fence and bring his arms up into a two-handed marksman's stance. Instinctively, Garwood ducked, trying to speed up a little. Ahead of him, the lines of cars lit up with the reflected flash; behind came the crack of an explosion—

And a yelp of pain.

Garwood braked to a halt and turned. Davidson was on the pavement twenty yards back of him, curled onto his side. A few feet in front of him was his gun. Or, rather, what had once been his gun . . .

Garwood looked around, eyes trying to pierce the shadows outside the fence. Neither of the other soldiers was anywhere in sight. Still in the car, or moving to flank him? Whichever, the best thing he could do right now was to forget Davidson and get moving.

The not-me generation. "Damn," Garwood muttered

to himself. "Davidson?" he called tentatively. "You all right?"

"I'm alive," the other's voice bit back.

"Where did you get hit?"

There was a short pause. "Right calf. Doesn't seem too bad."

"Probably took a chunk of your gun. You shouldn't have tried to shoot me—there are just as many people out there who hate guns as hate smoking." A truck with its brights on swept uncaringly past on the interstate behind Davidson, and Garwood got a glimpse of two figures inside the wrecked car. Moving sluggishly . . . which took at least a little of the load off Garwood's conscience. At least his little stratagem hadn't gotten anyone killed outright. "Are your men okay?"

"Do you care?" the other shot back.

Garwood grimaced. "Look, I'm sorry, Davidson, but I had no choice."

"Sure. What do a few lives matter, anyway?"

"Davidson—"

"Especially when your personal freedom's at stake. You know, I have to say you really did a marvelous job of it. Now, instead of your colleagues hounding *you* for whatever it is those equations are, all they have to do is hound *us*. All that crap about the dangers of this stuff getting out—that's all it was, wasn't it? Just crap."

Garwood gritted his teeth. He knew full well that Davidson was playing a game here, deliberately trying to enmesh him in conversation until reinforcements could arrive. But he might never see this man again. . . . "I wasn't trying to saddle you with this mess, Davidson— really I wasn't. I needed to strengthen the effect enough to stop the car, but it wasn't a tradeoff between my freedom and all hell breaking loose. You and your men can't possibly retain the equations I was calling out— you don't have the necessary mathematical background, for one thing. They'll be gone from your mind within minutes, if they aren't already."

"I'm so pleased to hear it," Davidson said, heavily

sarcastic. "Well, *I'm* certainly convinced. How about you?"

To that Garwood had no answer. . . . and it was long past time for him to get out of here. "I've got to go, now. Please—tell them to leave me alone. What they want just isn't possible."

Davidson didn't reply. With a sigh, Garwood turned his back and hurried toward the other end of the car lot and the street beyond it. Soon, he knew, the soldiers would be coming.

II

". . . one . . . two . . . *three.*"

Davidson opened his eyes, blinking for a minute as they adjusted to the room's light. He swallowed experimentally, glancing at the clock on the desk to his left. Just after three-thirty in the morning, which meant he'd been under for nearly an hour . . . and from the way his throat felt, he'd apparently been talking for most of that time. "How'd it go?" he asked the man seated beyond the microphone that had been set up in front of him.

Dr. Hamish nodded, the standard medical professional's neutral expression pasted across his face. "Quite well, Major. At least once we got you started."

"Sorry. I *did* warn you I've never been good at being hypnotized." A slight scraping of feet to his right made Davidson turn, to find a distinguished-looking middle-aged man seated just outside his field of view there. On the other's lap was a pad and pencil; beside him on another chair was a tape recorder connected to the microphone. "Dr. Saunders," Davidson nodded in greeting, vaguely surprised to see Backdrop's director looking so alert at such an ungodly hour. "I didn't hear you come in."

"Dr. Hamish was having enough trouble putting you under," Saunders shrugged. "I didn't think it would help for me to be here, too, during the process."

Davidson's eyes flicked to the notepad. "Did you get what you wanted?"

Saunders shrugged again, his neutral expression almost as good as Hamish's. "We'll know soon enough," he said. "It'll take a while to run the equations you gave us past our various experts, of course."

"Of course," Davidson nodded. "I hope whatever you got doesn't make things worse, the way Garwood thought it would."

"Dr. Garwood is a pessimist," Saunders said shortly.

"Maybe," Davidson said, knowing better than to start an argument. "Has there been any word about him?"

"From the searchers, you mean?" Saunders shook his head. "Not yet. Though that's hardly surprising—he had over half an hour to find a hole to hide in, after all."

Davidson winced at the implied accusation in the other's tone. It wasn't *his* fault, after all, that none of the damned "not-me" generation drivers on the interstate had bothered to stop. "Men with mild concussions aren't usually up to using car radios," he said, perhaps more tartly than was called for."

"I know, Major." Saunders sighed. "And I'm sorry we couldn't prepare you better for handling him. But—well, you understand."

"I understand that your security wound up working against you, yes," Davidson said. "If a fugitive is carrying a weapon, we're supposed to know that in advance. If the fugitive *is* a weapon, we ought to know *that*, too."

"Dr. Garwood as walking time bomb?" Saunder's lip twitched. "Yes, you mentioned that characterization of him a few minutes ago, during your debriefing."

Davidson only vaguely remembered calling Garwood that. "You disagree?"

"On the contrary, it's an uncomfortably vivid description of the situation," Saunders said grimly.

"Yeah." Davidson braced himself. "And now my men and I are in the same boat, aren't we?"

"Hardly," Saunders shook his head. The neutral expression, Davidson noted, was back in place. "We're going to keep the three of you here for awhile, just to be on the safe side, but I'm ninety-nine percent certain there's no danger of the same . . . effect . . . developing."

"I hope you're right," Davidson said. Perhaps a gentle probe . . . "Seems to me, though, that if there's even a chance it'll show up, we deserve to know what it is we've got. And how it works."

"Sorry, Major," Saunders said, with a quickness that showed he'd been expecting the question. "Until an updated security check's been done on you, we can't consider telling you anything else. You already know more than I'm really comfortable with."

Which was undoubtedly the *real* reason Saunders was keeping them here. "And if my security comes through clean?" he asked, passing up the cheap-shot reminder of what Saunder's overtight security had already cost him tonight.

"We'll see," Saunders said shortly, getting to his feet and sliding the pad into his pocket. "The guard will escort you to your quarters, Major. Good-night."

He left the room, taking the tape recorder with him, and Davidson turned his attention back to Hamish. "Any post-hypnotic side effects I should watch out for, Doctor?" he asked, reaching down for his crutches and carefully standing up. He winced as he put a shade too much weight on his injured leg.

Hamish shook his head. "No, nothing like that."

"Good." He eyed the other. "I don't suppose *you* could give me any hints as to my prognosis here, could you?"

"You mean as regards the—ah—problem with Dr. Garwood?" Hamish shook his head, too quickly. "I really don't think you're in any danger, Major. Really I don't. The room here didn't suffer any damage while Dr. Saunders was writing down the equations you gave him, which implies you don't know enough to bother you."

Davidson felt the skin on the back of his neck crawl. So Garwood had been telling the truth, after all. It was indeed pure knowledge alone that was behind his walking jinx effect.

He shook his head. No, that was utterly impossible. Much easier to believe that whatever scam Garwood was running, he'd managed to take in Backdrop's heads with it, too.

Either way, of course, it made Garwood one hell of a dangerous man. "I see," he said through stiff lips. "Thank you, Doctor. Good-night."

A Marine guard, dressed in one of Backdrop's oddly nonstandard jumpsuit outfits, was waiting outside the door as Davidson emerged. "If you'll follow me, Major," he said, and led the way to an undistinguished door a couple of corridors away. Behind the door, Davidson found a compact dorm-style apartment, minimally furnished with writing desk, chair, and fold-down bed, with a closet and bathroom tucked into opposite corners. Through the open closet door a half dozen orange jumpsuits could be seen hanging; laid out on the bed was a set of underwear and a large paper bag. "You'll need to put your clothing into the bag," the guard explained after showing Davidson around the room. "Your watch and other personal effects, too, if you would."

"Can I keep my cigarettes?"

"No, sir. Cigarettes are especially forbidden."

Davidson thought back to the car ride, and Garwood's disintegrating trick. "Because that effect of Garwood's destroys them?" he hazarded.

The Marine's face might have twitched, but Davidson wouldn't have sworn to it. "I'll wait outside, sir, while you change."

He retired to the hallway, shutting the door behind him. Grimacing, Davidson stripped and put on the underwear, wondering if it would help to tell Saunders that he'd already seen what the Garwood Effect did to cigarettes. The thought of spending however many days or weeks here without nicotine . . . Preoccupied, it was only as he was stuffing his clothes into it that his mind registered the oddity of using a *paper* bag instead of the usual plastic. A minor mystery, to go with all the major ones.

The Marine was waiting to accept the bag when he opened the door a minute later. Tucking it under his arm, he gave Davidson directions to the mess hall, wished him good-night, and left. Closing the door and locking it, Davidson limped his way back to the bed and shut off the nightstand light.

Lying there, eyes closed, he tried to think; but it had been a long day, and between fatigue and the medication he'd been given for his leg he found he couldn't hold onto a coherent train of thought, and two minutes after hitting the pillow he gave up the effort. A minute after that, he was fast asleep.

The jumpsuits hanging in the closet were the first surprise of the new day.

Not their color. Davidson hadn't seen any other orange outfits in his brief walk through Backdrop the previous night, but he'd rather expected to be given something distinctive as long as he was effectively on security probation here. But it was something else that caught his attention, some oddity in the feel of the material as he pulled it off its wooden hanger. Examining the label, he quickly found the reason: the jumpsuit was one hundred percent linen.

Davidson frowned, trying to remember what Garwood had said about the potential targets of his strange destructive power. *Engines, plastics, televisions*, had been on the list; *modern conveniences* had also been there. Did synthetic fibers come under the latter heading? Apparently so. He pulled the jumpsuit on, fingers brushing something thin but solid in the left breast pocket as he did so. He finished dressing, then dug the object out.

It was a plastic card.

Frowning, Davidson studied it. It wasn't an ID, at least not a very sophisticated one. His name was impressed into it, but there was no photo, thumbprint, or even a description. It wasn't a digital key, or a radiation dosimeter, or a coded info plate, or anything else he could think of.

Unless . . .

He licked his lips, a sudden chill running up his back. *Engines, plastics, televisions* . . . He'd been wrong; the card *was* a dosimeter. A dosimeter for the Garwood Effect.

Whatever the hell the Garwood Effect was.

He gritted his teeth. *All right, let's take this in a logical manner.* The Garwood Effect destroyed plastics; okay. It also ruined car engines and pistols . . . and cigarettes and ash trays. What did all of those have in common?

He puzzled at it for a few more minutes before giving up the effort. Without more information he wasn't going to get anywhere . . . and besides, a persistent growling in his stomach was reminding him he was overdue for a meal. *No one thinks well on an empty stomach,* he silently quoted his grandfather's favorite admonition. Retrieving his crutches from the floor by his bed, he clumped off to the mess hall.

After the linen jumpsuit, he half expected breakfast to consist of nuts and berries served in coconut shells, but fortunately Backdrop hadn't gone quite that far overboard. The dishware was a somewhat nonstandard heavy ceramic, but the meal itself was all too military standard: nutritious and filling without bothering as much with flavor as one might like. He ate quickly, swearing to himself afterward at the lack of a cigarette to help bury the taste. Manhandling his tray to the conveyer, he headed off to try and find some answers.

And ran immediately into a brick wall.

"Sorry, Major, but you're not authorized for entry," the Marine guard outside the Backdrop garage said apologetically.

"Not even to see my own car?" Davidson growled, waving past the Marine at the double doors behind him. "Come on, now—what kind of secrets does any-body keep in a garage?"

"You might be surprised, sir," the guard said. "I suggest you check with Colonel Bidwell and see if he'll authorize you to get in."

Davidson gritted his teeth. "I suppose I'll have to. Where's his office?"

Colonel Bidwell was a lean, weathered man with gray hair and eyes that seemed to be in a perpetual squint.

"Major," he nodded in greeting as Davidson was ushered into his office. "Sit down. Come to apply for a job?"

"More or less, sir," Davidson said, easing gratefully into the proffered chair. "I thought I could lend a hand in hunting down Dr. Garwood. Unless you've already found him, that is."

Bidwell gave him a hard look. "No, not yet. But he's in the Champaign-Urbana area—that's for damn sure—and it's only a matter of time."

Automatically, Davidson reached for a cigarette, dropping his hand to his lap halfway through the motion. "Yes, sir. I'd still like to help."

For a long moment Bidwell eyed him. "Uh-huh," he grunted. "Well, I'll tell you something, Major. Your file came through about an hour ago . . . and there are things there I really don't like."

"I'm sorry to hear that, sir," Davidson said evenly.

Bidwell's expression tightened a bit. "Your record shows a lot of bulldog, Major. You get hold of something and you won't let go until you've torn it apart."

"My superiors generally consider that an asset, sir."

"It usually is. But not if it gets you personally involved with your quarry. Like it might now."

Davidson pursed his lips. "Has the colonel had a chance to look over the rest of my file? Including my success rate?"

Bidwell grimaced. "I have. And I still don't want you. Unfortunately, that decision's been taken away from me. You're already here, and it's been decided that there's no point in letting you just spin your wheels. So. Effective immediately, you're assigned to hunter duty. Long-range duty, of course—we can't let you leave Backdrop until your updated security check is finished. You'll have a desk and computer in Room 138, with access to everything we know about Dr. Garwood."

Davidson nodded. Computer analysis was a highly impersonal way to track down a quarry, but he knew from long experience that it could be as effective as actually getting into the field and beating the bushes.

"Understood, sir. Can I also have access to the less secure areas of Backdrop?"

Bidwell frowned. "Why?"

"I'd like to get into the garage to look at my car, for one thing. Garwood may have left a clue there as to where he was headed."

"The car's already been checked over," Bidwell told him. "They didn't find anything."

Davidson remained silent, his eyes holding Bidwell's, and eventually the colonel snorted. "Oh, all right." Reaching into his desk, he withdrew a small card and scribbled on it. "Just to get you off my back. Here—a Level One security pass. And that's it, so don't try to badger me for anything higher."

"Yes, sir." The card, Davidson noted as he took it, was a thickened cardboard instead of standard passcard plastic. Not really surprising. "With your permission, then, I'll get straight to work."

"Be my guest," Bidwell grunted, turning back to his paperwork. "Dismissed."

"What in blazes happened to it?" Davidson asked, frowning into the open engine compartment. After what had happened to his cigarettes and gun, he'd rather expected to find a mess of shattered metal and disintegrated plastic under the hood of his car. But *this*—

"It's what happens to engines," the mechanic across the hood said vaguely, his eyes flicking to Davidson's orange jumpsuit.

Davidson gingerly reached in to touch the mass of metal. "It looks half melted."

"Yeah, it does," the mechanic agreed. "Uh . . . if that's all, Major, I have work to get to."

All right, Davidson thought grimly to himself as he clumped his way back down the corridor. *So this Garwood Effect doesn't affect everything the same way. No big deal—it just means it'll take a little more work to track down whatever the hell is going on here, that's all.*

What it didn't mean was that he was going to toss in the

towel and give up. Colonel Bidwell had been right on that count, at least; he did indeed have a lot of bulldog in him.

Dr. James Garwood was one of that vanishingly rare breed of scientist who was equally at home with scientific hardware as he was with scientific theory. A triple-threat man with advanced degrees in theoretical physics, applied physics, and electrical engineering, he was a certified genius with a proven knack for visualizing the real-world results of even the most esoteric mathematical theory. He'd been a highly-paid member of a highly respected research group until two years previously, when he'd taken a leave of absence to join the fledgling Backdrop Project. From almost the beginning it seemed he'd disagreed with Saunder's policies and procedures until, three months ago, he'd suddenly disappeared.

And that was the entire synopsis of Garwood's life since coming to Backdrop. Seated before the computer terminal, Davidson permitted himself an annoyed scowl. So much for having access to everything that was known about Dr. Garwood.

Of Garwood since his break there was, of course, nothing; but the files did contain a full report of the efforts to find him. The FBI had been called in early on, after which the National Security Agency had gotten involved and quickly pulled the rest of the country's intelligence services onto the case. In spite of it all, Garwood had managed to remain completely hidden until the report of yesterday's incident at the Springfield bus station had happened to catch the proper eye.

After three months he'd been caught . . . and promptly lost again.

Davidson gritted his teeth, forcing himself not to dwell on his failure. Bidwell had been right: too much emotional involvement had a bad tendency to cloud the thinking.

But then, there was more than one form of emotional involvement. Leaning back in his seat, stretching his

injured leg out beneath the desk, he closed his eyes
and tried to become Dr. James Garwood.

For whatever reason, he'd decided to quit Backdrop.
Perhaps he and Saunders had argued one too many
times; perhaps the presence of the Garwood Effect had
finally gotten too much for him to take. Perhaps—as
he'd claimed on the ride last night—he truly felt that
Backdrop was a danger and that the best thing for him
to do was to abandon it.

So all right. He'd left . . . and managed to remain
hidden from practically everybody for a solid three
months. Which implied money. Which usually implied
friends or relatives.

Opening his eyes, Davidson attacked the keyboard
again. Family . . . ? Negative—all members already in-
terviewed or under quiet surveillance. Ditto for relatives. Ditto for friends.

Fine. Where else, then, could he have gotten money
from? His own bank accounts? It was too obvious a
possibility to have been missed, but Davidson keyed for
it anyway. Sure enough, there was no evidence of large
withdrawals in the months previous to his abrupt departure from Backdrop. He went back another year,
just to be sure. Nothing.

Behind him, the door squeaked open, and Davidson
turned to see a young man with major's oak leaves on
his jumpsuit step into the room. "Major Davidson, I
presume," the other nodded in greeting. "I'm Major
Lyman, data coordinator for Backdrop Security."

"Nice to meet you," Davidson nodded, reaching back
to shake hands.

"Colonel Bidwell told me you've been co-opted for the
Garwood birdhunt," Lyman continued, glancing over
Davidson's shoulder at the computer screen. "How's it
going?"

"It might go better if I had more information on
Garwood's activities at Backdrop," Davidson told him.
"As it is, I've got barely one paragraph to cover two
years out of the man's life—the two most important
years, yet."

Lyman nodded. "I sympathize, but I'm afraid that's per the colonel's direct order. Apparently he thinks the full records would give you more information about what Backdrop is doing than he wants you to have."

"And Backdrop is doing something he doesn't want anyone to know about?" Davidson asked.

Lyman's face hardened a bit. "I wouldn't make vague inferences like that if I were you, Major," he said darkly. "You wouldn't have been allowed to just waltz into the Manhattan Project and get the whole story, either, and Backdrop is at least as sensitive as that was."

"As destructive, too." Davidson held a hand up before Lyman could reply. "Sorry—didn't mean it that way. Remember that all I know about this whole thing is that Garwood can use it to wreck cars and cigarettes."

"Yeah—the walking time bomb, I hear you dubbed him." Lyman snorted under his breath. "It's hoped that that . . . side effect, as it were . . . can be eliminated. Hoped a *lot*."

"Can't argue with that one," Davidson agreed. So his description of Garwood as a walking time bomb was being circulated around Backdrop. Interesting that what had been essentially a throwaway line would be so widely picked up on. He filed the datum away for possible future reference. "You think Garwood can help get rid of it if we find him?"

Lyman shrugged. "All I know is that my orders are to find him and get him back. What happens after that is someone else's problem. Anyway . . . my office is down the hall in Room One Fifty—let me know if you need anything."

"Thanks."

Lyman turned to go, then paused. "Oh, by the way . . . if your computer seems to go on the blink, don't waste time fiddling with it. Just call Maintenance and they'll take care of it."

Davidson frowned. "Computers go on the blink a lot around here?"

The other hesitated. "Often enough," he said vaguely.

"The point it, just tell Maintanence and let them figure out whether to fix or replace."

"Right."

Lyman nodded and left, and Davidson turned back to his terminal. So computers were among the modern conveniences subject to attack by the Garwood Effect . . . and it reminded Davidson of something else he'd planned to try.

It took a few minutes of searching, but eventually he found what he was looking for: a list of maintanence records, going all the way back to Backdrop's inception two years ago. Now, with a little analysis . . .

An hour later he straightened up in his chair, trying to work the cramps out of his fingers and the knot out of his stomach. If ever he'd needed confirmation of Garwood's story, he had it now. The amount of wrecked equipment coming up from the offices and experimental areas to Maintanence was simply staggering: computers, all kinds of electronic equipment, plastic-based items—the list went on and on. Even the physical structure of Backdrop itself was affected; a long report detailed instance after instance of walls that had been replastered and ceilings that had had to be shored up. That it was a result of Backdrop's work was beyond doubt: a simple analysis of the areas where damage had occurred showed steadily increasing frequency the closer to the experimental areas one got. To the experimental areas, and to Garwood's office.

And the analysis had yielded one other fact. The damage had been slowly increasing in frequency over the two years Garwood had been with Backdrop . . . until the point three months back when he'd left. After that, it had dropped nearly to zero.

Which meant that Garwood hadn't been lying. He was indeed at the center of what was happening.

A walking time bomb. Davidson felt a shiver run up his back. If Garwood remained at large . . . and if the Garwood Effect continued to increase in strength as it had over the past two years . . .

With a conscious effort he forced the thought from

his mind. Worry of that sort would gain him nothing. Somewhere, somehow, Garwood had to have left a trail of some sort. It was up to Davidson to find it.

He fumbled for a cigarette, swore under his breath. Leaning back in his seat again, he closed his eyes. *I am James Garwood*, he told himself, dragging his mind away from the irritations of nicotine withdrawal and willing his thoughts to drift. *I'm in hiding from the whole world. How exactly—exactly—have I pulled it off?*

III

. . . times e to the gamma one t.

Garwood circled the last equation and laid down the pencil, and for a minute he gazed at the set of equations he'd derived. It was progress of a sort, he supposed; he *had* gotten rid of the gamma zero factor this time, and that was the one the computer had been having its latest conniption fits over. Maybe this time the run would yield something useful.

Or maybe this time the damn machine would just find something else to trip over.

Garwood gritted his teeth. *Stop it*! he ordered himself darkly. Self-pity was for children, or for failures. Not for him.

Across the tiny efficiency apartment, the computer terminal was humming patiently as it sat on the floor in the corner. Easing down into a cross-legged sitting position on the floor, Garwood consulted his paper and maneuvered his "remote arm" into position. The arm was pretty crude, as such things went: a long dowel rod reaching across the room to the terminal with a shorter one fastened to it at a right angle for actually hitting the keys, the whole contraption resting on a universal pivot about its center. But crude or not, it enabled him to enter data without getting anywhere near the terminal, with the result that this terminal had already outlasted all the others he'd used since fleeing Backdrop. He only wished he'd thought of this trick sooner.

Entering the equations was a long, painstaking job,

made all the more difficult by having to watch what he was doing through a small set of opera glasses. But finally he hit the return key for the last time, keying in the simultaneous-solutions program already loaded. The terminal beeped acknowledgment, and with a grunt Garwood got stiffly back into his chair. His stomach growled as he did so, and with a mild shock he saw that it was ten-thirty. No wonder his stomach had been growling for the past hour or so. Getting up, rubbing at the cramps in his legs, he went over to the kitchen alcove.

To find that he'd once again let his supplies run below acceptable levels. "Blast," he muttered under his breath, and snared his wallet from the top of the dresser. There was a burger place a few blocks away that might still be open . . . but on the other hand, his wad of bills was getting dangerously thin, and when this batch was gone there wouldn't be any more. For a moment he studied the terminal's display with his opera glasses, but the lack of diagnostic messages implied that nothing immediate and obvious had tripped it up. Which meant that it would probably be chugging away happily on the equations for at least another half hour. Which meant there was plenty of time for him to skip the fast food and walk instead to the grocery store.

The overhead lights were humming loudly as Garwood started across the store's parking lot, and for a moment he fantasized that that he was out in some exotic wilderness, circled by giant insects made of equal parts firefly and cicada. Out in the wilderness, away from Backdrop and the curse that hounded him.

It might come to that eventually, he knew. Even if he was able to continue eluding the searchers Saunders had scouring the area, he still couldn't stay here. His carefully engineered sublet would last only another five weeks, his dwindling bankroll dropping near zero at about the same time. Leaving him a choice between surrender and finding a job.

Both of which, he knew, really boiled down to the

same thing. Any job paying enough for him to live on would leave a trail of paper that would bring Saunders's people down on him in double-quick time. Not to mention the risk he would present to the people he'd be working with.

He grimaced. A walking time bomb, that Intelligence major—Davidson—had dubbed him. A part of Garwood's mind appreciated the unintended irony of such a characterization; the rest of it winced at the truth also there.

The grocery store, not surprisingly, was quiet. Wrestling a cart that seemed determined to veer to the left, he went up and down the aisles, picking out his usual selection of convenience foods and allowing his nerves to relax as much as they could. There were probably some people somewhere who truly disliked supermarkets and the efficient long-term storage of food that made them possible; but if there were, the number must be vanishingly small. As a result, grocery stores were near the top of the short list of places where Garwood could feel fairly safe. As long as he stayed away from the cigarettes and smoking paraphernalia, he could be reasonably certain that nothing would break or crumble around him.

He collected as many packages as he estimated would fit into two bags and headed for the checkout. There, the teen-aged girl manning the register—or possibly she was a college student; they all looked equally young to him these days—gave him a pleasant smile and got to work unloading his cart. Listening to the familiar beep of the laser scanner, Garwood pulled out his wallet and watched the march of prices across the display.

The cart was still half full when a jar of instant coffee failed to register. The girl tried scanning it four times, then gave up and manually keyed the UPC code into her register. The next item, a frozen dinner, was similarly ignored. As was the next item . . . and the next . . . and the next . . .

"Trouble?" Garwood asked, his mouth going dry.

"Scanner seems to have quit," she frowned, tapping

the glass slits as if trying to get the machine's attention. "Funny—they're suppose to last longer than this."

"Well, you know how these things are," Garwood said, striving for nonchalance even as his heart began to pound in his ears.

"Yeah, but this one was just replaced Saturday. Oh, well, that's progress for you." She picked up the next item and turned back to her register.

Almost unwillingly, Garwood bent over and peered into the glass. Behind it, the laser scanner was dimly visible. Looking perfectly normal . . . *No,* he told himself firmly. *No, it's just coincidence. It has to be. Nobody hates laser grocery scanners, for God's sake.* But even as he fought to convince himself of that, a horrible thought occurred to him.

Perhaps it was no longer necessary for anyone to hate laser grocery scanners directly. Perhaps all it took now was enough people hating the lasers in self-guided weapons systems.

A dark haze seemed to settle across his vision. It had started, then; the beginning of the end. If a concerted desire to eliminate one incarnation of a given technology could spill over onto another, then there was literally nothing on the face of the earth that could resist Garwood's influence. His eyes fell on the packages of frozen food before him on the counter, and a dimly remembered television program came to mind. A program that had showed how the root invention of refrigeration had led to both frozen foods and ICBMs . . .

The girl finished packing the two paper bags and read off the total for him. Garwood pulled out the requisite number of bills, accepted his change, and left. Outside, the parking lot lights were still humming their cicada/firefly song. Still beckoning him to the safety of the wilderness.

A wilderness, he knew, which didn't exist.

The bags, light enough at the beginning of the walk, got progressively heavier as the blocks went by, and by the time he reached the door to his apartment house his arms were starting to tremble with the strain. Working the outside door open with his fingertips, he let it close behind him and started up the stairs. A young woman was starting down at the same time, and for an instant, just as they passed, their eyes met. But only for an instant. The woman broke the contact almost at once, her face the neutral inward-looking expression that everyone seemed to be wearing these days.

Garwood continued up the stairs, feeling a dull ache in the center of his chest. The "not-me" generation. Everyone encased in his or her own little bubble of space. *So why should I care, either?* he thought morosely. *Let it all fall apart around me. Why am I killing myself trying to take on decisions like this, anyway? Saunders is the one in charge, and if he says it'll work, then whatever happens is his responsibility. Right?*

The computer had finished its work. Setting the bags down, Garwood dug out his opera glasses again and studied the display. The machine had found three solutions to his coupled equations. The first was the one he'd already come up with, the one that had started this whole mess in the first place; the second was also one he'd seen before, and found to be mathematically correct but non-physical. The third solution . . .

Heart thudding in his ears, Garwood stepped to the table and reached to the ashtray for one of the loose cigarettes lying there. The third solution was new . . . and if it contained the build-in safeguard he was hoping to find . . .

He picked up one of the cigarettes. Squeezing it gently between thumb and fingertips, he gazed at the formula through his opera glasses, letting his eyes and thoughts linger on each symbol as he ticked off the seconds in his mind. At a count of *ten* he thought he felt a softness in the cigarette paper; at *twenty-two,* it crumbled to powder.

Wearily, he brushed the pieces from his hand into the garbage. Twenty-two seconds. The same length of time it had taken the last time . . . which meant that while it wasn't getting any worse, it wasn't getting any better, either.

Which probably implied this was yet another walk down a blind alley.

For a moment he gazed down at the cigarettes. A long time ago he'd believed that this field contained nothing but blind alleys—had believed it, and had done all he could to persuade Saunders of it, too. But Saunders hadn't believed . . . and now, Garwood couldn't afford to, either. Because if there weren't any stable solutions, then this curse would be with him forever.

Gritting his teeth, he stepped over to the counter and began unloading his groceries. Of course there was a stable solution. There *had* to be.

The only trick would be finding it before his time ran out.

IV

"Well," Davidson said, "at least he's staying put. I suppose that's *something*."

"Maybe," Lyman said, reaching over Davidson's shoulder to drop the report back onto his desk. "A broken laser scanner is hardly conclusive evidence, though."

"Oh, he's there, all right," Davidson growled, glaring at the paper. His fingertips rubbed restlessly at the edge of his desk, itching to be holding a cigarette. Damn Saunders's stupid rule, anyway. "He's there. Somewhere."

Lyman shrugged. "Well, he's not at any hotel or motel in the area—that much is for sure. We've got taps on all his friends around the country, checking for any calls he might make to them, but so far that's come up dry, too."

"Which means either he's somehow getting cash in despite the net, or else he's been holed up for nearly three weeks without any money. How?"

"You got me," Lyman sighed. "Maybe he had a wad of cash buried in a safe deposit box somewhere in town."

"I'd bet a couple of days' salary on that," Davidson

agreed. "But any such cash had to *come* from somewhere. I've been over his finances four times. His accounts have long since been frozen, and every cent he's made since coming to Backdrop has been accounted for."

Lyman grimaced. "Yeah, I know—I ran my own check on that a month ago. You think he could be working transient jobs or something? Maybe even at that supermarket where the laser scanner broke?"

Davidson shook his head. "I tend to doubt it—I can't see someone like Garwood taking the kind of underground job that doesn't leave a paper trail. On the other hand . . . do we know if he was ever in Champaign before?"

"Oh, sure." Lyman stepped around to Davidson's terminal, punched some keys. "He was there—yeah, there it is," he said over his shoulder. "A little over two and a half years ago, on a seminar tour."

Davidson frowned at the screen. Princeton, Ohio State, Illinois, Cal Tech—there were over a dozen others on the list. Silently, he cursed the bureaucratic foot-dragging that was still keeping his full security clearance from coming through. If he'd had access to all this data three weeks ago . . . "Did it occur to anyone that Garwood just *might* have made some friends during that trip that he's now turning to for help?"

"Of course it did," Lyman said, a bit tartly. "We've spent the last three weeks checking out all the people he met at that particular seminar. So far he hasn't contacted any of them."

"Or so they say." Davidson chewed at his lip. "Why a seminar tour, anyway? I thought that sort of thing was reserved for the really big names."

"Garwood is big enough in his field," Lyman said. "Besides, with him about to drop behind Backdrop's security screen, it was his last chance to get out and around—"

"Wait a second," Davidson interrupted him. "He was already scheduled to come to Backdrop? I thought he came here only two years ago."

Lyman gave him an odd look. "Yes, but Backdrop didn't even exist until his paper got the ball rolling. I thought you knew that."

"No, I did not," Davidson said through clenched teeth. "You mean to tell me Backdrop was *Garwood's* idea?"

"No, the project was Saunders's brainchild. It was simply Garwood's paper on—" he broke off. "On the appropriate subject," he continued more cautiously, "that gave Saunders the idea. And that made Backdrop possible, for that matter."

"So Garwood did the original paper," Davidson said slowly. "Saunders then saw it and convinced someone in the government to create and fund Backdrop. Then . . . what? He went to Garwood and recruited him?"

"More or less. Though I understand Garwood wasn't all that enthusiastic about coming."

"Philosophical conflicts?"

"Or else he thought he knew what would happen when Backdrop got going."

The Garwood Effect. Had Garwood really foreseen that fate coming at him? The thought made Davidson shiver. "So what it boils down to is that Saunders approached Garwood half a year before he actually came to Backdrop?"

"Probably closer to a year. It takes a fair amount of time to build and equip a place like this—"

"Or put another way," Davidson cut him off, "Garwood knew a year in advance that he was coming here . . . and had that same year to quietly siphon enough money out of his salary to live on if he decided to cut and run."

Lyman's face seemed to tighten, his eyes slightly unfocused. "But we checked his pre-Backdrop finances. I'm sure we did."

"How sure? And how well?"

Lyman swore under his breath. "Hang on. I'll go get another chair."

It took them six hours; but by the end of that time they'd found it.

"I'll be damned," Lyman growled, shutting off the microfiche record of Garwood's checking account and calling up the last set of numbers on the computer. "Fifteen thousand dollars. Enough for a year of running if he was careful with it."

Davidson nodded grimly. "And don't forget the per diem he would have gotten while he was on that seminar tour," he reminded the other. "If he skimped on meals he could have put away another couple of thousand."

Lyman stood up. "I'm going to go talk to the Colonel," he said, moving toward the door. "At least we know now how he's doing it. We can start hitting all the local landlords again and see which of them has a new tenant who paid in cash."

He left. *Great idea*, Davidson thought after him. *It assumes, of course, that Garwood didn't find a sublet that he could get into totally independently of the landlords. In a college town like Champaign that would be easy enough to do.*

The financial data was still on the display, and Davidson reached over to cancel it. The screen blanked; and for a long moment he just stared at the flashing cursor. "All right," he said out loud. "But why pick Champaign as a hideout in the first place?"

Because his seminar tour had taken him through there, giving him the chance to rent a safety deposit box? But the same tour had also taken him to universities in Chicago and Seattle, and either one of those metro areas would have provided him a far bigger haystack to hide in.

So why Champaign?

Garwood was running—that much was clear. But was he running *away* from something, or running *toward* something? Away from his problems at Backdrop, or toward—

Or toward a solution to those problems?

His fingers wanted a cigarette. Instead, he reached back to the keyboard. Everything about the Champaign area had, not surprisingly, been loaded into the computer's main database in the past three weeks. Now if he could just find the right question to ask the machine.

Five minutes later, on his second try, he found it.

There were men, Davidson had long ago learned, who could be put at a psychological disadvantage simply by standing over them while they sat. Colonel Bidwell, clearly, wasn't one of them. "Yes, I just got finished talking to Major Lyman," he said, looking up at Davidson from behind his desk. "Nice bit of work, if a little late in the day. You here to make sure you get proper credit?"

"No, sir," Davidson said. "I'm here to ask for permission to go back to Champaign to pick up Dr. Garwood."

Bidwell's eyebrows raised politely. "Isn't that a little premature, Major? We haven't even really gotten a handle on him yet."

"And we may not, either, sir, at least not the way Major Lyman thinks we will. There are at least two ways Garwood could have covered his trail well enough for us not to find it without tipping him off. But I think I know another way to track him down."

"Which is . . . ?"

Davidson hesitated. "I'd like to be there at the arrest, sir."

"You bargaining with me, Major?" Bidwell's voice remained glacially calm, but there was an unpleasant fire kindling in his eyes.

"No, sir, not really," Davidson said, mentally bracing himself against the force of the other's will. "But I submit to you that Garwood's arrest is unfinished business, and that I deserve the chance to rectify my earlier failure."

Bidwell snorted. "As I said when you first came in, Major, you have a bad tendency to get personally involved with your cases."

"And if I've really found the way to track Garwood down?"

Bidwell shook his head. "Worth a commendation in

my report. Not worth letting you gad about central Illinois."

Davidson took a deep breath. "All right, then, sir, try this: if you don't let *me* go get him, someone else will have to do it. Someone who doesn't already know about the Garwood Effect . . . but who'll have to be told."

Bidwell glared up at him, a faintly disgusted expression on his face. Clearly, he was a man who hated being maneuvered . . . but just as clearly, he was also a man who knew better than to let emotional reactions cloud his logic.

And for once, the logic was on Davidson's side. Eventually, Bidwell gave in.

He stood at the door for a minute, listening. No voices; nothing but the occasional creaking of floorboards. Taking a deep breath, preparing himself for possible action, he knocked.

For a moment there was no answer. Then more creaking, and a set of footsteps approached the door. "Who is it?" a familiar voice called.

"It's Major Davidson. Please open the door, Dr. Garwood."

He rather expected Garwood to refuse; but the other was intelligent enough not to bother with useless gestures. There was the click of a lock, the more elongated tinkle of a chain being removed, and the door swung slowly open.

Garwood looked about the same as the last time Davidson had seen him, though perhaps a bit wearier. Hardly surprising, under the circumstances. "I'm impressed," he said.

"That I found you?" Davidson shrugged. "Finding people on the run is largely a matter of learning to think the way they do. I seem to have that knack. May I come in?"

Garwood's lip twisted. "Do I have a choice?" he asked, taking a step backwards.

"Not really." Davidson walked inside, eyes automatically sweeping for possible danger. Across the room a computer terminal was sitting on the floor, humming to itself. "Rented?" he asked, nodding toward it.

"Purchased. They're not that expensive, really, and renting them usually requires a major credit card and more scrutiny than I could afford. Is that how you traced me?"

"Indirectly. It struck me that this was a pretty unlikely town for someone to try and hide out in . . . unless there was something here that you needed. The Beckman Institute's fancy computer system was the obvious candidate. Once we had that figured out, all we had to do was backtrack all the incoming modem links. Something of a risk for you, wasn't it?"

Garwood shook his head. "I didn't have any choice. I needed the use of a Cray Y-MP, and there aren't a lot of them around that the average citizen can get access to."

"Besides the ones at Stanford and Minneapolis, that is?"

Garwood grimaced. "I don't seem to have any secrets left, do I? I'd hoped I'd covered my trail a little better than that."

"Oh, we only got the high points," Davidson assured him. "And only after the fact. Once we knew you were here for the Beckman supercomputer it was just a matter of checking on which others around the country had had more than their share of breakdowns since you left Backdrop."

Garwood's lips compressed into a tight line, and something like pain flitted across his eyes. "My fault?"

"I don't know. Saunders said he'd look into it, see if there might have been other causes. He may have something by the time we get you back."

Garwood snorted. "So Saunders in his infinite wisdom is determined to keep going with it," he said bitterly. "He hasn't learned anything at all in the past four months, has he?"

"I guess not." Davidson nodded again at the terminal. "Have *you?*" he asked pointedly.

Garwood shook his head. "Only that the universe is full of blind alleys."

"Um." Stepping past Garwood, Davidson sat down at the table. "Well, I guess we can make that unanimous," he told the other. "I haven't learned much lately, either. Certainly not as much as I'd like."

He looked up, to find Garwood frowning at him with surprise. Surprise, and a suddenly nervous indecision . . . "No, don't try it, Doctor," Davidson told him. "Running won't help; I have men covering all the exits. Sit down, please."

Slowly, Garwood stepped forward to sink into the chair across from Davidson. "What do you want?" he asked carefully, resting his hands in front of him on the table.

"I want you to tell me what's going on," Davidson said bluntly. He glanced down at the table, noting both the equation-filled papers and the loose cigarettes scattered about. "I want to know what Backdrop's purpose is, why you left it—" he raised his eyes again— "and how this voodoo effect of yours works."

Garwood licked his lips, a quick slash of the tongue tip. "Major . . . if you had the proper clearance—"

"Then Saunders would have told me everything?" Davidson shrugged. "Maybe. But he's had three weeks, and I'm not sure he's ever going to."

"So why should I?"

Davidson let his face harden just a bit. "Because if Backdrop is a danger to my country, I want to know about it."

Garwood matched his gaze for a second, then dropped his eyes to the table, his fingers interlacing themselves into a tight double fist there. Then he took a deep breath. "You don't play fair, Major," he sighed. "But I suppose it doesn't really matter anymore. Besides, what's Saunders going to do?—lock me up? He plans to do that anyway."

"So what is it you know that has them so nervous?" Davidson prompted.

Garwood visibly braced himself. "I know how to make a time machine."

For a long moment the only sound in the room was the hum of the terminal in the corner . . . and the hazy buzzing of Garwood's words spinning over and over in Davidson's brain. "You *what?*" he whispered at last.

Garwood's shoulders heaved fractionally. "Sounds impossible, doesn't it? But it's true. And it's because of that . . ." he broke off, reached over to flick one of the loose cigarettes a few inches further away from him.

"Dr. Garwood—" Davidson licked dry lips, tried again. "Doctor, that doesn't make any sense. Why should a . . . a time machine—?" He faltered, his tongue balking at even suggesting such a ridiculous thing.

"Make things disintegrate?" Garwood sighed. "Saunders didn't believe it, either, not even after I explained what my paper really said."

The shock was slowly fading from Davidson's brain. "So what *did* it say?" he demanded.

"That the uncertainty factor in quantum mechanics didn't necessarily arise from the observer/universe interaction," Garwood said. "At least not in the usual sense. What I found was a set of self-consistent equations that showed the same effect would arise from the universe allowing for the possibility of time travel."

"And these equations of yours are the ones you recited to me when you wrecked my car and gun?"

Garwood shook his head. "No, those came later. Those were the equations that actually show how time travel is possible." His fingers moved restlessly, worrying at another of the cigarettes. "You know, Major, it would be almost funny if it weren't so deadly serious. Even after Backdrop started to fall apart around us Saunders refused to admit the possibility that it was our research that was causing it. That trying to build a time travel from my equations was by its very nature a self-defeating exercise."

"A long time ago," Davidson said slowly, "on that car

ride from Springfield, you called it subconscious democracy. That cigarettes disintegrated in your hand because some people didn't like smoking."

Garwood nodded. "It happens to cigarettes, plastics—"

"How? How can peoples' opinions affect the universe that way?"

Garwood sighed. "Look. Quantum mechanics says that everything around us is made up of atoms, each of which is a sort of cloudy particle with a very high mathematical probability of staying where it's supposed to. In particular, it's the atom's electron cloud that shows the most mathematical fuzziness; and it's the electron clouds that interact with each other to form molecules."

Davidson nodded; that much he remembered from college physics.

"Okay. Now, you told me once that you hated being hooked by cigarettes, right? Suppose you had the chance—right now—to wipe out the tobacco industry and force yourself out of that addiction? Would you do it?"

"With North Carolina's economy on the line?" Davidson retorted. "Of course not."

Garwood lips compressed. "You're more ethical than most," he acknowledged. "A lot of the 'not-me' generation wouldn't even bother to consider that particular consequence. Of course, it's a moot question anyway—we both know the industry is too well established for anyone to get rid of it now.

"But what if you could wipe it out in, say, 1750?"

Davidson opened his mouth . . . closed it again. Slowly, it was starting to become clear . . . "All right," he said at last. "Let's say I'd like to do that. What then?"

Garwood picked up one of the cigarettes. "Remember what I said about atoms—the atoms in this cigarette are only *probably* there. Think of it as a given atom being in its proper place ninety-nine point nine nine nine nine percent of the time and somewhere else the rest of it. Of course, it's never gone long enough to really affect the atomic bonds, which is why the whole cigarette normally holds together.

"But now *I* know how to make a time machine; and *you* want to eliminate the tobacco industry in 1750. *If* I build my machine, and *if* you get hold of it, and *if* you succeed in stamping out smoking, then this cigarette would never have been made and all of its atoms *would* be somewhere else."

Davidson's mouth seemed abnormally dry. "That's a lot of *ifs*," he managed.

"True, and that's probably why the cigarette doesn't simply disappear. But if enough of the electron clouds are affected—if they start being *gone* long enough to strain their bonds with the other atoms—then eventually the cigarette will fall apart." He held out his palm toward Davidson.

Davidson looked at the cigarette, kept his hands where they were. "I've seen the demo before, thanks."

Garwood nodded soberly. "It's scary, isn't it?"

"Yeah," Davidson admitted. "And all because I don't like smoking?"

"Oh, it's not just you," Garwood sighed. He turned his hand over, dropping the cigarette onto the table, where it burst into a little puddle of powder. "You could be president of Philip Morris and the same thing would happen. Remember that if a time machine is built from my equations, literally *everyone* from now until the end of time has access to the 1750 tobacco crop. And to the start of the computer age; and the inception of the credit card; and the invention of plastic." He rubbed his forehead wearily. "This list goes on and on. Maybe forever."

Davidson nodded, his stomach feeling strangely hollow. *A walking time bomb*, he'd called Garwood. *A time bomb*. No wonder everyone at Backdrop had been so quick to latch onto that particular epithet. "What about my car?" he asked. "Surely no one seriously wants to go back to the horse and buggy."

"Probably not," Garwood shook his head. "But the internal combustion engine is both more complicated and less efficient than several alternatives that were stamped out early in the century. If you could go back and nurture the steam engine, for instance—"

"Which is why the engine seemed to be trying to flow into a new shape, instead of just falling apart?" Davidson frowned. "It was starting to change into a steam engine?"

Garwood shrugged. "Possibly. I really don't know for sure why engines behave the way they do."

Almost unwillingly, Davidson reached out to touch what was left of the cigarette. "Why you?" he asked. "If your time machine is built, then everything in the world ought to be equally fair game. So why don't things disintegrate in *my* hands, too?"

"Again, I don't know for sure. I suspect the probability shifts cluster around me because I'm the only one who knows how to make the machine." Garwood seemed to brace himself. "But you're right. If the machine is actually made, then it's all out of my hands . . . and I can't see any reason why the effect wouldn't then mushroom into something worldwide."

A brief mental image flashed through Davidson's mind: a black vision of the whole of advanced technology falling to pieces, rapidly followed by society itself. If a superpower war of suspicion didn't end things even quicker . . . "My God," he murmured. "You can't let that happen, Doctor."

Garwood locked eyes with him. "I agree. At the moment, though, you have more power over that than I do."

For a long minute Davidson returned the other's gaze, torn by indecision. He could do it—he *could* simply let Garwood walk. It would mean his career, possibly, but the stakes here made such considerations trivial. Another possibility occurred briefly to him . . . "Why did you need the computer?" he asked Garwood. "What were you trying to do?"

"Find a solution to my equations that would allow for a safer form of time travel," Garwood said. "Something that would allow us to observe events, perhaps, without interacting with them."

"Did you have any luck?"

"No. But I'm not ready to give up the search, either. If you let me go, I'll keep at it."

Davidson clenched his jaw tightly enough to hurt. "I know that, Doctor," he said quietly. "But you'll have to continue your search at Backdrop."

Garwood sighed. "I should have known you wouldn't buck your orders," he said bitterly.

"And leave you out here, threatening a community of innocent bystanders?" Davidson retorted, feeling oddly stung by the accusation. "I have a working conscience, Doctor, but I also have a working brain. Backdrop is still the safest place for you to be, and you're going back there. End of argument." Abruptly, he got to his feet. "Come on. I'll have some of my people pack up your stuff and bring it to Backdrop behind us."

Reluctantly, Garwood also stood up. "Can I at least ask a favor?"

"Shoot."

"Can we drive instead of flying? I'm still afraid of what influence I might have on a plane's engines."

"If you can sit this close to that terminal without killing it, the engines should be perfectly safe," Davidson told him.

"Under the circumstances, 'should' is hardly adequate—"

"You're arguing in circles," Davidson pointed out. "If you get killed in a plane crash, how is anyone going to use your equations to build a time machine?"

Garwood blinked, then frowned. "Well . . . maybe I wouldn't actually die in the wreck."

"All right, fine," Davidson snapped, suddenly tired of the whole debate. "We'll put an impact bomb under your seat to make sure you'll die if we crash. Okay?"

Garwood's face reddened, and for a second Davidson thought he would explode with anger of his own. But he didn't. "I see," he said stiffly. "Very well, then, let's find a phone booth and see what Saunders says. You *will* accept suggestions from Saunders, won't you?"

Davidson gritted his teeth. "Never mind. You want to sit in a car for fourteen hours, fine. Let's go; we'll radio Chanute from the car and have them call in the change of schedule to Backdrop. And arrange for a quiet escort."

V

"I hope you realize," Garwood said heavily, "that by bringing me back you're putting everyone in Backdrop at risk."

Saunders raised polite eyebrows. Polite, stupidly unconcerned eyebrows. "Perhaps," he said. "But at least here we understand what's going on and can take the appropriate precautions. Unlike the nation at large, I may add, which you've just spent nearly four months putting at similar risk. Under the circumstances, I'm sure you'd agree that one of our concerns now has to be to keep you as isolated from the rest of the country as possible." He shrugged. "And as long as you have to be here anyway, you might as well keep busy."

"Oh, of course," Garwood snorted. "I might as well help Backdrop to fall apart that much soo—"

He broke off as a muffled cracking sound drifted into the room. "More of the plaster going," Saunders identified it off-handedly. "Nice to hear again after so long."

Garwood felt like hitting the man. "Damn it all, Saunders," he snarled. "Why won't you listen to reason? A working time machine *cannot be made*. The very fact that Backdrop is falling apart around me—"

"Proves that the machine *can* be made," Saunders cut him off. "If you'd stop thinking emotionally for a minute and track through the logic you'd realize that." Abruptly, all the vaguely amused patience vanished from his face, and his eyes hardened as they bored into Garwood's with an unexpected intensity. "Don't you understand?" he continued quietly. "When you left, the probability-shift damage to Backdrop dropped off to near zero. Now that you're back, the destruction is on the increase again."

"Which is my point—"

"No; which is *my* point," Saunders snapped. "The probability-shift effect cannot exist if a working time machine isn't possible."

"And yet that same effect precludes the manufacture of any such machine," Garwood pointed out. "As I've explained to you at least a hundred times."

"Perhaps. But perhaps not. Even given that the concept of time-travel generates circular arguments in the first place, has it occurred to you that a working time machine might actually prove to be a *stabilizing* factor?"

Garwood frowned. "You mean that if we have the theoretical capability of going back and correcting all these alterations of history then the wild fluctuations will subside of their own accord?"

"Something like that," Saunders nodded. "I did some preliminary mathematics on that question while you were gone and it looks promising. Of course, we won't know for sure until I have all the equations to work with."

"And what if you're wrong?" Garwood countered. "What if a working time machine would simply destabilize things further?"

A flicker of Saunders's old innocent expression crossed the man's face. "Why, then, we won't be able to make one, will we? The components will fall apart faster than we can replace them."

"In which event, we're back to the probability-shift effect being a circular paradox," Garwood sighed. "If it prevents us from building a time machine, there's no time travel. If there's no time travel, there's no change in probabilities and hence no probability-shift effect."

"As I said, time travel tends to generate paradoxes like that." Saunders pursed his lips. "There's one other possibility that's occurred to me, though. The man who brought you back from Champaign—Major Davidson— said in his report that you'd been trying to find an alternative solution to the time travel equations. Any luck?"

Garwood shook his head. "All I found was blind alleys."

"Maybe you just didn't get to look long enough."

Garwood eyed him. "Meaning . . .?"

"Meaning that one other possible explanation of the probability-shift effect is that there is indeed another set of solutions. A set that will let us build the machine and still be able to go back and change things."

Garwood sighed. "Saunders . . . don't you see that all you're doing is just making things worse? Isn't it bad enough that things fall apart around me?—do you want to see it happening on a global scale? Stabilization be damned: a time machine—a real, functional time machine—would be the worst instrument of destruction ever created. *Ever* created."

"All I know," Saunders said softly, "is that anything the universe allows us to do *will* eventually be done. If *we* don't build the machine, someone else will. Someone who might not hesitate to use it for the mass destruction you're so worried about."

Garwood shook his head tiredly. The discussion was finally turning, as he'd known it eventually would, onto all-too familiar territory: the question of whether or not the fruits of Backdrop's labor would be used responsibly by the politicians who would inherit it. "We've gone round and round on this one," he sighed, getting to his feet. "Neither of us is likely to change the other's mind this time, either. So if you don't mind, it's been a long drive and I'd like to get some rest."

"Fine." Saunders stood, too. "Tomorrow is soon enough to get back to work."

In the distance, the sound of more cracking plaster underlined his last word. "And if I refuse?" Garwood asked.

"You won't."

"Suppose I do?" Garwood persisted.

Saunders smiled lopsidedly and waved a hand in an all-encompassing gesture. "You talk too contemptuously about the 'not-me' generation to adopt their philosophy. You won't turn your back on a problem this serious . . . especially given that it's a problem partially of your own creation."

For a long moment Garwood considered arguing the latter point. It had been Saunders, after all, who'd pushed Backdrop into existence and then dragged him into it.

But on the other hand, it wasn't Saunders who knew how to build the damn time machine.

Wordlessly, he turned his back on the other and headed for the door. "Rest well," Saunders called after him.

His office, when he arrived there the next morning, was almost unrecognizable.

Two pieces of brand-new equipment had been shoehorned into the already cramped space, for starters; a terminal with what turned out to be a direct line to the Minneapolis Cray III supercomputer lab, and an expensive optical scanner that seemed set up to read typewritten equations directly onto the line. *So Saunders is capable of learning*, Garwood thought sardonically, careful not to touch either instrument as he gave them a brief examination. The electronic blackboard that had fallen apart shortly before he left Backdrop was gone, replaced by an old-fashioned chalk-on-slate type, and his steel-and-plastic chair had been replaced by a steel-and-wood one. Even his desk looked somehow different, though it took him a long minute to realize why.

All the piles of papers had been changed.

Silently, he mouthed a curse. He hadn't expected the papers to remain untouched—Saunders would certainly have ransacked his desk in hopes of finding the rest of his time-travel equations—but he hadn't expected everything to get so thoroughly shuffled in the process. Clearly, Saunders had gone about his task with a will and to hell with neatness; just as clearly, it was going to take most of the day to put things back where he could find them again. With a sigh, he sank gingerly into his new chair and started restacking.

It was two hours later, and he was not quite halfway

through the task, when there was a knock on the door. "Come in, Saunders," he called.

It wasn't Saunders. "Hello, Dr. Garwood," Major Davidson nodded, throwing a glance around the room. "You busy?"

"Not especially." Garwood looked up at him. "Checking to make sure I'm still here?"

Davidson shrugged fractionally, his gaze steady on Garwood. "Not really. I believe Colonel Bidwell has been able to plug the hole you got out by the last time."

"I'm not surprised." The look in Davidson's eyes was becoming just the least bit unnerving. "May I ask why you're here, then?"

Davidson pursed his lips. "The random destruction has started up again since we got in last night."

"This surprises you?"

Davidson opened his mouth; closed it. Tried again. "I'd . . . rather hoped you weren't so clearly the pivotal point of the effect."

"I thought we'd discussed all that back in Champaign," Garwood reminded him. "I'm the only one who knows how to build the machine, so of course the probability-shift effect centers around me."

Davidson's eyes flicked to the computer terminal/ optical scanner setup. "And Saunders wants you to let him in on the secret."

"Naturally. I don't intend to, of course."

"And if he doesn't give you that choice?"

"Meaning . . . ?"

"Meaning he tried once to use hypnosis to get your equations out of me. With you, the method would probably work."

Garwood's mouth felt dry. "He knows better than to try something that blatant," he said. Even to himself the words didn't sound very convincing.

"I hope so. But if he doesn't . . . I trust you'll always remember that there's at least one other person in Backdrop who recognizes the danger your knowledge poses."

Garwood nodded, wishing he knew exactly what the man was saying. Was he offering to help Garwood escape again should that become necessary? "I'll remember," he promised. "You're going to be here for awhile, then?"

Davidson smiled wryly. "They let me out on a tight rein to go after you, Doctor. That doesn't mean they want me running around loose with what I know about Backdrop. I'll be on temporary duty with the security office, at least for the foreseeable future." He paused halfway through the act of turning back toward the door. "Though I don't suppose the term 'foreseeable future' has quite the same meaning as it used to, does it?"

Without waiting for an answer, he nodded and left. *No, it doesn't,* Garwood agreed silently at the closed door. *It really doesn't.*

He thought about it for a long minute. Then, with a shiver, he turned back to his papers.

One by one, the leads faded into blind alleys . . . and two months later, Garwood finally admitted defeat.

"Damn you," he muttered aloud, slouching wearily in his chair as far away from his terminal as space permitted. "Damn you." An impotent curse hurled at the terminal, at the program, at the universe itself. "There has to be a way. There *has* to be."

His only answer was the vague and distant crash of something heavy, the sound muffled and unidentifiable. A piece of I-beam from the ceiling, he rather thought—the basic infrastructure of Backdrop had started to go the way of the more fragile plaster and electronics over the past couple of weeks. Saunders had spent much of that time trying to invent correlations between the increase in the destruction with some supposed progress in Garwood's mathematical work, and he'd come up with some highly imaginative ones.

But imaginative was all they were . . . because Garwood knew what was really happening.

Perversely, even as it blocked his attempts to find a

safe method of time travel, the universe had been busily showing him exactly how to transform his original equations into actual real-world hardware.

It was, on one level, maddening. He would be sitting at his typewriter, preparing a new set of equations for the optical scanner to feed into the computer, when suddenly he would have a flash of insight as to how a properly tuned set of asynchronous drivers could handle the multiple timing pulses. Or he'd be waiting for the computer to chew through a tensor calculation and suddenly recognize that an extra coil winding superimposed on a standard transformer system could create both the power and the odd voltage patterns his equations implied. Or he'd even be trying to fall asleep at night, head throbbing with the day's frustrations, and practically see a vision of the mu-metal molding that would distort a pulsed magnetic field by just the right amount to create the necessary envelope for radiating plasma bursts.

And as the insights came more and more frequently —as a working time machine came closer and closer to reality—the environment inside Backdrop came to look more and more like a war zone.

Across the room the terminal emitted a raucous beep, signaling the possibility of parity error in its buffer memory. "Damn," Garwood muttered again and dragged himself to his feet. Eventually he would have to tell Saunders that his last attempts had gone up in the same black smoke as all the previous ones, and there was nothing to be gained by putting it off. Picking up his hardhat, he put it on and stepped out of his office.

The corridor outside had changed dramatically in the past weeks, its soothing pastel walls giving way to the stark metallic glitter of steel shoring columns. Senses alert for new ripples in the floor beneath him as well as for falling objects from above, he set off toward Saunders's office.

Luck was with him. The passages were relatively clear, with only the minor challenge of maneuvering past shoring and other travelers to require his attention. He was nearly to Saunders's office, in fact, before he hit the first real roadblock.

And it was a good one. He'd been right about the sound earlier; one of the steel I-beams from the ceiling had indeed broken free, creating a somewhat bowed diagonal across the hallway. A team of men armed with acetylene torches were cutting carefully across the beam, trying to free it without bringing more down.

"Dr. Garwood?"

Garwood focused on the burly man stepping toward him, an engineer's insignia glittering amid the plaster dust on his jumpsuit collar. "Yes, Captain?"

"If you don't mind, sir," the other said in a gravelly voice, "we'd appreciate it if you wouldn't hang around here any longer than necessary. There may be more waiting to come down."

Garwood glanced at the ceiling, stomach tightening within him as he recognized the all-too-familiar message beneath the other's words. It wasn't so much interest in his, Garwood's, safety as it was concern that the cloud of destruction around him might wind up killing one of the workers. Briefly, bitterly, Garwood wondered if this was how Jonah had felt during the shipboard storm. Before he'd been thrown overboard to the whale . . . "I understand," he sighed. "Would you mind passing a message on to Dr. Saunders when you have the chance, then, asking him to meet me at my office? My phone's gone out again."

"A lot of 'em have, Doctor," the engineer nodded. "I'll give him the message."

Garwood nodded back and turned to go—

And nearly bumped into Major Davidson, standing quietly behind him.

"Major," Garwood managed, feeling his heart settle down again. "You startled me."

Davidson nodded, a simple acknowledgment of Garwood's statement. "Haven't seen you in a while, Dr. Garwood," he said, his voice the same neutral as his face. "How's it going?"

Garwood's usual vague deflection to that question

came to his lips . . . "I have to get back to my office," he said instead. "The workmen are worried about another collapse."

"I'll walk with you," Davidson offered, falling into step beside him.

Davidson waited until they were out of sight of the workers before speaking again. "I've been keeping an eye on the damage reports," he commented in that same neutral tone. "You been following them?"

"Not really," Garwood replied through dry lips. Suddenly there was something about Davidson that frightened him. "Though I can usually see the most immediate consequences in and around my office."

"Been some extra problems cropping up in the various machine and electronic fabrication shops, too," Davidson told him, almost off-handedly. "As if there's been some work going on there that's particularly susceptible to the Garwood Effect."

Garwood gritted his teeth. The Garwood Effect. An appropriate, if painful, name for it. "Saunders has had some people trying to translate what little he and the rest of the team know into practical hardware terms," he told Davidson.

"But they don't yet know how to build a time machine?"

"No. They don't."

"Do you?"

Again, Garwood's reflex was to lie. "I think so," he admitted instead. "I'm pretty close, anyway."

They walked on in silence for a few more paces. "I'm sure you realize," Davidson said at last, "the implications of what you're saying."

Garwood sighed. "Do try to remember, Major, that I was worrying about all this long before you were even on the scene."

"Perhaps. But my experience with scientists has been that you often have a tendency toward tunnel vision, so it never hurts to check. Have you told anyone yet? Or left any hard copies of the technique?"

"No, to both."

"Well, that's a start." Davidson threw him a sideways look. "Unfortunately, it won't hold anyone for long. If *I'm* smart enough to figure out what the increase in the Garwood Effect implies, Saunders is certainly smart enough to do the same."

Garwood looked over at Davidson's face, and the knot in his stomach tightened further as he remembered what the other had once said about Saunders using hypnosis against him. "Then I have to get away again before that happens," he said in a quiet voice.

Davidson shook his head. "That won't be easy to do a second time."

"Then I'll need help, won't I?"

Davidson didn't reply for several seconds. "Perhaps," he said at last. "But bear in mind that above everything else I have my duty to consider."

"I understand," Garwood nodded.

Davidson eyed him. "Do you, Doctor? Do you really?"

Garwood met his eyes . . . and at long last, he really *did* understand.

Davidson wasn't offering him safe passage to that mythical wilderness Garwood had so often longed for. He was offering only to help Garwood keep the secret of time travel out of Saunders's grasp. To keep it away from a world that such a secret would surely destroy.

Offering the only way out that was guaranteed to be permanent.

Garwood's heart was thudding in his ears, and he could feel sweat gathering on his upper lip. "And when," he heard himself say, "would your duty require you to take that action?"

"When it was clear there was no longer any choice," Davidson said evenly. "When you finally proved safe time travel was impossible, for instance. Or perhaps when you showed a working time machine could be built."

They'd reached the door to Garwood's office now. "But if I instead proved that the probability-shift effect would in fact keep a working time machine from actually being built?" Garwood asked, turning to face the other. "What then?"

"Then it's not a working time machine, is it?" Davidson countered.

Garwood took a deep breath. "Major . . . I want a working time machine built even less than you do. Believe me."

"I hope so," Davidson nodded, his eyes steady on Garwood's. "Because you and I may be the only ones here who feel that way . . . and speaking for myself, I know only one way to keep your equations from bringing chaos onto the world. I hope I don't have to use it."

A violent shiver ran up Garwood's back. "I do, too," he managed. Turning the doorknob with a shaking hand, he fled from Davidson's eyes to the safety of his office.

To the relative safety, anyway, of his office.

For several minutes he paced the room, his pounding heart only gradually calming down. A long time ago, before his break from Backdrop, he'd contemplated suicide as the only sure way to escape the cloud of destruction around him. But it had never been a serious consideration, and he'd turned instead to his escape-and-research plan.

A plan which had eventually ended in failure. And now, with the stakes even higher than they'd been back then, death was once again being presented to him as the only sure way to keep the genie in the bottle.

Only this time the decision wasn't necessarily going to be his. And to add irony to the whole thing, Davidson's presence here was ultimately his own fault. If he hadn't skipped out of Backdrop six months ago, the major would never even have come onto the scene.

Or maybe he would have. With the contorted circular logic that seemed to drive the probability-shift effect nothing could be taken for granted. Besides, if Davidson hadn't caught him, perhaps someone less intelligent would have. Someone who might have brushed aside his fears and forced him onto that airplane at Chanute AFB. If that had happened—if the effect had then precipitated a crash—

He shook his head to clear it. It was, he thought bitterly, like the old college bull sessions about free will versus predestination. There were no answers, ever; and you could go around in circles all night chasing after them. On one hand, the probability-shift effect could destroy engines; on the other, as Davidson himself had pointed out, it logically shouldn't be able to crash a plane that Garwood himself was on . . .

Garwood frowned, train of thought breaking as a wisp of something brushed past his mind. *Davidson . . . airplane . . . ?*

And with a sudden flood of adrenaline, the answer came to him.

Maybe.

Deep in thought, he barely noticed the knock at the door. "Who is it?" he called mechanically.

"Saunders," the other's familiar voice came through the panel.

Garwood licked his lips, shifting his mind as best he could back to the real world. The next few minutes could be crucial ones indeed. . . . "Come in," he called.

"I got a message that you wanted to see me," Saunders said, glancing toward the terminal as he came into the room. "More equipment trouble?"

"Always," Garwood nodded, waving him to a chair. "But that's not why I called you here. I think I may have some good news."

Saunders's eyes probed Garwood's face as he sank into the proffered seat. "Oh? What kind?"

Garwood hesitated. "It'll depend, of course, on just what kind of latitude you're willing to allow me—how much control I'll have on this—and I'll tell you up front that if you buck me you'll wind up with nothing. Understand?"

"It would be hard not to," Saunders said dryly, "considering that you've been making these same demands since you got here. What am I promising not to interfere with this time?"

Garwood took a deep breath. "I'm ready," he said, "to build you a time machine."

VI

Within a few days the Garwood Effect damage that

had been occurring sporadically throughout Backdrop's several fabrication areas jumped nearly eight hundred percent. A few days after that, repair and replacement equipment began to be shipped into the complex at a correspondingly increased rate, almost—but not quite— masking the even more dramatic flood of non-damage-control shipping also entering Backdrop. The invoice lists for the latter made for interesting reading: esoteric electronic and mechanical equipment, exotic metals, specialized machine tools for both macro and micro work, odd power supplies—it ran the entire gamut.

And for Davidson, the invoices combined with the damage reports were all the proof he needed.

Garwood had figured out how to build his time machine. And was building it.

Damn him. Hissing between his teeth, Davidson leaned wearily back into his chair and blanked the last of the invoices from his terminal screen. So Garwood had been lying through his teeth all along. Lying about his fears concerning time travel; lying about his disagreements with Dr. Saunders; lying about how noble and self-sacrificing he was willing to be to keep the world safe from the wildfire Garwood Effect a time machine would create.

And Davidson, that supposedly expert reader of people, had fallen for the whole act like a novice investigator.

Firmly, he shook the thought away. Bruised pride was far and away the least of his considerations at the moment. If Garwood was building a time machine . . .

But *could* he in fact build it?

Davidson gnawed at the inside of his cheek, listening to the logic spin in circles in his head. Garwood had suggested more than once that the Garwood Effect would destroy a time machine piecemeal before it could even be assembled. Had he been lying about that, too? It had seemed reasonable enough at the time . . . but then why would he and Saunders even bother trying? No, there had to be something else happening, something Garwood had managed to leave out of his argument and which Davidson hadn't caught on his own.

But whatever it was he'd missed, circumstances still left him no choice. Garwood had to be stopped.

Taking a deep breath, Davidson leaned forward to the terminal again and called up Backdrop's cafeteria records. If Garwood was working around the clock, as Davidson certainly would be doing in his place . . . and after a few tries he found what he was looking for: the records of the meals delivered to the main assembly area at the end of Backdrop's security tunnel. Scanning them, he found there had been between three and twelve meals going into the tunnel each mealtime since two days before the dramatic upsurge in Garwood Effect damage.

And Garwood's ordering number was on each one of the order lists.

Davidson swore again, under his breath. Of course Garwood would be spending all his time down the tunnel—after their last conversation a couple of weeks ago the man would be crazy to stay anywhere that Davidson's security clearance would let him get to. And he'd chosen his sanctuary well. Down the security tunnel, buried beneath the assembly area's artificial hill, it would take either a company of Marines or a medium-sized tactical nuke to get to him now.

Or maybe—just maybe—all it would take would be a single man with a computer terminal. A man with some knowledge of security systems, some patience, and some time.

Davidson gritted his teeth. The terminal he had; and the knowledge, and the patience. But as for the time . . . he would know in a few days.

If the world still existed by then.

VII

The five techs were still going strong as the clocks reached midnight, but Garwood called a halt anyway. "We'll be doing the final wiring assembly and checkout tomorrow," he reminded them. "I don't want people falling asleep over their voltmeters while they're doing that."

"You really expect any of us to *sleep?*" one of the techs grumbled half-seriously.

"Well, *I* sure will," Garwood told him lightly, hooking a thumb toward the door. "Come on, everybody out. See you at eight tomorrow morning. Pleasant dreams."

The tech had been right, Garwood realized as he watched them empty their tool pouches onto an already cluttered work table: with the project so close to completion they *were* going to be too wired up for easy sleep. But fortunately they were as obedient as they were competent, and they filed out without any real protest.

And Garwood was alone.

Exhaling tiredly, he locked the double doors and made his way back to the center of the huge shored-up fabrication dome and the lopsided monstrosity looming there. Beyond it across the dome was his cot, beckoning him temptingly . . . Stepping instead to the cluttered work table, he picked up a screwdriver set and climbed up through the tangle of equipment into the seat at its center. Fifteen minutes later, the final connections were complete.

It was finished.

For a long minute he just sat there, eyes gazing unseeingly at the simple control/indicator panel before him. It was finished. After all the blood, sweat, and tears—after all the arguments with Saunders—after the total disruption of his life . . . it was done.

He had created a time machine.

Sighing, he climbed stiffly down from the seat and returned the screwdrivers to their place on the work table. The next table over was covered with various papers; snaring a wastebasket, he began pushing the papers into it, tamping them down as necessary until the table was clear. A length of electrical cable secured the wastebasket to a protruding metal plate at the back of the time machine's seat, leaving enough room for the suitcase and survival pack he retrieved from beneath his cot. Two more lengths of cable to secure them . . .

and there was just one more chore to do. A set of three video cameras stood spaced around the room, silent on their tripods; stepping to each in turn, he turned all of them on.

He was just starting back to the time machine when there was a faint sound from the double doors.

He turned, stomach tightening into a knot. It could only be Saunders, here for a late-night briefing on the day's progress. If he noticed that the cameras were running—realized what that meant—

The doors swung open, and Major Davidson stepped in.

Garwood felt an instantaneous burst of relief . . . followed by an equally instantaneous burst of fear. He'd specifically requested that Davidson not be cleared for this part of Backdrop . . . "Major," he managed to say between suddenly dry lips. "Up—ah, rather late, aren't you?"

Davidson closed the doors, his eyes never leaving Garwood's face. "I only hope I'm *not* here too late," he said in a quiet voice. "You've done it, haven't you?"

Garwood licked his lips, nodding his head fractionally toward the machine beside him. "Here it is."

For a long moment neither man spoke. "I misjudged you," Davidson said at last, and to Garwood's ears there was more sorrow than anger in the words. "You talked a lot about responsibility to the world; but in the end you backed down and did what they told you to do."

"And you?" Garwood asked softly, the tightness in his stomach beginning to unknot. If Davidson was willing to talk first . . . to talk, and to listen . . . "Have you thought through the consequences of *your* actions? You went to a lot of illegal trouble to get in here. If you kill me on top of that, your own life's effectively over."

A muscle in Davidson's cheek twitched. "Unlike you, Doctor, I don't just talk about responsibility. And there *are* things worth dying for."

Unbidden, a smile twitched at Garwood's lips. "You know, Major, I'm glad you came. It gives me a certain measure of hope to know that even in the midst of the 'not-me' generation there are still people willing to look beyond their own selfish interests."

Davidson snorted. "Doctor, I'll remind you that I've seen this nobility act of yours before. I'm not buying it this time."

"Good. Then just listen."

Davidson frowned. "To what?"

"To the silence."

"The—?" Davidson stopped abruptly; and all at once he seemed to get it. "It's *quiet*," he almost whispered, eyes darting around the room, coming to rest eventually on the machine beside Garwood. "But—the Garwood Effect—you've found a way to stop it?"

Garwood shook his head. "No, not really. Though I think I may understand it a bit better now." He waved a hand around the room. "In a sense, the trouble is merely that I was born at the wrong time. If I'd lived a hundred years earlier the culture wouldn't have had the technological base to do anything with my equations; if I'd been born a hundred years later, perhaps I'd have had the time and necessary mathematics to work out a safe method of time travel, leaving my current equations as nothing more than useless curiosities to be forgotten."

"I'd hardly call them useless," Davidson interjected.

"Oh, but they are. Or didn't you notice how much trouble the various fabrication shops had in constructing the modules for this machine?"

"Of course I did," Davidson nodded, a frown still hovering across his eyes. "But if the modules themselves were falling apart . . . ?"

"How was I able to assemble a working machine?" Garwood reached up to touch one of the machine's supports. "To be blunt, I cheated. And as it happens, *you* were the one who showed me how to do it."

Davidson's eyes locked with him. "Me?"

"You," Garwood nodded. "With a simple, rather sarcastic remark you made to me back in my Champaign apartment. Tell me, what's the underlying force that drives the Garwood Effect?"

Davidson hesitated, as if looking for a verbal trap. "You told me it was the possibility that someone would use time travel to change the past—" He broke off, head jerking with sudden insight. "Are you saying . . . ?"

"Exactly," Garwood nodded. "There's no possibility of changing the past *if my machine can only take me into the future.*"

Davidson looked up at the machine. "How did you manage that?"

"As I said, it was your idea. Remember when I balked at flying back here and you suggested putting a bomb under my seat to make sure a crash would be fatal?" Garwood pointed upwards. "If you'll look under the seat there you'll see three full tanks of acetylene, rigged to incinerate both the rider and the machine if the 'reverse' setting is connected and used."

Davidson looked at the machine for a long moment, eyes flicking across the tanks and the mechanism for igniting them. "And that was really all it took?" he asked.

"That's all. Before I installed the system we couldn't even load the modules into their racks without them coming apart in our hands. Afterwards, they were still touchy to make, but once they were in place they were completely stable. Though if I disconnected the suicide system they'd probably fall apart en masse."

Slowly, Davidson nodded. "All right. So that covers the machine. It still doesn't explain what's happened to your own personal Garwood Effect."

"Do you really need an explanation for that?" Garwood asked.

Davidson's eyes searched his. "But you don't even know how well it'll work," he reminded Garwood. "Or if there are any dangerous side effects."

That thought had occurred to Garwood, too. "Ultimately, it doesn't matter. One way or another, this is my final ticket out of Backdrop. My equations go with me, of course—" he pointed at the secured wastebasket— "and all the evidence to date indicates Saunders and his team could work till Doomsday without being able to reproduce them."

"They know how to make the modules for this machine," Davidson pointed out.

"Only some of them. None of the really vital ones—I made those myself, and I'm taking all the documentation with me. And even if they somehow reconstructed them, I'm still convinced that assembling a fully operational machine based on my equations will be impossible." He paused, focused his attention on the cameras silently recording the scene. "You hear that, Saunders? Drop it. Drop it, unless and until you can find equations that lead to a safer means of time travel. You'll just be wasting your own time and the taxpayers' money if you don't."

Turning his back on the cameras, he climbed once again up into the seat. "Well, Major," he said, looking down, "I guess this is good-bye. I've . . . enjoyed knowing you."

"That's crap, Doctor," Davidson said softly. "But good luck anyway."

"Thanks." There were a handful of switches to be thrown—a dozen strokes on each of three keypads—and amid the quiet hum and vibration of the machine he reached for the trigger lever—

"Doctor?"

He paused. "Yes, Major?"

"Thanks," Davidson said, a faint smile on his lips, "for helping me quit smoking."

Garwood smiled back. "You're welcome."

Grasping the trigger lever, he pulled it.

The President's Doll

It started—or at least *my* involvement in the case started—as a brief but nasty behind-the-scenes battle between the Washington Police and the Secret Service over jurisdiction. The brief part I was witness to: I was at my desk, attention split between lunch and a jewelry recovery report, when Agent William Maxwell went into Captain Forsythe's office; and I was still on the same report when they came out. The nasty part I didn't actually see, but the all-too-familiar glint in Forsythe's eyes was only just beginning to fade as he and Maxwell left the office and started across the crowded squad room. I noted the glint, and Maxwell's set jaw, and said a brief prayer for whoever the poor sucker was who would have to follow Forsythe's act.

So of course they came straight over to me.

"Detective Harland; Secret Service Agent Maxwell," Forsythe introduced us with his customary eloquence. "You're assigned as of right now to a burglary case; Maxwell will give you the details." And with that, he turned on his heel and strode back to his office.

For a second Maxwell and I eyed each other in somewhat awkward silence. "Burglary?" I prompted at last, expecting him to pick up on the part of the question I wasn't asking.

He did, and his tight lips compressed a fraction more. "A very special burglary. Something belonging to President Thompson. All I really need from you is access to the police files on—"

"Stolen from the White House?" I asked, feeling my eyebrows rise.

"No, the doll was—" He broke off, glancing around at the desks crowding around us. None of the officers there were paying the least bit of attention to us, but I guess Maxwell didn't know that. Or else mild paranoia just naturally came with his job. "Is there some place a little more private where we can go and talk?" he asked.

"Sure," I said, getting to my feet and snaring my coat from the chair back as I took a last bite from my sandwich. "My car. We can talk on the way to the scene of the crime."

I was very restrained. I got us downstairs, into the car, and out into Washington traffic before I finally broke down. "Did you refer to this burglared item as a 'doll'?" I asked.

Maxwell sighed. "Yes, I did," he admitted. "But it's not what you're thinking. The President's doll is—" He broke off, swearing under his breath. "You weren't supposed to know about this, Harland—none of you were. There's no reason for you to be in on this at all; it's a Secret Service matter, pure and simple. Left at the next light."

"Apparently Captain Forsythe thought differently. He gets like that sometimes—very insistent on having a hand in everything that happens in this town." I reached the intersection and made the turn.

"Yeah, well, this one is none of his business, and I'd have taken him right down on the mat if time wasn't so damn critical." Maxwell hissed through his teeth.

"So what files do you need?" I asked after a minute. "Professional burglars or safecrackers?"

He glanced over at me. "Nice guess," he conceded. "Probably both. We've checked over security at the—office—and it took a real expert to get in the way he did."

"Whose office?"

"Pak and Christophe. Doctors Sam and Pierre, respectively."

"Medical doctors?"

"They say yes. I say—" Maxwell shook his head. "Look, do me a favor; hold off on any more questions until we get there, okay? They're the only ones who can explain their setup. Or at least the only ones who can explain it so that you might actually believe it."

I blinked. "Uh . . ."

"Right at the next light."

Gritting my teeth, I sat on my curiosity and concentrated on my driving.

Dr. Sam Pak was a short, intense second generation Chinese-American. Dr. Pierre Christophe was a tall, equally intense first generation Haitian. Pak's specialty was obvious; the lettering on their office door proclaimed it to be the Pak-Christophe Acupuncture Clinic. It wasn't until the two doctors led us to the back room and opened the walk-in vault there that I found out just what it was Christophe supplied to the partnership.

Believing it was another matter entirely.

"I don't believe it," I said, staring at the dozen or so row planters lining the shelves of the vault. Stuck knee deep into the planters' dirt were rows of the ugliest wax figures I'd ever seen. Figurines with bits of hair and fingernail stuck on and into them . . . "I don't believe it," I repeated, *"Voodoo acupuncture?"*

"It is not that difficult to understand," Christophe said in the careful tones and faint accent of one who'd learned English as a second language. "I might even say it is a natural outgrowth of the science of acupuncture. If—"

"Pierre," Pak interrupted him. "I don't think Detective Harland came here to hear about medical philosophy."

"Forgive me," Christophe said, ducking his head. "I am very serious about my work here—"

"Pierre," Pak said. Christophe ducked his head again and shut up.

I sighed. "Okay, I'll bite. Just how is this supposed to work?"

"You're probably familiar with at least the basics of acupuncture," Pak said, reaching into the vault to pluck out one of the wax dolls from its dirt footbath. "Thin needles placed into various nerve centers can heal a vast number of diseases and alleviate the pain from others." His face cracked in a tight smile. "From your reaction, I'd guess you also know a little about voodoo."

"Just what I've seen in bad movies," I told him. "The dead chickens were always my favorite part." Christophe made some sort of disgusted noise in the back of his throat; I ignored him. "Let me guess: instead of sticking the acupuncture needles into the patient himself, you just poke them into his or her doll?"

"Exactly." Pak indicated the hair and fingernail clippings on the doll he was holding. "Despite the impression Hollywood probably gave you, there *does* seem to be a science behind voodoo. It's just that most of the practitioners never bother to learn it."

I looked over at Maxwell, who was looking simultaneously worried, tense, and embarrassed. "And you're telling me the President of the United States is involved in something this nutzoid?"

He pursed his lips. "He has some pains on occasion, especially when he's under abnormal stress. Normal acupuncture was effective in controlling that pain, but it was proving something of a hassle to keep sneaking Dr. Pak into the White House."

" 'Sneaking'?"

He reddened. "Come on, Harland—you watch the news. Half of Danzing's jibes are aimed at the state of the President's health."

And whether or not he was really up to a second term. Senator Danzing had played that tune almost constantly since the campaign started, and would almost certainly be playing it again at their first official debate tonight in Baltimore. And with the election itself only two months away . . . "So when the possibility opened up of getting his treatments by remote control, he jumped at it with both feet, huh?" I commented. "I can just see what Danzing would do with something like this."

"He couldn't do a thing," Maxwell growled. "What's he going to do, go on TV and accuse the President of dealing in voodoo? Face it—he'd be laughed right off the stage, probably lose every scrap of credibility he has right then and there. Even if he got the media interested enough to dig out the facts, he'd almost certainly still wind up hurting himself more than he would the President."

"He could still make Thompson look pretty gullible, though," I said bluntly. "Not to mention reckless."

"This wasn't exactly done on a whim," Maxwell said stiffly. "Drs. Pak and Christophe have been working on this technique for several years—these dolls right here represent their sixth testing phase over a period of at least eighteen months."

I looked at the dolls in their planters. "I can hardly wait to see the ads when they have their grand opening."

Maxwell ignored the comment. "The point is that they've been successful in ninety-five-plus percent of the cases where plain acupuncture was already working—those figures courtesy of the FBI and FDA people we had quietly check this out. Whatever else you might think of the whole thing, the President didn't go into it without our okay."

I glanced at the tight muscles in his cheek. "Your okay, but not your enthusiasm?" I ventured.

He gritted his teeth. "The President wanted to do it," he growled. "*We* obey *his* orders, not the other way around. Besides, the general consensus was that, crazy or not, if the treatment didn't help him it also probably wouldn't hurt him."

I looked at Pak and Christophe, standing quietly by trying not to look offended. "*Did* it help?"

"Of course it did," Christophe said, sounding a little hurt. "The technique itself is perfectly straightforward—"

"Yeah. Right." I turned back to Maxwell. "So what's the problem? Either Dr. Pak moves into the White House until after the dust of the election has settled, or else Dr. Christophe goes ahead and makes Thompson a new doll. Surely he can spare another set of fingernail clippings—he can probably even afford to give up the extra hair."

"You miss the point," Maxwell grated. "It's not the President's pain treatments we're worried about."

"Then what—?"

"You mean you have forgotten," Christophe put in, "how voodoo dolls were originally used?"

I looked at the doll still in Pak's hand. "Oh, hell," I said quietly.

"Our theory is that it is the protein signature in the hair and nail clippings that, so to speak, forms the connection between the doll and the subject," Christophe said, gesturing broadly at the dolls in the vault. "Once that connection is made, what happens to the doll is duplicated in what happens to the subject."

I gnawed at my lip. "Well . . . these dolls were made specifically for medical purposes, right? Is there anything about their design that would make it impossible to use them for attack purposes? Or even to limit the amount of damage they could do?"

Christophe's brow furrowed. "It is an interesting question. There was certainly no malice involved in their creation, which may be a factor. But whether some other person could so bend them to that purpose—"

"If you don't know," I interrupted brusquely, "just say so."

"I do not know," he said, looking a little hurt.

"What's all this dirt for?" Maxwell asked, poking a finger experimentally into one of the row planters.

"Ah!" Christophe said, perking up. "That is our true crowning achievement, Mr. Maxwell—the discovery that it is the soil of Haiti that is the true source of voodoo power."

"You're kidding," I said.

"No, it's true," Pak put in. "A doll that's taken away from Haiti soon loses its potency. Having them in Haitian soil seems to keep them working indefinitely."

"Or in other words, the doll they stole will eventually run out of steam," I nodded. "How soon before that happens? A few hours? Days?"

"I expect it'd be measured in terms of a few weeks, maybe longer. I don't think we've ever gotten around to properly experimenting with—"

"If you don't know," I growled, "just say so."

"I don't know."

I looked at Maxwell. "Well, that's something, anyway. If it takes our thief long enough to figure out what he's got, it won't do him any good."

"Oh, he knows what he's got, all right," Maxwell said grimly. "Unless you really think he just grabbed that one by accident?"

"I suppose not," I sighed, glancing back at the rows of figurines. None of the others showed evidence of even having been touched, let alone considered for theft. "Dr. Christophe . . . is there anything like a—well, a *range* for this . . . effect of yours? In other words, does the President have to be within five miles, say, of the doll before anything will happen?"

Christophe and Pak exchanged looks. "We've treated patients who were as far as a hundred miles away," Pak said. "In fact—yes. I believe President Thompson himself was on a campaign trip in Omaha two months ago when we treated a stomach cramp."

Omaha. Great. If this nonsensical, unreal effect could reach a thousand miles across country, the thief could be anywhere.

Maxwell apparently followed my train of thought. "Looks like I was right—our best bet is to try and narrow down the possibilities."

I nodded, eyeing the vault door. This wasn't some cheap chain lock substitute Pak and Christophe had here—only a genuine professional would have the know-how to get into it. "Alarm systems?" I asked.

"I've got the parameters," Maxwell said before either of the others could speak. "You think I've proved sufficient urgency now for us to head back and dig into your files?"

The President's life, threatened by the melding of two pseudosciences that no one in his right mind could possibly believe in . . . except maybe that the combination happened to work. "Yeah, I think you've got a case," I admitted. "How's the President taking it?"

Maxwell hesitated a fraction too long. "He's doing fine," he said.

I cocked my eyebrow at him. "Really?" I asked pointedly.

His jaw clenched momentarily. "Actually . . . I'm not sure he's been told yet. There's nothing he can do, and we don't want to . . . you know."

Stir up psychosomatic trouble, I finished silently for him. Made as much sense as any of the rest of it, I supposed—

"Wait a second," I interrupted my own thought. "I remember reading once that for acupuncture to work the subject has to believe in it, at least a little. Doesn't the same apply to voodoo?"

Christophe drew himself up to his full height. "Mr. Harland," he said stiffly, "we are not dealing with fantasies and legends here. Our method is a fully medical, fully *scientific* treatment of the patient, and whatever he believes or does not believe matters but little."

Maxwell looked at Pak. "You agree with that, Doctor?"

Pak pursed his lips. "There's some element of belief in it, sure," he conceded. "But what area of medicine doesn't have that? The whole double-blind/placebo approach to drug testing shows—"

"Fine, fine," Maxwell cut him off. "I suppose it doesn't matter, anyway. If the President has enough belief to get benefit out of it, he probably has enough to get hurt, too."

Pak swallowed visibly. "Mr. Maxwell . . . look, we're really sorry about all this. Is there anything at all we can do to help?"

Maxwell glanced at me. "You think of anything?"

I looked past him at the rows of dolls. There was still a heavy aura of unreality hanging over this whole thing. . . . With an effort I forced myself back to business. "I presume your people already checked for fingerprints?"

"In the entryway, on the windows, on the vault itself, and also on the file cabinet where the records are kept. We're assuming that's how the thief knew which doll was the President's."

"In that case—" I shrugged. "I guess it's time to get back to the station and warm up the computer. So unless you two know of a antidote to—"

I broke off as, for some reason, a train of thought I'd been sidetracked from earlier suddenly reappeared. "Something?" Maxwell prompted.

"Dr. Christophe," I said slowly, "what would happen if a given patient had *two* dolls linked to him? And different things were done to each one?"

Christophe nodded eagerly. "Yes—I had the exact same thought myself. If Sam's acupuncture can counteract any damage done through the stolen doll—" He looked at Pak. "Certainly you can do it?"

Pak's forehead creased in a frown. "It's a nice thought, Pierre, but I'm not at all sure I can do it. If the dolls are both running the same strength—"

"But they won't be," Maxwell interrupted him. "The Haitian dirt, remember? You can keep yours stuck up to its knees in the stuff, while theirs will gradually be losing power." He shook his head abruptly. "I can't *believe* I'm actually talking like this," he muttered. "Anyway, it's our best shot until we get the first doll back. I'm going to phone for a car—have all the stuff you'll need ready in fifteen minutes, okay?"

"Wait a second," Pak objected. "Where are we going?"

"The White House, of course," Maxwell told him. "Well, Baltimore, actually—the President's there right now getting ready for the debate tonight. I want you to be right there with him in case an attack is made."

"But the doll will work—"

"I'm not talking about the damn doll—I'm talking about the problem of communications lag. If the President has to tell someone where it hurts and then they have to call you from Baltimore or the White House and then *you* have to get the doll out and treat it and ask over the phone whether it's doing any good—" He broke off. "What am I explaining all of this for? You're going to be with the President for the next few days and that's that. As material witnesses, if nothing else."

He hadn't a hope of getting that one to stick, and he and I both knew it. But Pak and Christophe apparently didn't. Or else they were feeling responsible enough that they weren't in any mood to be awkward. Whichever, by the time Maxwell got his connection through to the White House they'd both headed off to collect their materials and equipment, and by the time the car arrived ten minutes later they were ready to go. Maxwell gave the driver directions, and as they drove off he and I got back in my car and returned to the station.

"Well, there you have it," I sighed, leaning back in my chair and waving at the printout. "Your likeliest suspects. Take your pick."

Maxwell said a particularly obscene word and hefted the stack of paper. "I don't suppose there's a chance we missed any helpful criteria, is there?"

I shrugged. "You sat there and watched me feed it all in. Expert safecracker, equally proficient with fancy vaults and fancy electronic alarm systems, not dead, not in jail, et cetera, et cetera."

He shook his head. "It'll take *days* to sort through these."

"Longer than that to track all of them down," I agreed. "Any ideas you've got, I'll take them."

He gnawed at the end of a pencil. "What about cross-referencing with our hate mail file? Surely no ordinary thief would have any interest in killing President Thompson."

"Fine—but most of your hate-mail people aren't going to know about the President's doll in the first place. We'd do better to try and find a leak from either the White House or Pak and Christophe's place."

"We're already doing that," he said grimly. "Also checking with the CIA regarding foreign intelligence services and terrorist organizations. These guys—" he tapped the printout— "were more of a long shot, but we couldn't afford to pass it up."

"Nice to occasionally be included in what's going on," I murmured. "How's the President?"

"As of ten minutes ago he was fine." Maxwell had been calling at roughly fifteen minute intervals, despite the fact that the Baltimore Secret Service contingent had my phone number and had promised to let us know immediately if anything happened.

"Well, that's something, anyway." I glanced at my watch. It was nearly four o'clock; two and a half hours since we'd left the voodoo acupuncture clinic and maybe as many as sixteen since the doll had been stolen.

And something here was not quite right. "Maxwell, don't take this the wrong way . . . but what the hell is he waiting for?"

"Who, the thief?"

"Yeah." I chewed at my lip. "Think about it a minute. We assume he knows what he has and that he went in deliberately looking for it. So why wait to use it?"

"Establishing an alibi?" Maxwell suggested slowly.

"For murder with a *voodoo doll?*"

"Yeah, I suppose that doesn't make any sense," he admitted. "Well . . . maybe he's not planning to use it himself. Maybe he's going to send out feelers and sell the doll to the highest bidder."

"Maybe," I nodded. "On the other hand, who would believe him?"

"Holding it for ransom, then?"

"He's had sixteen hours to cut out newspaper letters and paste up a ransom note. Anything like that shown up?"

He shook his head. "I'm sure I'd have been told if it had. Okay, I'll bite: what *is* taking him so long?"

"I don't know, but whatever he's planning he's up against at least two time limits. One: the longer he holds it, the better the chance that we'll catch up with him. And two: the longer he waits, the less power the doll's going to have."

"Unless he knows about the Haitian soil connection . . . no. If he'd known he should have helped himself to some when he took the doll."

"Though he *could* have a private source of the stuff," I agreed. "It's still a fair assumption, though. Could he have expected us to have Pak standing by waiting to counteract whatever he does? He might be holding off then until Pak relaxes his guard some."

"The theft went undiscovered for at least a couple of hours," Maxwell pointed out. "He could have killed the President in his sleep. For that matter, he could have done it right there in the vault and never needed to take the doll at all."

"Point," I conceded. "So simple murder isn't what he's looking for—complicated murder, maybe, but not simple murder."

"Oh, my God," Maxwell whispered suddenly, his face going pale. "The debate. He's going to do it at the *debate*."

For a long second we stared at each other. Then, simultaneously, we grabbed our jackets and bolted for the door.

It was something like forty miles to Baltimore; an hour's trip under normal conditions. Maxwell insisted on driving and made it in a shade over forty-five minutes. In rush hour traffic, yet.

We arrived at the Hyatt and found the President's suite . . . and discovered that all our haste had been for nothing.

"What do you mean, they won't cancel?" Maxwell growled to VanderSluis, the Secret Service man who met us just inside the door.

"Who's this 'they' you're talking about?" the other growled back. "It's the *President* who won't cancel."

"Didn't you tell him—?"

"We gave him everything you radioed in," VanderSluis sighed. "Didn't do a bit of good. He says canceling at the last minute like this without a good reason would be playing right into Danzing's rhetoric."

"Has he been told . . .?"

"About the doll? Yeah, but it didn't help. Probably hurt, actually—he rightly pointed out that if someone's going to attack him using the doll, hiding won't do him a damn bit of good."

Maxwell glanced at me, frustration etched across his face. "What about Pak and Christophe?" he asked VanderSluis. "They here?"

"Sure—down the hall in seventeen."

"Down the *hall?* I thought I told them to stick by the President."

"They're as close now as they're likely to get," VanderSluis said grimly. "The President said he didn't want them underfoot while he was getting ready for the debate."

Or roughly translated, he didn't want any of the media bloodhounds nosing about to get a sniff of them and start asking awkward questions. "At least they're not back in Washington," I murmured as Maxwell opened his mouth.

Maxwell closed his mouth again, clenched his teeth momentarily. "I suppose so," he said reluctantly. "Well . . . come on, Harland, let's go talk to them. Maybe they'll have some ideas."

We found them in the room, lounging on the two double beds watching television. On the floor between the beds, the room's coffee table had been set up like a miniature surgical tray, with Pak's acupuncture needles laid out around a flower pot containing Christophe's replacement doll. It looked as hideous as the ones back in their Washington vault. "Anything?" Maxwell asked as the doctors looked up at us.

"Ah—Mr. Maxwell," Christophe said, tapping the remote to turn off the TV. "You will be pleased to hear that President Thompson is in perfect health—"

"He had some stomach trouble an hour ago." Pak put in, "but I don't think it had anything to do with the doll. Just predebate tension, probably. Anyway, I got rid of it with the new doll."

Maxwell nodded impatiently. "Yeah, well, the lull's about to end. We think that the main attack's going to come sometime during the debate."

Both men's eyes widened momentarily, and Christophe muttered something French under his breath. Pak recovered first. "Of course. Obvious, in a way. What can we do?"

"The same thing you were brought here for in the first place: counteract the effects of the old doll with the new one. Unfortunately, we're now back to our original problem."

"Communications?" I asked.

He nodded. "How are we going to know—fast—what's happening out there on the stage?"

I found myself gazing at the now-dark TV. "Dr. Pak . . . how are you at reading a man's physical condition from his expression and body language?"

"You mean can I sit here and tell how President Thompson is feeling by watching the debate on TV?" Pak shook his head. "No chance. Even if the camera was on him the whole time, which of course it won't be."

"Maybe a signal board," Maxwell suggested, a tone of excitement creeping into his voice. "With individual buttons for each likely target—joints, stomach, back, and all."

"And he does, what, pushes a button whenever he hurts somewhere?" I scoffed.

"It doesn't have to be that obvious," Maxwell said, reaching past Christophe to snare the bedside phone. "We can make it out of tiny piezo crystals—it doesn't take more than a touch to trigger those things. And they're small enough that a whole boardful of them could fit on the lectern behind his notes—Larry?" he interrupted himself into the phone. "Bill Maxwell. Listen, do we have any of those single-crystal piezo pressure gadgets we use for signaling and spot security? . . . Yeah, short range would be fine—we'd just need a booster somewhere backstage . . . Oh, great . . . Well, as many as you've got . . . Great—I'll be right down."

He tossed the phone back into it cradle and headed for the door. "We're in," he announced over his shoulder. "They've got over a hundred of the things. I'll be right back." Scooping up a room key from a low table beside the door, he left.

I looked at my watch. Five-fifteen, with the debate set to begin at nine. Not much time for the kind of wiring Maxwell was talking about. "You think it'll work?" I asked Pak.

He shrugged uncomfortably. "I suppose so. The bad part is that it means I'll be relying on diagnostics from someone who is essentially an amateur."

"It's *his* body, isn't it?"

Pak shrugged again, and for a few minutes the three of us sat together in silence. Which made it even more of a heart-stopping jolt then the phone suddenly rang.

Reflexively, I scooped it up. "Yes?"

"Who is this?" a suspicious voice asked.

"Cal Harland—Washington Police."

"Oh, yeah—you came with Maxwell. Has he gotten back with those piezos yet?"

I began to breathe again. Whatever was up, at least it wasn't a medical emergency. "No, not yet. Can I take a message?"

"Yeah," the other sighed, "but he's not going to like

it. This is VanderSluis. Tell him I called and that I just took his suggestion in to the President. And that he scotched the whole idea."

My mouth went dry all at once. "He *what?*"

"Shot it down. Said in no uncertain terms that he can't handle a debate and a damn push-button switchboard at the same time. Unquote."

"Did you remind him that it could be his *life* at stake here?" I snapped. "Or even fight dirty and suggest it could cost him the election?"

"Just give Maxwell the message, will you?" the other said coldly. "Leave the snide comments to Senator Danzing."

"Sorry," I muttered. But I was talking to a dead phone. Slowly, I replaced the handset and looked up to meet Pak's and Christophe's gazes. "What is the matter?" Christophe asked.

"Thompson's not going for it," I sighed. "Says the signal board would be too much trouble."

"But—" Pak broke off as the door opened and Maxwell strode into the room, his arms laden with boxes of equipment.

"Hell," he growled when I'd delivered VanderSluis's message. "Hell and *hell*. What's a little trouble matter when it could save his life?"

"I doubt that's his only consideration," Pak shook his head. "Politics, again, Mr. Maxwell—politics and appearances. If any of the press should notice the board, there are any number of conclusions they could come to."

"None of them good." I took a deep breath. "But damn it all, what does he want you to do?—defend him without his cooperation?"

"Probably," Maxwell said heavily. "There's a long tradition of that in the Secret Service." He took a deep breath. "Well, gentlemen, we've still got three and a half hours to come up with something. Suggestions?"

"Can you find the robber and get the doll back?" Christophe asked.

"Probably not," Maxwell shook his head. "Too many

potential suspects, not enough time to sort through all of them."

"A shame the thief didn't leave any hair at the scene of the crime," I commented, only half humorously. "If he had, we could make a doll and take him out whether we knew who he was or not."

Maxwell cocked an eye at Christophe. "Anything you can do without something from his body?"

Christophe shook his head. "Only a little bit is required, Mr. Maxwell, but that little bit is absolutely essential."

Maxwell swore and said something else to Christophe . . . but I wasn't really listening. A crazy sort of idea had just popped into my head . . . "Dr. Christophe," I said slowly, "what about the doll itself? You made the thing—presumably you know everything about its makeup and design. Would there be any way to make a—I don't know, a counteracting doll that you could use to destroy the original?"

Christophe blinked. "To tell the honest truth, I do not know. I have never heard of such a thing being done. Still . . . from what I have learned of the science of voodoo, I believe I would still need to have something of the stolen doll here to create the necessary link."

"Wait a minute, though," Pak spoke up. "It's all the same wax that you use, isn't it? That strange translucent goop that's so pressure-sensitive that it bruises if you even look at it wrong."

"It is hardly that delicate," Christophe said with an air of wounded pride. "And it is that very responsiveness that makes it so useful—"

"I know, I know," Pak interrupted him. "What I meant was, would it be possible to link up with the stolen doll since you know what it's made of?"

"I do not think so," Christophe shook his head. "Voodoo is not a shotgun, but a very precise rifle. When a link is created between doll and subject it is a *very* specific one."

"And does that link work both ways?" Maxwell asked suddenly.

There was something odd in his voice, something that made me turn to look at him. The expression on his face was even odder. "Something?" I asked.

"Maybe. Dr. Christophe?"

"Uh . . ." Christophe floundered a second as he back-tracked to the question Maxwell had asked. "Well, certainly the link works both ways. How could it be otherwise?"

For a moment Maxwell didn't say anything, but continued gazing off into space. Then, slowly, a grim smile worked itself onto his face. "Then it might work. It might just work. And the President should even go for it—yeah, I'm sure he will." Abruptly, he looked down at his watch. "Three and a quarter hours to go," he said, all business again. "We'd better get busy."

"Doing what?" Pak asked, clearly bewildered.

Maxwell told us.

The Hyatt ballroom was stuffed to the gills with people long before President Thompson and Senator Danzing came around the curtains, shook hands, and took their places at the twin lecterns. Sitting on the end of the bed, I studied Thompson's television image closely, wishing we'd been allowed to set up somewhere a little closer to the action. TV screens being what they were, it was going to be pretty hard for me to gauge how the President was feeling.

The moderator went through a short welcoming routine and then nodded to Thompson. "Mr. President, the first opening statement will be yours," he said. The camera shifted to a mid-closeup and Thompson began to speak—"

"Stomach," Maxwell said tersely from behind me.

"I see it," Pak answered in a much calmer voice. ". . . This should do it."

I kept my own eyes on the President's face. A brief flicker of almost-pain came and went. "He's looking okay now," I announced.

"Unfortunately, we can't tell if the treatment is working," Pak commented. "Only where the attack is directed—"

"Right elbow," Maxwell cut him off.

"Got it."

"Thank you, Mr. President," the moderator cut smoothly into Thompsons's speech. "Senator Danzing: your opening statement, sir."

The camera shifted to Danzing and I took a deep breath and relaxed a bit. Only for a second, though, as an angled side camera was brought into play and Thompson appeared in the foreground. "Watch it," I warned the other. "He's on camera again."

"Uh-huh," Maxwell grunted. "—stomach again."

"Got it," Pak assured him. "Whoever our thief is, he isn't very imaginative."

"Not terribly dangerous, either, at least so far," I put in. "Though I suppose we should be grateful for small favors."

"Or for small minds," Maxwell said dryly. "It's starting to look more and more like murder wasn't the original object at all."

"I do not understand," Christophe spoke up.

Maxwell snorted. "Haven't you ever heard of political dirty tricks?"

The camera was full on Danzing again, and I risked a glance around at the others hunched over the table set up between the two hotel beds. "You mean . . . all of this just to make Thompson look wracked by aches and pains on camera?"

"Why not?" Maxwell said, glancing briefly up at me. "Stupider things have been done. Effectively, I might add."

"I suppose." But probably, I added to myself, none stranger than this one. My eyes flicked to the table and to two wax figures standing up in flower pots of Haitian soil there: one with a half dozen acupuncture needles already sticking out of it, the other much larger one looking more like a pincushion than a doll.

But those weren't pins sticking into it. Rather, they

were a hundred thin wires leading *out* of it. Out, and into a board with an equal number of neatly spaced and labeled lights set into it . . . and even as I watched, one of the tiny piezo crystals Christophe had so carefully embedded into his creation reacted to the subtle change in pressure of the wax and the corresponding light blinked on—

"Right wrist," Maxwell snapped.

"Got it," Pak said. Belatedly, I turned back to my station at the TV, just in time to see the President's arm wave in one of his trademark wide-open gestures. The arm swung forward, hand cupped slightly toward the camera . . . and as it paused there my eyes focused on that hand, and despite the limitations of the screen I could almost imagine I saw the slight discolorations under his neatly manicured fingernails. Would any of the reporters in the ballroom be close enough to see that? Probably not. And even if they did, they almost certainly wouldn't recognize Christophe's oddly translucent wax for what it really was.

Or believe it if they did. Doll-to-person voodoo was ridiculous enough; running the process in reverse, person-to-doll, was even harder to swallow.

The picture shifted to Danzing. "He's off-camera again," I announced, getting my mind back on my job.

The battles raged for just over an hour—the President's and Senator's verbal battle, and our quieter, behind-the-scenes one. And when it was over, the two men on the stage shook hands and headed backstage . . . and because I knew to look for it, I noticed the slight limp to the President's walk. Hardly surprising, really—though I've never tried it, I'm sure it's very difficult to walk properly when your socks are full of Haitian dirt.

The Secret Service dropped me out of the investigation after that, so I don't know whether or not they ever actually recovered the doll. But at this point it hardly matters. The President's clearly still alive, and by now the stolen doll is almost certainly inert. I haven't seen Pak or Christophe since the debate, either, but from the excited way they were talking afterwards I'd guess that by now they've probably worked most of the bugs out of the new voodoo diagnostic technique that Maxwell came up with that night. And I suppose I have to accept that all medical advances, whether they make me uncomfortable or not, are ultimately a good thing.

And actually, the whole experience has wound up saving me a fair amount of money, too. Instead of shelling out fifteen dollars for a haircut once a month, I've learned to do the job myself, at home.

I collect and destroy my fingernail clippings, too. Not paranoid, you understand; just cautious.

Banshee

The bar was a small, roadside spot nestled almost invisibly among the mountains of south-central Wyoming. It had probably once been a tourist trap of sorts. I guessed, before newer roads had drained traffic away and left it struggling to survive on the flyspeck towns loosely grouped around it. How it was managing to do so I couldn't guess; even at four o'clock on a Tuesday afternoon a decent bar ought to have had more than three cars huddled together in its parking lot. In my mind's eye I envisioned an interior to the place as dreary as its exterior, aching with a sense of failure, and the thought of facing that nearly made me pass it up. But I hadn't eaten since breakfast and my stomach had been rumbling for the past two hours . . . and besides, perhaps my patronage would help a little. Pulling my old rust bucket into the lot, I climbed out into the hot sun and went inside.

I'd been right about the bar being largely deserted; but on the plus side, the decor was not nearly as depressing as I'd feared it would be. Old and somewhat faded, it had nevertheless been well cared for. Which, coincidentally, was how I viewed the waitress who reached my side as I settled down at my chosen table. "Afternoon," she said with a smile as she set down a water glass in front of me. "Our special today is home-barbequed chicken with . . ."

"Sounds good," I agreed, when she'd finished her description, "but I think I'll just have a medium-rare burger and a glass of beer."

"You got it," she said, smiling again as she marked it down on her pad and moved back toward the kitchen. The chicken actually *had* sounded better, but the burger was cheaper, and taking that instead would enable me to shift a little more of my limited resources into her tip. Silly, perhaps, but I'd always felt that a little sacrificial scrimping was well worthwhile when it would help brighten someone's day.

Taking a long swallow of water, I moved the glass across the table and pulled out my map. I'd need to find a motel eventually, but I wanted to get at least a little closer to where I'd be hiking before I quit for the day. If I picked up Eleven and got at least to Woods Landing . . .

"Hey! You!"

I looked up to see the barman waving the phone in my direction, an odd expression on his face. "Phone's for you," he announced.

My tongue froze against my teeth. "It . . . what?" I managed.

His expression grew a little odder. "Your name Sinn?"

My stomach tightened against its emptiness. No one knew where I was . . . which meant no one could possibly have called me. But someone had. "Yes . . . yes it is," I told him. "Adam Sinn."

"Yeah, well, guy wants to talk to you. C'mon—I don't want my phone tied up all afternoon."

I got my legs under me and walked over . . . and halfway there the only conceivable possibility clicked into place. After nearly a year . . . For a second I considered turning around, getting back into my car,

and heading for parts unknown. I would have a perfect
right to do so; neither Griff nor Banshee had the slightest legal hold over me any more.

I reached the bar and accepted the phone from the
barman. Licking my lips, I took a deep breath and held
the instrument to my ear. "Hello?"

"Adam? *God*—I was afraid we weren't going to find
you."

My jaw clenched painfully, and I knew with absolute
certainty that my year away from Banshee had abruptly
come to an end. Griffith Mansfield was the archetypical
iron-calm man, with a manner and matching voice that
were as even and steady as set concrete even at the
worst of times. In my two years with Banshee I'd never
once heard that voice as shot through with tension as it
was now, and it sent an ice-cold spike digging into my
stomach. "What's the matter?" I forced myself to ask.

"Full-fledged hell has just broken loose, that's what's
the matter," he growled, "and we're right square in the
middle of it. Where are you?"

"What do you mean, where am I? *You* called *me*,
remember?"

"Yeah, yeah, let me check the readout." The line
went blank for a moment, and the spike digging into
my stomach took an extra turn as I realized Griff really
didn't know where I was. *Checking the readout* meant
he'd been on something like the FBI's Search-Spot
system . . . and last I knew the FBI was *not* in the
habit of lending their magic phone equipment out to
hole-in-the-wall agencies like Banshee. Which meant
he hadn't been exaggerating: all hell really *had* broken
out. "Adam? Okay, I got you. Look, there's a small
private airstrip about four miles south of you, at the
west end of Lake Hattie. Go there and wait; they'll be
sending a T-61 from Warren AFB for you."

I licked my lips again without noticeable effect as my
intention of pointing out to him that I was no longer
under his jurisdiction died a quiet death. First the
FBI's phone search machine, now an Air Force general's commuter jet casually laid on to carry a civilian

cross country. Whatever was happening, it was becoming less and less likely that anyone was going to let my personal preferences get in the way. "Griff . . . can you at least give me a hint of what's happening? Has something happened to the rest of the Jumpers?"

"No, no, everyone's fine. As to the rest of it, you'll get everything we know on the plane—if you don't find out sooner. I understand they're going to release it to the media in a few minutes."

"Griff—"

"Look, Adam, trust me; I wouldn't be asking you to come back if it wasn't vitally important. I'll see you soon." There was a click and he was gone.

"Damn," I said softly to the dead line. Laying the phone back on the counter, I looked up to find both the barman and the waitress staring at me with what seemed to be a combination of awe and suspicion . . . and in the waitress's eyes, at least, I could see the dawning realization that she was about to lose possibly her only customer of the afternoon.

That, at least, I could do something about. Digging out my wallet, I found a twenty and handed it to her. "Keep the change," I told her. At least now I could give without having to take quite so much thought for the morrow: whatever Banshee's other financial difficulties, Griff had always insisted on good salaries for his Jumpers . . . and it looked very much like I was about to become a Jumper again.

I reached the airstrip in ten minutes, and was sitting in my car listening to the radio when the news broke.

Somewhere over western Colorado, Air Force One had just crashed. With the President of the United States aboard.

The T-61's pilot didn't have much more for me than I'd already heard on the radio, mainly because there wasn't much more that anyone knew at this stage. Air Force One had been on its way to Washington from President Jeffers's Sierra retreat when the pilot suddenly announced he'd lost the right inboard engine.

Seconds later the radio went silent altogether, and the jets that were scrambled for an overflight reported wreckage strewn across a large swath of smoking cliffside forest. There had been no confirmation of casualties or survivors as yet, but from the sound of things there wasn't much call for optimism. Little to do now but clean up the wreckage, both physical and psychological . . . and to find out, for the record, what had gone wrong.

The latter would be Banshee's job.

We arrived about an hour and a half after leaving Wyoming. A police car was waiting at the end of the runway for me, a lukewarm box of take-out chicken in the back seat reminding me that I'd never gotten the early dinner I'd planned. Indirect evidence of two things: that Griff was getting his balance back, and that sometime this evening I was indeed going to have to Jump. Two of Banshee's Jumpers did best on empty stomachs, but I wasn't one of them. The thought of what was coming tightened the knot in my stomach; but the hunger down there far outclassed the nervousness, and by the time we pulled up at the familiar nondescript building fifteen minutes later I'd worked my way through all three pieces of chicken and was polishing off the last of the biscuit.

Griff was waiting for me at the front door. "Adam," he nodded, gripping my hand briefly as he pushed the door open. "Thanks for coming. I really appreciate it."

"No trouble," I told him, not entirely truthfully. We stepped out of the entryway airlock . . . and I found myself face to face with a dress-uniformed Marine.

"He's one of our people," Griff told the Marine before I could get my tongue unstuck. The guard nodded incuriously; but even as we passed him I could feel his eyes giving me an unobtrusive but thorough once-over. I'd seen that kind of apparent unconcern once or twice before, always from truly professional guards who used it as a way to throw people off-guard.

Professional guards at Banshee. "The place has changed," I murmured.

"The Marines are just on loan," he shook his head. "Courtesy of a Washington VIP named Shaeffer. He's in the lounge updating things for Hale and Kristin."

"What about Morgan? Or has he quit?"

"No, he's still with us. He's downstairs getting prepped."

I blinked. "You've got a Jump going already?"

"We will as soon as the model of Air Force One is ready. Shaeffer insisted on particularly fine detailing, and the modelers just finished it a few minutes ago."

"Actually, I was surprised more by the speed than the delay," I told him.

Griff snorted. "Yes, well, for a change, the budget overseers aren't going to be a problem. It's amazing," he added with a trace of bitterness, "the kind of money people are willing to throw around when someone important gets killed."

I nodded silently.

We reached the lounge and went in. The Washington VIP was there, all right, easily distinguishable by his expensive business suit and taut look. He was standing over the lounge table talking across a map to Hale Fortner and Kristin Cosgrove and—

I stopped just through the doorway, so abruptly that Griff stepped on my heel. "*Rennie?*" I hissed.

Griff squeezed past me into the room. "We needed everyone we could get, Adam—"

"How on Earth did you get him to come back?" I whispered. The painful scene that had taken place when Rennie Baylor was fired from Banshee flooded back from my memory.

"Look, this is no time to dredge up past disagreements," Griff hissed back. "Not for me, not for any of us—and if I can stand him for three days, so can you. Okay?"

I took a deep breath and got my feet moving again. True, it was Griff, not me, with whom Rennie had had most of his friction . . . but that didn't mean the rest of us hadn't suffered with him from the sidelines. Still, for three days—and under such circumstances—I would do my best to make do.

"—came down about here, among a real mess of hidden ravines and tricky cliff faces," the VIP was saying as we came up to the table. He looked up, eyes flicking past Griff to lock briefly onto me. "Mr. Sinn," he nodded in greeting. "Shaeffer—special aide to President Jef—" He broke off, his mouth compressing in brief pain before he could recover himself. "Have you been briefed?"

"Just the basics," I told him, his tight expression inducing another flicker of pain within me. Shaeffer, clearly, had been very close to the President. "Air Force One lost its right wing—somehow—and went down out in Colorado."

He nodded. "That's about all we've got at the moment. The search-and-rescue team hasn't been working for very long; so far they haven't got anything."

"No survivors, in other words," Kristin interjected quietly.

Shaeffer's lip tightened. "Yeah." He took a deep breath. "Well. Banshee's job will be to find out what happened to the plane. As I've already explained to Dr. Mansfield, you've got essentially a blank check—go ahead and do as many Jumps as it takes to get the job done right. Understood? Dr. Mansfield, how much longer will it be before you can get someone back there?"

Right on cue, the lounge's lights flickered. "Immediately, Mr. Shaeffer," Griff answered. "I'm afraid it's not much of a show, but if you'd like we could head downstairs and you could see Banshee in action."

"I'm not here to play tourist," Shaeffer bit out. "I'll be in the communications center if you need me; let me know as soon as the Jump is over."

Griff reddened slightly. "Yes, of course." He turned and quickly left the lounge, heading left toward the elevator. Shaeffer nodded to each of us in turn and followed, branching to the right toward the room where our modest radio, wire, and computer-net equipment were kept.

And I was left alone with the other Jumpers.

For a moment we all just looked at each other. Then Kristin stirred. "You haven't kept in touch very well, Adam."

I shrugged fractionally. "I've been pretty busy," I told her. It was more or less true.

"So have we," Hale said, more than a little tartly. "Work load's increased considerably since you cut out on us."

My eyes flicked to Rennie. "Don't look at me," he said blandly. "*I* was fired; *you're* the one who deserted."

"That's putting it a little strongly, isn't it?" I asked . . . but the indignation I'd intended to put into the words died somewhere en route. I hadn't been able to tell them the reasons then, and down deep I knew I couldn't tell them now, either.

"Yeah, Rennie, desertion's much too harsh a word," Hale chimed in. "It's not strickly desertion when the captain advises you to get off a sinking ship."

"What's *that* supposed to mean?" I asked him.

"I think you know," he ground out. "You've always been Griff's favorite Jumper—that's common knowledge. I think he warned you that we were about to be snowed under by a huge work load and suggested you take off and leave the rest of us more expendable Jumpers to struggle under the pile."

"That's not true," I said, trying hard to keep my voice steady.

Hale snorted. "Of course not. It was just pure coincidence. Sure."

Clenching my jaw, I leaned over the table for a look at the map Shaeffer had left behind. It was an impressive job, larger scale even than the standard 7.5-minute topographic ones I used for backpacking. The crash site was marked by a large red oval near one end, and my recently filled stomach did a couple of turns at the thought of having to go back and watch it happen. "Did

Shaeffer say anything about surveying the crash sight, or just watching for the primary cause?" I asked.

"That's the way," Rennie said with mock approval. "When you can't win, change the subject."

I focused on Kristin. "Did he say anything about surveying the crash site?" I repeated.

"Not to us," she said. "But, then, we're just the Jumpers. We don't count for anything in that sort of decision-making."

"If you're wondering specifically about body trackings," Hale put in, "I'm sure you'll get a shot at one. They've become almost standard for us these days."

I shivered. Watching people die in mid-air explosions was bad enough . . . but to follow the bodies down as they fell to earth, seeing up close the burned and battered shells that had once been human beings . . .

"Unless, of course," Rennie suggested, "you want to talk to Griff about exempting you from anything particularly unpleasant."

I gritted my teeth. "I'll do my share of whatever comes up. See you later." Turning my back on them, I headed out of the lounge.

For a long moment I stood leaning against the hallway wall, slowly bringing my trembling knees under control again. I hadn't really expected to be welcomed back with open arms, but the sheer intensity of the others' hostility had hit me like ice water in the face. Clearly, Griff had kept his promise not to tell them why I'd left Banshee; whether or not I could survive three days under that kind of pressure wasn't nearly as clear.

But I would, of course. For whatever reason, Banshee needed me here . . . and I'd always been there when people needed me.

Taking a deep breath, I turned left and headed for the elevator.

The Banshee building's basement always reminded me of a cartoon I'd seen a long time ago in which one of the characters had bragged that "the house itself isn't much, but you should see the rec room." A one-time basement and subbasement had had their walls and the dividing floor knocked out to create a single vast space, with nothing to break it up but strategically placed pillers put in to support the rest of the building above it. The result was a room the size of a small warehouse . . . a room the Banshee equipment still filled to over-flowing.

A small sign on the cabinet nearest the elevator proclaimed all this stuff to be the property of the U.S. Government Time Observation Group, Banshee's official name. Official or not, though, I'd never heard anyone refer to us by that name, even in official correspondence. Probably, I'd always suspected, because no one up there really took us seriously. With a staff numbering in the low twenties and an operating budget under four million a year, we were hardly a drop in the bucket as far as Washington was concerned. Not to mention the fact that the whole thing was generally considered either ghoulish or a waste of money by most of the handful of officials who knew anything about it.

I don't know who coined the name Banshee for the group. I know only too well why it had stuck.

There was absolutely nothing theatrical about a typical Banshee Jump, a fact that had disappointed more than one official visitor over the years. There were no revolving lights warning of high-voltage, no large and blinking status boards, no armies of steely-eyed techs huddled over displays under dark-room-red lighting. The lights were normal, our three operators had a tendency to slouch in their seats; and even the Jumper, Morgan Portland, might simply have been asleep on his contour couch amid the handful of sensor leads sprouting from his arm- and headbands. It would have taken a close look at the EEG display—and some knowledge of how to interpret the readings—to realize that Morgan was essentially registering as dead.

All of us Jumpers had long since come to the conclusion that no one really knew how the Banshee apparatus worked.

Oh, all the parts were understood, to one degree or

another—that much was certain. The mathematicians could show you all the equations and formulas and tell you how they implied time reversal; the various scientists could show you how the equations related to the real universe, both in physical equipment and in brain and mind structure; and the engineers could show you how all this boiled down to several million dollars' worth of apparatus. There were even those who claimed to understand how a person's consciousness could be decoupled from his body for up to an hour at a time without any major ill effects. But when you put all of it together, no one *really* knew how or why the whole thing worked the way it did. No one knew why there was a seventy-two-hour limit on how far back in time a Jumper's consciousness could go, no one knew why only certain very specific types of people could Jump in the first place . . . and no one knew how it was our disembodied consciousnesses could sometimes be seen by those about to die.

It had first happened to me on my seventh Jump, and it would forever color all my thoughts about Banshee. A little girl, maybe seven years old, had spotted me as I floated by an airport locker in hopes of seeing the person who had planted a bomb there. At least I assume she saw me; the expression on her face could hardly have been explained by anything else in the immediate vicinity. Her mother had pulled her away a moment later and plopped them both down in a waiting lounge, but she'd continued to glance nervously back in my direction. Two minutes later the bomb had blown out the bank of lockers and most of the roof overhead.

The girl and her mother had been among the casualties.

I shuddered with the memory and forced her face from my mind . . . and cursed once more the unfeeling idiot who'd taken his inspiration from that and similar incidents to hang the name *Banshee* on us.

A motion off to the side by one of the RF generator cabinets caught my eye; Griff, doing a walkthrough of the equipment. He saw me as I started toward him and changed course to meet me. "So . . . how did it go up there with the others?" he murmured.

"Not exactly your TV-style homecoming," I retorted softly. There was no reason for anyone to whisper while a Jump was in progress, but people invariably did so anyway. "I wish you'd told me Rennie was going to be here. And maybe prepared me a little for the sour apples from everyone else."

He sighed. "I'm sorry, Adam; really I am. If it'd been up to me, you wouldn't be here at all—that despite the fact you're still the best Jumper we ever had. But Schaeffer insisted we bring both you and Rennie back."

"Did you point out to him that three Jumpers are perfectly adequate to handle the half-dozen or so Jumps it'll take to figure out what happened?"

"I tried, but he wouldn't budge." Griff scratched his ear thoughtfully. "What makes it even stranger is that he seemed to know an awful lot about us—must've actually been keeping up with the reports we've filed into the bureaucratic black hole back in Washington."

"Very flattering. Doesn't explain why he's out here being underfoot instead of directing things from the White House, though."

"No, it doesn't," Griff agreed. "Maybe he thinks he can help. Or else needs to at least *feel* like he's helping."

"If he wants to help, he'd do better to be in Washington helping brief Vice President McCallum on his new office."

Griff shrugged fractionally. "From what I've read, Shaeffer and Jeffers go back a long way together, since Jeffers's first stint as mayor in Phoenix. There are other people available to brief McCallum; I get the feeling Shaeffer's more out for vengeance."

I shivered. "In other words, we'd better get him the cause of the crash in double-quick time, or else?"

"We can hope he's more sensible than that. But there's a strong tendency in people to look for scapegoats when things go wrong."

I thought back to the other Jumpers upstairs. "Yeah.

Well . . . we'll just have to see to it that we do our job fast and get out from in front of the gunsights."

My last word was punctuated by the *snap* of circuit breakers shunting the end-point power surge to ground. Across the room, Morgan's body threw itself suddenly against the couch's restraints. A moment later his eyes opened a crack and he burped loudly.

We were at his side by the time the operators had the straps off. "What'd you get?" Griff asked, helping him up into a sitting position.

"It was the right inboard engine, aw right," Morgan nodded tiredly, massaging the sides of his neck. "Smoke trail out o' it just 'fore it caught fire and blew to shreds."

"Did you get inside the wing and see where the fire started?" Griff asked.

"Sorry—didn't have time. I was too busy backtrackin' the line o' smoke." His eyes met mine and I braced myself for a repeat of the confrontation upstairs. But he merely nodded in greeting and shifted his attention back to Griff. "I've seen a lot o' engine-fire plumes, Griff—this'un didn't look right at all."

Griff swore under his breath. "Shaeffer thought it might be something like this. Okay; come on upstairs and we'll take a look at the blueprints."

Morgan nodded and swung his feet over the side of the couch. "Dr. Mansfield," one of the operators called, "you want us to get ready to cycle again right away?"

"Yes," Griff answered, taking Morgan's arm. "Hale will be down immediately for prepping. We'll be Jumping again as soon as you and he are ready."

"Why the break-neck rush?" I asked Griff as he helped Morgan navigate away from the couch. "It's—what, after six already?"

"Shaeffer's in a hurry," Griff said tightly. "For now, that's all the reason any of us need. Give me a hand, here, will you?"

Morgan's report was strong evidence; but it took two more hours and a Jump by Hale before Shaeffer was willing to come to the official conclusion all of us had guessed at.

President Jeffers's plane had been sabotaged.

"Something in the engine or fuel line," Shaeffer growled, tapping his clenched fist on the blueprints of the VC-25A's right wing. "Something that could start a fire despite the flame retardants in the fuel."

"Implies a pretty drastic breach of security," Rennie murmured.

Shaeffer threw him a hard look but kept his temper in check. "I would think so, yes. Finding out just how the bomb was introduced should show where and how big that hole is. Dr. Mansfield, I want another Jump tonight. How soon before the equipment can be ready?"

"Half an hour at the least," Griff told him, glancing at his watch. "But I'd like to point out that it's already coming up on eight o'clock and the Jumpers will need both a good night's sleep and some wind-down time before that."

"They'll get all the rest they need," Shaeffer said shortly. "Allow *me* to point out that you've still got three Jumpers you haven't even used yet."

I looked over at Kristen, saw her mouth twist sourly. Being treated like merchandise or pack animals had always been especially annoying to her. She caught me watching her, looked quickly away.

"Well . . . I suppose we could go ahead," Griff said slowly, looking around the table at the rest of us. "Late-night Jumps can be rougher than usual, though—biological rhythms and all, you understand—"

"We're up against a time crunch here, Doctor," Shaeffer snapped. "How many times am I going to have to repeat that?"

"Yes, but we've *got* three da—"

"I'm not talking about the damn three-day limit—" Shaeffer broke off abruptly, and for a second a strange look flicked across his face. "We're dealing with the media here, Doctor," he continued in a more controlled tone. "The American people want some answers, and I intend to get those answers for them. So. Who's next?"

Griff grimaced and turned to Kristin; moving my head, I managed to catch his eye. "I can take it, Griff," I said. "Evening Jumps never bothered me much." It wasn't quite true, but it was close enough.

Griff's lip twitched, but he nodded. "Yes . . . all right, fine. If that's all, then, Mr. Shaeffer . . . ?"

Shaeffer nodded, and the group began to break up. I got out fast and headed toward the elevator; but even so, Morgan managed to catch up with me before I reached it. "Left my jacket downstairs after my Jump," he commented. "Mind if I tag along down with you?"

"No, of course not," I said as he fell into step beside me. "How bad is it?"

"The crash?" He shrugged, a nervous twitch of shoulders beneath his shirt. "Not too bad, leastwise not as long as you're up in the air. Not goin' be much fun at ground level."

"They never are."

"No."

We'd reached the elevator before he spoke again. "So . . . how you been doin'? We ain't heard much from you since you left."

"Judging by my reception earlier, it's just as well," I told him, hearing an unaccustomed trace of bitterness in my voice.

He nodded heavily. "I talked to Kristin after my Jump. You know, she was kinda hurt the way you just upped and left."

"I didn't just 'up and leave'—"

"You know what I mean. Woulda helped, you know, if you'd told us why you were quittin'."

I looked at him sharply. Had he figured it out? "I had my reasons," I said.

"I reckon you did. But Kristin and Hale don't take a lot on faith. S'pose it's a little late to worry 'bout now. So what do you think of this mess?"

"What's there to think about it?" I replied grimly.

The elevator arrived and we got in. "Like you say, it's a mess."

"What 'bout Shaeffer?"

"What about him?"

"Strikes me as a mite . . . over-wrought, I s'pose."

I snorted. "He *has* just lost both his employer and a long time friend. How would you *expect* him to act?"

"I'd expect him to be mad as a hornet," Morgan nodded. "Nothin' wrong with that. But there's somethin' under the anger that bothers me. I get a feelin' he's hidin' somethin' big up his sleeve. Somethin' he wants to do, but at the same time is scared of doin'."

I bit at my lip. Morgan had grown up in a backwoods area of Arkansas, and people tended to assume he wasn't particularly bright. But what he lacked in book learning he more than made up in people-sense . . . and if he thought there was something odd about Shaeffer, it was time for me to start paying better attention to the man. "Maybe he's involved in the discussions of revenge against whoever's responsible," I suggested slowly. "McCallum's never struck me as the sort to call in military strikes—maybe it's Shaeffer's job to convince him otherwise."

"Maybe." Morgan shook his head. "Well, whatever it is, I 'spect we'll hear 'bout it soon enough."

The elevator door opened and we stepped out. "See you later," Morgan said as he scooped up his jacket from a chair near the contour couch. "Good luck."

"Thanks." Squaring my shoulders, I headed over to be prepped.

Twenty minutes later, wired and tubed and mildly sedated, I was lying on the contour couch and we were ready for my Jump. "Okay," one of the operators called. "Here we go. Countdown: six . . . three, two, one, *mark.*"

And abruptly I found myself in brilliant sunlight, floating beside Air Force One as it soared over the mountains on its unknowing way to death.

To see the past like this had been a horrible shock to me the first time, and though its impact had diminished since then I didn't think it would ever fade away completely. There was an *immediacy* to the experience; a sense of objective, 360-degree reality, despite the obvious limitations, that was nothing at all like viewing the event on a TV screen. For me, at least—and probably for most of the others, too—that sense came with a suffocating feeling of helplessness and stomach-churning frustration. I was here—really *here*—at the actual real-life scene of a real-life disaster about to happen . . . and there was nothing I could do to prevent it.

Griff had once brought in a psychiatrist who'd tried to tell us that everyone felt similarly when they saw disasters that happened to have been caught on film. If that revelation was supposed to make us feel better, it hadn't worked.

But all this was standard reflex, the thoughts and emotions that had come in one form or another with every Jump I'd made, and even as the frustration rose in my throat, the old professional reflexes came up to cut it back. Gritting my teeth—a sensation I could feel despite having no real body at the moment—I moved forward over the wing and dipped beneath its surface.

It was dark inside the wing, but there was enough light coming in from somewhere for me to make out the details of the fuel tanks and piping and all. It was eerily quiet, of course—vision on Jumps is as crystal clear as if we'd brought our physical retinas back in time with us, but there's no sound or other sensory input whatsoever. Like being wrapped in soundproof plastic, Kristin had once described it. For me it was just one more macabre touch amid the general unpleasantness.

I floated around inside the wing for several minutes, keeping a close watch for anything that might precede the explosion about to take place. From the settings the operators had made I knew I'd have fifteen minutes before the engine caught fire, but time sense distortion was a normal part of Jumping and I didn't want to be caught unawares. I'd been tethered to the right inboard engine pylon, the tether length adjusted to let me get nearly out to the outboard engine in one direction or to the fuselage in the other. The tether was even more of a witchgadget than most of the Banshee equipment as a whole, consisting mainly of a charged electrical lead attached to a specific spot on a scale model of whatever your target vehicle or building was. With a tether in place a Jumper would stick with that piece of metal or wood or plasterboard through hell and high water; without it, there was no way to hold your position even in a stationary building.

The experts could just barely explain the mechanism. The rest of us didn't bother trying.

I was just starting to drift toward the engine itself when the Ping-Pong ball caught my eye.

I'd poked around planes like this one a lot during my time with Banshee and in some ways knew more about them than their designers did; and I was pretty sure there weren't supposed to be Ping-Pong balls floating around inside the fuel lines. Maneuvering around in front of it, I leaned in for a closer look . . . and it was then that I saw that the ball wasn't alone. A dozen more were coming down the line toward the right inboard engine, and a quick check showed that two or three more were already clustered up against the engine intake itself.

There had been a lot of times I'd wished I could touch something on a Jump, and this was one of them. But there was still a lot I could learn with vision alone. The balls were coated with something waxy looking—a gasoline-soluble paraffin, most likely. They were smaller than regulation Ping-Pong balls, too, small enough to have been dropped into the plane's fuel intake or perhaps even hosed in through the nozzle along with the fuel.

I settled down near the engine, watching the balls clustered there, and waited for the clock to tick down . . . and suddenly the balls began spouting clouds of bubbles. I had just enough time to notice that flickers

of flame were starting to dance at the balls' surfaces
when the whole thing blew up in front of me.

For a second I lost control, and an instant later had
snapped back behind the wing to the full length of my
tether. The trail of smoke Morgan and Hale had mentioned was coming out of the engine. In a handful of
seconds the engine would explode and everyone aboard
would die . . . and if I ended the Jump right now, I
wouldn't have to watch it happen.

I stayed anyway. White House cartes blanches or
not, someone was shelling out a quarter of a million
dollars for this trip. They might as well get their money's worth.

Morgan had been right; it wasn't nearly as bad as
some I'd seen. The right inboard engine caught fire and
blew up on schedule, sending pieces of itself through
the air toward me. I ducked in unnecessary reflex and
watched as the rest of the wing caught fire, blazing
more fiercely than it had any right to. The plane tilted
violently, but for the moment the wing and the pylon I
was tethered to were still attached and I stayed with it.
Then the wing just seemed to disintegrate . . . and as I
fell behind the plane with the tumbling debris I watched
it arc almost lazily down toward the tree-covered slope
ahead.

And coming to Earth far behind the crash site, there
was no longer any reason for me to stay. I let go of the
past, wishing as always that I could just as easily release
the trauma of what I'd just seen; and a disoriented
moment later, I was back on the couch.

The operators unstrapped me and began removing
the tubes and wires. . . . and as my eyes and brain
refocused I became aware of Kristin's face hovering
over me. "Kristin," I croaked, trying to get moisture
back into my mouth. My eyes were just the opposite:
they were streaming freely. I turned my head to the
side, feeling an obscure embarrassment at her seeing
me like this.

If Kristin noticed, she gave no sign of it. "Griff sent

me to get you," she said. "He wants all of us in his office right away."

I blinked away the tears; and even as I struggled to sit up I noticed the tightness about her eyes. Still mad at me, I decided . . . until I realized her eyes were focused off in space somewhere. "Is anything wrong?"

She licked her lips briefly. "I don't know, but *something* sure as blazes is happening. Griff and Shaeffer have been closeted up there since you left for your Jump . . . and Griff wasn't sounding too good when he told me to come get you."

I swallowed, hard, and concentrated on getting my blood up to speed again. With Kristin supporting me, we were upstairs in Griff's office five minutes later.

She was right: the whole gang was there . . . and one look at Griff's and Shaeffer's stony faces set my stomach churning. Something had indeed happened . . . I looked at Griff, but it was Shaeffer who spoke. "Your report, Mr. Sinn?" His voice matched his expression.

I gave it to him without elaboration, describing as best I could the Ping-Pong balls in the fuel line and the way they'd behaved. Shaeffer listened like a man who already had the answers and was merely looking for some confirmation, and when I'd finished he nodded. "The searchers on the scene already came to pretty much the same conclusion," he said grimly. "Catalyst bombs, sounds like—gadgets that get the fuel and the degraded fragments of flame retardant to react together."

"Never heard of them," Rennie said.

"They're not exactly on-shelf technology. We've developed a type or two, and there are maybe two or three other countries doing similar work. That could be a blunder on the saboteur's part—exotic equipment makes any trail easier to trace. All right, Mr. Sinn, thank you." He took a deep breath, looked around at each of us in turn . . . and his expression seemed to get a little stonier. "And here now is where we get to the sticky part. I imagine you've been wondering why I came to Banshee in person instead of directing your investigation from Washington. It's because I want you to do something I don't believe you've ever tried before. Something—I'll say this up front—that could turn out to be dangerous." He paused, and the tip of his tongue swiped at his upper lip. "I've read everything President Jeffers ever received on Banshee, and he and I both noted with a great deal of interest that you've been . . . seen . . . on more than one occasion by the people you've been observing."

Kristin shifted in her seat . . . and a horrible suspicion began to drift like a storm cloud across my mind.

"Now, tell me," Shaeffer continued, sweeping his gaze across us Jumpers, "did any of you, during your Jumps the past few hours, ever get a look inside Air Force One itself?"

Hale, Morgan, and I exchanged glances, shook our heads. "That why Griff set the tethers so short?" Morgan asked. "So we couldn't get inside?"

A flicker of surprise crossed the rock that was Shaeffer's expression. "I hadn't expected you to notice," he said. "Yes, that's precisely why I had Dr. Mansfield set them that way. You see . . . as of yet, the searchers at the crash site have located only a few of the bodies from the wreckage. It occurred to me early on that due to an unusual set of circumstances back at the President's retreat no outsiders actually saw him get onto that plane. And now you've told me that none of you have seen him there, either.

"Which means . . . perhaps he never was aboard to begin with."

A brittle silence settled, vise-like, around the table. "Are you suggestin'," Morgan said at last, "that you want us to go back there and change the past?"

His sentence ended on a whispered hiss. I looked back at Shaeffer, and to me it was abundantly clear that he knew exactly what it was he was suggesting . . . and that he was just as scared about it as the rest of us were.

But it was equally clear he was also determined not to let those fears stand in his way. "There's nothing of changing the past about it," he said firmly. "We don't know—none of us do—exactly what happened on that flight. If we don't *know* what the past is, how can we be changing it?"

" 'If a tree falls alone in the forest, is there any sound?' " Hale put in icily. "Do you have any *idea* what will happen if we meddle like this?"

"No—and neither do you," Shaeffer replied. "Face it, people, no one knows what changing even a *known* fact of history would mean. A *known* fact, notice, which is *not* what we're talking about doing here."

"Oh, aren't we?" Hale retorted. "All right, fine—let's assume for the moment that somehow we keep President Jeffers out of Air Force One. It's been over six hours now since the crash. Are you going to try and tell us that he and his whole Secret Service detachment have been sitting around listening to the news and *no one's* bothered to pick up a phone to let the world know he's still alive? Come *on*, now, let's be serious. We keep Jeffers out of the plane and we've changed history—pure and simple."

"Maybe not," Shaeffer said stubbornly. "It's possible he could be lying low while the crash is being checked out. Especially if sabotage is a possibility, he might want to give the perpetrators a false sense of security. You might recall that for days after the Libyan raid back in 1986 Quaddafi disappeared—"

Hale snorted. "Jeffers wouldn't duck and hide, and you know it. That shoot-from-the-hip style of his was practically his trademark."

"Maybe lying low wasn't his idea," Shaeffer snapped. "Maybe someone persuaded him to do so."

I felt my hands start to tremble. "Shaeffer . . . are you saying *you've* been in touch with him?"

Kristin caught her breath and murmured something inaudible. But Shaeffer shook his head. "No, of course not. Do you think I want to risk frogging up your chances by contacting someone out there?"

"But if you call and find that he's there—" Rennie began.

"And if he *isn't*, then that's it," Shaeffer snapped back. "Right?" He glared around at all of us.

Morgan cleared his throat. "Mr. Shaeffer, we all of us understand how you feel 'bout . . . what's happened to President Jeffers. But denyin' the facts isn't gonna—"

"What 'facts,' Mr. Portland?" Shaeffer cut him off. "We have no *facts* at this point—just speculations and possibilities."

I looked at Griff, who had yet to say a word. "Griff . . . ?"

"Yes, Griff, say something, will you?" Hale cut in. "Explain things to this idiot. Or has the wow-value of the big-city bureaucrat short-circuited your ability to think straight?"

Griff cocked an eyebrow, but that was the extent of his reaction to Hale's harshness. "If you're asking whether or not I'm going along with Mr. Shaeffer's idea, the answer is a qualified and cautious yes. We're talking about the chance to save a man's *life* here."

"Oh, for God's sake," Hale snarled, his eyes flicking around the table once before returning to Griff. "Will you for one minute look past the lure of a real budget and *think* about what we're being asked to do here? We're being asked to *change the past*—Shaeffer's weaseling phrases be damned, that's what's really at stake here. Don't you *care* what that might mean?"

For a moment Griff gazed steadily back at him. "Certainly, Hale, you have a point," he said at last. "Certainly this could prove dangerous. But have any of you stopped to consider the other side of the coin? If there's a single factor that consistently shows up on your psych evaluations, it's the frustrations Banshee creates in you— the stress of seeing disasters you can't do anything to prevent. Denials: anyone?"

I glanced around the table even as I realized that, for me, all further arguments were moot. The chance to save a life that would otherwise be lost—a life whose loss was filling an entire nation with grief and pain— was all the motivation I needed.

Besides which, Griff happened to be right. All of us hated the helplessness we felt during Jumps; hated it with a passion. If we really *could* do something about the disasters we had to witness . . .

"So," Griff continued after a moment. "Then consider what we've got here: a chance to see whether or not the past *can* be safely changed. Doesn't that seem like something worth taking a little risk to find out?"

"And if it leads to disaster?" Hale demanded. "What then? It doesn't matter a damn how pure or noble our motives were if we screw things up royally. I say we just forget the whole idea and—"

"Mr. Fortness, you're relieved of duty," Shaeffer said quietly.

The words came so suddenly and with such conviction behind them that it took a moment for me to register the fact that the man giving the order had no authority to do so. An instant later everyone else seemed to catch on to that fact, too, and the awkward silence suddenly went rigid. "Someone die and leave you boss?" Hale growled scornfully.

"That's enough, Hale," Griff said quietly. "Go back to your room."

From the looks on the other's faces it appeared they were as flabbergasted as Hale was. "Griff—you don't mean—" Kristin began.

Griff looked at her, and she fell silent. The awkward silence resumed as Hale got up from the table, face set in stone, and left the room. I half expected him to slam the door on his way out, but he apparently was still too stunned by it all to be thinking in terms of theatrics. Griff let the silence hang in the air another couple of seconds before looking back at Kristin. "I believe, Kristin," he said, "that the next Jump is yours. I know it's getting late, but I'd appreciate it if you'd try anyway. If you feel up to it, that is."

A muscle twitched in Kristin's cheek as she threw a glance at Shaeffer's tight face and stood up. "I'll try, Griff. Sure. Shall I go downstairs and start getting prepped?"

"Please. I'll be there shortly to set the tether and slot coordinates and see you off."

She nodded and left the room. Shaeffer watched her go, then turned back to lock Morgan, Rennie, and me into a searchlight gaze. "I realize that in a tight-knit organization like Banshee strangers like me are not especially welcome," he said, his soft voice underlaid with steel. "But at the moment I don't give a nickel damn about your feelings. We have less than sixty-six hours to get President Jeffers off that plane and into temporary hiding; and the longer it takes us, the greater the danger of exactly the sort of thing happening that you've all voiced concerns about." He paused, as if waiting to see if any of us would follow Hale's lead. But we said nothing, and after a moment Shaeffer turned to Griff. "All right, Dr. Mansfield. Let's get started."

"Now remember," Shaeffer said, leaning close to Kristin as if she were asleep or deaf or both. "You go right up in front of the President's face and hover there where he can see you—*don't* get out of his sight. If he doesn't seem to see you, or else ignores you, come back and we'll try again. Under *no* circumstances are you to stay long enough to see him climb up the steps to the plane. Understand?"

I half expected Kristin to remind him that this was the third replay of these same instructions and that she'd caught them all the first time around. But she merely nodded and closed her eyes. Griff gave the high sign, and with the usual flickering of lights she was gone.

Taking a deep breath, I moved away from Griff and Shaeffer, lingering by the two-foot model of Air Force One and the tiny model limo that now sat on the table beside it. The tether lead's alligator clip was attached to the limo; Shaeffer was pushing this contact as far back as he reasonably could, all the way back to the President's drive to the landing field. Passing the models, I kept going, heading for the rows of equipment cabinets at the building's west end. My father had always gone for a walk in the woods when he needed to think through a particularly knotty problem, and during my two years at Banshee I'd discovered that the maze of gray cabinets back here was an adequate substitute.

I hoped the magic still worked.

Upstairs, half an hour ago, I'd made my decision . . . but with Shaeffer's pep talk beginning to fade, things no longer looked nearly so clear cut. The greatest good for the greatest number, and attention paid whenever possible to the individual; those were the rules I'd been taught as a child, the standards against which I'd always measured my actions. But to make such judgments required information and wisdom . . . and I could find nothing in past experience that seemed to apply to this case.

How was I supposed to weigh the pain and suffering that could be caused by changing the past?

"Hello, Adam."

I jerked out of my reverie and spun around. Rennie stood there, leaning against one of the computer cabinets, arms crossed negligently across his chest. Blocking my way out.

I made a conscious effort to unclench my teeth. "Rennie," I said with a curt nod. "You taken to wandering the Banshee room, too?"

"Hardly," he sniffed. "I just noticed you head back here and thought I'd see what Banshee's own little White Knight was up to."

I felt my teeth clamp together again. I'd hoped a year might have changed Rennie at least a little, but it was becoming clear that it hadn't. "Just looking for a little peace and quiet," I told him shortly. "If you'll excuse me—"

"Must be a great thrill for you," he continued, as if I hadn't spoken. "A chance to save a real person from real death—why, I'll bet you're so happy about it you haven't even bothered to consider that you might skewer a few billion innocent people on your lance in the process."

"If you're talking about Hale's rantings, yes, I'm aware of the risks involved. You can also drop that 'White Knight' business any time."

He radiated innocence. *"You're* the one who tagged yourself with that title—or had you forgotten? The White Knight: defender of the lame, guardian of the helpless, picker-up of those fallen flat on their faces—"

"Do you have something to say?" I interrupted. "If not, you're invited to step aside."

"As a matter of fact, I do." Abruptly, all the mockery vanished from his face, and his expression became serious. Though with Rennie, I reminded myself, expressions didn't necessarily mean anything. "I wanted to see if you were as taken in by this whole pack of manure as you'd looked upstairs."

"If you're referring to Shaeffer's plan," I said stiffly, "I think it's worth trying, yes. At least as long as he continues to go about it in a rational manner."

Rennie snorted. "You mean that frog spit about not letting Kristin see if Jeffers actually gets on the plane because if she does that'll make that a 'known' fact? Word games; that's all it is. We know Jeffers got on that plane, Adam—whether we actually saw it or not, we *know* he got on it. Anybody who tells you otherwise is either kidding himself or lying through his teeth."

"Keep that sort of thing up and you'll be joining Hale in exile upstairs," I warned him.

"Maybe I ought to," he shot back. "That'd be the surest way to cancel this whole thing. Especially if I can get Kristin and Morgan to join me—I'd like to see you handle all the Jumps alone, especially with the breakneck schedule Shaeffer's trying to run."

Abruptly, I was very sick of this conversation. "I can do it all if I have to," I bit out. "Though I expect you'll find Kristin and Morgan have better ethics than you give them credit for."

"Maybe," he shrugged. "Or maybe *you'll* find that they can see beyond the life of a single man. The way White Knights like you don't seem capable of doing."

Clamping my teeth together, I walked toward him, ready to flatten him if he gave me even the slightest cause to do so. But he was smarter than that, even flattening himself slightly up against one of the cabinets to give me room to pass. I brushed by him without a word . . . but I couldn't help but notice the small smile playing across his lips as I passed.

A moment later I was back in the more open areas of the Banshee room . . . and I'd made up my mind. Whatever legitimate points Rennie may have had, I knew from long and painful experience that everything he did always had an ulterior motive buried somewhere within it. And in this case that motive wasn't hard to find.

He was out to destroy Griff.

The seeds of the conflict had been there from almost the very beginning, when Rennie's perfectionism had run straight into Griff's severe lack of administrative skill. It had become a simmering feud by the time he and I had left Banshee.

I had gone voluntarily; Rennie hadn't. Which had almost certainly soured his feelings toward Griff even more.

Standing across the room by the couch, Griff half-turned from his tete-a-tete with Shaeffer and beckoned to me. "Adam," he said as I joined them, "Mr. Shaeffer and I are going to head upstairs and see if anything new has come in from the crash site. Would you mind waiting here with Kristin, just in case she finishes her Jump before we get back?"

"No problem," I assured him. . . . and as he and Shaeffer headed for the elevator I realized that I had no choice anymore as to where I stood on this experiment. Rennie was willing to scuttle the chance to save President Jeffers's life in order to give Griff a black eye; and if I had to join Shaeffer in order to stand by Griff, then that was it. End of argument.

I looked down at Kristin's closed eyes, her dead-looking face. The trauma of coming back from a Jump had always been hard on her, and Griff clearly was still maintaining his old practice of making sure either he or another Jumper was on hand to comfort her during those first few seconds of disorientation.

Griff would never win any awards for administration

or appropriations appearances . . . but he took good care of the people in Banshee. For me, that was what really mattered.

Pulling up a chair, I sat down next to Kristin and waited for the Jump to end.

As it turned out, Griff's precaution proved unnecessary. He and Shaeffer were back in the basement, looking over a computer printout, when the circuit breakers snapped and Kristin gasped for air.

They were beside me instantly. "Well?" Shaeffer demanded.

Griff shushed him and held Kristin's hand until her eyes slowly came back to focus. "Griff?" she whispered in a husky voice.

"Right here," he assured her. "That was a long Jump; how do you feel?"

"Okay." She took a deep breath. "Okay."

"What happened?" Shaeffer asked, hope and apprehension struggling for prominence in his voice.

But Kristin shook her head. "He didn't see me," she said. "I'm almost sure he didn't. He was talking to one of his people all the way to the airfield, and it was sunny and—" she broke off, squeezing her eyes shut as a shudder went up through her. "He didn't see me."

I looked at Shaeffer; but if he was discouraged it didn't show. "All right, we'll just try it again," he said grimly. "Dr. Mansfield, do you have any idea whether or not the Banshee images accumulate? In other words, will the President see only one of them no matter how many Jumpers have visited that particular time frame?"

"I have no idea," Griff admitted. "We don't even know what these images are that people see. The Jumpers don't see them, certainly—they never see each other, no matter how many of them are present in a particular slot."

"It's entirely possible that only those about to die can see them," Rennie's voice came from behind me. I jumped; I hadn't heard him come up. "That was the way a real banshee operated, wasn't it?"

"Depends on which legends you listen to," I told him shortly. Kristin's eyes flicked briefly to mine, then turned away.

"Try to recall we're talking reality here, not legends," Shaeffer said tartly. His eyes studied Rennie for a second. "I believe it's your turn now, Mr. Baylor."

I looked at Griff, expecting him to remind Shaeffer that it was after ten o'clock and that he'd pushed the usual late-night limits by a couple of hours already. But he remained silent, his attention also on Rennie.

Rennie, however, wasn't nearly so reticent. "I was under the impression, Mr. Shaeffer, that the goal here was to rescue the President, not turn Banshee's Jumpers inside out. It's getting late, and if you keep this up you're going to kill us."

"Mr. Baylor, if you don't understand what the hell we're doing here, please ask Dr. Mansfield to explain it to you," Shaeffer bit out icily. "The longer it takes us to make contact with President Jeffers, the greater the risk of changing known history. Remember? Whenever one of you finally gets seen by the President, I'm banking on him recognizing the image as that of a Banshee Jumper and coming to the proper conclusion."

"That he's going to die?"

Shaeffer's brow darkened. "Of course not—that he needs to stay incommunicado until the risk of changing the past is over. Except that from his point of view it'll be the future, of course."

"Would he really think things out that clearly?" Kristin asked.

"If he doesn't, there could be trouble," Shaeffer admitted. "But I think he will. He's been following Banshee's progress closely ever since you were first set up—he's fascinated by the whole concept."

"So how do you expect him to know when he can come out?" I asked Shaeffer. "You think he can postpone letting the world know he's still alive for a full three days?"

"That's precisely the reason I'm pushing to make contact as soon as possible," Shaeffer snapped. "Once we know he's off the plane, I can call California and let whoever's answering the phone know that he can come out. Understand?" He didn't wait for an answer, but turned back to Rennie. "Mr. Baylor? It's your turn."

I held my breath . . . but apparently Rennie wasn't yet ready for the big confrontation. "All right," he said heavily. "I don't suppose I can fight you, Griff, *and* Adam on this one, can I?" Turning his back on us, he stepped over toward the prep area.

"This isn't supposed to be a fight—" Griff began.

Shaeffer cut him off with a hand motion. "Ms. Cosgrove," he said to Kristin, "whenever you feel ready, I'd like you to come upstairs for a short debriefing."

"I'm ready now," she said, struggling to sit up. Griff put an arm around her shoulders and helped her get her feet on the floor.

We were halfway to the elevator when Rennie's voice stopped us. "I trust you realize, Mr. Shaeffer, that if President Jeffers *does* see me we'll change known history right then and there."

Shaeffer turned back, annoyance on his face. "You're assuming he won't think fast enough to avoid making any phone calls —"

"Actually, I was referring to the fact that Kristin has already seen this same slot of history and knows he didn't react to her presence. *Her* presence or, presumably, anyone else's."

We all stood there a long moment, grouped around Kristin, as the silence thickened like paste in the air. "God," Griff said at last, very softly. "He's right. We can't send him back to the same slot."

Shaeffer's eyes were defocused. "We don't *know* how the President would react, though. Do we? He could have seen but not have given any indication . . . damn." He took a deep breath, looked at Kristin. "Damn it all. Ms Cosgrove, where was he when you ended the Jump?"

"He was just getting out of the car and starting toward the landing strip. It was so sunny I figured that if he hadn't seen me inside the car he wouldn't see me out—"

"Yes, yes," Shaeffer cut her off. "Damn, Dr. Mansfield, can you hit that same end point with the next Jump?"

"No problem," Griff assured him. "The instruments record both ends of the Jump and we can get it to the exact second. But if he was already at the strip—"

"Then we don't have much time left," Shaeffer said harshly. "I know, damn it. But we don't have any choice."

Griff nodded. "I'll set the coordinates myself. Adam . . . ?"

I took his place at Kristin's side, and he headed over to the control board. Shaeffer watched him go, then turned back toward the elevator with a hissing breath. "Come on, you two. Let's get upstairs."

Kristin's debriefing was short, calm, and—at least as near as I could tell—totally worthless. Jeffers had gotten into his limo with some aides and Secret Service men, gone straight to the semi-private landing strip where Air Force One was waiting, and headed off toward the plane on foot. If there were a banshee or ghost where Kristin was hovering, neither he nor any of the others ever saw it.

Afterwards, Kristin let me escort her back to her room, but she was clearly not in a talkative mood and we reached the door with barely a dozen words having passed between us. She went inside, and I trudged two doors down to where my old room had been set up for me.

It looked about the same as I remembered it, with the minor exception of a new television replacing the ancient model that had been there before. I resisted the lure of the remote control while I got undressed . . . but even before I crawled into bed I knew I was too wired up to sleep right away. Flicking the set on, I began to scan the channels.

Unsurprisingly, there wasn't much on except latenight summaries of President Jeffers's death.

It was thoroughly depressing. The cold hard facts themselves were bad enough, even though the media didn't yet know what we did about the cause of the crash. But for me, the interspersed segments of national and world response were even worse. Mine had been one of the landslides of votes that had reelected Jeffers a year ago, but it wasn't until now that I really understood on a gut level how truly popular with the people he'd been. The cameras showed at least half a dozen candlelit memorial marches from cities all across the country and even one or two from overseas. People talked about the shock and the fear and the pain . . . and I lay there and soaked it in, hurting right along with them.

Hurting with people, after all, was part of what being a White Knight meant.

White Knight. A college friend had first coined that nickname for me, and for a long time I'd felt proud of it. It was a statement of my ability to care for people; to serve them and to take whatever bits of their suffering that I could onto myself. It was a fine, noble calling—and I was good at it. It was almost second nature now for me to take the smallest piece of meat at dinners and cookouts, or to give up my days off helping people move or do home repairs. My ability to sacrifice for others enabled me to give away my money, even if I had to do without something myself.

It had enabled me to quit Banshee almost a year ago. And to not tell anyone why.

I watched the news for another half hour, until I couldn't take it any more. Lying in the dark, listening to the unfamiliar sounds of big-city traffic around me, I finally fell asleep.

The news that it was sabotage broke sometime during the night, and by morning the news programs were hauling in experts to give their speculations as to who was responsible and why. Combined with the eulogies still pouring in from leaders around the world, it made it that much harder, an hour later, to watch a man already dead walking casually across the tarmac toward his plane.

And to labor in vain to warn him. The others had been right: the sunlight was far too bright for the President to have any hope at all of seeing anything as insubstantial as a ghost.

Mine, Shaeffer had told me before the Jump, was to be the last effort in this particular slot, and so I kept at it all the way up the stairway. But it was no use. I did every kind of aerial maneuver I could think of to try and get his attention, but not once did he so much as take a second look in my direction. Eventually, he passed the limit of my tether, fastened to Air Force One's door, and vanished into the communications section at the front of the plane.

Third strike, and Banshee was out.

I came back to find Griff and Shaeffer leaning over me. "Well?" Griff demanded.

"Uh-uh," I shook my head. The motion sent a brief spasm of pain splitting through my skull. "He never saw me."

Griff seemed to slump. "Damn," he breathed, "Mr. Shaeffer . . . I'm sorry—"

"It's not over yet," Shaeffer cut him off, icy calm. "All right; if we can't stop him getting on the plane, the next step is to try and get him *off* it before the balloon goes up." He stepped back from the couch and gestured, and as I struggled up onto my elbows I saw Morgan standing nearby. "Mr. Portland, you're next. You'll be Jumping as soon as the equipment is ready."

Morgan nodded silently. His eyes met mine for an instant, and then he turned away from us.

I should have realized right then that something was wrong. But with the Jump and my recovery from it taking all my attention, Morgan's odd reaction missed me completely. "If you're going to try and get him off," I told Shaeffer, working myself to a vertical position, "you'll need to have the tether a lot further forward.

When I left he was heading into the forward section of the plane."

Shaeffer nodded abstractly. "He'll be back in his private section before take-off, though. That's where we'll have to try and get to him."

"Ah," Griff said, offering me a hand as I swung my legs off the couch and more or less steadied myself on my feet. "You're talking about getting him out *during* the flight, then?"

"Right. There are parachutes stored near both exit doors. If we can contact him, all he'll have to do is grab one, open the door, and jump."

"Is that all?" an unexpected voice cut in.

We all turned around. "Hale, you were told to stay upstairs," Griff growled.

"So that Shaeffer can dismantle the stability of the universe in peace and quiet?" Hale snorted. "Fat chance."

I looked at Griff. He shrugged fractionally in return, a worried frown starting to settle onto his face. Hale had always been something of a borderline neurotic anyway, but this seemed to me to be a pretty drastic slippage. "Hale—" I began.

"*You* just shut up," he snapped back. "You cut out on us once— coming back now just because Griff wants a yes-man on his side doesn't win you any points."

I opened my mouth, closing it again in confusion . . . and only then did I spot Rennie lounging against the wall near the elevator.

And finally understood.

That confrontation among the equipment cabinets hadn't been an effort to convince me to join him in opposing Griff. Instead, he'd been trying to drive me solidly onto Griff's side . . . so that he could use the others' animosity toward me as a lever to get *them* on his side.

"Hale, if you have any specifics to bring up," Griff said soothingly, "we're willing to discuss them—"

"I have one," Rennie spoke up, strolling over. "Mr. Shaeffer, you're talking as if all the President has to do is open the door and jump out and that's that. Right?"

"He was in the Air Force for six years," Shaeffer said stiffly. "He knows how to handle a parachute."

"I'm sure he does. Has it occurred to you that if the pilot radios that they've got an open door the known past will be changed?"

I looked at Shaeffer, the muscles of my shoulders tightening. "*Would* they broadcast something like that?" I asked. "Or would it just show up on the flight recorder?"

"Depends on whether the pilot was on the radio at the time it happened, I suppose," he said. "If he wasn't . . ."

"And when someone notices the President is missing?" Hale shot back.

Shaeffer took a deep breath. "All hell breaks loose," he admitted grudgingly.

For a moment we all looked at each other. "Well?" Griff said at last. "What now, Mr. Shaeffer?"

Morgan cleared his throat. "If President Jeffers recognizes us as being from Banshee, as you've suggested he might, wouldn't he realize he has to give the pilot instructions not to mention his departure?"

"Oh, come on," Rennie scoffed. "I, for one, have no intention of just hoping he'll think of all these things on the spur of the moment—hell, Shaeffer, you've been working on this scheme for twelve hours or more and you still missed this angle."

"Rennie—"

"No, Dr. Mansfield, he's right," Shaeffer cut Griff off. "If we're going to do this safely, we've got to make sure the President winds up with only the options we want him to have."

I glanced at Rennie, saw a touch of surprise flicker across his face. Shaeffer's acceptance of his argument seemed to have pulled some of the wind out of his sails. "It gets worse," he said, a bit less belligerently. "If he jumps out of the plane anywhere near civilization, we get exactly the same problem."

"Yes, I'd caught that corollary, thank you," Shaeffer returned tartly. "Let me think."

For a moment the only sound in the room was the steady drone of a hundred cabinet fans. "All right," Shaeffer said at last. "He was in the air for approximately ninety minutes before the crash. We'll start fifteen minutes before the end."

"And what if he spots Morgan immediately?" Rennie growled.

"What if he does?" Shaeffer countered. "What's he likely to do?"

A slight frown creased Rennie's forehead as, for the second time in so many minutes, Shaeffer seemed to have taken him by surprise. "I thought the whole point of this exercise was to get him to pull the ripcord on the flight."

"Sure . . . but put yourself in his shoes for a second. What would you do if you were President and saw a Banshee appear in front of you?"

Rennie's frown darkened. "This isn't any time for guessing games, Shaeffer," he bit out. "If you've got some brilliant idea—"

"We wouldn't be lookin' in on him if the plane was just gonna crash," Morgan said slowly.

"What was that?" Shaeffer asked, an oddly tense look in his eye.

Morgan was frowning off into space. "Well, our business here's s'posed to be findin' out how these things happen . . . and if he was gonna crash, we oughta be concentratin' on the wings or engines or somethin'. If one o' us just sits there and watches him, maybe he'll think it's somethin' else gonna happen."

Griff inhaled sharply. "Like maybe . . . assassination?"

Shaeffer nodded, almost eagerly. "Right—exactly right. I'm expecting him to assume he's going to be the target of a simple attack, and that you're there to find out which of his aides is the one involved."

"So he'll sit there and make sure the door is locked," Griff nodded. "Makes sense."

"Or else he'll assume that there's a bomb in his private section," Hale put in.

Shaeffer's expression soured a little. "In which case he'll call for a quick search of the plane," he said shortly. "Either way, the thought of jumping shouldn't even cross his mind . . . until you start leading him out toward the exit."

I looked at Morgan, back to Shaeffer. "And what if the President doesn't notice him?" I asked.

"He will, Shaeffer said grimly. "This is our last chance, and we're damn well going to make sure he sees something this time. So. Dr. Mansfield, you'll be sending Mr. Portland into the slot T minus fifteen minutes to T minus six minutes—no later, understand? Ms. Cosgrove will be next, and after that Mr. Baylor here—all of them Jumping into the same fifteen-to-six minute time slot."

I looked at Griff, saw his eyebrows go up. "Didn't we decide," I said carefully, "that sending more than one person into the same slot—?"

"As each comes back," Shaeffer went on as if I hadn't spoken, "you will *immediately* administer a sedative, before there can be any indications one way or the other as to what the Jumper has seen or done. Understand?"

For a long moment Griff just stood there, looking as flabbergasted as I felt. Beside me, Morgan stirred. "Mr. Shaeffer," he said hesitantly, "I'd be the first to admit I'm not all that smart. But are you tryin' to say that if we don't know what the other Jumpers saw, then a lot of the problems go away?"

Shaeffer's mouth compressed into a tight line. "I'm hoping the paradoxes will, yes," he said. "It ought to work—it's a version of the Schrödinger's cat setup—" He broke off, took a deep breath. "Anyway, we have to risk it; and we have to risk it *now,* Mr. Portland."

I looked at Morgan, expecting him to nod and take his position on the couch. "No," he said quietly.

I stared at him. We all did, for what seemed to be a very long time. "What did you say?" Shaeffer asked at last, very softly.

"I said no," Morgan told him, equally softly. "Sorry, Mr. Shaeffer, but even the way you got it I don't think it's safe enough. And if you're wrong . . ." He shook his head. "It all goes bad real quick."

"And you came to this conclusion all by yourself?" Shaeffer growled pointedly.

Morgan's forehead creased. "Just 'cause I never had much schooling doesn't mean I ain't got any common sense," he said without rancor.

"And common sense is important in abstract physics, is it?" Shaeffer bit out. He shifted his glare to Hale and Rennie. "All right. Which of you two put him up to this? Or would you rather the Marines upstairs ask the questions?"

"You don't need to do that," Morgan sighed. "It was Rennie who told me that you couldn't fiddle things so's it wouldn't be dangerous."

"Common sense may not be the best thing to go by here, Morgan," Griff put in quietly. "What about your sense of honor, your loyalty to the rest of us? What do *they* tell you?"

Morgan gave him a long look. "It's 'cause of that that I'm just quittin' straight out," he said. "Otherwise I'd prob'bly do what Hale thought I should: Jump, but stay as far as I could away from President Jeffers."

"Son of a bitch," Shaeffer ground out, turning his glare on Hale as his hand dipped briefly into his side coat pocket. "You're under arrest—both of you."

"On what charge?" Rennie asked calmly. "You had no legal authority to drag me back here to Banshee in the first place—there's been no declaration of martial law, and I wasn't served any kind of papers, Federal or otherwise. You have no power over me, Shaeffer—you *or* Griff. Arrest me and I'll sue your eyes out."

Behind him, the elevator opened to reveal two Marines. "These men are under house arrest," Shaeffer told them, pointing to Hale and Rennie. "Take them to their rooms *and make sure they stay there*." He looked at Morgan. "Last chance, Portland. Are you going to join them?"

Without a word, Morgan stepped over beside Rennie and Hale. Shaeffer nodded to the Marines and the entire group disappeared back into the elevator.

And as the doors closed on them, all of the starch suddenly seemed to go out of Shaeffer's backbone. His hands went up to rub his face and he actually staggered, and I found myself wondering just how much sleep he'd gotten the night before. Probably not much. "Dr. Mansfield, you'd better call Ms. Cosgrove down here."

I looked at Griff. "There's no way we can do this with just two Jumpers," I said.

He took a deep breath and nodded. "Adam's right, Mr. Shaeffer. Especially if you still plan to go with sedation after each Jump."

"I'd say it's obvious that idea's not going to work as is," Shaeffer bit out. "Just get Ms. Cosgrove down here—let me worry about procedure."

Griff pursed his lips and for a moment I thought he was going to argue. Then, without a word, he stepped over to the control board phone.

Kristin arrived about fifteen minutes later, looking even worse than Shaeffer did. Her eyes were red and half-lidded, her hair had the disheveled look of someone who'd spent the night doing more tossing and turning than actual sleeping, and her feet seemed to drag as she walked toward us from the elevator. I stepped forward to take her arm; she sent me a half-hearted glare and pulled back from my grasp. "What's going on, Griff?" she asked.

"Mutiny," he told her grimly. "You and Adam seem to be the only Jumpers on our side at the moment."

"We—*what*?"

"Ms. Cosgrove," Shaeffer interrupted her, stepping over from the control station. "I understand you're still recovering from last night's Jump, but I'm afraid I'm going to have to ask you to do another one this morning."

Kristin closed her eyes, and I saw a muscle in her cheek twitch. "All right," she sighed. "What am I supposed to do?"

"Same thing you tried to do yesterday; get President Jeffers to see you," Shaeffer told her. "We're going to put you in his private office on Air Force One fifteen minutes before the engine catches fire. When he sees you, you will stay in the room, hovering in front of him, until the clock in the room shows three minutes before the crash. That was—what, three-twenty-five, Pacific Time?"

"Right," Griff nodded. "The engine fire probably started a minute or two before that, though.

"Point," Shaeffer agreed, forehead furrowed in thought. "Yeah. All right, then make it three-twenty. At three-twenty exactly, Ms. Cosgrove, you are to move to a spot in front of the door and then end the Jump. Understood?"

Kristin hesitated. "What if he doesn't see me . . . ?"

"He has to," Shaeffer said, very quietly. "He has to."

For a moment none of us said anything. Then Shaeffer took a deep breath. "No point in delaying it. This is it; let's go."

The lights flickered, Kristin's body sagged on the couch, and I turned to Shaeffer to wait for the other shoe to drop.

It did so immediately. "Mr. Sinn, I want you to wait in your quarters," he said. "When Ms. Cosgrove returns, she'll be put under immediate sedation, but I don't want there to be any chance at all she'll say something you'll hear."

Griff turned back from the control board, his eyes wide. "I thought you said—"

"I said the plan would need modification," Shaeffer cut him off. "This is that modification: adapting it to only two players. Problems?"

"Yes," I said with a sigh. "It isn't going to work."

"It's a perfectly reasonable—"

"No, it's not!" I snarled. For once, I was tired of tiptoeing around other people's feelings. "Think about it a second, Shaeffer. Whatever Kristin experiences on that plane, a long nap isn't going to make her forget it.

You're the one who mentioned Schrödinger's cat awhile back—do you really know how that experiment was supposed to work, or were you just spouting words?"

Shaeffer held his temper with obvious effort. "A gun is set up so that if a particular radioactive atom in a test sample decays in a given time, the gun goes off and kills the cat. If it doesn't decay, the cat lives."

So he *did* know. "Right," I nodded. "Do you also remember why there's no way to know what actually happened?"

Shaeffer pursed his lips. "If you open the box, the cat automatically dies."

"Right," I said softly. "Were you ultimately planning to kill Kristin?"

He closed his eyes and exhaled between his teeth; a hissing sound of defeat. "Then this really *is* it. Isn't it."

My stomach churned with sympathetic pain. "Hang onto the bright side," I urged him. "He *might* see her; and if he does, I'll be able to talk to Kristin about it before I do my own Jump. Which means I'll know what the situation is before I go into it."

He gave me an odd look, as if being comforted by what he clearly regarded as an underling was outside his usual experience. Then, turning, he wandered off toward the elevators, hands clasped tightly behind him. Griff and I exchanged glances and silently settled down to wait.

We waited nearly ten minutes; and when it came, the snap of circuit breakers made me jump. We were crowded over Kristin's couch within seconds, all three of us. She gasped, eyes fluttering—

"What happened?" Shaeffer snapped. "Answer me! What *happened?*"

"Uh . . . uh . . . Griff," she managed, hand reaching up to grip at Griff's sleeve. Her eyes were wet as she blinked tears into them; wet, and strangely wild. "Griff—oh, God. It *worked*—it really worked. *He saw me!*"

President Jeffers's Air Force One office was small but

sumptuous, something that rather jarred against his
public image as one of the common people. The room's
decor registered only peripherally, though, as I concentrated my full attention on the man standing behind the
oaken desk in shirtsleeves and loosened tie . . . the
man who was likewise concentrating his full attention
on me.

Or, more precisely, on my Banshee image. Or, even
more precisely, on Kristin's Banshee image. According
to the clock I could just see on the side wall—and the
settings Griff had used—I would be overlapping her
Jump for another thirty seconds. Enough time for me to
orient myself and to get into position in front of the
office door where she would be when she ended her
Jump. Ready to take over from her.

Assuming, of course, it wasn't just Kristin's image
Jeffers could see. In that case, I'd have to abort the
Jump and we'd be forced to wait until Kristin could try
it again.

I watched the second hand on the clock . . . and
when the half minute was up, I began to drift back
toward the door. Holding my nonexistent breath.

Jeffers's eyes adjusted their focus to follow me.

I continued to ease back; and with my full concentration on him, it was a shock when the universe suddenly
went dark around me. For a second I lost control and
snapped to the length of my tether toward the front of
the plane before my brain caught up with me and I
realized that I had simply gone into the honey-combed
metal of the office door. Fortunately, Jeffers moved
slower than I did, and I was back in the corridor outside his office when he hesitantly opened the door. His
eyes flicked momentarily around, found me again. His
lips moved—soundlessly, of course, as far as I was
concerned. But Griff had long ago made all of us learn
how to lip-read: *Am I supposed to follow you?*

I nodded and pointed toward the rear of the plane,
watching Jeffer's face closely. There was no reaction
that I could detect. Whatever it was he was seeing, it

didn't seem to match the nonexistent body my subconscious persisted in giving me during Jumps. Which meant hand motions, expressions—body language of all sorts—were out.

Which left me exactly one method of communication. I hoped it would be enough.

Carefully—mindful of both the deadline breathing down Jeffers's neck and the danger of him losing track of me if I moved too fast—I began backing down the corridor toward the rear of the plane. For a moment Jeffers held his ground, a whole raft of conflicting emotions playing across his face. Then, almost reluctantly, he followed. I had another flicker of darkness as someone came up from behind and walked through me, nodding greetings to Jeffers as they passed. For a bad second I thought Jeffers was going to point me out to the other man; but it was clear that he still wasn't entirely sure he wasn't hallucinating, and after a few casual words he left the other and continued on toward me. I got my breathing started again and resumed my own movement, and a minute later we were standing across from the rear door.

And I ran full tilt into my inability to speak or even pantomime. The parachutes were racked across from the door, inconspicuous but clearly visible . . . but moving over and hovering by them didn't seem to give Jeffers the hint. I tried moving away, then back again— tried backing directly into and through one of the neat packs and then back out—tried moving practically to Jeffer's nose, back to the chutes, and then to the door.

Nothing.

I gritted my teeth. With the usual fouling of my time sense I had no idea how many seconds we had left before the balloon went up, but I knew there weren't a lot of them. There had to be some other way to get the message across to Jeffers—there *had* to be—but for the life of me I couldn't come up with one. Back and forth I went, parachute to door back to parachute, repeating the motions for lack of anything better to do, all the whole racking my brain trying to think of something else—*anything* else—that I could do. Back and forth . . .

On what must have been the tenth repetition, he finally got it.

You want me to jump from the plane? his lips said. I started to nod, caught myself, and instead tried moving my whole body up and down.

For a wonder, he interpreted the gesture properly. *Is someone going to shoot us down?* he asked.

Close enough. I nodded again and moved back to the parachutes. Any second now—

Jeffers didn't move. *What about the others?* he asked, his hand sweeping around in a gesture that encompassed the entire plane *I can't just leave them to die.*

I blinked, feeling my stomach tightening within me. Jeffers's ability to think and care about average American people had been one of my major reasons for voting for him in the first place; to have that asset suddenly turn into a liability was something I would never have expected. I thought furiously, trying to figure out some way to answer him—

From outside came a dull *thud* . . . and an instant later the floor beneath Jeffers tilted violently, throwing him through me and into the parachute rack.

I spun around, heart thudding in my ears, half expecting to see him sprawled on the floor, dazed or unconscious from the impact. It was almost a shock to find him on his feet, fully alert—

And pulling on one of the parachutes.

I didn't stop to try and figure it out. Pulling laterally to the direction of my tether, I ducked outside for a moment, trying to estimate how much time Jeffers had before we were too close to the ground. Thirty seconds, perhaps, depending on whether the winds would be blowing him toward or away from the mountain sloping away directly beneath us. I went back inside, and to my mild surprise found Jeffers already in harness and fighting his way uphill along the sloping floor toward the door. I held my breath . . . and as the plane almost leveled for a second, he lunged and managed to catch the lever before the floor angled beneath him again.

I glanced back toward the parachute rack again to fix in my mind exactly which chute he'd taken; and as I did so, something skittering along the wall caught my eye. It was a flat package, covered in bright orange: one of the emergency packs that were supposed to be clipped to the front webbing of each of the chutes. I looked back at Jeffers, but before I could get in position to see his chest the plane almost-leveled again—

And in a single convulsive motion he shoved the door hard against the gale of the air outside and squeezed his way out.

I dropped straight down through the floor and luggage compartment, falling as far below the crippled plane as my tether allowed. Below and behind me, Jeffers tumbled end over end, shirt billowing in the breeze. If he'd hit something on the way out—if he was unconscious—

The drogue chute snaked its way out of the pack, followed immediately by the main chute. It filled out, stabilized . . . and for the first time the reality of what I'd just done hit me.

We'd used the Banshee machinery to save a man's life.

All the private agony I'd had to endure throughout my time at Banshee—all the pent-up frustration of watching disasters I couldn't stop—all of it seemed to flow out of me in that one glorious moment. All the millions of dollars—all the backhanded bureaucratic comments we'd had to put up with—it was suddenly worth it. Let them scoff now! We'd saved a life—a President's life, no less. And on top of it, we'd even done so without any of Rennie's and Hale's fears about changing the past coming true. The minute I was back, Shaeffer could direct the searchers at the crash site to move their operations back a couple of miles to where I could see Jeffers coming down. . . .

And as my attention shifted from Jeffers's parachute to the rocky, tree-covered slope below, the flood of wonder and pride washing over me evaporated. Beyond his landing area, perhaps a mile further down the slope, a small village was clearly visible.

A village he'd be able to walk to in an hour.

I don't remember much about the minutes immediately following the Jump. There was, I know, a lot of shaking of my arms and some fairly insistent use of my name, but for some reason I was unable to really come out of it, and after a short time the voices and hands faded into blackness and disturbing dreams.

Eventually, though, the dreams faded. When I was finally able to drag myself back to full awareness, I found I was back upstairs in my room, lying on my bed with an intravenous tube running into my arm. I lifted the arm slightly, frowning at the tube.

"Just relax and don't try to move," a voice said from my other side.

I turned my head, and with a complete lack of surprise found Griff sitting beside the bed. "What—?" I managed to croak before my voice gave out.

"You came out of the Jump in something approximating a hysterical state," he said. "Babbled something about Jeffers bailing out and changing the past and then collapsed. Shaeffer's had them pumping stuff into your arm ever since."

I glanced again at the needle and shivered. "How . . . what time is it?"

He checked his wrist. "Almost four-thirty."

Which meant I'd been out of commission for something close to three hours. "What's been happening with the search?"

Griff shrugged fractionally, the lines around his eyes and mouth tightening a bit. "Nothing, as far as I know. Shaeffer's been running back and forth between here and the communications room, not wanting to launch anything major until he could talk to you and find out just what you were talking about back there."

A shiver went down my back. "He got out of the plane," I whispered. "The parachute opened okay, and he was on his way down. . . . but there was a town an hour's walk downslope of him. There's no way he could have missed it."

Griff swore under his breath as he scooped up the phone and punched at the buttons. "Get me Shaeffer . . . Mr. Shaeffer? This is Griff. Adam's awake, and we've got a hell of a problem. . . . Okay, and if you've got more of those maps maybe you'd better bring them . . . Right."

He hung up and looked back at me. "You think you'll be able to locate the exact spot where he went down?"

I shivered again. "With that town sitting practically beneath him? Of course I can."

He pursed his lips and fell silent.

Shaeffer arrived a couple of minutes later, a stack of his fine-detail maps in his arms. "Glad to see you awake," he said shortly, his mind clearly on other things as he all but pushed Griff out of his chair and sat down, laying the maps across my chest. "Show me."

I propped myself up on my elbows and began sorting through them. Someone had sketched out the plane's trajectory across the maps in red, and it took me only a minute to find the one I needed. "Here," I said, tracing a circle around the spot with my finger. "He came down about here."

Shaeffer's eyes were shining as he glanced at the number in the map's corner and then at the spot I'd indicated. "All right," he breathed. "All right. Important point, now: did you notice whether or not he had an orange emergency pack attached to his parachute?"

"No, he didn't. In fact, I think I saw it on the floor just before he jumped out. It must have come off while he was getting into the chute."

Shaeffer grunted. "Good. I guess. Eliminates the problem right away of why there wasn't a transponder for the search team to tag onto. Unfortunately, it also means he didn't have any food or water with him, either. Any chance he could have had trouble with the landing itself? Would another Jump be a good idea?"

I sighed. "I don't know. Shaeffer . . . what about that town down there?"

"What about it?"

"Well, it's *there*—right in the most obvious path for him to have taken. But it's been twenty-five hours now since he landed, and . . ." I shrugged helplessly.

"Maybe he's been smarter than all of you gave him credit for," Shaeffer said. "Maybe he realized that you were from the future and knew to wait until we came looking for him. Or maybe he didn't notice the town at all on his way down, in which case staying near his landing site was the only rational thing to do." Abruptly, he got to his feet. "Whichever, there's one easy way to find out."

"You going to send out the searchers right now?" Griff asked.

Shaeffer arched his eyebrows. "As Mr. Sinn just pointed out, he's spent approximately twenty-five hours in the Colorado Rockies. It would be rather a waste of effort to have gotten him out of the plane and then let him die of exposure, now, wouldn't it?"

I took a deep breath. "I want to make another Jump first."

They both looked at me. "Why?" Shaeffer asked.

"I just . . . want to see what happened after he landed."

"In an hour or two we'll be able to *ask* him what happened," Shaeffer said scathingly. "Besides, you need more rest before you can Jump again."

"And besides, if I don't know what happened, I won't be taking any further risk of changing the past?"

Shaeffer's lip twitched. "Something like that," he said. "Look, I don't have time for this. The past is secure, Mr. Sinn—the fact that we're still here and all our memories are still intact proves that. Right? The important thing now is to go out there and bring him home. There'll be plenty of time later for speculation and back-patting." With a nod to Griff, he pulled open the door and left.

I looked at Griff. "Griff . . . ?"

He shrugged. "I don't know, Adam," he admitted. "Everything certainly *feels* okay. Though if our memories are also malleable I suppose feelings aren't necessarily a good indication." He locked eyes with me. "I don't think it's necessary . . . but if you want to do another Jump, I'll okay it."

I hesitated; but Shaeffer was right. Whatever had happened, the very fact that Jeffers was still lost out there implied that what we'd done hadn't significantly altered the known past. "No, that's all right," I sighed. "I guess I can wait until Jeffers tells us himself what happened."

"Okay," Griff said softly. "In that case, you'd better concentrate on getting some rest."

"I think I can manage that," I agreed, closing my eyes.

The lights went out, the door opened and closed, and I was alone. *So that's it,* I thought. *Looks like all the worry was for nothing . . .*

The opening of the door snapped me out of the doze I'd been drifting into, and I opened my eyes to see Morgan framed in the doorway. "Adam?" he whispered. "You awake?"

"Yeah," I told him. "Come in, but leave the overhead light off if you don't mind."

"Okay." He closed the door behind him and groped his way to the bedside, where he flicked on the small lamp there. "So," he said, eyeing me closely. "You did it, huh?"

"Shaeffer seems to think so. He tell everyone already?"

"Not really, but when Hale and Rennie and me were let outta our rooms, it was a pretty good clue. So tell me what happened."

I gave him all of it, and when I'd finished he sat silently for a long moment. "Well?" I prompted. "What do you think?"

"I don't like that town bein' there so close. Worries me pretty bad, if you want to know the truth."

"It worries me, too," I admitted. "But since Jeffers never showed up there everything must be safe—"

"It must, huh? S'pose the only reason nothin's happened yet is 'cause we can still change it?"

"I . . . don't follow you."

He took a deep breath. "We still got somethin' like forty six hours to go back and try to get the President to do somethin' we want 'fore that slot's closed, right? Well, maybe we're s'posed to do somethin' else to him . . . and maybe if we *don't*, it'll suddenly happen that he *did* get to that town after all, and that he was picked up twenty hours ago—"

He broke off, and as I looked into his eyes I shivered. A temporarily shattered but still-fluid past sitting there on hold was a possibility that hadn't even occurred to me. From the expression on Morgan's face it was clear he didn't care for the idea at all; I knew it sure had *me* scared. "What do you think we should do about it?" I asked.

He snorted. "It's not *we*, Adam: it's *you*. Shaeffer let us out of our rooms, all right, but he ain't gonna let us downstairs anytime soon, leastwise nowhere near the couch."

"So what do you think *I* should do about it?" I growled.

His eyes held mine. "Go back there," he said bluntly. "Go back there and . . . stop him."

"Stop him how? Put out my foot and trip him?"

He didn't even notice the sarcasm. "You're the guy that got him outta the plane—I figure he'd follow you anywhere you took him. So . . . lead him off to a ravine somewhere and get him to fall in."

I stared up at him, not believing what I was hearing. "Are you *crazy*?" I said at last.

"It's the only way," he insisted. "You pick the ravine right and you can make him walk miles out of his way 'fore he can get out."

"And if I pick the ravine wrong and the fall kills

him?" I snapped. "That would fix things up good, wouldn't it?"

His eyes dropped away from my gaze. "He was dead once already, Adam," he said quietly. "All you'd be doin' is puttin' the universe back like it was s'posed to be."

"No," I bit out. "That's *not* all I'd be doing. I'd be committing murder."

"Then get him lost or somethin'. Lead him away from the town, so far off he couldn't find his way back."

"Morgan, that town's barely a *mile* away—and I'll only have an hour back there before I have to end the Jump. How can I get him *that* lost *that* fast?"

"Then droppin' him into a ravine's your only shot. Our only shot." He took a deep breath. "I know it's risky. But you're just gonna have to take that risk."

"Oh, right. *I* have to take the risk. But of course you'll be with me in spirit, right?"

"Hey, friend, I'm in this a whole lot tighter than that," he grated. "Me and everyone else in the world. We'll all have to suffer whatever happens if the past gets changed. Maybe you oughtta try thinkin' about that for a change."

Slowly, I shook my head. "I'm sorry, Morgan. I can't deliberately risk someone's life over an unknown and possibly even nonexistent set of consequences. I just can't."

A look of contempt spread over his face. "That's it, huh? You're gonna spout fancy words and all that and then just go ahead and take the easy way out. Like you usually do."

"I've never in my entire life taken the easy way—"

"*Damn it all, will you shut that crap up?*"

I shrank back against my pillow, stunned at the totally unexpected outburst. "Morgan—"

"*Every* time," he snarled. "Every single damn time I've seen you have a choice, you always took the easy way. Maybe you didn't think so, but you did."

"Yeah?" I snarled back. "Well, maybe you just haven't ever seen the whole picture."

"And maybe it's *you* who hasn't. You talk up a good fight with that White Knight stuff of yours, but you know what?—you ain't a White Knight at all. All you are is what we used to call a professional martyr. You make a little sacrifice that costs you something and figure that's proof you've done somebody some good."

Somehow I found my voice again. "That's unfair. You have no idea what I do and how I do it."

"No? You want me to tell you why you quit Banshee? And why it hurt all of us more'n it helped?"

I swallowed the retort that came to me. "I'm listening," I managed to say instead.

He took a deep breath. "Griff told you Banshee's money was gonna be cut, and you did some figuring and found out that even with Rennie being bounced out there wasn't gonna be enough left for four Jumpers. So instead o' workin' out a deal—lettin' us all go part-time, maybe—you just up and quit."

I felt my face go red. All my efforts to keep them from finding out why I'd done it . . . "Do the others know?"

His lip twisted. "No, 'course not. How you think Kristin would feel if I told you you'd quit your job for her? 'Specially since it good as trapped her here?"

"She'd probably—what?" I interrupted myself as the last words registered. "What do you mean, trapped her? She's earning more now than she ever has in her life."

He sighed. "That's just what I meant, Adam. Don't you see?—this Banshee job's pretty much a dead-end one. There just ain't anywhere to go with it. But the money's too good for her to just walk away and start somethin' new from scratch. Same for Hale and me, for different reasons."

"Oh, really?" I scoffed. "So tell me, where would you suggest someone with Hale's abrasive personality might go?"

"Again, that's what I meant," he said wearily. "Here at Banshee Griff hasn't got much choice but to put up with him, so there's no reason for him to try and change himself." He hesitated. "For me . . . heck, we all know I'm just a hick from the backwoods. Right? I don't have much schooling, and until I do I can't really find any better job than I've got right here. Now, if I was only workin' part of the year here, I could maybe go off to college somewhere, maybe get a degree. But stuck here, on call all the time . . ." He shook his head.

For a long moment I gazed at him in silence, thoughts spinning like miniature tornadoes in my brain as a horrible ache spread throughout my being. Had I really been the cause of all that? It was inconceivable—what I'd done had been to *help* them, not hurt them. And yet, Morgan's arguments were impossible to refute.

And impossible to ignore.

"It pretty well boils down," Morgan said at last, "to what my Ma used to call *tough love*. Like taking off a bandaid—short hurt for long help. If you can't do that . . . maybe you oughtta stay clear of that White Knight business of yours."

I took a deep breath. All the shadows of the past—all the sacrifices I'd made for others—rose up en masse to haunt me. How many of them, I wondered, had been useless? How many had been worse than useless? And perhaps most painful of all was the fact that it was too late to do anything about any of them.

Almost any of them. "Pick up the phone," I told Morgan, sitting up in bed. Gritting my teeth, I pried up a corner of the tape holding the intravenous needle in place against my arm and ripped it free. *Like a band-aid*, he'd said. . . . "Griff's probably in the communications room. Find him and tell him I want to do that Jump after all. And tell him I'll want another look at those maps of Shaeffer's."

From ten thousand feet up, the sun that fatal afternoon had been shining from high in a cloudless sky, seemingly bathing the world in light and heat. From ground level, however, things were considerably different. The sun, still high in absolute terms, was nevertheless almost at "sundown" as it approached a long ridge towering up in the west. The view off to the south was even more sobering, as the thin haze of white frost visible on the peaks there was mute testimony to the fact that the sun's heat was more illusion than reality. In half an hour or less, when the sun disappeared behind the mountains, the temperature on the slope would begin its slow but steady slide.

Jeffers clearly knew it, too. I'd timed the Jump to arrive after he was down, and by the time I got there he was standing in the middle of the cracker-box-sized clearing where he'd landed, industriously gathering up the parachute silk. Hovering behind him, I watched as he wadded it up and draped it around himself in a sort of combination vest and sari, securing it tightly around him with belt and tie.

I felt terrible.

Never before had I done even two Jumps in a single day, let alone three: and now I knew why Griff was usually so strict on the one per day rule. Nausea, dizziness, and a steadily increasing fatigue dragged hard at me, distracting me from the task at hand. *Please,* I begged silently, *let him just sit down and wait for rescue. Conserve his energy . . .*

With a final tug on his tie, Jeffers took a minute to look around him. His eyes lingered on the plume of smoke in the distance, and I saw his fists clench in impotent anger. Then, taking a deep breath, he squared his shoulders and started off downslope.

Toward the town below.

I groaned inwardly. So he *had* seen the village during his descent . . . and my last chance to avoid making the hard choice was gone. *Tough love,* I reminded myself; and moving out in front of Jeffers, I hovered before his eyes and waited for him to spot me.

He did so within a handful of steps. *Are you the same one?* his lips said. I tried the up-down motion again and he nodded understanding. *You're not still tethered to the plane, are you?*

In answer I moved over behind him to the parachute

pack still strapped to his back. *Good. Can you lead me to the town I saw when we were coming down?*

I swallowed hard, and moved out ahead of him. Morgan had been right; there was no trace of the hesitation he'd shown back aboard the plane as he set out to follow me.

He trusted me.

Clamping my teeth against both the guilt and a sudden surge of nausea, I kept going. *Tough love*, I repeated to myself. *Tough love.*

It worked for over half an hour. We tramped through groves of spindly pines and over hard angular rock, always heading toward the south, and for awhile I dared to hope I could simply get him lost and leave it at that. If I could get him turned around sufficiently he might hesitate to strike out on his own after I left him. Even if he knew—and he might not—that my time limit meant that wherever I led him he would never be more than an hour's walk from the town.

But even while I hoped, I knew down deep not to rely on wishful thinking. So I kept us going the proper direction . . . and five minutes short of my goal, the bubble burst.

Without warning, too. One minute I was leading Jeffers across a particularly rough section of ground, a patch littered by dozens of branches apparently blown off the nearby trees by a recent windstorm; the next, he abruptly stopped and frowned up at the sky. *We're heading southwest*, he told me. *Wasn't that town more due west?*

I suppose I should have anticipated that he'd eventually notice the direction we were heading and come up with some kind of plan to allay any suspicions. But between the physical discomfort I was going through and the even more gnawing emotional turmoil I hadn't thought to do so. I had a rationale, certainly—that I was leading him to the town via the safest path available—but with all communication one-way there was no way for me to relay such a complex lie to him. Even if my conscience would have let me do so.

He was still watching me. Carefully, I did my "nod" and then continued on a couple of yards in the direction I'd been leading him. He watched for a few seconds and then, almost reluctantly began to follow. I breathed a sigh of relief. Five minutes more of his trust was all I needed. . . . five minutes, and I would be able to betray that trust.

Tough love. Tough love.

Three minutes later, we reached the ravine.

It was both wider and deeper than I'd envisioned it from Shaeffer's maps, probably fifty feet from rim to rim at this spot and a hundred feet or more from rim to bottom. It was also considerably starker than I'd expected. There were stunted trees lining both rims and along the very bottom, but the sides themselves were nothing but rock and gravel and an occasional clump of grass or small cacti.

And with the sun now behind the western mountains, the growing gloom was beginning to mask what lay below.

Jeffers spotted the ravine as we approached, of course, and for a moment he stood at the edge, peering as far over as the gently rolling slope permitted. *What now?* he asked.

In answer, I drifted over the edge and moved a few feet down the side, scanning the area immediately beneath me as I did so. I had indeed led us to the precise place I'd hoped to: barely thirty feet down, the increasingly steep side abruptly became sheer, dropping almost straight down to the trees below. Together with the loose gravel of the sides . . . I returned my attention to Jeffers, praying that he wouldn't look any further, but just trust me and step out over the edge.

But whatever trust he still had in me wasn't nearly that blind. *Isn't there some other route?* he asked, not moving. *This doesn't look very safe to me.*

Again, there was nothing I could do to communicate with him except to repeat my motion into the ravine. Rubbing at his jaw, he looked both ways along the edge, as if trying to decide whether he should instead try to go around it. But the slopes in both directions were at least as intimidating as what he could see of the ravine—I'd made sure that would be the case when I chose this place. For another minute his eyes searched the area around us, looking perhaps for a place where he could tether one of the lines from his parachute as a safety rope. But it was clear that none of the half dead trees in the vicinity would stand up to any force, and after a minute he clenched his teeth and nodded. Holding gingerly onto the nearest trees for support, he stepped onto the slope and started down.

He got five steps before he lost it.

He screamed, or perhaps swore, as the ground slid abruptly out from under his feet and he started down. Dropping down on his butt, he rolled over and flattened his torso against the rocky slope, hands scrabbling for purchase. But there was nothing there to grasp onto; and as the slope steepened, his hands ceased their attempts as he seemed to realize that he was doomed. Faster and faster he went, his passage throwing up dust and clouds of tiny stones as he fell down and down toward the bottom and certain death—

And an instant later hit and collapsed onto the wide granite ledge thrusting its way out of the side of the ravine.

For an awful minute I thought all my careful planning had been in vain, that the fall had in fact killed or lethally injured him. Then, to my vast relief, he rolled over and levered himself stiffly into a sitting position. He looked at the ledge, glancing up, then eased forward to peer over the edge at the sheer drop below. And then his eyes found me . . .

I forced myself to look back at him, to accept the expression of betrayal on his face. Morgan had been right on this one, too: tough love meant short pain. . . . and there was still enough of the martyr in me to want to claim some of that pain for myself.

Though no doubt both Jeffers and Shaeffer would be able to find plenty of pain for me at the end of the

Jump. But that was all right. I'd saved Jeffers's life, and I'd saved the past, and that was all that counted.

Smiling to myself, I left.

I found Morgan, Kristin, and Griff sitting around the lounge TV when I finally felt well enough to leave my room. On the screen, coincidentally, was President Jeffers, giving his first public speech since his rescue. The two days of rest seemed to have done *him* a lot of good, too.

"Hey—Adam," Griff half turned as I came into the lounge. "How're you feeling?"

"Groggy, but pretty good otherwise," I told him, pulling up a chair next to his and nodding in turn at Kristin and Morgan. "I'm a little surprised I didn't wake up in Leavenworth."

He snorted gently. "What, you think Jeffers is going to hold a grudge?"

"The thought had crossed my mind."

"He had a lot of time out there to figure out why you did what you did. Shaeffer's a little madder, I'll admit, but I think he understands, too." He'd exhaled loudly. "So. Rumor has it Banshee's going to be getting a fairly dramatic budget increase. Would you ever consider coming back?"

I shrugged. "I don't know. It depends on a lot of things."

"Such as?"

Such as whether my coming back would help the other Jumpers. *Really* help them, not just hurt me. "Oh, you know. Things."

Griff grunted. "Well, anyway, I hope you do. Especially now that there's a whole new area waiting for us to work in."

"You mean changin' the past?" Morgan put in quietly.

Something about the way he said that . . . "You okay, Morgan?" I asked, craning my neck to look at him.

His expression, too, was . . . strange. "Listen," he said, nodding toward the TV.

I shifted my attention to the set. ". . . will seek out

those responsible for this cowardly attack on me—and through me on the American people. I am further directing the Pentagon to draw up contingency plans for punitive military action should we find evidence of foreign governmental involvement . . ."

I licked my lips. "He sounds serious."

"He's angry, and he's bitter," Kristin said. "He lost a lot of friends on that plane."

Morgan took a deep breath, exhaled it slowly. "Tell me," he said slowly, "any of you ever heard o' Hezekiah?"

Griff glanced a frown toward me. "One of the kings of ancient Israel, wasn't he?"

"Of Judah, yes," Morgan nodded. "A good one, too . . . except that when God told him it was time for him to die, he fought and kicked against the decision. And God backed down—gave him another fifteen years to live."

A cold shiver worked its way up my back. "And . . . ?"

"And durin' that time he had himself a son who wound up bein' one of the worst kings Judah ever had. And helped to destroy the whole country."

I looked back at the TV. . . . at the image of *th* whose death I'd helped to reverse. "I hope, quietly, "that kind of history doesn't repeat itself.

Morgan nodded. "Me, too."